INHARMONIC

THE MUSIC MAKER SERIES, BOOK ONE

A. K. R. SCOTT

First Paperback Edition published 2017.

Cover Design: Deranged Doctor Designs
Select Map Images: Tiffany Munro, aleksm/shutterstock
Tree Images: Pagina/shutterstock

ISBN-10: 0-9985083-1-4
ISBN-13: 978-0-9985083-1-3

www.akrscott.com

CONTENTS

For my Family

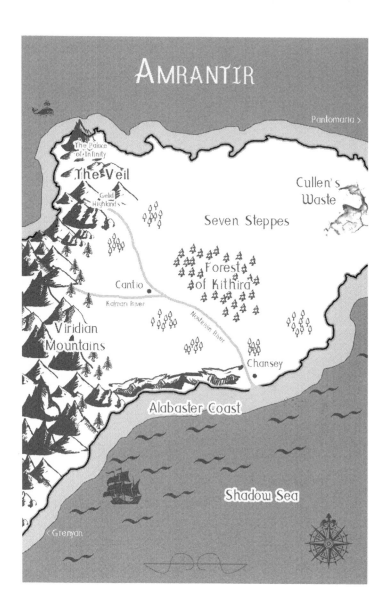

Music has the power to create real and tangible change.

— GRANDMASTER MUSICIAN THADDEUS WESTBROOK,
DEAN OF THE MUSIC CONSERVATORY

Chapter One

Thhhhhpt!

The dart connected with its target, making up with impressive force what it lacked in accuracy. Nadja stooped to pick up the dun-colored weasel, its lifeless body still warm in her hands.

"Not bad," muttered Luca.

"Not bad," said Nadja. "I finally got one, and all you say is 'Not bad'? Look. Not two inches off my mark." She hoisted her prey up to his nose for closer inspection.

Luca chuckled. "I wouldn't want you to be solely responsible for keeping us fed, but your skills with the blowpipe are improving."

"Well, this little guy will make the most delicious meal I've had all week," said Nadja, placing the weasel into her game bag. After a string of unsuccessful days in the grass, stalking small prairie animals with Luca, the thrill of her first kill made the long, hot hours seem worth it. After all, marrying Luca meant becoming a Tulmen. As was the tradition of the Wanderers, a woman adopted the occupation of her husband—the one who spoke for her.

Luca Tulmen was born and raised a hunter, as was his father before him, and his father before him.

"It's getting late in the day," said Luca. "We should make our way back to camp."

"Afraid to be alone with me after dark?" Nadja smirked.

"Certainly not," said Luca, his tanned face taking on a deeper hue. "But I will have no one suggesting any impropriety between us. Especially the day before the celebration."

"I was only teasing," said Nadja with a half smile, as she set off to lead the way back to camp.

The grass crunched under their feet as they walked along in silence. A sporadic breeze gave momentary relief from the midsummer sun as it whipped and whirled across Nadja's skin, only to whisk away sooner than she would have liked. To the east, across the Seven Steppes, patches of tall, golden grass alternated with small matted clumps of various flora. It looked like a thousand tufted cushions scattered across the grassland as far as the eye could see. The otherwise flat landscape was broken here and there by small, rolling hills and dry, shallow riverbeds eagerly awaiting the coming rainy season. Before long, summer would give way to autumn, and it would be time to move south towards the Forest of Kithira.

Nadja closed her eyes, remembering her last winter by the sea, and inhaled as another breeze touched her face. The bumpy grassland reminded her of the ocean just before a storm—choppy and full of power. Her mother,

Jamila, had been a Marimen, a daughter of the sea, before she had married Nadja's father. Fralo Filamen was a weaver who died when Nadja was just a year old. Jamila never remarried, and as she no longer had a husband to speak for her, reverted to the authority of her father. Jamila lent her novice cloth-making skills as needed, but her real talents were best used in the company of other seamen, fishing and diving. It was this deep love of river and sea which she had passed to Nadja.

Nadja's game bag was heavy on her shoulder as she imagined future days spent crouched and hidden, hunting animals of all sizes, not daring to breathe or move for fear of frightening away the next week's meals. The hunters played an important role in the survival of the tribe. But, she would miss the blissful freedom of plunging into the cool sea, feeling the water wrap around her body, and moving through the world in graceful, fluid strokes, much like the fish she sought. She would have to learn to read the tracks of land animals much like she had learned to read the currents.

Cresting the top of one of the smaller hills, they caught sight of the Wanderer encampment on the flat plain below them.

"Have you finished your preparations for tomorrow's celebration?" asked Luca, coming up alongside her.

Nadja nodded. "Mostly. My mother has decided to make a few last-minute alterations to my dress, but otherwise, everything is ready."

"I am looking forward to seeing this mysterious dress of yours."

"So am I," she chuckled. Her mother had been working in secret for months, crafting the dress Nadja would wear to their betrothal celebration. Normally the bride-to-be would have some say in what she would don for such a special event. However, having always preferred function over fashion, Nadja was glad to leave all of those decisions to her mother, who had exquisite taste and a great eye for detail.

She glanced up at Luca and pondered her future husband. Most people would call him handsome, and they would be right. He was taller than other young men his age, and at twenty-four, he was four years older than she. His ebony hair, which matched hers in color, hung in a long ponytail down his back. His almond-shaped eyes were dark and thoughtful, reflecting a wisdom beyond his years. And, though he was reserved, he was also very kind.

As they approached the edge of camp, Luca reached up and touched her arm, turning her to face him.

"You did well today," he said.

"Thank you," she said, smiling up at him.

Luca drew his eyebrows together and looked down at her as if trying to decide what to say next.

His gaze dropped to the ground, and he cleared his throat. "I know I am not good at conveying my more . . . intimate feelings. But, please do not mistake my reserve for indifference." He slid his hand down her arm and took both of her hands in his. Stepping closer, his eyes captured hers and sparked with something more than friendship.

"I love you, Nadja Filamen. I am honored you would accept me as your Promised One. And when you stand with me, and we commit our lives to each other, you will make me the happiest man to ever see his wedding day."

As he leaned in, Nadja held her breath and closed her eyes. When she felt his lips leave a gentle kiss on her forehead, she sighed and opened her eyes once more.

Luca leaned back, smiling at her.

"Until tomorrow," he said, releasing her hands and turning towards his tent.

"Tomorrow," she whispered, making her way towards the tent she shared with her mother.

It wasn't that she didn't love Luca. Of course she loved him. They had known each other from childhood. And, even though their parents had promised them to one another at a young age, she had the right to break that promise if she chose to. As a woman, it was one of the few important decisions which was her own. But, she would be a fool to do so. He came from a respectable family, and he placed his faith in the traditions and beliefs of their people. He would take care of her. He would speak well for her. He was a good match.

Nadja's nose twitched as the heavenly scent of freshly cooked bacon filled her nostrils, followed almost at once by the sweet smell of honeyed rolls. With a deep breath, she inhaled the familiar aroma which always brought with it fond memories of her mother. Through one cracked eyelid, she saw Jamila approaching her cot with a plate piled high with not just bacon and rolls, but eggs and dried fruit. Nadja's stomach growled.

"Good morning, sweetheart," cooed her mother, placing a kiss on her head. "Time to get up. You have a big day ahead of you."

The day of the celebration. Nadja sat up and rubbed her face. She heard the clinking of plates and cups as she stretched. She swung her legs over the side of her cot and padded over to the small table where Jamila had placed her breakfast. Their domed tent held two cots, a table and two chairs, a water basin, and two chests which held clothing, blankets, and items of personal value. It wasn't big, but it was enough for the two of them. The furniture surrounded a central fire pit used for heating purposes only. Any cooking happened in one of the communal pits outside.

Nadja sank into a chair, picked up a crispy strip of bacon and devoured it. "What time is it?" she yawned.

"Almost midday," replied Jamila.

Nadja's eyes flew open. "Midday?" she exclaimed. "Why did you let me sleep so long?" She jumped up from the table, shoving a roll between her teeth. Running over to her chest, she knelt down and dug through the contents, searching for something decent to wear.

Jamila laughed. "Calm down. You have plenty of time to get ready for the celebration. It doesn't even begin until sundown."

"Bf mff abwff mmmfabbaba?" Nadja replied, still turning the chest inside out. She bit through the roll and chewed frantically. "I haven't gone over the song order with the musicians ..."

"That's taken care of."

". . . and I haven't met with Mrs. Tulmen, I mean Naaro, to discuss the organization of the attendants."

"I've already spoken with her."

"When?"

"While you and Luca were out hunting yesterday."

"How did you find time to do that?"

Jamila crossed the dirt floor and knelt beside her daughter, placing an arm around her shoulders and giving them a squeeze. "The only thing you need to worry about is enjoying this day. Come on," she said, pulling Nadja to her feet, "there is something I want to show you."

Nadja's shoulders relaxed as she stood and wondered, not for the first nor the last time, at the strong, capable, warm, and loving woman who had held her hand through so many of life's moments, just as she was doing now.

Jamila was a fine woman, a beauty in her youth as much as she was now. Nadja had inherited her mother's long raven locks along with her sense of adventure and love of music. Without a male influence in their day-to-day lives, Jamila had developed a strong back and rough-edged demeanor when interacting with people outside of their family. But she had always been loving and kind. The fine lines which now decorated the edges of her onyx eyes and tawny forehead were the smallest evidence of the difficulties accompanying the life of a widow. Not that she couldn't have remarried. She'd had offers. Nadja suspected her mother had never fully recovered from the loss of her father, and couldn't, in good conscience, accept a proposal from one man while her heart still held fast to the memory of another.

It was a bold choice. In a nomadic tribe where women could not take part in decision-making of any importance, even as far as being forbidden to entreat the Elders for help when needed, a woman without a husband was almost unheard of. It was the man's duty to represent and speak for his family. Jamila's father, Goran, had agreed to once again accept responsibility for Jamila when Fralo died. But he largely left his daughter and granddaughter to their own devices. And so, Jamila and Nadja were gifted a rare element of independence in the way they lived their lives. It was a freedom Nadja would forfeit when she married Luca.

Jamila ran her fingers along the wood grain of her trunk. She lifted the lid and reached inside, removing a small package wrapped in a light wool fabric and tied with a leather cord. With the bundle in one hand, she untied the cord with the other and peeled away the layers of fabric.

Grasping the contents of the package, she let the wrappings fall away.

Like the gentle rain, an emerald cascade of wispy cloth drifted towards the floor. Nadja's eyes fell first on the bodice of the dress. Hundreds of tiny, sparkling green seed beads flowed at a diagonal from the right shoulder of the sleeveless gown, surging and spilling across the front, fading out as they reached the fitted waist. An undercurrent of lighter blue beads followed suit, whirling and swirling a merry dance in harmony with the green. The skirt was fashioned from countless strips of long jewel-colored crepe cut in wave patterns. The overall effect was that of a verdant kelp forest, imbuing the entire dress with movement and fluidity.

"Oh, Mother," breathed Nadja, at a loss for anything else to say.

Jamila chuckled. "Well, don't just stand there, try it on."

She helped Nadja into the dress, fastening the buttons up the back. Stepping back to take in the entire form of her daughter, Jamila smiled and nodded in approval. A quick search in her trunk produced a silver handheld mirror, which had been a gift from her grandmother. She turned the mirror towards Nadja. "I thought it would bring out your eyes."

Nadja's reflection confirmed it. Her emerald eyes had always stood out as her most distinctive feature, and an anomaly among her tribe. Jamila had once or twice remarked that she'd heard of a great-great so-and-so having eyes of the same shade, but that was all anyone knew. Though Nadja resented them in her youth, having been teased as a child, she grew to embrace and appreciate their striking appearance. Her dress caused them to come alight as they never had before.

"It's stunning," said Nadja. "I don't know what to say."

Jamila dropped the mirror onto her cot and placed her hands on Nadja's shoulders, searching her face. "Do you love him?"

Nadja paused, then smiled. "Of course."

Jamila lifted her right hand and caressed Nadja's cheek, smiling in return. "Then that is all you need to say."

"Thank you, Mother!" said Nadja, throwing her arms around her mother's waist in a tight squeeze.

Without warning, emotions flowed from her—some which she didn't even realize she was feeling. Love, appreciation, and humility joined with nervousness about the upcoming season of celebration and with trepidation about the new life she would soon enter. All of these feelings intermingled to form the salty torrent now moistening Jamila's shoulder.

"Nadja! Where are you? Come and see what they have set up outside of camp!" Kizzy's voice floated into the tent, giving warning she was not far behind it.

Nadja released her mother with enough time to wipe the moisture from her eyes and nose. Her cousin burst into the tent in a flurry of limbs and syllables, her long braid flapping wildly behind her, and her sweet round face beaming with a cherubic glow which brightened the windowless room.

"And, oh my gosh, you have to see my dress!" she exclaimed, rotating in a swirl of purple and gold, and looking like a dainty, dazzling spinning top. "It was going to be a surprise, but I couldn't wait to tell you. You'd never believe how much I had to beg mother and father to let me be one of your attendants, but I am, after all, almost fifteen. And what does it matter, just a few months, anyway? And it's not like I'll be able to attend for sisters of my own— and you are the closest thing I have to a sister."

Kizzy paused for a breath and looked at Nadja as if seeing her for the first time. Rushing forward, Kizzy grabbed Nadja's hands and swung her arms out wide. "Oh Nadja! You look—"

"Stunning," finished Pili. Kizzy's mother leaned against one of the smooth wooden poles which formed the door frame. She grinned at Nadja, trying to catch her breath. Her apron bore evidence of flour and various fruit concoctions, and a bit of dried dough, missed during washing, still clung to her forearm. She favored her sister, though rounder in the face and hips, and contentment in life and family had given her a free and easy smile.

"Thank you." Nadja smiled in return. "As do you, little cousin," she said, pulling Kizzy into a warm hug. "Now, I want to hear all about how you got your father, of all people, to agree to let you join in."

"Oh, well, that part was mother's doing," said Kizzy.

Pili laughed. "I may be getting older, but I still have my charms," she said, giving Jamila a knowing look.

"That anyone can get Harman to do anything he doesn't want to still amazes me," Jamila said, chuckling. Then, noting her sister's disheveled appearance she asked, "How is the food coming?"

"Well, for the most part. But Syerra's oldest girl has managed to burn half of the venison pies, and we've run into a snag with one of the dessert courses."

"I had better come with you," said Jamila, crossing to the open tent flap. Then, she glanced back over her shoulder calling, "You girls have fun," before leaving them to their confidences.

"I cannot believe you're getting married!" exclaimed Kizzy, flopping onto Nadja's cot in a dramatic heap.

"I'm not getting married *yet*," said Nadja, relaxing onto Jamila's. "The Betrothal Celebration is just the beginning of the wedding festivities. We won't actually be getting married for another month."

"I know, but it's still so exciting and romantic," Kizzy swooned. "And Luca is so handsome." She sighed. "You're lucky you were promised to someone so nice to look at. Fish-faced Fectamen is the same age as Luca. You could just as easily have been promised to him."

"Don't make fun of Woral," scolded Nadja, playfully. "He's a nice man, and I'm sure he will make Moira an excellent husband. And besides, you know that promising is about more than age. Luca comes from a very respectable family, and his father was good friends with mine. Our parents believed our marriage would be mutually beneficial."

"Well, it will also be 'mutually beneficial' that the two of you are good-looking people. It might help settle disagreements sooner. What's the point of arguing with someone when all you want to do is kiss their face? Although, Luca isn't much of a talker, anyway." Kizzy rolled over onto her stomach, giving Nadja a mischievous look. "Not that you'll be doing a lot of talking in the beginning," she said, grinning and wiggling her eyebrows.

Nadja's face grow hot as she looked wide-eyed at her cousin. "And what do you know about that?" she laughed nervously, picking up a limp pillow and tossing it at Kizzy's head.

"Enough," said Kizzy in a fit of giggles, dodging the pillow.

"Yes, he is handsome. And kind. And good," said Nadja, smiling down into her hands.

"So, you love him then?" panted Kizzy, recovering from her laughter.

Nadja's eyes grew distant as she raked her nails back and forth over her palm.

"I care for him very much. And I do find him attractive. It's just different than I thought it would be, that's all."

Kizzy pushed herself up off of the cot and crossed the floor, wrapping her arms around her cousin. "The two of you will be so happy. I just know it!"

Nadja sighed. "I hope so."

Chapter Two

Drumbeats thumped and pressed into the crowd of revelers, twisting and turning them in myriad directions at once. The rhythm forced even the most reserved in attendance to join the throng. Their bodies melted together to form a single giant creature made of hundreds of arms and legs and heads vibrating together in time to the beat. Tambourines added a lighter cadence, while the stringed instruments laid a melodic layer atop the musical trifle, already rich with brass and winds.

Nadja smiled up at Luca as she spun around him, her leafy skirt whipping him gently in the legs. He returned her smile, laughing down at her and complementing her spins with a few steps of his own. He grabbed her hands and swiveled her towards him, pulling her against his chest as the musicians brought their song to a close. For a moment longer he held her there, searching her flashing green eyes with his. Their chests rose and fell as each of them tried to catch their breath. Neither of them spoke as Nadja returned his searching look with one of her own. Then, as quickly as the music had drawn back the curtain of reserve which usually covered Luca's features, it fell back into place.

"You must be thirsty," he said, placing a hand on the small of her back and leading her through the maze of torches towards their seats.

Nadja relaxed down into the soft leather-covered cushion positioned conspicuously beneath an arbor festooned with prairie flowers and colored ribbons.

"I'll be right back."

As soon as Luca disappeared into the crowd, a rough hand encircled Nadja's bicep, giving a gentle squeeze.

"The two of you looked so lovely out there," beamed Naaro Tulmen, settling herself onto the cushion next to Nadja.

Nadja cringed inwardly, but smiled at her mother-in-law-to-be. "Thank you. And thank you for all you did to help my mother prepare for the celebration. It was so kind. Everything turned out beautifully."

"Yes it has." Naaro looked out over the crowd, taking in the scene with a self-satisfied look. "I can only imagine how hard it must be to get through a normal day without a husband, let alone to try to plan and coordinate everything that leads up to a wedding. It was my duty, and a joy, to take charge of the situation."

In truth, Jamila had done the bulk of work in making the celebration come to life, though to hear Naaro tell it, it was *she* who had single-handedly managed the whole affair.

"It was a lot of work, but it will all be worth it when you two are married." Then, turning to smile at Nadja, Naaro continued. "And especially so when I finally get to greet my grandchildren. How soon do you think that might be?"

"Oh . . . well . . . I mean . . ." Nadja stammered, crimson creeping up her neck to warm her cheeks for the second time that day.

"I asked Luca, but you know how he is. Always tight-lipped about personal matters. Well, as long as you don't wait too long."

"Oh?"

"There's no sense in putting off motherhood. It's such a wonderful privilege, and your duty, you know."

"Mmm."

"Have you given any thought to how many you might want? The more the merrier, I say."

In truth, Nadja had given a lot of thought to that. The role of a woman was made clear to Nadja, as it had been to every other girl born into her tribe, from an early age. A girl should be good and quiet in manner, diligent in her duties and learning, and obedient to her parents until she married. As a woman, the authority which once belonged to her father would be transferred to her husband, and she would likewise transfer her obedience to him. She would become his complement, learn his trade, and bear and raise their children. In return, she would receive his protection and loyalty. He would ensure her needs were met. She would never worry about political or economic matters because he would speak for her.

But Nadja had grown up without a father. She was a product of her mother's strength and wisdom. She saw her mother work and struggle and make a life for them on her own. Yes, being a widow afforded Jamila more than a modicum of protection against unwanted advances, out of the respect other men had for her deceased husband. And, officially, Jamila's father spoke for her. But, Nadja's grandfather always held the thoughts and opinions of his daughters in high regard. Any time Jamila faced an issue which required her Speaker's intervention, Goran simply acted as her mouthpiece. Jamila lived a good life on her own terms, not merely as someone else's complement. Nadja's heart longed to keep hold of the freedom she had always known, but Jamila's situation was an anomaly. Still, it left Nadja questioning the values and traditions of her tribe and wondering if their way truly was the best way.

Naaro continued to prattle on about the joys of motherhood, and her anticipated joys of grand-motherhood, when Luca returned with two cups of blackberry wine.

"And how is my handsome boy enjoying the celebration?" chirped Naaro, rising to accept the cup Luca offered her.

Luca's mouth turned up in a half smile, looking self-conscious at his mother's puerile endearment.

"Very much so," he replied, leaning in to place a kiss on her cheek.

"Good, good! Well, I know you two have so much to discuss," she said, sending an awkward and not-so-inconspicuous wink in Nadja's direction. "I will rejoin your father. Enjoy yourselves!" Naaro flitted back into the crowd.

"I hope I wasn't interrupting," said Luca, handing Nadja the other glass of wine and taking up the seat left vacant by his mother. "You two looked deep in conversation."

Nadja took a much-needed sip of the sweet brew, its fruity tang slipping down her throat and relaxing the tension in her neck and shoulders. She chuckled and turned to Luca, raising an eyebrow. "I'll give you three guesses as to the topic of that conversation."

"Ahh," he smiled, with a knowing nod. "I only need one. She talks of little else these days. Not that I blame her. She always hoped for a large family, but it was not to be. I think our marriage has renewed that hope in her."

Nadja took another sip of the wine, passing her eyes over the darkening horizon. Without thinking, she turned to Luca.

"Do you ever wonder if there is more out there?"

"More than what?"

"More than this. More than getting married and having children and following the same path our parents and their parents, and their parents walked."

"Of course there is, but nothing that interests me."

"But have you ever wanted to see for yourself? Other people and places, I mean. I've heard the Viridian Mountains are the most brilliant green, and their tops disappear right up into the clouds. And, a merchant in Chansey once told me about the capital city and how some of the buildings are almost as tall as the mountains themselves. And, I once heard there are master musicians who can actually drive away oncoming storms."

Luca's features darkened. "I've seen the Waste," he said. "I've seen enough to know how lucky we are to live protected by our beliefs and traditions, and not to be influenced by the outside."

The light bowing of a familiar tune floated over to them, alerting them the musicians were about to begin another song. "Of course, you're right," murmured Nadja, casting her eyes down, though not at all deterred in her course of thought. Then brightly she added, "It was just talk, anyway."

At that moment, Kizzy emerged from the crowd, bounded over to the arbor and pulled Nadja to her feet. "They want you! The band is about to play 'Yours, Forever,' and Mrs. Tulmen wants you to sing."

Nadja groaned, "In front of everyone? I don't think so."

"Oh, come on. She only wants to show off her future daughter-in-law," said Luca.

Nadja's palms felt clammy, and her heart plunged into the pit of her stomach. "But I don't even have a half-decent voice. I may not be a master musician, but I have ears enough to know *that*. I'm much more comfortable playing my flute."

Struck with the idea, she turned to her cousin. "Kizzy, run to my tent and bring back my flute. I'll try to stall until you get back."

"Got it!" said Kizzy, as she hurried away.

"It's just one song," said Luca, looking disappointed.

"Yes, well, she will still be able to show me off. But at least with my flute it'll be to everyone's advantage."

They meandered towards the raised platform, which held the carousing musicians. When they reached the makeshift stage, Nadja glanced back over her shoulder in time to see Kizzy trotting along on the outskirts of the crowd, making her way towards the empty camp. Nadja's tent was on the north end of camp, and she mentally willed her cousin to pick up the pace. Turning back towards the band, she waved at the leader.

"Hello there, Nadja!" crowed the bandleader, stooping to grin at her. His wobbly gait coupled with the purple stains on his shirt were proof he'd gotten an early start on the wine.

"Hi, Devyn. Look, I know Naaro wants me to sing 'Yours, Forever,' but I was thinking—"

"Wonderful!" he interrupted. Then standing tall he shouted, "Brothers and Sisters! The lovely bride-to-be, Miss Nadja Filamen, will do us the great the pleasure of joining us for the next song."

A cheer rose from the crowd, but all Nadja heard was the pounding din of the blood rushing through her ears. She caught her breath as Devyn reached down and hoisted her up onto the platform before settling back into his chair. He raised his horn to his lips, gave one elegant upbeat, and the band struck the first chord with a sweet sincerity hardly to be believed from a group of men who had, until just a moment ago, been the most boisterous of the merrymakers.

Nadja froze. Her eyes were saucers, darting back and forth as she scanned the crowd in a panicked search for Kizzy. Where was that girl? Based on where she was when Nadja last saw her, she should be back to this edge of town by now.

Just a few more moments . . .

A single note hung in the air like a ripe peach just waiting to be plucked.

Nadja had missed her entrance.

The band expertly picked up and replayed the previous eight bars of introduction as Nadja's eyes made one last desperate pass over the crowd. With no sign of her cousin, Nadja resigned herself to the fact that she would have to sing the song whether she wanted to or not. She closed her eyes and took a deep breath, swallowing her anxiety as the band once again cued her entrance.

It was a sweet love song with a simple but honest narrative which played at odds with the intricate melodic line. Nadja warbled her way through the first verse, catching her breath where she could, while her nerves added an extra dash of vibrato to her mediocre voice. She wished to be anywhere in the world other than on that stage at that moment. The smile she forced to her lips as she began the first chorus looked more like a pained grimace. Out of the corner of her eye, she caught sight of Jamila standing behind the desserts table, a serving spoon in hand and a warm smile across her face. Jamila bobbed an encouraging nod, and Nadja transformed.

Who was this jelly-legged girl standing petrified before a crowd of people she had known all her life?

Nadja felt her back straighten and her chin lift. Her clenched fists relaxed at her side, and she looked into the crowd, making eye contact with every person in turn.

She was the daughter of Jamila Filamen. A woman who stood tall and strong when met with adversity. A woman who made her own way and most certainly did *not* make excuses. Nadja was marrying Luca and her mother-in-law wanted to show her off. This was her life. At that moment she chose to do everything in her power to be worthy of it, finding enjoyment where she could and rising to meet any challenges that came along, with determination and grace.

As Nadja began the second verse, her grimace melted into a real smile. Her new confidence worked its unique magic on her voice in a way that only confidence could, changing it from a timorous, hushed twitter into a warm mantle of tones, swathing the listeners in comfort and lulling them into a relaxed reverie.

Nadja tilted her head and locked eyes with Luca, who was looking up at her with curious interest. She sang the final verse to him. A story of lovers reunited and undying love and devotion flowed from her lips, and she sang every word as if singing only for him.

A strange, puzzled look flitted across Luca's features. Then suddenly, the cloud lifted and a wide smile covered his face as he stared back at her in frank admiration. His eyes danced with amusement and longing. The heat of his gaze increased with each passing beat, and Nadja seemed unable to tear her eyes away from him as she sang the last few words.

The crowd erupted into thunderous applause, breaking their connection and snapping Nadja's attention forward. She returned the acclaim with a gracious bow as Naaro skittered across the platform, basking in the praise and glowing like the noontime sun. Nadja allowed her mother-in-law to lead her off the stage while the band struck up the next song. A wave of relief washed over her when her feet landed back on the ground.

"Marvelous! Absolutely marvelous!" crooned Naaro. "I must say I was a bit worried about you at the start. But, you turned it around and really came into your own by the second verse. Well done, my dear!"

"Well done, indeed."

Luca appeared next to Nadja, slipping an arm around her waist and pulling her close. She stiffened at his unexpected gesture, then relaxed against his side.

"Thank you both. I hope it was all right," she said. And then, in a low voice, "Singing is not one of my greater talents, but you'd have trouble finding anyone who plays the flute as well as I do."

Naaro nodded conspiratorially.

"Speaking of my flute, has either of you seen Kizzy?"

"Oh no dear, not since earlier this evening,"

"She hasn't returned from the, ah, errand you sent her on," said Luca.

Nadja furrowed her brow. "I need to go check on her."

Luca tightened his grip on her waist. "I'm sure she's fine," he said, taking her hand in his and raising it to his lips. "And we still have so many things to discuss."

She looked up at him in surprise, caught off guard by his public display of affection. "You're right, of course," she said sweetly, "and I'll only be gone for a few moments. Would you mind getting me a drink of water? I'm parched after that song. I'll meet you back at the arbor in a few minutes."

Leaving no room for argument, Nadja pried herself away from Luca's grasp and made a beeline towards the camp.

The chatter and music faded away as she approached the empty camp. The sun was gone, and the new moon did nothing to light her path. The festival fires cast dancing shadows along the edge of camp. Their light, and the warmth they provided, faded to nothingness as she neared the camp's center. Her soft footfalls along the dirt path rang out like pounding fists in the silent settlement. Still no sign of Kizzy. The empty stillness of the camp sent a shiver up Nadja's spine.

"Kizzy?"

Maybe she'd had trouble finding the flute. Or maybe she made it back to the festival, and they missed each other in passing. Nadja decided to peek in at her tent to be sure. Wrapping her arms around herself, she picked up her pace.

When she got to her tent, she lifted the flap and called into the blackness. No answer.

Satisfied Kizzy must have returned to the festival, Nadja closed the flap and headed back through the camp, scolding herself for not bringing a lantern, or a cloak for that matter, along with her.

She had not gone more than twenty paces when a sudden muffled sound reached her ears. Nadja froze, listening intently.

Silence.

"Kizzy?"

Another muffled noise was the reply. Nadja jerked her head in the direction of the sound and moved towards it, being careful not to stumble in the darkness. She maneuvered her way through the maze of tents until she reached the western edge of camp, still searching for the origin of the sound.

"Kizzy, is that you?"

A sharp cry cut through the cold night air. Nadja rushed forward, her eyes searching to pinpoint the location of the cry, when she noticed a faint glowing outline of a door in the distance.

The smokehouse.

Her heart caught in her throat as she ran towards the small makeshift building. The tall, dry prairie grass sliced at her bare legs and grabbed at pieces of her skirt, fighting to immobilize her. She heard a loud *thump* and saw the walls of the smokehouse shake in protest. As she approached the building, she reached out a trembling arm and flung the door wide, her nostrils filling with the spicy scent of curing meats.

Nadja froze in horror.

An enormous dark figure was hunched on the floor over the body of Kizzy, who lay on her back, thrashing in protest. Shreds of purple and gold littered the floor, remnants of the fabric which once covered her now exposed chest, and blood ran like a red ribbon down her face.

"Help me!" she screamed, as the monster's fist cracked against her jaw.

Her body went still.

The monster stood abruptly, bringing himself up to his full height and turning his attention to Nadja. His cruel eyes bored into hers. She opened her mouth to scream, but no sound came. An evil smile spread across his face as he raised his hands and moved towards her.

And then a high-pitched sound escaped Nadja's lips. It was small at first, but soon built in strength and volume. Her whole body began to vibrate uncontrollably with the incessant crescendo, and suddenly it was not just one pitch, but a chorus of dissonant tones which seemed to emanate from her very core.

The monster's eyes grew wide, and he drew his eyebrows together in confusion as he pulled his hands back to cover his ears.

Never taking her eyes off of him, Nadja's fear, panic, and fury fueled her auditory assault. Flashes of light popped before her eyes and the room spun around her. The last thing she remembered was seeing the monster fall to his knees, his eyes bulging and blood streaming from his nose and ears.

And then everything went black.

Chapter Three

Nadja's eyes flew open as she gasped for breath, her lungs straining to fill with air. Panting, she pulled her knees up to her chest and eased onto her side. The smokehouse floor was hard beneath her, and her head throbbed with every heartbeat.

"Nadja!" Kizzy's face blurred, then came into focus as Nadja blinked up at her through the haze. "Nadja, are you all right?" Her voice was fragile and trembling as she grabbed Nadja by the elbows and helped her to sit.

Nadja was mostly dead weight, and the muscles in her abdomen quivered with the effort to right herself. The back of her neck tightened as she lifted her head to face Kizzy, summoning every last ounce of will. Even still, she felt as though she was moving through a giant pit of tar. She opened her mouth to speak, but choked on her words. Her throat felt raw as if she had swallowed a handful of rusty nails. Dark, fuzzy shapes dotted her vision, and she squeezed her eyes shut a few times, blinking them into focus. Opening them wide, she scanned the room until her eyes came to rest on the body.

Nadja jolted, pushing herself away from the sprawled form. Adrenaline fueled her movements and brought back some of her strength. Everything came flooding back to her.

Kizzy.

The attack.

Her scream.

Turning, she grabbed her cousin by the shoulders. "Are you all right?" she croaked.

Kizzy nodded. She flung herself into Nadja's arms as a soft sob bubbled up from her chest. Nadja held her for a moment, and then they turned their attention to the body.

It was lying on its side, unmoving, with its face towards the ground. Nadja picked up a piece of leftover charred wood and nudged it. Nothing. A second poke, this time with more force, yielded the same result. She glanced at Kizzy, then put the end of the stick against its shoulder and shoved with all her might.

The two girls let out an involuntary squeal as the monster flopped onto its back. But it wasn't a monster. It was a man. A large man, to be sure, but still a man. They recognized him at once. It was Baulo Oramen, one of the tribal Elders and the Wanderers' delegate to the capital. His bald head glistened with sweat, and bloody trails flowed over the coarse texture of his salt-and-pepper beard and mustache. His mouth, which had come open when they'd rolled him over, displayed a crooked bow of malformed teeth, and his thick, unmoving tongue lay like a dead fish against his cheek.

"I think he's dead," whispered Kizzy.

"Dead," echoed Nadja, staring at the body in disbelief. "What happened?"

"I don't know." Kizzy shook her head.

Nadja pinned her cousin with her gaze. "Kizzy," she said. "What happened?"

Kizzy's eyes welled up with tears, and the story rushed from her mouth in a disjointed tumble of words and emotion. Nadja pieced together that Baulo had surprised Kizzy on her way to pick up Nadja's flute and dragged her to the smokehouse. If Kizzy's bare chest and the remnants of her dress were not evidence enough of his intentions, the things he said to her were. Nadja shuddered as Kizzy recounted every last filthy and vile thing he had uttered.

"And then you came in the door, and that's the last thing I remember until I woke up. Then I saw you both on the ground, and I was so worried he had gotten to you!"

"Are you . . . ?" Nadja fumbled with her words. "Did he . . . ?"

"I don't think so," Kizzy whispered, looking at the ground.

"Oh thank goodness!" Nadja pulled her cousin to her chest and closed her eyes with a deep sigh. When she opened them, her gaze fell on the body.

Realization and panic flooded her senses, a precursor to another jolt of adrenaline.

She had killed him.

Somehow she knew, down to the core of her being, that she—her . . . scream—had been the cause of his death.

Nadja's stomach muscles twitched. The trembling worked its way across her chest and back. It spread out until it reached the tips of her fingers and toes, until her whole body was vibrating.

What were they going to do? How could they possibly explain their current state? A child, a young woman, and a dead body—of an Elder, no less. Nothing about this situation boded well.

Nadja's breathing came harder and faster.

They could say they were attacked by an outsider.

No. Who would believe the two females had survived while Baulo, an exceptional warrior in his youth, had fallen?

It was hopeless.

She would die.

The penalty for murder was execution. Never mind Baulo had attacked Kizzy. He was one of the most respected Elders in the tribe. Nadja had little faith her accusations would be taken seriously, even with Kizzy's damaged state as evidence. It was the word of a woman against the reputation of an Elder.

At that moment, they heard soft footfalls approaching the smokehouse.

This was it.

Nadja squeezed her eyes shut and rocked back and forth, willing it all to disappear and hoping she might disappear along with it.

The door swung wide.

Jamila took one step inside, then stumbled back, taking in the gruesome scene before her. Her face blanched as she reached up a hand to cover her mouth.

"Oh my." Her voice faded to nothing.

The three of them stared at each other as seconds ticked by like infinity.

Jamila dropped her hand, and her mouth formed a hard line. Nadja knew that look. It was the face her mother wore into battle. Jamila rushed forward to grab an arm of each girl. "Tell me what happened. Quickly."

As soon as Nadja began to recount their nightmare, she could see the wheels in Jamila's head turning. Kizzy gasped as Nadja filled in the gap between the time Baulo knocked her unconscious and the time she awoke. When Nadja confessed her guilt, Jamila's features softened, and pity fluttered across her face. "Oh my poor, sweet girl," she whispered. "If only I'd gotten here sooner."

"How are you here?" asked Nadja.

"I wanted to tell you how proud I was of your song. I saw you join Luca and Naaro when you left the stage, but by the time I reached them, they said you had come back to camp to find Kizzy. When I didn't see either of you return after a few moments, I came to check on you." Jamila's voice cracked. "I'm so sorry I didn't make it here before."

Jamila embraced them with a fierceness which took their breaths away. Pulling back, she glanced over to where Baulo lay and then down at the ground. "There were rumors . . ."

Nadja and Kizzy exchanged puzzled looks. Before either one could say anything, Jamila snapped to them, her face now a solid mask of strength and determination.

"We must hurry," she said, jumping to her feet.

Nadja and Kizzy rose to their feet as best as their varying states of injury allowed.

"Gather up every last scrap of fabric," commanded Jamila. The girls moved to obey. "Be sure you get them all. Did either of you touch the body?"

Nadja replied that she had used a piece of wood to roll him over.

"Get that stick and bring it with us. We'll burn it in the fire pit in our tent along with the torn bits of Kizzy's dress. Kizzy, go home and change your clothes. Stay in your tent. Even better, stay in your bed, and do not come out until morning. When your parents ask about the dress and your injuries, tell them you lost your way in the dark and fell down the hill into the riverbed on the east side of camp when you came to search for Nadja's flute. Nadja and I will return to our tent and take care of a few other details." Jamila led them out of the smokehouse. Turning back, she cast one last look of disgust at what remained of the monster. "And remember. We were never here."

Even though the camp was deserted, the three of them stayed silent and kept to the shadows as they made their way back. They arrived at Kizzy's tent in a matter of minutes. As soon as Kizzy was changed and safely tucked in her bed for the night, Jamila and Nadja hurried to their own tent. Once through the flap, Jamila glanced back over her shoulder at Nadja. "Get your pack. You must leave. Now."

Jamila lit the fire, tossing in the dress scraps and bit of wood. Then she turned, hurried to her chest, threw open the lid and dug down to uncover a small box containing a quill, a tiny ink well, a few sheets of paper and a nub of wax. She sat at the table and scribbled furiously.

Nadja stood in stunned silence, watching her mother's movements with a sense of disbelief. "What do you mean, I have to leave?"

Jamila continued writing with her head down, her eyebrows knit in concentration. Her voice was calm and low as she spoke. "You must go. If anyone uncovers what happened, you know what the consequences are."

"But if I run, won't that be a clear admission of guilt?"

"Not if I can help it. And besides, if you stay, it will only be worse."

"And what about Kizzy?"

"She won't breathe a word of what happened to anyone. You also know what the punishment is for a girl who seduces a man outside of her marriage."

"But she didn't seduce him! He attacked her!"

"I know that." Jamila sighed. "But if he had succeeded in his attack and you had not come to her aid, it would have been his word against hers. And you can be certain he was counting on that to ensure her silence. As it stands now, it is still his reputation against her word. She won't tell a soul. Kizzy will be fine. Her father will make sure of that."

Jamila folded the paper and slid it across the table.

"But where will I go?"

"I'm sending you to your uncle in Cantio. He will help you and keep you safe." She gave Nadja a sharp look. "Stop standing there like a statue. Pack quickly and lightly. There is no time to lose." Taking a fresh sheet of paper, she dipped the quill into the ink and began to write again.

The urgency in her voice prompted Nadja to action. She flew back and forth across the room, gathering anything that might help her on her journey. A few changes of clothes, some dried meat and fruit and the leftovers from her breakfast, a canteen of water, her flute, and blowpipe. For a few moments the only sounds accompanying her movements were the staccato scratches of the quill against the paper.

Jamila folded the second piece of paper. Walking over to the fire to heat the nub, she dripped the melted wax onto the paper to seal it. She handed it to Nadja.

"Your uncle goes by the name Tau Machinal. He is a barge captain in Cantio. Give him this letter when you find him. He will know what to do."

Nadja shot a questioning look at the other piece of paper still lying on the table.

"That is a letter from you telling me you had second thoughts about marrying Luca. Something about wanting to find adventure and see the world and such nonsense," Jamila said dryly. She returned to her chest. This time she produced a little, round tin which Nadja had never seen. Jamila opened the tin and carefully dumped the contents into Nadja's hand. Nadja's eyes marveled as she looked at a small mound of creamy, lustrous pearls. They often found pearls while diving for oysters in the late winter months when the Wanderers traveled up the Alabaster Coast. But the pearls should have been brought back to camp and used for bartering with outsiders for supplies which were easier to trade for than to make themselves. Jamila had taken a great risk in keeping some for herself.

She gave Nadja a wan smile. "I was saving these for a time when we might need it. It would appear that time is now. You'll need something to barter with along your way, and these should help you make it to Cantio with little trouble." She walked over to Nadja's cot and scooped up the mirror which had been cast aside in the excitement of the morning. "Take this too. It's silver and will fetch a good price."

Nadja protested, "I can't take that. It's too precious to you."

Jamila grabbed Nadja and pulled her to her chest, wrapping her arms tightly around her daughter. "*You* are too precious to me," she choked, and kissed the top of

Nadja's head. "If you don't trade the mirror, give it back to me when I see you again."

Nadja clung to her mother. She buried her head in Jamila's neck, indulging for one moment in the comfort she always felt in her mother's strong arms. She closed her eyes and inhaled her mother's scent, lavender mixed with fresh rain, trying to build a memory which would carry her through whatever came next.

Too soon Jamila released her and backed away, reaching up with her hand and wiping a single tear from her cheek. "Go southwest into the Forest of Kithira. The closer you get to Cantio, the more well-traveled the area becomes, and the more roads you'll find. If you can find a main road, you should have no trouble making your way into the city. If not, well, you'll reach the river sooner or later, and you'll know where to go from there."

Nadja fastened her cloak around her, shouldering her pack and taking her blowpipe in hand. "What about you? What will you do?" she asked, the sinking feeling returning to her stomach.

"I will be fine. I'll go back to the celebration and tell them you became suddenly ill and have gone to bed for the night. I won't return home until well into the early-morning hours once the celebration has ended. Only then will I 'discover' your letter. They won't send out a search until everyone has had a chance to recover from tonight's festivities. That gives you a half-day head start. And, Nadja," Jamila squeezed Nadja's arm, "they will send out a search. Please stay hidden."

"I will."

"I'll go first. Give me just enough time to reach the edge of camp, then go." Jamila grabbed Nadja for one final embrace. "I love you," she whispered.

"I love you too," Nadja replied.

And Jamila was gone.

Nadja picked up a small lantern near her bed and lit it. Then, she stood in the middle of the tent, her eyes glued to the flap, and focused on her escape. Mentally, she began slowly counting to fifty. She didn't dare look around the tent, or the thought of leaving her home, her family, and the safety of everything she had ever known would weigh too heavily on her heart and possibly shake her resolve.

. . . forty-eight . . . forty-nine . . . fifty.

She opened the flap and stepped out into the night.

Chapter Four

Nadja's entire body cried out in protest.

She had been walking for about six hours, and the fear and adrenaline which powered her flight in the beginning had long since worn off. She was exhausted and needed to find somewhere to rest. Being alone at night in the steppes was asking for trouble, and she felt lucky to have made it this far without encountering any.

The grass under her feet had become a soft carpet, and a welcome reprieve from the prickly brush which had paved the first part of her journey. The chilly night air had already formed a light dew on the sod. The forest was near. Another day's walk, and she could disappear into the trees, taking shelter among the densely packed hardwoods and finding solace in the shade. Even now, still hours from the forest edge, the shrubs of the prairie were transforming into tall trees, scattered here and there like welcoming outposts, guiding her towards the arboreous haven.

Nadja's steps slowed as she leaned on her blowpipe. The weapon had made itself useful as a walking stick, and she was relieved to have something to help keep her upright as she stumbled along in the night. The lantern dimmed, and the night air was cool on her face. She took a deep breath and closed her eyes, savoring the caress of a breeze as it lifted her hair and dried the sweat soaking the back of her neck.

Without warning, a piercing scream shot through the darkness and snapped Nadja back to attention. She swung around, raising her lantern just in time to catch a flash of white swoop down a few steps to her left. She let out a cry as she stumbled backwards, losing her balance and falling to the ground. The lantern flew from her hands. It landed on its side just out of reach, and its contents spilled out over the damp grass. She looked up and saw the owl ascending into the starry sky, a plump, wriggling mouse clutched in its talons. The steady beat of its wings kept time in the night as the lantern faded to nothingness.

Nadja froze, listening to the sound of the owl disappear into the dark. Once it was out of earshot, a thick silence settled on her shoulders, giving her an uneasy feeling in the pit of her stomach. She reached out and pawed the ground around her, finally landing on the broken lantern. She silently cursed herself for not packing something to use to start a fire. With no moon and no fire to light her way, finding somewhere to settle in for the night would be next to impossible. Planting one end of her blowpipe in the ground, she pulled herself up to standing and adjusted her pack. She strained her eyes to see anything which might give her a clue about what to do next. Thankfully, the night was clear. And, while the stars didn't cast enough glow to illuminate the surrounding area, she could see the outlines of the few lonely trees against the night sky. Thinking it would be safer to spend the night in one of those trees rather than on the ground, she pointed her feet at the closest one and began dragging herself towards it.

After a few steps, the anxious twitch in Nadja's stomach began to nag her. It was probably just a culmination of the entire night's events coupled with the fact she was now without light or fire. But the more steps she took, the more anxious she became.

And then, she realized why. Ever since her encounter with the owl, the prairie had gone silent. Not just back to its restful tranquility, but completely silent. No scuttling feet of nocturnal vermin. No far off calls of other birds of prey. Even the wind was still.

The sweat returned to Nadja's neck, and fear tickled the nerves in her spine. The silhouette of the tree in the distance grew larger as she got closer, and she focused her sight on it. She picked up her pace, her feet following the new tempo of her heartbeat.

Then quietly, from the darkness some distance behind her, she heard a faint howl.

Alarm bells rang in her head as she moved faster, her legs burning, somewhere between a walk and a run. Another howl, closer this time, caused every hair on her body to stand on end. Was it the same creature or another one? She dared not look back to find out. It was too dark to see anything that wasn't right on top of her. And it didn't matter, anyway. She recognized the sound of those howls.

Wolves.

It might be one or one hundred, the outcome would be the same for her. Nadja was proficient in many skills: diving, fishing, gathering, and hunting small game. But nothing which might be defined as "fighting off large wild animals" was in her repertoire. When her fight-or-fight response cued, there was only one option. Run.

Nadja shot forward, her foot slipping on the damp grass. She tripped, but caught herself, and picked up speed. A growl echoed through the darkness, breaking the silence behind her as the wolf pack seemed to match her movements. She could tell from the different origins of the sounds there were at least three or four of them.

The tree was just ahead of her now, and a tiny glimmer of hope lit within her heart. She was close enough to see individual limbs, so if she could make it to the tree, she wouldn't have to climb blindly.

The wolves were closing in on her. She put on another burst of speed, racing towards the safety of the tree.

She got there with no time to spare. Running at full speed, she dropped her blowpipe and leapt upward, grabbing the lowest branch with both hands. Using her momentum to gain height, she hooked one leg over the branch to pull herself up.

Her body jerked as she was snatched back with a snarl. One of the wolves had his teeth buried deep in her pack and was bringing her down along with it. She wrapped her arms and leg around the branch, holding on for her life. Knowing she didn't have the strength to win this tug-of-war, Nadja let go with her right arm long enough for her pack to slip away into the waiting swarm.

The wolves interest in her pack bought her enough time to strengthen her grip on the branch and pull herself up on top of it. The tree was rough and its jagged bark cut into her hands as she scrambled her way up and out of the reach of the wolves. When the branches got thinner and smaller, she anchored her feet as best as she could and hugged the leader limb to her chest.

When the tumult below her subsided, Nadja relaxed her grip on the tree and settled into a V where two larger limbs met. An occasional noise from below signaled the wolves were still there. She would have to wait them out. She tightened her cloak around her and tried to get comfortable.

There, the shock of the night dissipated, and the weight of everything she had been through hit her like a blow to the head. And now, with her meager supplies being looted by a pack of wolves, she truly had nothing and no one. To return to her tribe was suicide and continuing on her journey meant almost certain death. Nadja's heart broke, and she wept as one mourning the loss of a loved one. But for her, it was the loss of everyone she had ever loved. Her body racked with sobs, and she stuffed the edge of her cloak into her mouth in a feeble attempt to muffle the noise. She cried until exhaustion overcame her and swept her away into a fitful slumber.

Nadja crossed into the Forest of Kithira and removed her cloak, soaking in the coolness of the shade. Still wearing her green dress, it had been necessary to keep her bare skin protected underneath her cloak as she finished her journey through the steppes. The heavy cloak was both a blessing and a curse as it protected her from sunburn but gave her body heat no means of escape.

Daybreak had come too early and brought with it another blistering day. Nadja awoke, stiff and dehydrated, in the safety of her tree, her eyes matted with the crusted remnants of dried tears. The wolves had given up hope of enjoying her for dinner during the night, probably because they had filled their bellies with the rations from her pack, leaving her with nothing to eat. Thankfully, her canteen remained intact. But, after walking all day on an empty stomach, the water was almost gone. Finding water was her first priority. Food was a close second.

The forest stretched out tall and dense before her. Setting her pack on the ground, she took a deep breath in and exhaled slowly, closing her eyes and tuning her ears to the sounds of the forest.

A soft breeze rustled to her right, coming in from the northwest, and swooping and shushing through the high treetops. The corners of her mouth twitched upward as a puff of air broke through the canopy and swirled around her, ruffling the tatters of her skirt and cooling her sun-baked face. She detected a light rhythmic thumping as if someone was tapping out a pattern of lazy beats on a fluffy pillow. She angled her ears towards the cadence and followed it from right to left as the formation of hawks passed overhead and deeper into the forest. Opening her eyes, she shouldered her pack and followed suit.

The ground gradually grew soft and moist, and after an hour of picking her way through the trees, Nadja came to the banks of a small bubbling stream. She knelt at the water's edge and gulped the elixir, relishing its restorative properties as it relieved her parched lips and throat. Once she had drunk to her limit and filled her canteen, she peeled off her dress and shoes and sank into the stream with a sigh, enjoying the brief reprieve. The water was only about knee deep, and Nadja laid her head back, reveling in the swirls and eddies which massaged her tired and aching body. Her scalp tingled in response to her fingers as she scrubbed the debris from her hair. After a time all too brief, the muscles in her swollen and blistered feet began to cramp from the cold, and she begrudgingly dragged herself from the water.

Nadja pulled on a clean white shirt and long tan skirt. Though skirts were standard dress for Wanderer women, they were not without any sense of utility. Some tasks were simply too difficult to do in a long skirt. She reached between her legs and grasped the back hem, finding the little loop sewn there. Pulling the hem back up through her legs, she fastened it to a button hidden in her waistband. She pulled on her soft leather slippers, now worn thin with days of walking. They were a perfect choice for her betrothal celebration, but Nadja lamented not changing into a pair of sturdy boots before fleeing camp. Then, she turned her thoughts to supper.

The sun was setting, and since she had neither light nor fire, she would need to work fast if she wanted to eat before morning. Grabbing a few sharp stones, she made quick work of a branch from a nearby young tree. She positioned herself on a stone outcrop over the stream with her makeshift spear and waited. While the stream was a boon for water and a bath, it lacked for food. After a half hour, it became clear the single small trout she'd managed to spear early on was her only food for the night. Using the sharp stones and her fingers, she gutted the fish and rinsed it in the stream as the sun was setting. She devoured the meat, picking through the bones and trying not to waste a single piece. The trout lessened her hunger pains, but did not fill her belly.

With the setting sun, the air turned crisp. Nadja pulled on her cloak and put together a makeshift camp. A large elm tree a short distance from the stream marked the edge of a small clearing in the trees. The base of the elm was carpeted with moss. A few colorful flowering plants peppered the ground, taking advantage of the break in the canopy and stretching up towards the sun's window. Nadja relaxed onto the soft and dank moss, resting her back against the elm. With nightfall at hand, and nothing to do until morning, she was left with nothing to distract her from her own thoughts.

It was hard to believe just a day earlier she had been laughing and dancing at her betrothal celebration, preparing to marry Luca and begin her new life as a wife and mother. How could so much change over the course of just a few hours? One moment, she was celebrating a new life, and the next she was fighting just to stay alive.

Nadja stood up and crossed over to where she'd tossed her dress. Scooping it up, she walked back to the tree and resumed her seat. She looked at the once vibrant green dress, now a shade of sickly gray in the moonlight. She ran her hands along the intricate pattern of beads her mother had lovingly and diligently hand-stitched and let the streamers of skirt slip through her fingers. Bringing the fabric up to her cheek, she closed her eyes and allowed her mind to take her back home, if but for a moment. She felt her mother's embrace and the warmth of conversation and laughter with Kizzy. She breathed in the aroma of a delicious boar roasting over the cooking pit and felt the freedom of diving in the sea. She snuggled into the comfort and safety of her people, the tribe and way of life she knew. She felt the heat of the sun and remembered a time when figuring out the puzzle of Luca was her biggest worry.

Nadja opened her eyes and gazed down at the dress, a reminder of the life which was no longer hers. It was of no use to her now, but she could not bring herself to part with it. Instead, she folded it carefully and tucked it into her pack.

Tears pricked at the corners of her eyes, but they would not come. Shaping her pack into something resembling a pillow, Nadja laid next to the protective elm. Her heart was full and heavy, in stark contrast to the evening before when she had stood before the celebrating crowd and sung with determination and joy. Tonight her song was different.

Nadja parted her lips, and a quiet, doleful tune issued forth, carrying with it her sadness and loss. The minor melody gave vent to her aching heart, and as she keened her way through the song, her grief flowed from her like the ignorant stream dancing just a few feet away. It was to this eerie lullaby she finally fell asleep.

> *Hearken to me and heed my song*
> *For time is close at hand, at hand*
> *Till sleep descends on me at last*
> *With its final command*
>
> *When darkness comes to close my eyes*
> *And stillness rests on me, on me*
> *And mists surround my body there*
> *How grateful will I be*
>
> *Weep not for me, for when I sleep*
> *In peace I find reprieve, reprieve*
> *And no more sorrows shall I keep*
> *And no more heart to grieve*

Dawn broke, and Nadja awoke, her nostrils filled with scent of dirt and decay. She was facedown in the moss, her cheek scratchy and damp, and she realized she must have rolled off of her pack during the night. She sat up and rubbed her eyes. Blinking them into focus, she froze.

A pit formed in her stomach as she took in her surroundings.

The clearing, which had been home to a sweet collection of verdant leaves and bright flowers, was now a dried bed of brown, dead vegetation. Once proud and colorful blooms now hung their heads in drab shame, and the grass stood sharp like thousands of little pikes. The destruction stretched out about eight paces in all directions, creating an almost perfect circle of wasted earth.

Nadja's legs trembled as she stood and picked up her pack. Her eyes traced a path up the trunk of the old oak. Overhead brown and brittle leaves, made almost golden in the early-morning sun, rustled ominously in the breeze.

Nadja backed away, her shoes crunching in the devastation underfoot. What could cause something like this? A disease? But what kind of disease worked so quickly? The clearing had been full of life only hours before.

Something wasn't right. This was unnatural.

Nadja's feet finally found soft ground as she stepped out of the circle, and relief washed over her. Turning and heading towards the stream, she cast one last puzzled glance over her shoulder. That was a mystery which would have to remain one. She still had a long way to go.

Chapter Five

Nadja followed the stream for a day or so until it turned and headed east. Still with no light or fire, she survived on fish and what she could forage. Her Aunt Pili married into a family of gatherers, so Nadja had gleaned rudimentary knowledge of some wild edible plants from Kizzy.

Parting ways with the meandering stream, Nadja settled on a direct southwesterly route. She was learning the forest a little more every day—which trees made for the best shelter, where small and edible animals preferred to make their homes. She practiced a few minutes each day with her blowpipe because, though she had no fire source at present, she needed to vary her diet once she solved that problem.

At her current pace she was still about nine day's journey from Cantio. Though she had left the stream behind, finding a new source of fresh water was still top priority, which was why the darkening afternoon sky was a welcome sight. A rumble of thunder in the distance drew her attention back over her right shoulder.

That's when she saw it.

An enormous tree rose out of the ground like it was trying to pull the earth up along with it. Its serpentine branches wound around in every direction. The bottom ones were low enough for her to reach and as big around as some of the other mature trees standing near it. The trunk was so large Nadja reckoned it would take at least twenty men standing hand in hand to reach around it. Roughly textured bark of gray speckled with white mottled with patches of smooth burnt umber. It was bumpy and knobby and gnarled, looking as though it had borne the trials of the last thousand years. A large indentation along the side of the trunk could have been the thumbprint of some fairytale giant of long ago. The smallest of the smooth, pale green leaves was as big as her hand and sprouted out in chaotic bunches. Like the unruly wild child among his well-mannered peers, the tree looked completely out of place.

Nadja marveled at the ancient hardwood. Never had she seen anything like it. She approached reverently, her hand outstretched, and ran her fingers over the exquisitely painted bark.

A sudden boom of thunder, this time only a few minutes away, broke the spell and pulled her back to the task at hand. Determining she could take shelter in the thumbprint, she grabbed one of the low branches and climbed. Once her pack was stowed, she set to work twisting and setting the leaves to funnel the rainwater into her canteen. The air was still, and Nadja hoped her setup would hold through the storm. No sooner had the thought floated through her mind than the tree rocked with a sudden blast of air, followed by a thunderous downpour. The canteen flew through the air, landing who-knows-where, and Nadja backed as far into the huge thumbprint as possible. With just enough space between her body and the edge of the opening, Nadja settled in as best as she could. The branches of the old tree creaked and moaned, protesting the gusting winds. But the hardwood stood firm. Occasionally a shifting wind blew the rain sideways, peppering Nadja with cold, needly droplets. But, for the most part, she remained safe and dry in her hiding place. Bunching up her pack, she leaned against it, trying to get comfortable. It would be a long night.

The storm subsided while she slept. The hot morning sun mixed with the storm's soggy aftermath, creating a heavy, sticky layer of humidity which was difficult to breathe. Nadja's half-hour search of the surrounding woods produced her canteen, which was indeed filled—with mud. With a sigh, she left the shelter of her tree and continued towards Cantio.

By the afternoon, she'd traced another water source. The forest grew denser and darker by the minute. She heard the bubbling before she saw it, and followed the sound to its origin. It was a small but deep spring, a little wider than the span of her blowpipe and twice in length. Vegetation grew lush and thick along the bank opposite her, and a few persistent rays of afternoon sun pierced the branches overhead, giving the pool a welcoming glow amidst the darkness surrounding it. After a day's walking with no water, and a handful of berries to eat, she dropped her belongings and knelt at the water's edge with relief. She cupped her hands and dipped them into the spring, breaking its mirrorlike quality and rippling the surface. After washing and refilling her canteen, she took a deep breath and leaned over, dunking her head into the water to escape the heat and humidity of the day, if only from the neck up. The minutes ticked by as her lungs, trained by a lifetime of diving, held strong. When she could hold her breath no longer, she came up for air, flipping her now wet hair behind her. She wiped the water from her eyes with her sleeve and leaned down to take another sip.

The water had returned to its glassy stillness, and before Nadja's fingers touched the surface again, she noticed her reflection . . . and someone else's.

Trying not to make any sudden movements, Nadja slowly looked up and discovered she wasn't the only one enjoying the watering hole. Across the water, a few feet away, a large ghost cat stood motionless, its unblinking yellow eyes boring into her own. One of the most feared predators in the Forest of Kithira, the black cat was almost invisible among the dark shadows and abundant flora outlining the other side of the spring. An incessant low, purring noise emanated from deep within the animal, and it watched Nadja with interest. Nadja's heartbeat quickened as it hurried to push adrenaline through every inch of her body. Soon, the sound of the blood rushing through her ears matched the rhythm of the cat's purr.

She couldn't outrun it. A ghost cat could run faster than any human. The trees were no option either. Ghost cats were climbers. And even if she had time to get her blowpipe loaded and in position before the cat was on her, the small darts were no match for the sleek feline.

Almost imperceptibly, Nadja crept her right hand towards her improvised fishing spear, never taking her eyes off the cat. The cat's tongue flicked out, running along the edges of its muzzle, and Nadja glimpsed the flashing white fangs underneath. Those fangs could easily snap her little spear.

The ghost cat crouched. In a blink, it sprang across the pool with a roar, claws outstretched. The cat slammed into her with the force of a charging bull, knocking her away from the spear and onto her back. Her head slammed against the ground. She screamed as the animal's razor-like claws dug into her shoulders and pinned her to the forest floor. The ground beneath her back was spongy, and the weight of the cat caused her to sink down. Nadja lifted her feet, trying to connect with the beast's belly, all the while frantically groping for the spear with her right hand. She threw up her left arm, shielding her face and neck as the cat aimed its fangs at that very spot. Instead, the animal's gaping maw clamped down on her forearm, its teeth sinking in almost to the bone. The cat yanked and pulled at Nadja's arm, tearing bits of flesh and muscle in a frustrated attempt to uncover its true target. The violent shaking inched the pair towards the water's edge.

The water!

Seizing her only means of escape, Nadja's fingers finally found the spear. With every ounce of her strength, she swung her arm in a wide arc. The sharpened tip of the spear connected with the soft flesh of the ghost cat's neck. Its tip sank in only about an inch before snapping off, momentarily stunning the beast. The cat swayed, releasing its hold on Nadja long enough for her to roll onto her stomach and make for the water. Halfway in, the cat's paws connected with her back, flattening her to the ground. Nadja thrashed against the weight of the predator, splashing water in a feeble attempt to distract it. She knew the cat's next move. A bite to the back of her neck and a swift severing of her spinal cord.

She squeezed her eyes shut.

Thunk!

The weight lifted. Stunned, Nadja lay unmoving for a beat. Then her survival instinct kicked in, and she took a deep breath and rolled into the water.

Nadja's body sank to the bottom of the spring as a stream of bubbles rose to the surface, transforming the crystal clear pool into a frothing crimson cauldron.

Chapter Six

A log popped and crackled, startling Nadja awake. She opened her eyes and gazed up at the cream-colored ceiling. In the hazy moment between sleep and waking, she drew her eyebrows together trying to remember when she and her mother had swapped their leather hut coverings for canvas. Puzzled, she lifted her hand to brush the hair out of her eyes and gasped as the movement sent bolts of pain shooting up the length of her arm and through her shoulder.

Now fully awake, she sat up slowly and surveyed the area. Of course she wasn't at home. She looked around at the small tent, then down at her bandaged arm.

"Good afternoon, Pretty Lady."

Nadja jumped at the greeting and twisted to face the opening, biting her lip as her shoulders burned.

"I wouldn't move so fast, if I were you," rolled the velvety baritone, "unless you want to reopen some of those wounds."

Nadja stared at the man crouched inside the entrance. He had a handsome face, with chiseled angular features, topped with a mop of wavy brown hair. His sapphire eyes sparkled with mirth, and he appeared to be about the same age as she. Nadja wasn't so injured that she didn't appreciate how attractive he was. Nor was she so affected that she let down her guard.

"Who are you?" she demanded.

"Well, I'd say I'm your hero," he said, flashing her a perfect grin. When his reply elicited a cold stare from Nadja, his face sobered. "I heard your screaming and found you wrestling with a ghost cat. You took a pretty good beating and fell into the spring. I fished you out, brought you to my home away from home," he said, gesturing to the tent, "patched you up and let you sleep it off."

"How long have I been asleep?"

"About a day."

"A whole day?" Nadja exclaimed, pushing back the blankets and struggling to her feet. That was a whole day she should have spent putting distance between her and the Wanderer camp.

"Whoa, slow down," said the man, reaching in to take her elbow.

As Nadja stood, she felt a cool breeze rush up her legs. Looking down, she discovered not only was she wearing an enormous shirt which hung to her knees, but she was most certainly not wearing any pants.

With a squeal, she tumbled down and desperately tried to pull the blankets around her waist. Her cheeks flamed with embarrassment.

"Up or down, make up your mind," said the man.

"Where are my clothes?" she squeaked.

"They are hanging out by the fire."

Nadja glared at him, pulling the blankets up to her chin.

The man let go of her elbow and held up his hands. "Like I said, I pulled you out of the spring. You were soaked, and your clothes were in no better shape than you were. Would you have rather I'd left you as you were? You'd have had plenty of time for an infection set in."

"No," said Nadja, casting her eyes to the ground.

"And if your dignity is what you're worried about," he continued solemnly, "you have my word I was a complete gentleman."

Nadja was silent for a moment, then lifted her eyes to meet his. "Thank you."

"But I can't promise I'm always a gentleman," he grinned and winked at her before scooting back out of the tent. A moment later he opened the flap and tossed in her dry clothes. "Come on out when you're ready. Supper is on the fire." Before closing the flap, he flashed her another smile. "And my name is Pax."

Nadja dressed as quickly as she could. The smell of roasting meat rolled into the tent, causing her stomach to clench and rumble. Her skirt was in good shape, but the shoulders and sleeve of her tunic were shredded beyond all levels of decency. As she removed the tunic and cast it aside, she noticed a pair of matching dotted arcs across either side of her chest. She gingerly touched the puncture wounds left by the cat's claws. They were tender, but seemed to be healing well. Reaching up and across her body with her right arm, she found the ones it had left across the back of her shoulder. They felt about the same as the ones on the front. With her left arm out of commission she couldn't check the other side, so she rolled both of her shoulders to compare pain level and range of movement. About the same. Satisfied, she put Pax's voluminous shirt back on, pulling up the bottom hem, as best as she could with one arm, and knotting it at her waist.

She left the tent and took in her surroundings as her eyes adjusted to the afternoon sun. The camp was small, clearly just for one, but well situated in a little glade. An empty spit bridged a modest fire, and to the left of that, a double bit axe stood in the middle of a perfectly split woodpile. Its generous size suggested her rescuer hadn't planned on going anywhere for a few days. She turned her head in his direction and caught her breath.

He was standing in front of a stump, preparing the food. Even with his back to her, she could tell the dim light in the tent hadn't done him justice. He was much larger than he'd appeared crouching in the doorway of the tent. A generous head taller than she was, his shoulders and back were large and broad. The muscles in his arms were powerful and defined in a way which comes from years of manual labor. The sun's rays illuminated errant strands of golden hair hidden within his chestnut mane and deepened the color of his already tanned skin. He turned at that moment and spied her, causing her stomach to flutter in a most peculiar way.

"You know, you might just wear my shirt better than I do," he joked.

"Mine is a bit beyond repair," she said, turning hurriedly and glancing around the camp in an attempt to hide her rosy cheeks. "Have you seen my pack? I have another one I can change into."

"Nope. But, I wasn't worried about that at the time. Here, eat something. It will help you get your strength back. I'll see if I can find your pack."

He handed Nadja a plate of roasted rabbit, a few chunks of bread and cheese, and a deep purple plum. Her eyes grew wide, and she practically drooled at the spread. But, she simply took the plate and said, "Thank you."

"You're welcome."

She settled down on the ground in front of the fire and looked up at him again. "No, I mean it. Thank you. You probably saved my life."

Pax nodded and lifted one side of his mouth in a charming, crooked smile. "I'll be back in a little while. There's more bread and cheese and fruit in the sack over there if you're still hungry after you finish your plate," he said, pointing to the stump. Then, he turned and headed into the forest.

Nadja wasted no time digging into her meal. After days of nothing but raw fish and foraged scraps, the smoky rabbit meat and creamy cheese were something out of a dream. The plum burst in her mouth as she bit into it, sending sweet juicy rivulets running down her chin and leaving a sticky trail behind. She giggled at the sensation, recalling the time her mother purchased a watermelon from a merchant ship in Chansey, and they sat along the seashore eating until they were stuffed and covered in pink stains.

A half hour later, her hunger satisfied, she was sucking the last bits of rabbit off of the bones when a rustling in the undergrowth announced Pax's return.

"I believe this belongs to you," he proclaimed, setting the pack next to her. "And I found your walking stick as well." He handed her the blowpipe.

"Thank you," said Nadja, turning her head to hide her smirk.

"That hike worked up an appetite. Any meat left?"

Nadja's face fell, and she eyed her empty plate in embarrassment. "Oh, um, I thought everything on the plate was for me," she stammered. "I didn't realize there was nothing else left." She looked up to see his eyes twinkling in merriment and the corners of his mouth threatening to betray him.

"Just kidding," he said as his lips melted into an easy smile. "I ate while you were sleeping." He walked over to the stump and fished out a chunk of bread. "But I could use a snack."

Settling down onto the ground next to her, he tore off a piece of bread and popped it into his mouth. "So, what's your story?"

Nadja stiffened as she fortified her protective mental barrier and searched for a believable story. Slowly, she lowered her plate to the ground. "What do you mean?"

"Well, you could start by telling me your name."

Warning bells rang I her head. "Uh, I'm nobody important," she offered, lamely.

Pax looked thoughtful for a moment. "All right, Pretty Lady. What are you doing out here in the middle of the woods?"

Nadja slid her plate away from her and shifted on the soft grass, scooting closer to the fire. The sun was setting, and the air was turning cooler. Clearing her throat, she replied, "I'm headed west to visit family." It wasn't a lie, technically.

She saw the wheels turning in his head as he chewed his last bit of bread and stared at her small pack, which was obviously not stocked for travel of any great length. He opened his mouth to say something else, but she cut him off.

"What about you? What are you doing out here in the middle of the forest?" she asked, trying to divert the focus from herself. Her plan worked easily.

He leaned towards her and lowered his voice. "I'm on a quest," he said with an air of mystery.

The scent of pine and earth washed over Nadja as he drew near to her, momentarily shaking her guard. "What kind of quest?" she asked.

"The kind only for the strong and courageous," Pax said with intensity, leaning in closer and closer to Nadja.

"It's the kind of quest which either refines or destroys a man. And if I find what I'm searching for, it will bring honor and fortune to my entire family." He was almost nose-to-nose with her now.

"And what is it you seek?" she breathed.

Pax brought his lips within inches of her ear. "I seek," he whispered, "the great and elusive Auldwood Oak." With that, he leaned back lazily on his elbows and chuckled, polishing off the last bite of bread.

Confusion flitted across Nadja's features but shifted into annoyance as she realized he was teasing her again.

"A tree," she said flatly.

"Ahh, but it's not just any tree. The wood from the Auldwood Oak is the rarest and most coveted crafting material of luthiers across Amrantir. They say it's as light as a feather, but as strong and sturdy as Mount Stalwind. And the resonance produced by instruments made from it is almost otherworldly. But, like I said, they're extremely rare."

"Have you seen one before?" she asked.

"No."

"But, you know where one is."

"Nope."

"Then how do you expect to find one?"

"The roots of the Auldwood Oak run deeper than any other tree in the forest. They grow gigantic, and there are stories of some living to be thousands of years old. They're rare for two reasons. One, they only produce seeds once every hundred years or so. And, two, their roots release a toxin into the soil which prevents any other Auldwood seeds from taking root within a day's ride of the parent tree. So, in order for a new tree to grow, the seed has to travel a long way to find suitable ground. And, I figure since I'm already a week into my search and I haven't seen one yet, I must be getting closer."

Nadja suspected his finishing logic, but decided not to challenge him on it. Instead she asked, "Why is finding this tree so important to you?"

Pax sat up and rested his elbows on his knees. "You know, you haven't yet asked me what happened when I found you being attacked by the ghost cat."

Nadja had wondered, but her memories of the attack were hazy. She remembered the cat charging her. She remembered its hot breath on her neck and feeling like she couldn't breathe because of its weight on her chest. She remembered trying in vain to get to the water before, as if by some miracle, the weight lifted. Then the water enveloped her and made her wounds burn even more.

Pax stood and walked over to the woodpile. He gripped the axe with one hand and pulled it free, swinging it loosely from side to side as he walked back toward Nadja. When he was within striking distance, his relaxed features drew together into a look of intense focus, and his eyes turned to lock onto a spot to her right. Then, in one swift and fluid movement, his muscles rippled as he brought the axe up behind his back and over his head, gripped the handle with his other hand, and launched it forward. The axe flew straight, turning end over end, and embedded one of its sharp blades into a large tree at the edge of camp.

Nadja jumped at the *crunch* which crackled the air as the axe connected with the tree.

Then it all made sense, why the ghost cat seemed to disappear mid-attack, and why Pax didn't have a scratch on him. She was grateful he had dispatched the cat, but upset to think a tiny miscalculation on his part could have ended her instead. She chose to focus on the positive.

"Impressive."

"I'm a woodsman," he shrugged, pulling the axe free from the tree. "It's a family business. If I could find an Auldwood Oak, it would be a windfall for us." He hesitated, then added, "I'm also a bit of a woodworker myself," rubbing the back of his neck and appearing, for the first time, to lose a tiny bit of that confidence which had, until then, seemed inexhaustible.

"Really?" Nadja's interest piqued. "What kinds of things do you make?"

"Anything, really. Furniture, toys. But what I like making most is musical instruments."

Nadja nodded. "Yet another reason to find the Auldwood Oak."

"Exactly."

"So, you make stringed instruments?"

"Yes. But I make wind instruments as well," said Pax, crossing to the tent. He opened the flap and reached inside, digging through a small leather bag. Returning to Nadja, he said, "This isn't much, but it's something I've been working on while I've been wandering the woods." He sat back down beside her and opened his fingers.

In his hand rested an expertly crafted oaken ocarina. It stretched across the length of his large palm, from wrist to fingertips, and reminded Nadja of a knobbed cane handle.

"May I?" she asked, glancing up at Pax, who nodded in reply.

Still favoring her left arm, she reached over with her right, lifted the ocarina from his hands and placed it in her lap. She turned it over, noting the smoothness of the seams and the symmetrical curve of both sides. The wood was silk to the touch, except near the finger holes. She held the instrument up to her eyes for a closer inspection and was pleasantly surprised to find each finger hole was decorated with a unique, tiny design of dots, curls, and swoops. Pax relaxed his stiff posture as she smiled in appreciation. She brought the mouthpiece to her lips and blew a long, mellow, and haunting note which hung in the air for a few seconds after she stopped.

"It's beautiful," she said, turning to smile at him for the first time.

"Thank you." He returned her smile with one of his own. Then, taking the ocarina from her outstretched hand, he rubbed his thumb absently back and forth across the holes and shrugged. "It's just a hobby."

"Hobby or not, you have a talent. Do you sell your work?"

Pax grunted, and his smile faltered. "No. Like I said, I'm a woodsman, not a craftsman. Felling trees and refining raw materials, that's what we do. I make things just for fun."

Nadja studied him. "It's clear you love the process. The carvings alone are so intricate. They must have taken hours to do, and no one spends that kind of time on something they do 'just for fun.'"

"I do," he replied.

They sat in silence for a moment. Then, afraid she might be wading into turbulent waters, Nadja pulled back and said, "Well, whether you call yourself a craftsman or not, I'd certainly say you are. And a fine one, too. Thank you for showing me the ocarina."

They both turned their attention to the fire. The sun had almost disappeared behind the trees, and the flickering flames leapt in a warm, cheerful dance, hypnotizing Nadja and lulling her into a relaxed and calm state of mind. It was the first time she felt peace since fleeing her home.

After a few moments, Pax jumped up. "We had better get your dressing changed before it's completely dark and all we have to see by is the campfire."

He placed the ocarina on the stump and gathered clean bandages from the makeshift clothesline, where, Nadja guessed, her own clothes had hung to dry.

Pax settled himself back down next to Nadja and began removing the bandages from her forearm. The white material gradually turned pink as he uncovered layer after layer, and Nadja gritted her teeth against the pain. When the old bandages were gone, she assessed the damage.

The wound was deep and jagged. Bits of flesh had been replaced in some semblance of order. Though the wound did not appear to be infected, the surface of her arm glistened with a light sheen. She flinched as Pax dabbed at the gash with his fingertips. The bleeding had waned to a slight ooze, and the wound was healing well after only a day.

With a frown, Pax reached into his pocket and removed a small tin. Letting go of her arm, he took off the lid and dug his fingers into the little pot of shiny white ointment. He reached over and rubbed the salve down the length of her forearm, gently massaging it into her wound. The pain relief was immediate, and Nadja looked up at him in surprise.

"Oh, come on," he said, meeting her eyes with a half smile. "You don't really think a seasoned woodsman like myself wanders off on a quest unprepared, do you? Let's just say you don't spend your days playing with sharp objects without getting your fair share of cuts."

"But the pain is gone!" exclaimed Nadja as Pax began to wrap her arm with the fresh bandages.

"I'm sorry to say that effect is only temporary, but the salve does help the wound heal and keeps infection from setting in."

"What's in it?"

"I'm not sure. It's my mother's recipe, and none of us leave home without it." Pax finished tying up the bandages and handed the tin to Nadja. "You might want to rub this on your other wounds too. Since you're awake now, I guess you can handle that part. Although, if you'd like, I could help you with that, too," he said, flashing her a grin.

Nadja arched an eyebrow and returned his smile with one of her own. "Thank you, but you have already done so much for me. I'd hate to trouble you further," she replied with a chuckle, slipping the tin into her skirt pocket.

"Speaking of my mother," said Pax, his face becoming more serious, "she should take a look at your arm. I'm no healer, and she has seen more than one of us through some pretty bad injuries. She'll be able to get you patched up properly and make sure you don't take a turn for the worse."

Nadja's body turned to stone as Pax spoke. The comfort of the evening dissolved in an instant, replaced by a sense of claustrophobia, as if all the trees surrounding their little glen were pressing in on her, trapping her where she sat.

What was she thinking, relaxing by the fire, enjoying the company of the handsome stranger who had come to her aid? She had killed a man! She had fled the scene, and if, or when, the Elders learned the truth of the matter, she would be found and killed for her crime. Her only hope was to make it to her uncle in Cantio, and she had already lost a full day's progress. And now, Pax wanted to take her to his family's home. This was not a part of the plan.

Pax searched her face.

Clearing her throat, Nadja tried to relax her muscles and chose her words carefully. "I don't think that's necessary." she said, her lips pulling into a tight smile.

"I do," he replied. "Your arm should have stopped bleeding by now. And I have no other supplies or medicines to help you. But, if you'll come with me back to my family's home, my mother will have everything you need."

"That is kind of you, but my family is expecting me in a few days, and I've already lost a whole day of travel time. I don't want to worry them."

"We can send a messenger to them as soon as we reach home to let them know you're safe. Surely they will understand your delay considering the circumstances. Where did you say they lived?"

Nadja paused for a beat, her eyes narrowing. "I didn't."

"Look, I just want to make sure you'll be all right." Pax let out an exasperated sigh. "I tell you what. It's late, and you still need some good rest. Why don't you sleep on it and see how you feel when you wake up? You can take the tent. I'll be comfortable out here by the fire. We can talk about it again in the morning."

"Fine," Nadja agreed. No way was she going to feel differently in the morning, but she seized the opportunity to end the conversation. Then, in an effort to draw his mind away from that line of thinking, she changed subjects.

"I was wondering something about what you said earlier. If you haven't seen an Auldwood Oak before, and you don't know where one is, how will you know when you've found it?"

Pax's eyes lit up. "Oh, I'll know. My grandfather helped fell one over fifty years ago. He said it's enormous—way bigger than any other trees in the forest, with multicolored bark and branches which are bent and twisted like a thousand snakes. And there will be no others like it as far as the eye can see."

"Multicolored bark? Do you mean gray and white and a sort of orangish brown?"

"Yes," replied Pax, eyeing her curiously.

"With bunches of big, light green leaves."

"Yes." Pax's hand shot out and grabbed Nadja's good arm, giving it a gentle squeeze. "How do you know that?"

"I've seen it. I took shelter in a tree just like that only two nights ago. It was beautiful, like some magical thing from a children's fairy story."

"And do you remember where it was?" Pax's body was practically vibrating with anticipation.

A smile crept over Nadja's face. "It's no more than a day's walk east of the spring."

Pax leapt to his feet and let out a whoop of joy. The firelight flickered in his eyes, and excitement shone on his face like a beacon. Nadja thought she glimpsed the little

73

boy he had once been grinning out at her. She stood up, giggling along with him.

"Do you know what this means?" he asked, swooping her into his arms and twirling her around. "You, Pretty Lady, have solved my quest!" He set her down and took her face in his hands. Before Nadja knew what was happening, he pressed a swift kiss to her lips. Then, just as quickly, he released her.

"Tomorrow, at first light," he continued, pacing back and forth in front of the fire, "I'll pack camp and head east. Once I locate the tree, I can go home to get help with the felling. From what my grandfather told me, it'll be more than a one-man job." His movements halted as he turned and looked at Nadja, who was still standing like a statue where he placed her. "Oh, no! I'm sorry, I almost forgot. We'll head home first. Mother can take care of your injuries, and I'll gather help while we're there."

Nadja tried to shake the spinning sensation in her head and gathered her thoughts. "But you're so close. And I really am feeling much better. If you leave in the morning, you can make it to the tree before nightfall."

"No," said Pax, taking her by the hand. "Getting your wounds seen to is the most important thing right now. That Auldwood Oak has probably stood there for over a thousand years. It can wait a few more days."

Nadja's hand warmed in his grip, and her lips still tingled from his kiss. Suddenly uncomfortable, she pulled away.

"Well then. We had better turn in for the night. It sounds like we have quite a day ahead of us tomorrow." With that, she retrieved her pack.

"Here," said Pax, walking toward the stump. "Bring your lantern. I noticed it was out of oil when I found your things. You'll need it. That tent is as dark as pitch once the sun sets." He refilled her lantern and lit the little wick.

"Thank you."

Nadja turned and headed towards the tent. When she reached the flap, she stopped and turned back to see Pax arranging his bedroll near the fire.

"Pax?" she called.

"Yes?"

"Thank you again, really, for all you've done for me."

She saw his white teeth gleam in the darkness and knew he was giving her another one of his heart-stopping grins.

"Sleep well, Pretty Lady."

Nadja entered the tent and dimmed her lantern to almost nothing.

She sat in the darkness for what seemed like hours. Pax's breathing had fallen into an even rhythm of sleep a while ago, but she wanted to make sure he was down for the night before making her move. She raised the wick of her lantern slightly and brought it near the leather bag in which Pax kept his ocarina. Digging through its contents, her fingers brushed past small carving tools, a handful of rough stones, and various other supplies before finding what she was hoping for. Matches. She took out the packet and removed only a handful before placing the rest back into his bag. As she did so, she also palmed one of the stones.

She stored the matches and stone in her own pack and removed the tin her mother had given her. The contents of the tin bumped and rattled around, and she did her best to muffle the noise as she removed a few of the pearls. Once she was sure her movements had not disturbed Pax, she lifted the tent flap and crept towards the stump. Being short and light had always given Nadja the advantage of stealth when playing games with the other Wanderer children, and it still served her well in her adulthood. When she reached the stump, she dug into the rations bag, removing a few pieces of bread and fruit, being sure to leave a few days' worth for Pax. She slipped her hand into her pocket and wrapped her fingers around the tin of ointment Pax had given her. He didn't mean it to be a permanent gift, but right now, it was the only medicine she had. She withdrew her hand, leaving the tin where it was.

She hated taking from him after all he had done for her, adding thief to her growing list of crimes. Placing the pearls on top of the stump, she knew they would more than cover the monetary loss of the things she had taken. She also hoped they would also help lessen the anger and frustration she was sure Pax would feel when he awoke to find her gone. But he was determined to help her whether she wanted his help or not. He may have the best intentions, but the last thing she wanted was to drag someone else into her own mess. She hoped the lure of the Auldwood Oak would be enough to keep him from trying to find her. The longer she stayed with Pax, the closer any possible Wanderer scouts could come. And what if he found out what she had done?

No. Getting to Cantio and to her uncle was her one chance.

Steeling her resolve, Nadja glanced one last time at Pax's sleeping form and disappeared into the forest's shadows.

Chapter Seven

The next few days disappeared in a blur. Nadja's wounds were healing rapidly, thanks to Pax's ointment. Between his rations and what game she was able to bag with her blowpipe, now that the pain in her arm was tolerable, she kept her belly full. She spent her days on foot and her evenings by the fire playing familiar and comforting tunes on her flute. While most of her thoughts focused on survival, from time to time she let her mind drift back to her meeting with Pax. He was so kind to her. She knew she owed him her life, and she hated the way she had left him, a literal thief in the night. She thought of the way his lips felt when he kissed her.

Her first kiss.

Others in Amrantir might find it strange he had been Nadja's first kiss, but as a female of the Wanderer tribe, it wasn't out of the ordinary. She was betrothed to Luca for most of her life, so none of the other boys in the village ever dared steal a kiss. And Luca, even as they celebrated their betrothal, had never really kissed her, holding instead to the staunch Wanderer tradition of saving the first kiss for their wedding day. The memory of the way Pax's solid arms had wrapped around her waist as he spun her around, and the dizziness in her head when his lips had pressed against hers caused her stomach to flutter and her face to grow warm.

Nadja made good time, and when she came across a road a few days after leaving Pax, she was filled with a renewed sense of hope. She didn't follow the road directly, choosing instead to keep it in sight as she traveled under the cover of the forest, still wary of anyone she might meet along the way. Each passing day, she saw more people traveling along the road, letting her know she was getting closer to Cantio. On one day in particular, she chanced to emerge from the forest when she spotted a traveling peddler walking in the opposite direction. Her once sweet pair of leather slippers, now riddled with holes and barely clinging to her feet, were replaced by a pair of sturdy walking boots and extra-thick socks.

Two days later, as she ate her midday meal under the shade of an elm, the mellow tones of an instrument Nadja did not recognize floated past on the late summer breeze. The tune wasn't one she knew, but the effortless sound of the notes piqued her interest. She packed away the uneaten portion of crust, shouldered her pack, and crept towards the sound.

A few minutes later, the forest opened. Keeping to the trees to avoid discovery, she surveyed the swath of land before her. Long ago, the area must have looked much like the surrounding forest. But, now, it was a lush, verdant vineyard. Row upon row of grapevines dripped with densely packed bunches of deep, purple orbs. Every vine was ripe for harvesting, except for a small patch along the north edge. The ground in that area was dry and scorched as if touched by fire. The music came from that direction, and Nadja watched in wonder.

Small, green shoots surrounded by halos of rich soil had been replanted at intervals beneath the repaired trellis wire. A woman strolled along the rows playing a wind instrument whose body and bell wrapped around her torso, up and across her back, and over her right shoulder. As she passed a shoot, the vine sprung to life, darting upwards and snaking around the wire. New leaves burst forth and tiny tendrils coiled like springs opposite them. In the space of a moment, the young vine transformed before her eyes, matching the rest of the vineyard in appearance, but for the grapes. It wouldn't be ready for this year's harvest, but it would flower and bloom in the spring along with the rest of the vines.

Nadja shuddered as the woman continued to play, and the process repeated itself over and over again. Such blatant disregard for the natural order of things was one of the main reasons the Wanderers lived apart from the rest of Amrantir. Repulsed by the sight before her, Nadja retreated into the safety of the forest and continued on her way.

One afternoon, a week after leaving Pax's camp, the sound of rushing water met her ears. She picked up her pace and continued to follow the road. The sound grew louder until the road curved suddenly, crossing Nadja's path and forcing her out of the forest.

She recognized the Nostirivin River, even though she had never seen this part of it before. The yearly migration of the Wanderers never took them this far north, but Nadja would know that river anywhere. Half of her childhood was spent in and around its waters. Nadja's heart leapt for joy, knowing her journey was almost at an end. Turning south, she followed the road as it wound its way along the banks of the river. Two days later, Nadja caught her first glimpse of Cantio.

Situated where the Kalmari joined with the Nostirivin River, Cantio shone before her like the crown of Amrantir. A singular smooth, stone wall encompassed the ring-shaped city, and though Nadja had never visited it herself, she'd learned a little about the capital over the years. The city itself was laid out in three concentric circles, with the outer two divided, by roads, into five equal sections each. Most of the city's residents, primarily comprised of the Amrantirian elite, lived in the outer ring. The middle ring was filled with markets, theaters, and businesses of all sorts, with one-fifth dedicated exclusively to housing the Delegates Hall, among other governmental buildings.

But most impressively, rising from the center circle, was the Music Conservatory. Its bright, cream-colored limestone walls glittered in the midday sunlight like a great jewel. The conservatory stood like a castle, the tallest building in Cantio by far, and the foundation upon which the identity of Amrantir rested. This was where musicians and craftsmen came to hone their skills before beginning work in their chosen profession. The Music Conservatory was often spoken about with much derision within the Wanderers. They were outliers in their beliefs that music should only be used for enjoyment, and not to manipulate the natural world. Whatever Nadja's opinion about the purpose of the conservatory, she could not deny the feeling of wonderment it instilled.

Sensing it might be a good idea to do so, she disassembled her blowpipe and tucked the three short pieces into her pack. As she did, her hand brushed against a bundle of smooth, green fabric. Her dress. Of all the things she carried with her, this was the most poignant reminder of a life that could have been, but never would be. She walked to the edge of the river and tossed the dress into the water. The flowing material rolled and undulated away from her with the bouncy current, traveling along with the will of the river. Nadja watched until it disappeared. Then, she focused her eyes on the city and shouldered her pack once more, surprised to find it much lighter than it had been.

As she crossed the bridge spanning the Nostirivin River and leading to one of the three city gates, her heartbeat quickened. Her singular focus on reaching Cantio and her uncle was slowly being overtaken by feelings of anxiousness and uncertainty. Her steps slowed as she approached a gate flanked by a pair of towering stone trumpeters. For a moment, she considered returning to the forest. She had grown comfortable in her protective cocoon of solitude and anonymity over the past week. Entering the city gates was the quickest way to eliminate her chance at both. Her hesitance didn't last long, however. As safe as she felt in her isolation, Nadja imagined the life of a recluse was probably worse than death. With a deep breath, she entered the city.

The outer ring was not terribly crowded. It was early afternoon, and many of the city's residents were at work or school now. As she turned southward, Nadja's gaze was seized by the buildings which lined the ring road. A strange mixture of practical and whimsical, the homes were unlike any she had seen before. Roofs and window gables rose at steep, sharp angles, as if surprised to see her. Curved wooden accents framed doorways and windowsills, smiling or frowning at her, depending on their mood. While every house was different, the visual flow from house to house was harmonious, as if each told a small part of a much greater story.

Nadja pried her eyes away from the curiosities around her, lowered her chin, and turned her attention back to finding her uncle. Thanks to her mother she had a name and a profession, which was a good start.

Apart from being the heart of music and the governmental seat of the country, Cantio was also the most important inland port. Almost all imports and exports were required to pass through Cantio before entering or leaving the country. The wharf lay just outside the east city wall, covering every bit of land between the

Kalmari and Nostirivin Rivers. What better place to look for a barge captain?

As Nadja passed out of the southeastern city gate onto the wharf, she stepped into a different world. Unlike the sleepy neighborhood streets inside the city wall, the wharf was a cacophony of voices and machines, street and animal sounds. What appeared to be thousands of people scurried in all directions, coming in and out of buildings, lifting boxes and freight to and from carts, looking like an anthill which had just been kicked over. Past the maelstrom, she could see ships of various shapes and sizes moored along the banks of both rivers. Most of the ships were smaller than the ones she had seen in Chansey, which made sense. Many of the larger vessels which did well at sea were just too big to make it upriver to Cantio.

She made her way past the rows of identical buildings which bordered the wall and picked her way through the crowd, wondering where to begin. Giant warehouses loomed overhead, striping the road with shadows. The buildings past the warehouses were smaller, less imposing. Nadja spotted a large sign reading "Cantio Custom House" and turned in that direction.

The crowd grew denser the closer she got to the custom house. People bumped into one another, and hundreds of conversations melded together to form a thick drone. All at once, one voice rose above the rest.

"And I never want to see your face again!" came the shrill cry from an open doorway just ahead.

A man stumbled backwards out of the opening, quickly regaining his balance, but continuing to take a few steps backwards.

"Aww, come on, sugar," he replied, straightening his shirt. "She's just an old friend of mine."

Nadja curved wide to avoid the scuffle, but the compact crowd made maneuvering difficult.

"Old friend?" the woman shouted, tossing a coat out onto the ground in front of the man. "Old friend!?" A boot shot through the air and smacked the man in the chest.

Nadja couldn't see the woman in the shadows of the doorway, but whoever she was, she had a good arm.

"I'm sure you kiss all of your old friends that way, you rat!" the woman screeched. The other boot flashed through the air, this time with a precise trajectory. The door slammed, and the man ducked just in time to avoid getting hit.

At least, Nadja thought he did. He must have. Because the next thing she knew, she was lying on her back with a terrible headache, squinting up into a pair of chocolaty-brown eyes.

Chapter Eight

"Hey, are you all right?"

The man slipped his arm under her shoulders and helped her sit up. Nadja reached up and touched her forehead.

"You're probably going to have a pretty nice bump there," he said, brushing a lock of sandy blond hair back from his eyes. "Sorry about that. That one was meant for me."

"No," said Nadja. "I mean, yeah, I'm fine."

"Think you can stand?" he asked.

"I think so."

The man helped Nadja to her feet and grabbed her pack.

"I can carry that," said Nadja, reaching for it.

"Nope," the man replied. "You just took a boot to the face for me. The least I can do is carry your pack. Where are you headed?"

"The custom house."

"The custom house it is," he said. They began walking slowly in that direction. The man glanced at

Nadja every few steps. "You know," he said, "you should get some ice for that."

"I'll be fine," said Nadja.

"If you say so."

They walked along for a few moments in silence. Nadja noticed how the crowd seemed to part for them as they passed. No doubt it was due to the man's size. He was taller than most other people and looked as solid as a boulder.

"I'm sorry about your lady friend back there," said Nadja, breaking the silence.

The man chuckled. "Oh, don't worry about that. Tessa likes a good row every now and then. She likes the fighting almost as much as she likes the making up."

"Oh."

"But what about you?" asked the man, scratching at the day's growth of whiskers which darkened his cheeks and chin. "I haven't seen you around the wharf before. You don't look like you're much for heavy lifting, and you don't have the look of a sailor. Or the smell for that matter. And as for other . . . ah . . . professions, I wouldn't put you there either. So, what's your business here?"

At first, Nadja was taken aback by his direct questioning. However, his comment about her smell made her glad she had sneaked in a bath and changed into her last set of clean clothes the night before. And, his apparent familiarity with the wharf made her think he might be able to help her.

"I'm looking for someone. Tau Machinal. He's a barge captain."

The man's eyebrows rose in surprise. "Tau Machinal?" he said.

"Yes."

"Well then, you, sugar, are in luck. Most everyone around here knows who that is, and I happen to know him better than most." The man turned down a side road leading away from the custom house and towards the docks.

"How do you know him?" asked Nadja.

"I work security for him. Everything shipped in or out of Amrantir has to come through Cantio. That's a lot of valuable cargo. It's my job to make sure none of it goes missing before it gets where its needs to go."

Nadja cut her eyes towards him, again noticing how he towered over the rest of the crowd. "You must be good at your job," she offered.

He smiled down at her, and Nadja could see why he would have lady troubles. Too many ladies brings trouble. "That I am, sugar. That I am."

After a few moments, they stepped up onto the small porch of a rather unimposing wooden building. A faded sign posted to the left of the door read "Montgomery & Co. Shipping." The door creaked on its hinges as the man opened it.

Following him inside, Nadja found herself in a small room which held a few uncomfortable-looking chairs and a long desk stretching almost the entire width of the room. Behind it sat an elderly, dour-looking man.

"Hey Branson, I need to see Tau," said Nadja's guide, leaning casually across the desk.

"Is he expecting you?" The old man's gravelly voice sounded as if he hadn't used it in so long spider webs had formed in his throat. His eyes narrowed suspiciously at Nadja.

"No, but this young lady needs to speak with him."

"Regarding?"

Both men turned and looked expectantly at Nadja.

Clearing her throat, she replied, "A personal matter."

The old man assessed Nadja in silence. His eyes narrowed even further, if that was possible. So much so, Nadja wonder if he had fallen asleep. Then, he turned abruptly and disappeared through a blue door to the right of the desk.

A few minutes later, he emerged.

"You may go in," he croaked.

"Thank you, Branson," said the younger man, clapping the older one on the shoulder as they passed.

Nadja heard the old man grumble under his breath.

The office they entered stood in stark contrast to the barren and utilitarian front room. Rich, dark mahogany accented the walls and thick green drapes hung from the windows. The furniture was ornately carved from the same wood which covered the walls, and the stuffed seat coverings were practically bursting. Nadja's footsteps silenced the moment they met the plush rug which covered most of the floor. In front of the window, opposite the door through which they had entered, stood a large mahogany desk, behind which sat a rather imposing figure.

The man appeared to be in his early forties with wavy, shoulder-length black hair and brown eyes. His tanned skin spoke of hours spent in the sun, and his mouth was framed by a thick black mustache and closely-cropped beard. His heavy, black eyebrows and sharp features gave him a stern countenance, but Nadja thought she detected something familiar in it.

"Wheedler," the dark man spoke, nodding at Nadja's companion. His voice was low and calm, but possessed a command which demanded attention. "I thought you were bringing a shipment down from Wailing Gap today."

"We made it in ahead of schedule. The load is on its way to Chansey as we speak," replied Wheedler. "Good to see you made it back in one piece."

"I always do. To what do I owe this visit?"

"Well, I was taking care of some business after we settled everything up at the dock, and I happened to run into this young lady who said she was looking for you." Wheedler raised an eyebrow and gave the man, whom Nadja assumed to be Tau, a slightly comical smile.

"Really? And what business brings you here?" asked the dark man, looking at Nadja for the first time since she had entered the room.

Nadja shrank back from his gaze, her stomach churning with nervous anticipation. "Are you Tau Machinal?" she asked.

"I am."

Unsure of what to say next, Nadja retrieved her pack from Wheedler and removed the letter her mother had written. She didn't care to share her story with anyone who didn't need to know, but Wheedler didn't seem interested in going anywhere else. She handed the letter to Tau and stood in silence as he broke the seal and began to read.

The minutes passed like hours as Tau's eyes moved back and forth across the letter once, twice, and then a third time. The churning in Nadja's stomach grew worse when he finally lowered the letter and pinned her with his gaze. He scrutinized her in silence for a few moments. She felt as if his eyes could see right into her soul, and perhaps they could. She squirmed, shifting back and forth on her feet, fighting the urge to turn and flee. After what seemed like an eternity, his eyes snapped to Wheedler and his face relaxed somewhat.

"Wheedler, I have a shipment of minerals coming in from the Waste tonight. I'd like you and Brooks to accompany it down to Chansey first thing in the morning. It's for one of our more valued clients, and I need my best on this one."

"Yessir," replied Wheedler.

"Thank you. That will be all."

Wheedler looked disappointed at the dismissal, but didn't argue.

"Thank you for your help," said Nadja, as he headed out the door.

"Any time, sugar." He smiled and closed the door behind him.

Nadja turned back to face Tau.

"Hello, Niece," he said.

"Hello, Uncle," was all she could think of to reply.

Tau rose from his seat and crossed over to a small, low table next to the window. "Would you care for some tea?" he asked.

Not at all what she had been expecting, Nadja simply nodded her head in reply.

"If you were hoping for something stronger, I'm afraid you'll have to look elsewhere. I have never cared for alcohol."

Tau hefted an elaborate silver teapot and filled two matching teacups. He handed one to Nadja and motioned for her to sit. She obeyed, taking the tea from him and eyeing the cup and saucer. They were dainty, yet masculine, but didn't seem to match with the man who now sat across from her. Lifting the cup to her lips, she sipped. The tea had a floral flavor with a slightly bitter, though not unpleasant, finish. As the warm liquid slid down her throat, her muscles relaxed. She took a deep breath and savored the taste on her tongue. After two weeks of nothing but water to drink, the tea was a welcome change.

"It seems you find yourself in an unfortunate situation," he began.

"That's an understatement," replied Nadja, taking another sip of her tea.

"Mmm." Tau resumed his seat behind the desk. "Nadja, I have read your mother's letter, and I know why she sent you here. But I want to hear, in your own words, what brought you to my doorstep."

Nadja sighed and closed her eyes. The last thing she wanted to do was go back to the beginning and relive the whole thing over again. But, her uncle was her only hope for staying safe. So, she took a deep breath and told him everything. Kizzy. Baulo. Her scream. Her blackout. And, the dead man.

When Nadja finished her story, she was afraid to meet his gaze. They sat in silence once again. When she finally looked up, she didn't see the disgust or judgement she had expected to find. Instead, it was something more like pity. No sooner had she looked at him than his expression once more went blank, and he finished his tea.

"Who else have you spoken with since you arrived in Cantio?"

"No one, except Wheedler."

"And what did you tell him?"

"Nothing. Just that I was looking for you, and that it was a personal matter."

"Did you tell him your name?"

"No."

Tau's shoulders relaxed a bit. "Good," he said, rising and walking to the small table to replace his cup. "When I left the Wanderers, I made a clean break. I no longer go by my family name as you do. No one in Cantio knows I was once a part of the tribe, and I have worked very hard to keep it that way." He turned to look out the window.

"Why did you leave?" asked Nadja.

Tau said nothing, but continued to stare out the window for a few moments. "I go by Machinal, and as my niece, now so do you. Nadja Filamen no longer exists. Nadja Machinal is your future. You, like me, are an immigrant from Grenyan." He turned to face her. "As for the reason you are here, well, I will need a little time to think on that. You may stay with me for now, but that is not a permanent solution. We need to find a way for you to become invisible, at least for the time being. If the Elders believe you have merely run away, as your mother tells them, then tradition suggests they will only search for a few months. If, however, they discover you are responsible for Baulo's death, it could be much, much longer. If you choose to stay here, you must do exactly as I say. These are my terms. Do you agree?"

Nadja sat in thought. She wasn't sure what she was expecting her uncle to do once she found him. Wave his hand and make everything magically disappear? That was silly. Perhaps she thought she would live with him and keep out of sight. But what kind of life would that be? She had already separated herself from her past, but he was asking her to erase it altogether and replace it with an entirely fictitious one. Did she have any other choice?

"Take it or leave it!" a high-pitched voice screeched from behind her.

Nadja jumped up and whirled around to face the door, her teacup clanging as it bounced across the floor. At first, she saw no one. Then, as she looked closer, she could make out a small gray form at eye level. It was about a foot and a half tall and covered in feathers.

"Don't rush her," said Tau, walking over and removing the bird from its perch. "My apologies," he said to Nadja. "He likes to chime in at the most inappropriate times. Nadja, this is Monty. Monty, Nadja."

The absurdity of the situation was not lost on Nadja, but her uncle acted as if introducing people to his parrot was the most natural thing in the world.

"Um, it's a pleasure to meet you, Monty," she said.

Tau coughed and passed his hand in front of his mouth as his shoulders shook. Monty tilted his head to the side, and his pupils expanded and contracted as he studied her.

"May I touch him?" Nadja asked, her hand already approaching the bird.

"He doesn't respond well to strangers," Tau was saying as Monty first dodged Nadja's hand, then moved his head to brush underneath her fingertips.

"Hmm," Tau finished.

Nadja smiled as she ran her fingers across Monty's head and down his soft neck. "Where did you get him?"

"I inherited him along with the shipping company."

"You own this company?" Nadja gaped. "But mother said you were a barge captain."

"I was, for a time. I still captain runs to and from Chansey a few times a year. A handful which require extra attention. But usually I leave the safety and security of my shipments in the capable hands of my guards, one of whom just escorted you to my office." Tau nodded towards the door through which Wheedler had exited.

"How did you inherit the business? Grandfather never owned a shipping company. And why the bird?"

Tau sighed, obviously annoyed with all of the questions. "My predecessor was a good businessman, and a kind man. He never married or had children, but he would have been a good father—was much like a father to me. He found Monty when he was just a little chick and doted on him for the rest of his life." He regarded Monty thoughtfully. "But, the thing about this kind of bird is that it can live for a very long time. Monty is almost as old as I am, but I imagine he still has many years ahead of him."

As Tau spoke, Monty crept his way up Tau's arm to perch on his shoulder.

"And out of respect for your predecessor, you continue to care for him," finished Nadja.

"Correct."

"So, you're sort of like brothers," said Nadja, stifling a giggle of her own.

Tau frowned at her. "Not in the least." He walked back to his desk and straightened the papers which littered the top. "I have given you my terms, Niece. I have no desire to rush your decision, so take as much time as you need."

Nadja didn't need any more time. Her decision was made the moment she fled the Wanderer camp.

"I agree to your terms," she replied hastily, stooping to retrieve the roving teacup and placing it on the small table.

Tau finished straightening his desk and came around to Nadja. "Then let me show you to your room, such as it is."

They passed through a doorway which led into a small stairwell. Another door in the stairwell led outside to the back of the building, but Nadja followed Tau up the winding staircase to the second floor. Leaving the stairwell, they entered an apartment which took up the top floor of the building.

Nadja had expected it to be furnished in the same way as her uncle's office, but was pleased to find it was simply arranged. A stone fireplace and modest kitchen anchored one end of the room. Animal skin rugs, a couch, and a few chairs filled the rest of the space. Opposite the fireplace, a doorway led into a single bedroom, and a large bookcase took up most of the far corner. The corner opposite that one housed an enormous and ornately decorated golden bird cage, complete with perch, swing, and toys. Its opulence contrasted the relative simplicity of the rest of the apartment.

"Unfortunately, my home is a little small for more than one person, but you are welcome to sleep on the couch. We can move it close to the fire if you find it cool in the evenings. I myself do little cooking, but there are a few things to eat in the cupboard if you get hungry. Some of the amenities enjoyed within the city haven't yet reached the wharf. There is a pump at the basin over there, and it drains by itself. However, that is the extent of my indoor plumbing. You can find the necessary facilities out back."

As he spoke, Tau walked around the room, pointing out the different items within the apartment before stopping next to the bird cage. He opened the door, and Monty hopped from his shoulder, flew to a small container of water on the floor of the cage, and immediately began bathing.

Tau turned back to Nadja, appraising her appearance. "How many changes of clothes do you have? Your pack doesn't look like it holds much."

Nadja's face reddened. "Well, I have one other set, but they need to be cleaned."

"I will order you new ones tomorrow. As for now, it's nearing supper time. I'll go out and get something for us to eat while you get settled."

Tau headed for the door. "And don't leave the apartment unless it's absolutely necessary."

Nadja nodded. "Thank you, Uncle Tau."

Tau grunted and closed the door behind him.

Chapter Nine

". . . As warrrm and sweet as the first spring raaaain
Whose pitter-pat echoooes the sweet refraaaain
Of my hearrrt as I gaze at the face so fair
Of the lovely ladyyy with the long dark haaaair!"

Nadja cringed as Monty squawked his way through the chorus of "The Lady with the Long Dark Hair" for the eighth time that morning. She awoke to his serenade just before sunrise, her muscles like cold taffy. The couch was a welcome reprieve after two weeks of nights spent either on the ground or in trees, but it was small, and she wasn't able to stretch out to her full length. Her uncle had yet to come out of his room, though Nadja couldn't fathom how he slept through Monty's musical offerings.

She made herself useful scrounging up breakfast for the two of them. The cupboard yielded a few staples. Nadja mixed up a batch of fry bread which she paired with a gobbet of salt pork she found tucked away on a high shelf. She had just finished warming the pork when Tau emerged.

"Good morning," said Nadja, setting the food on the table. "I hope you don't mind I made breakfast."

"Not at all. It looks delicious." Tau busied himself steeping a pot of tea, then joined Nadja at the table.

Nadja sipped from the cup Tau placed in front of her. Unlike the sweet and mellow flavor of yesterday's tea, this one was dark and smoky with a hint of cocoa. It helped clear the remaining cobwebs from Nadja's head, and she eagerly downed half of the cup.

"I have given a lot of thought to your situation," began Tau. He tore off a piece of fry bread and dipped it in his tea before popping it into his mouth.

Nadja's stomach dropped, and she replaced the bit of pork she had just picked up from her plate, suddenly without an appetite. She felt safe now she had found her uncle. His strong and calm demeanor, though not sentimental, made her feel protected if nothing else. She had agreed to his terms knowing they would likely mean finding her way on her own, but she didn't think he would have made a decision so soon.

"You will begin instruction at the Music Conservatory."

Nadja's mouth fell open as she stared at her uncle. Of all the things he could have suggested that possibility had never crossed her mind.

Tau looked at her, his expression unreadable. "You grew up in the tribe, so I assume you have some musical skill, do you not?" he asked.

"Well yes, but—"

"Excellent. The entrance auditions are scheduled to begin a week from today. They will run for two days, so you have between now and then to prepare." Tau's attention returned to his plate as Nadja continued to stare at him.

"I can't go to the conservatory!" she exclaimed.

"Why not?"

"Well, I can think of two good reasons. One, while, yes, I am pretty good with my flute, I am not at the level of a professional musician, which is what people at the conservatory are training to be. Also, using music to manipulate nature, it's just wrong."

Tau didn't reply right away. Instead he sat back in his chair and studied her intently, just as he had in his office the day before.

"I have no doubt," he began slowly, "a woman with the determination and resourcefulness to survive for two weeks in the wilderness with little more than the clothes on her back can prepare for the conservatory auditions in one week's time." Tau leaned forward and took a sip of his tea. "As to your other objection, why do you believe using music in that way is wrong?"

"Nature maintains its own balance," stated Nadja. "It is both arrogant and foolish to believe we can disrupt that balance without consequences."

"Spoken like a true daughter of the tribe," said Tau, with a sad smile. "Tell me, Nadja, when you harvest from a bed of oysters, or when one of your hunters takes down a doe to provide food for the people, does that not also disrupt nature? You change the oysters' male to female balance and take away a food source from other marine life, and a young deer is likely orphaned when its mother becomes your dinner. We are a part *of* nature, not apart *from* it."

"Yes, but we take only what we need, and over time the balance is restored."

"Agreed. But what would you say to the farmer whose crops are being swarmed by beetles? Would you say, 'I'm sorry, but you'll just have to do without food this winter?' Or would you send for the town's master musician to drive away the pests and save the crop?"

When Nadja did not reply, Tau continued. "Music can be a valuable tool, and, when used responsibly, can do so without causing permanent damage."

"Like the Waste?" Nadja's question was more of an accusation.

Tau did not argue her point, but gave her a moment to think over the things he'd said. After a beat, he continued.

"Now you have told me why you think my plan is unsuitable, allow me to share with you the reasons I believe it is the best course of action. The conservatory itself is an island within the city. Students and teachers have little reason to venture from the grounds, and few outsiders have reason to enter them. The full length of study there takes four years. Should you need to remain in hiding for any great length of time, you can continue on there. And finally, as you have so perfectly illustrated, the whole idea of the Music Conservatory and what it stands for is distasteful, if not offensive, to the Wanderers. It would be the last place they would look for one of their own."

They continued their breakfast in silence. Nadja picked at her bread and pork, mulling over what her uncle had said. She hated to admit it, but his plan was a solid one.

So, what was really bothering her?

Yes, the whole idea of the Music Conservatory didn't sit well with her. She'd learned from as early as she could remember that using music as a tool in the way it was taught at the conservatory was wrong and dangerous. And she understood why. That wasn't something she was going to change her mind about just because her uncle made a few intriguing points.

But, if she was honest with herself, her biggest reason for not wanting to go was that she felt safe right where she was. For the first time since leaving the Wanderer camp, she wasn't looking over her shoulder or fighting to survive. It felt right. True, Uncle Tau had not been a part of the tribe in a long time, since before she was born. But there was still a sense of kinship. He was family.

And now, he was asking her to leave that, no sooner than she had found it, and step into a world completely foreign to her. He wanted her to surround herself with people so unlike her, and to make them believe she belonged there.

Tau finished his breakfast and rose to take his plate and cup to the sink. Nadja did the same, standing beside him as he washed and dried his dishes.

"You're right," she said as he put his clean dishes away. "The conservatory is a good plan. It's just a lot to consider all at once." She cleaned and put away her own plate and cup.

As he waited in silence for her answer, she realized how different her life had already become. Had they been standing amongst her people—*his* people—she would have no choice. He would be within his right to initiate his plan without her agreement. But as they were, standing side by side in front of the little sink in his apartment, the independence and freedom she'd gained the moment she left the Wanderers became startlingly clear. She marveled at the thought. The choice was hers.

"I will do as you say. Not out of deference to you because you are my uncle," she added, "but because I gave you my word."

A broad smile melted Tau's stoic countenance. "Well said, Nadja. To hear you speak like that, one could hardly guess your true heritage."

Chapter Ten

As Nadja stepped onto the Music Conservatory grounds, she took a steadying breath. The gate she passed through was set in the low wall which separated the conservatory from the rest of the city. Large trees stood guard around the inside perimeter, rising much higher than the wall and providing a bit of privacy. Lush, green grass carpeted almost the entire grounds, which were ample, housing not only the imposing main building but several smaller buildings as well. The sun shone brightly, and a late summer breeze swirled around Nadja's legs, ruffling the hem of her lightweight skirt and foretelling the coming autumn.

Uncle Tau had not disappointed in his promise of new clothes. Within two days, she had a new wardrobe, one which, according to her uncle, was indicative of a new Grenyan immigrant. Black, gray, burgundy, and navy made up the majority of the palette, with a few lighter pieces thrown in at Nadja's request. The tops were simple and functional. The bottoms were evenly divided between skirts and pants due to Uncle Tau's insistence most

Grenyan women wore pants almost exclusively. But Nadja, who had never worn a pair of pants in her life, preferred the comfort of the skirts, all of which included cleverly hidden pockets in the side seams, as was the Grenyan style. Whether in pants or skirts, her foreign dress would draw notice from the average Cantio resident. But it lent credence to her immigrant status. Her boots, the only part of her attire which remained from her journey through the forest, tapped a slow but steady beat on the cobblestone road leading to the conservatory.

As she approached the glittering structure, it seemed to grow larger, almost filling her entire field of vision by the time she stopped in front of it. A tangled mass of people funneled into a line as they climbed the front stairs and disappeared through one of the enormous open doors. Nadja hesitated for a moment, taking in the scene and tightening her grip on her flute. Then, she joined the throng. To her surprise, the line moved swiftly.

Before she knew it, she was passing through the front entrance into the atrium. The conservatory's entryway was a large, open space. A vaulted ceiling soared three stories above her and was covered entirely in glass, forming a clear mosaic of varied polygons through which the sun beamed, lighting and warming the room.

The mosaic peaked in the center of the ceiling where a beautiful stained glass panel rained down vibrant colors onto the people below. Nadja couldn't help but stare up at it. The panel depicted two figures facing one another. Both had their right arms raised, palms touching. The figure on the right held a trumpet in its left hand while the figure on the left was empty handed. Music notes bordered the panel, and Nadja squinted, trying to make out the tune in her head.

"Name?"

Startled, Nadja jerked her attention away from the panel. While she was distracted by her surroundings, the line had continued to move. She now stood in front of a table, looking down at a perky young woman.

"Uh," Nadja stammered, trying to collect her thoughts. "Nadja F—Machinal."

"Hmmm, Nadjaf. What an interesting name," beamed the woman as she sifted through the papers in front of her. "Ah, here you are! Though it looks like they misspelled your name . . . there we go, fixed," said the woman, making a small mark with her pencil. "And what instrument will you be playing, Nadjaf?"

"The flute, though it's a bit different than most other flutes. It's made of coral and—"

"Oh, no matter," said the woman, smiling up at Nadja. "It's not so much what you play as how you play it!" She handed Nadja the paper. Then, as if repeating herself for the hundredth time, she took a deep breath and droned, "Head left down that hallway. If you wish to warm up, you may do so in the Dead Room. There is a monitor stationed outside the door, so if you have any questions, just ask him. You will need to be at the Concert Hall a few minutes before your scheduled audition time.

If you need help getting there, one of the monitors can assist you. Best of luck! Name?"

Nadja realized the woman was now talking to the man behind her, so she moved aside and started in the direction the woman had indicated. A few dozen paces ahead of her, she could see a man about her age seated in a chair against the wall with his nose in a book and a handful of papers on his lap. Next to him was a doorway. As she drew closer, she read the words "Dead Room" in fluid cursive on a sign posted to the left of the door. She smiled tentatively at the bored-looking monitor as she reached for the door handle.

Stepping through the door, she found herself in a small vestibule containing nothing more than another door. The tiny room was silent, and she wondered if she was the only person taking advantage of the warm-up space. Curious, she reached forward and pulled open the second door. Sound leaked out as soon as the door cracked, but it had a strange timbre.

Nadja's eyes widened as she entered. Patterns of large acute wedges, each of which was more than the length of her forearm, covered the walls. She couldn't tell what they were made of, but the wedges had a porous quality.

She felt her step spring as she walked into the room. Looking at her feet, she saw the same wedges below her. Only, she wasn't stepping on them. Instead, she was suspended on a thick wire mesh which attached at every wall and floated above the wedges. The same shapes hung from the ceiling giving the whole room a cavelike and otherworldly feeling.

There were more than a dozen people scattered around the room. One man stood in a far corner playing a trombone, interspersing his melody with strange honking noises. A clarinetist cocooned herself within a circle of chairs and sat in the middle with her eyes closed, flying up and down octave upon octave of scales. Other musicians were stretching, fluttering their lips, rubbing their faces or, as Nadja assumed, going through their own unique preperformance rituals. The majority sat or stood around the outer edge of the room facing the walls.

Nadja picked her way to the back of the room. Her ears caught the notes of individual players as she passed but only for the moment she was closest to them. Something about this room played with the basic nature of sound, devouring it as soon as it came into being. Following the other musicians' leads, she filled in an empty spot along the back wall. Nadja unpacked her flute and began to warm up as best as she could.

Even with the relative quiet of the room, she found herself distracted now and then by the musicians on either side of her. The violinist to her right bowed at an incredible rate. Notes tripped and jumped from her instrument with such technical perfection Nadja's feelings of self-doubt rose to the surface.

The musician to her right, a young man who looked barely older than Kizzy, played an instrument Nadja had never seen. It was a strange amalgamation of multiple pipes and mouthpieces and appeared to be powered by a bellows he worked with both feet. The instrument itself was a curious sight to behold, but the tones emanating from it were pure and beautiful. He played a difficult and heavily ornamented piece. As Nadja listened, her feelings of unworthiness grew exponentially.

What was she doing here? How could she have let her uncle convince her she had half a chance of gaining acceptance into the conservatory? She'd already counted well over a hundred hopefuls between the crowd gathered outside and the people in the warm-up rooms. There were only thirty seats available for the new year, and those seats were open not only to musicians, but craftsmen as well. She was kidding herself to think she had any chance of getting in.

Conversation was almost nonexistent within the Dead Room. Every once in a while, the monitor would open the door and recite a handful of names. Each time, a few people would gather their belongings and head out of the door, only to have their empty spots filled by the trickle of new arrivals. As soon as Nadja collected herself well enough to blow a few warm-up notes into her flute, she heard her name called.

Nadja bounced her way back across the room and into the hallway. Sensing a tingling in her shoulders, she glanced back and saw the violinist who had been warming up next to her following close behind. They exited the Dead Room together and met the monitor outside.

"Names?"

"Nadja Machinal."

"Helaine Vastrof," replied the violinist.

"Your audition times are coming up. Head towards the atrium and take a left once you get there. The Concert Hall will be right in front of you, but stay to the left, go past the main entrance and under the staircase to the backstage door. You'll see the other hopefuls waiting there." The monitor glanced at his paper. "Helaine, you'll go after Colby Bertramaine. Nadja, you're after Helaine. Good luck."

Dismissed, the two women made their way back towards the atrium. Nadja peered at Helaine. The violinist was choking her bow with one hand and hugging her instrument to her chest with the other. Her wavy blonde hair cascaded down her back, almost to her waist. Her brown eyes stared straight ahead, and worry lines drew a *V* between her eyebrows.

"I heard you warming up. You play beautifully."

Helaine's head twisted to face her. "Do you really think so?" she asked, her voice hesitant and strained. "I'm just not sure if I've chosen the right piece for this audition. And it is *the* audition, isn't it? I mean, there will probably be others, but none as important as *this* one. And I'm terrible at auditions. Oh, I don't mind playing solo or anything like that, but something about an audition, and knowing there are people out there *judging* you. It's almost too much to bear, isn't it?"

"I suppose so. I hadn't really thought about it like that. This is my first audition."

Helaine's eyes widened. "Your first audition? Oh my word! Lucky. Well, you picked a doozy to start off with." Her mouth snapped shut, and she turned her eyes to the floor. "I'm sorry. I tend to ramble when I'm nervous. I don't mean to dump worry on you."

Nadja sighed. "It's all right. From what I heard, if half of the people here play as well as you do, I don't stand a chance."

A shy smile curled the corners of Helaine's mouth. "Thank you. I'm sorry to say I didn't hear you play. I was too focused on my own warm-up. But I'm sure you'll do fine. My violin teacher always says you only have yourself to give. So give it all, and don't hold anything back."

By the time Helaine finished speaking, they had arrived at the backstage door. Nadja returned Helaine's smile, and they joined the line behind two other musicians.

The door swung open, and another monitor popped her head out. "Sylvia Neuronin," she said, holding the door open just wide enough for the next hopeful to pass through.

A few moments later Nadja heard the buzzing, quirky tones of a bassoon floating through the closed door and out to her waiting ears. Sylvia was playing a dance song of some sort, and Nadja giggled as the bassoon's unique sounds brought to mind a vision of a cow in fancy dress skipping in time through a field of daisies. Her giggles halted, however, when she heard the instrument issue a trio of wrong notes before falling silent.

Everyone in the hall froze, and Helaine flashed a look of fear at Nadja. No one breathed as they all strained to hear what came next.

Sylvia picked up her piece a few measures before the missed notes and made it past the sticky part with no problem. The hall collectively exhaled, then froze again as the bassoon hit another snag only a handful of beats past the first one.

Nadja's own heartbeat grew louder in her ears in the silence that followed. The atmosphere seemed ready to ignite at any moment. While it was true, they were all in competition for few available spots, each of the waiting musicians felt empathy for Sylvia. They all knew how easily they could be in the same position.

The monitor's head reappeared through the crack in the backstage door. "Colby Bertramaine."

The waiting musicians cast sympathetic and encouraging glances at Colby as he disappeared.

Nadja's anxiety level grew as she got closer to that door, listening to the auditions as they played out through it. Colby first, then Helaine, had both done excellent jobs. Before she knew it, the monitor called her name.

Nadja stepped through the door and followed the monitor through the dimly lit area, listening to her instructions.

"Play your audition piece first. They might ask you a few questions after you've finished. Once they dismiss you, continue across the stage and exit through the door at the end of the opposite wing."

Nadja's footsteps echoed through the Concert Hall as she emerged from the wing and crossed to the center of the stage. The space was vast and open, taking Nadja's breath away. The room stretched upwards a good four stories. Curved wooden panels like soft caramel rippled in wide waves across the ceiling, and the wooden walls of the lower levels of seating curved outwards away from the stage. In stark contrast to the Dead Room, every little sound came to life in the Concert Hall.

Nadja positioned herself towards the audience and looked up. She counted ten people sprinkled here and there throughout the first few rows of seats—six men and four women. Some were reclining. Some sat straight and alert. All were looking at her.

"Whenever you're ready," said a distinguished-looking older gentleman.

Nadja took a deep breath and counted to five as she exhaled. Raising the flute to her lips, she blew a few long notes to check the sound in the room. The resonance of the notes she produced was even more pronounced than her footsteps had been. The tones were clear and crisp and rang out like an invitation to the listeners. Nadja's palms began to sweat. Never had she played in a more acoustically perfect setting. The room itself would enhance her performance as long as she played well. But, it would also make obvious any mistakes she might make along the way.

Steadying her nerves, she reminded herself why she was here. This was her chance to start over. If she could gain admittance into the conservatory, she would be protected and safe. She could build a new life as a new person and not live in fear, looking over her shoulder for the rest of her life. She pushed the thoughts and feelings of self-doubt out of her mind. Negative thoughts beget negative actions, and the last thing she needed to do was stand in her own way.

Nadja inhaled and began her piece. It was a well-known piece from a classic Amrantirian comedy. The song had alternating fast and slow sections, allowing Nadja to show off a range of styles. She made a few mistakes along the way, but nothing terrible, and when she finished her piece, she felt like she'd done a good job. However, if they were looking for perfection, her good job wouldn't be good enough.

Lowering her flute, she stood in silence and waited.

"Nadja . . . Machinal, correct?" asked the older gentleman.

"Yes," she replied.

"It says here you are an immigrant from Grenyan. What made you decide to come here and pursue the study of music, such as we provide?"

Nadja was prepared for this question. She had worked with her uncle to develop a history for her new persona with enough detail to be believable.

"I come from a musical family. But, music in Grenyan is not valued in the same way as it is in Amrantir. I love to play music, but I also want to be of use to the people around me. The idea of combining my love for music and my desire to help others made the conservatory an obvious choice for me," she answered.

There was a brief pause as the listeners pondered her answer or scribbled down notes.

"Your instrument has a peculiar look. Can you tell us about it?"

Nadja looked in the direction of the questioner. A petite woman with short curly white hair and tortoise-shell eyeglasses smiled up at her.

Seeing no reason to lie, Nadja held up the pink-hued instrument and replied "It's carved from coral. It was my mother's, and she gifted it to me when I was little. I believe she bought it in a seaside market somewhere before I was born."

"Interesting" the woman replied, looking down to write some notes of her own.

A man who looked barely older than Nadja spoke up next. "Hundreds of candidates are hoping to get one of the limited spots we have available," he drawled, sounding bored and peevish. "Why in the world should we should choose you?" He stared at her critically.

Nadja's muscles tightened. This wasn't a question she was prepared for. She shifted her weight back and forth between her feet, trying to come up with an answer for him. The truth wouldn't work. She couldn't tell him she needed a safe place to hide for an unforeseen amount of time.

Ten pairs of eyes were on her, and she felt the weight of every one of them. She gulped, the sound echoing throughout the hall.

"I have to be here. I left behind my family and friends to journey here, hoping to finding something better. For me, there is no alternative. I may not be the most talented musician to audition, but I learn fast and I work hard. If you allow me to stay, you can be sure I will do whatever it takes to prove you've made the right decision."

Silence lingered, and then the white-haired woman approached the older gentleman and whisper something in his ear. They conversed momentarily. Then, the woman returned to her seat and said, "Do you have anything else you can play for us?"

Nadja's brows drew together. The audition requirements only included one prepared piece, and that's what she had practiced. Under the scrutiny of her judges, her brain refused to cooperate as she frantically searched her mind for something else to play. Only one song bubbled to the surface, and Nadja tried in vain to push it away. It was a lullaby, the one her mother sang to her as a child. A plain melody with little ornamentation, it was too simplistic to offer as another audition piece. But, in the urgency of the moment, no other options came to mind. Instead of continuing to stand there like a statue, Nadja raised her instrument and closed her eyes.

The low, slow strain soared through the Concert Hall like a soft summer breeze. Nadja thought of her mother as she played. The memories of thousands of drowsy evenings spent in their tent listening to her mother sing the familiar words warmed her heart. The song may not have contained the excitement inherent in a quick tempo or technically dazzling passages, but as Nadja's heart connected with those sweet memories it bled into her song.

When she finished, she lowered her flute and opened her eyes.

"Thank you," said the older gentleman, smiling at her this time. "You are dismissed."

Nadja turned to her right and left the stage.

Nadja and Tau sat at his table enjoying a quiet breakfast. The windows were open, inviting in the late summer breeze, and the aroma of cinnamon rolls filled the air. Since Nadja's arrival, Tau had increased his cupboard inventory, and she took full advantage of it. As was the case every morning, Monty serenaded them with whatever song fluffed his feathers. Today, it was "Brave Siris Cullen."

The three of them had fallen into a pleasant rhythm over the past few weeks. Nadja stayed mostly in the apartment, contributing to the household with light cooking and chores since she didn't venture out alone and wasn't able to seek employment. Her uncle was a tidy man, so there wasn't much cleaning to do. She spent the rest of her time exploring Tau's bookshelves, playing her flute, or, in the evenings, chatting with Monty and her uncle.

An unexpected knock at the door interrupted their meal. Tau rose to answer, motioning for Nadja to remain seated and quiet. He opened the door. Nadja heard a brief muffled exchange, but couldn't make out any specific words. Then, her uncle closed the door and returned to the table. Resuming his seat, he placed an envelope in front of her.

"A messenger from the Music Conservatory," he said.

Nadja's hands trembled as she picked up the envelope. With great care, she opened it and removed a single piece of paper.

"Well?" prompted Tau.

Nadja unfolded the paper and read:

"On behalf of The Music Conservatory of Amrantir and its distinguished faculty, I am pleased to offer you a seat among this year's new class. Please reply at your earliest convenience with your acceptance or regrets.

Sincerely,
Grandmaster Musician Thaddeus Westbrook."

Chapter Eleven

The air was thick with excitement and anticipation as Nadja passed through the Music Conservatory's entrance for the second time. This time, however, she entered as a bona fide student. People scurried to and fro throughout the atrium carrying luggage, cleaning, or just in a general state of hustle.

Her grip tightened on the handle of her small trunk as she looked around trying to decide where to go. Peering upwards, her spirit lifted as she gazed up at the atrium's stained glass panel. The rainbow cascaded down and painted the floor beneath it, beckoning her to bathe in its colors.

She had done it. She was home.

Granted, this new home was nothing she had ever imagined, but she was safe and hidden. The relief which came from knowing she wouldn't have to live in a state of perpetual fear and paranoia made her want to dance. She giggled to herself as the temptation to run beneath the stained glass and twirl in its bright hues almost overcame her.

"My, aren't we in a good mood?" came a light, singsongy voice.

Nadja's chin jerked down and her cheeks reddened. A stunning redhead approached her with a notebook in one hand and a pencil in the other. Nadja though she was, with her sparkling blue eyes and a petite but curvaceous figure, one of the most beautiful women she had ever seen.

"I'm excited to be here," Nadja admitted, embarrassed to be caught gawking like a teenager.

"I'm sure you are," replied the woman with a tight-lipped smile. "My name is Laurel Willowcroft, Adept Musician. And you must be," she peeked at her notebook, "Nadja Machinal."

"Yes."

"It's my job to greet the new apprentices and point them in the right direction. Though I must say, you're nearly the last apprentice to arrive. I had almost given up on you."

"Oh," said Nadja, confusion crossing her face, "I thought the assembly started at noon."

"And so it does. However, most new apprentices like to arrive early and settle into their rooms first. No matter," said Laurel, snapping her fingers and waving at a young man hurrying past. "Timothy can take your luggage to your room, and you can settle in after the Apprentice Assembly. Did you leave them outside?"

"Who?"

Laurel's foot tapped against the slate floor. "Your bags. Did you leave them outside?"

"No," replied Nadja, indicating her little trunk. "I brought it in."

"Oh." Laurel wrinkled her nose.

With her simple attire and meager belongings, Nadja felt small and deficient as the gorgeous adept assessed her. Then, as if struck by a sudden idea, Laurel tilted her head to the side and smiled another close-mouthed smile.

"Well, at least you've made it easy for Timothy," she said, sending him off with Nadja's trunk.

As Timothy hurried away, leaving Nadja empty handed, Laurel flipped to another page of her notebook and turned it towards Nadja.

"Living quarters for students are on the third floor," she said, displaying a map of the conservatory and pointing to a small room with her pencil. "This is your room. You can take the open staircases on either side of the Concert Hall to get there. However, I suggest you go directly to the hall now. The assembly will begin in about ten minutes."

She reached into the back of her notebook and pulled out a sheet of paper. "Here is your class schedule," she said, handing it to Nadja. "Any questions?"

Nadja shook her head. "No, thank y—"

"Welcome to the Music Conservatory." Laurel spun on her heels and hurried away.

Nadja turned her feet towards the Concert Hall. It was easy enough to find since that was where she'd auditioned. But this time, instead of going around backstage, she entered through the main house doors.

Even from the back of the room Nadja could hear the twitter of conversations coming from the front. The other apprentices were scattered amongst the first few rows. Some were chatting in small groups while others sat alone, taking in their surroundings or scribbling in notebooks.

Not wanting to draw attention to herself, she took a seat in the first empty row behind the other apprentices and surveyed her surroundings.

The hall was just as impressive from this vantage point as it had been from the stage. The warm tones of the winding wood were comforting and inviting. Plush house seats were covered in a deep burgundy fabric accented with gold embellishments. The seats were interspersed with little two-person couches upholstered to match the chairs. Mirrored lanterns lined the walls, amplifying their light, and a glistening golden chandelier hovered overhead.

Nadja's seat bumped as someone settled into the row behind her, but she was so absorbed in her surroundings she hardly noticed.

"You owe me a shirt," a deep voice rumbled softly, tickling her ear.

Nadja gasped and almost jumped out of her seat. She whirled around to face the speaker and froze as she locked onto a pair of dazzling sapphire eyes. Her face blanched, and the moisture disappeared from her mouth, leaving a wad of cotton in its place. Her brain panicked as she tried to rationalize the presence of the man seated behind her.

Pax reclined back in his seat, amusement dancing in his eyes and a half smile on his lips.

"What are you doing here?" she stammered in hushed tones.

"I could ask you the same question."

Nadja twisted forward only to find herself face-to-face with the man and woman seated in front of her. No doubt they had heard her squeak and were curious about the cause. After regarding her for a moment, they turned towards the front and resumed their conversation, though this time in a purposefully quieter tone.

"I thought you were visiting family." Pax's breath tickled her other ear causing her to tilt her head involuntarily towards his mouth.

"I did. And now I'm here," said Nadja, turning again to face him. His unexpected appearance unnerved her as did his proximity. Her gaze dropped to his mouth as she remembered his kiss. Her face regained its color and a little more than its previous warmth, and the hair on the back of her neck stood at attention.

Snapping her eyes back to his, she was annoyed to see a slow smile spread across his face. He knew he was making her uncomfortable, and he was enjoying it.

Nadja narrowed her eyes and cleared her throat. "What about you? Shouldn't you be chopping down a tree somewhere?" she hissed.

"I should. But a pretty lady recently told me I had the makings of a fine craftsman. I decided to submit some of my work to the faculty of the conservatory on the slim chance they might agree. Looks like they do."

"You're a new student?"

"Pax Raynor, Apprentice Craftsman," he said, inclining his head with an air of mock superiority.

Though caught off guard by his unexpected arrival, Nadja realized it was just another hurdle she would have to leap in order to maintain her ruse and position in her new safe haven. She thought back to their time together. Had she said or done anything to give herself away? Had she led him to believe anything she could not easily explain?

No.

In her single-minded resolve to preserve her anonymity and safety she had not even given him her name.

The tension in her shoulders eased as she pasted on her best impression of a warm smile.

"Nadja Machinal, Apprentice Musician."

"Nadja." Pax rolled her name over his tongue as if savoring the taste. His eyes danced briefly, then darkened. "Well, Nadja, I have a few questions for you."

Nadja's smile melted like snow on a warm spring day. She opened her mouth to say something she hoped would turn the conversation away from the unfortunate direction it was heading.

"Welcome, apprentices, to the Music Conservatory. And congratulations!" The commanding voice echoed through the Concert Hall.

Nadja turned away from Pax and towards the stage which was now filled with a dozen or so people. She was relieved to see that, in her distracted state, she had not noticed the familiar faces take their seats. She recognized the one standing and addressing them as the older gentleman who had asked her questions during her audition. The top of his head was bald, but he wore a cropped halo of white hair around the sides and back. His thick white-and-gray eyebrows mirrored the color of his tidy mustache and goatee. His eyes held genuine warmth as he smiled and opened his arms in a gesture of welcome.

"I am Grandmaster Musician Thaddeus Westbrook, Dean of the Music Conservatory of Amrantir," he began, lowering his voice along with his arms. "It is my great privilege to welcome you as apprentices, and future master musicians and craftsmen of Amrantir. The skills you will learn during your time at the conservatory will serve not only you, but your community and your country for years to come.

"Every one of you is a fine musician or craftsman in his or her own right. But, there is so much more to mastering music than the ability to play a beautiful melody or to craft the instrument used to do so. Music has always been something more than the sum of its notes, rhythms, and dynamics. Music has the power to create real and tangible change.

"As we all know, some music has additional levels of complexity and precision. This music is intended for more than mere enjoyment. This music can harness and divert energy. It can quench dry and barren lands with desperately needed rain, and it can, quite literally, move mountains.

"It is my sincere hope that you will take advantage of every opportunity which presents itself in your time here. That you learn and master both the art and science of music and craft. That you become a mover of mountains."

He paused for a breath and smiled at the crowd.

There was something about Grandmaster Westbrook which calmed Nadja's nerves and set her at ease. While she took issue with some of the things he had said, particularly the moving-mountains bit, she had to admit she felt an instant affection for the gentleman.

He introduced the rest of the faculty members. Nadja glanced at her course schedule and noted her instructors. Among them were the other two who had questioned her during her audition. The white-haired woman, Meliina Kero, would be her private-lessons tutor and teach the Music History class. The bored-looking and rather snobbish younger man who would lead the Music for Enjoyment class was Xavier Pennequois.

As Grandmaster Westbrook continued the introductions, Nadja's attention was divided between the other instructors on her course schedule—Deotys Stallworthy: Music Theory and String Technique, Rafe

Gilmoren: Sound Theory, Petra Dappacas: Percussion Technique—and more pressing matters.

Namely, what to do about Pax.

Nadja had a good idea about the types of questions he wanted to ask her, and she was certain she had no desire to answer them. Pax's presence was a glaring mar on the otherwise clean slate of her new life at the conservatory. She would have to address the issue somehow.

At the moment, she hoped avoidance would be the simplest solution. Pax was on the craftsman track. Most likely, they would be in different classes, since his focus would be making instruments while hers was playing them. She resolved to do her best to avoid him in the hope he might eventually lose interest.

By this time Grandmaster Westbrook had completed his introductions and was issuing a few closing remarks. As soon as he dismissed them, Nadja jumped up from her seat and bumbled her way to the end of the row. Unfortunately, Pax detected her attempted escape and matched her movements, blocking her path in the aisle.

"Excuse me," said Nadja, giving him a curt smile and stepping aside to go around him.

Pax reached out and grabbed her hand, pulling her almost close enough to him to raise the eyebrows of passersby. The aroma of the forest washed over her, clouding her initial shock and annoyance. As she looked up at his humorless face, a quivering sensation in her stomach began warring with her determination to put as much space between the two of them as possible.

The skin along her forearm tingled as Pax reached over with his other hand and gently pushed up the sleeve of her blouse. Finally breaking eye contact, he looked down and studied the red scar.

"Looks like you'll live."

"Just as I said." Nadja swallowed as Pax's rough thumb traced the length of the damage.

Pax huffed. He met her eyes again, his face filled with a mixture of confusion and earnestness. "Why did you disappear?"

"I told you," she said, gathering her wits and trying to ignore the feeling of her hand in his. "I needed to get to my family. And you needed to get to the Auldwood Oak. You did a fine job patching me up. I would have just delayed your quest."

Pax dropped her hand and reached up, rubbing his face in frustration. His head tilted to the side as he contemplated her. With the physical link between them broken, Nadja's head cleared, and she shifted her weight back and forth between her feet, looking for the opportunity to escape. Just as Pax opened his mouth, no doubt to reprimand her, they were joined by two grinning girls. Actually, they were women, but the way they tittered and giggled between one another, one would hardly guess them long past the age of dolls and imaginary tea parties.

"Hello! I'm Selina, and this is Vatara," said the first girl, offering Pax a floppy wrist. Her fingers reminded Nadja of the wriggling bait she used to catch fish.

Pax returned the greeting with a pleasant smile, accepting the proffered paw and giving it a firm shake. He reached out to offer the same greeting to Vatara and was met with another awkward handshake and a just-too-loud laugh.

The two women peppered Pax with a barrage of questions and compliments.

Nadja cringed inwardly. Pax's attractiveness was undeniable. She would freely admit that if for no other reason than to declare otherwise would go against all natural aesthetic sensibilities. But, the sight of Selina and Vatara practically throwing themselves at him turned her stomach in much the same way a week-old trout left rotting on the riverbank would.

Yet, in her discomfort Nadja offered a silent thank-you to the pair for providing her escape. While Pax was held captive politely answering their long list of questions, Nadja melted into the rest of the passing crowd and disappeared through the exit.

Chapter Twelve

The dark metal hinges of the wardrobe door creaked softly as Nadja pushed closed the smooth cedar panel. It had taken her less than twenty minutes to unpack and put away all of her belongings. She had arrived in Cantio with little more than the clothes on her back, and apart from her new wardrobe, she'd obtained nothing else she could truly call her own. Her blowpipe, pearls, and silver mirror were tucked away behind the lengths of unused pants in a back corner of the wardrobe, and the rest of her garments took up no more than a third of the space.

The warmth emanating from the fireplace hugged her back as she paced across the hardwood floor towards the room's one large window. Though it was still early autumn, the changing winds which infiltrated the higher floors of the conservatory brought with them a chill. Nadja pulled open the shutter and looked out over the conservatory grounds.

From her room she could see the perfect arc of the grounds' wall. Her room faced the governmental zone of the middle ring. The Delegates Hall stood tall and imposing compared to the surrounding buildings, and she watched the people come and go.

Each region of Amrantir selected a delegate to represent them in the capital. The delegates convened at the midpoint of each season under the leadership of their appointed delegate prime to make decisions regarding the safety, economic growth, and general well-being of the country. The Wanderers, even though they belonged to no dedicated geographic region, had their own delegate as well. Nadja's stomach sank as she realized the tribe must appoint someone new to represent them. Because of her, Baulo could no longer fill that role.

She shook her head, trying to ward off the ache threatening to settle in, and moved away from the window. Flopping down on her bed, she picked up her flute from the bedside table and leaned back, surveying her surroundings.

The room was spacious and luxurious compared to the tent she had shared with her mother. Two full-sized beds draped with downy comforters and plush pillows were positioned atop a thick carpet of deep blue and gold. They sat facing one another, each with a matching bedside table and bookcase. In the middle of the room was a small round table with two chairs, and matching wardrobes flanked the fireplace on the opposite wall. In the space between the window and Nadja's wardrobe was a basin complete with running water. The rest of the necessary facilities were a short walk down the hall, but after weeks spent trekking to and from her uncle's backyard, she welcomed the small inconvenience in exchange for indulging in the miracle of indoor plumbing.

Nadja blew a light stream of air into her flute and silently fingered through a familiar tune. Having taken the bed by the window, she faced the one next to the door and wondered about her roommate. The woman must have arrived early to settle in and, from the looks of it, brought a team of decorators along with her. Her side of the room had suffered an attack of lavender and teal. Colorful pillows accented the already plump head of the bed while swaths of sheer material draped artfully around the furniture. Small framed paintings decorated the walls and bedside table, and her bookcase overflowed with books, music, and sundry knickknacks. A violin case lounged carelessly on top of an enormous trunk which took up the space at the foot of the bed. The whole effect was made even more overwhelming when contrasted with the stark appearance of her own side.

Glancing at the other wardrobe, Nadja's curiosity got the better of her. She laid her flute on the bed and crept over to the wardrobe, easing the door open to peek inside. At the same moment, the sound of a rattling doorknob met her ears.

Nadja closed the wardrobe and jumped back as the room door swung open. A familiar blonde with a cheery round face and an armload of books crossed the threshold.

"It's you!"

The woman hurried in Nadja's direction, then stopped short and regained her composure, a slight blush on her face. "I mean, it's so nice to see a familiar face. I'm Helaine Vastroff. It's so nice to officially meet you." She extended her hand in greeting.

Nadja returned her smile with one of her own. "Nadja Machinal."

"Nadja. What a lovely name. I'm so glad you're here, Nadja. Please forgive me for rambling on and on during our audition. I was absolutely worried sick with thinking I caused you more anxiety than you were probably already feeling, and right before it was your turn to perform. But, you must have done well, because here you are!" Helaine reached out and held Nadja's hand between her two.

"And here you are," replied Nadja with a light chuckle.

The two studied each other in silence for a moment before Nadja spoke. "I heard you play your audition," she said, gesturing towards the violin case. "You did a beautiful job. How long have you been playing?"

"For almost as long as I can remember," replied Helaine, tossing the books onto the small table and settling on her bed. "My father is a master musician and works with the copper mines on the edge of the Gelid Highlands. He plays the violin and so, of course, my violin education began as soon as I was able to hold it."

Nadja mirrored her new roommate, and the two began that awkward dance of first acquaintance. It was not long, however, before they fell into a comfortable conversation. Nadja responded to Helaine's questions with as little detail as possible, telling her she was an immigrant from Grenyan who wanted nothing more than to become a graduate of the conservatory.

Nadja learned Helaine was an only child who had few friends growing up in the sparsely populated border between the Viridian Mountains and the Gelid Highlands. Like her father and his parents before him, Helaine was expected to do well at the conservatory and choose a position somewhere as a master musician. She was shy, but had a sweet temperament which made her instantly likable, and Nadja felt lucky to be paired with her.

"Though, I must confess," said Helaine, biting her lip. "I may not be the tidiest roommate. I tend to let things lie where they land. It's one of my many faults."

Nadja laughed. "I have plenty faults of my own. Let's make a deal. I'll try my best to see past yours if you try to see past mine."

"It's a deal," smiled Helaine, the worry lines across her forehead vanishing. "All right, I just have to ask," she said, bolting upright on the bed and locking eyes with Nadja. "What is going on with that?"

Nadja glanced beside her where Helaine pointed. "My flute?"

"Yes! I noticed it at the audition, but was afraid to ask you about it then. It's pink!"

"It's made from coral. My mother gave it to me when I was little, and it's my favorite instrument."

"You play others?"

"Well, mostly just auxiliary percussion instruments. And I do sing, poorly and to myself, sometimes. But this flute is who I am." Nadja picked up the flute and studied it wistfully, circling her thumb over the small indentions around the finger holes which had begun to form after years of playing.

Helaine hesitated. "May I hear something?"

Nadja smiled and nodded. She played a short Wanderer folk tune with a bright and up-tempo melody. When she finished, she put down the flute and looked at Helaine, who had her eyes closed and was wearing a blissful look.

"Cinnamon apples," sighed Helaine as she opened her eyes.

Nadja didn't know how to reply to that comment. She sent a questioning look to Helaine, who responded by coming to her feet and pacing back and forth between the fireplace and her bed.

"I'm so sorry. I meant to say that was lovely, and you do play well."

Still puzzled, but flattered, Nadja giggled. "Is 'cinnamon apples' a popular expression up north?"

Helaine laughed ruefully. "No, it isn't." She sighed, this time with an air of exasperation, and sat back down on her bed.

Nadja watched her fidget with the pillows, packing a few around her seat, and hugging one to her chest. When she at last seemed comfortable, Helaine gave Nadja a solemn look.

"Since you and I are going to be roommates this year, there's something I think you need to know about me. Oh, it's not a great secret or anything, but it is something I don't usually talk about. But, since you *are* my roommate, I think it's better I get it out in the open with you. That's what friends do, right? And I do hope we'll be friends." Helaine lowered her chin in embarrassment.

Not sure where the conversation was leading, Nadja gave Helaine a reassuring smile. "I would like that very much."

This seemed to give Helaine the confidence she needed.

"I have a condition of sorts. It's something which has come down through generations of my family, popping up from time to time. My mother doesn't have it, but her mother did."

"What kind of condition?"

Helaine took a deep breath. "I can smell sound."

Nadja's eyebrows crept towards her hairline as Helaine's words hung in the air.

She squeezed her eyes shut and shook her head, trying to collect her thoughts. "What do you mean, 'smell sound'?"

"Just that. I can smell sound . . . well music, mostly. Something about music triggers the part of my mind linked to my sense of smell. When I play my violin, for example, I get the distinct scent of rain. For my grandmother, it was her sense of sight. She could see colors in the music. But for me, it's smell. Violin music smells like rain, and your flute smells like—"

"Cinnamon apples," finished Nadja, nodding her head with understanding. "But that's amazing!"

"Sometimes. But imagine the rain and cinnamon apple smells mixing with mint, sweet jasmine, smoke, and mushrooms. It can make enjoying certain ensembles, much less playing in them, difficult."

"I see what you mean."

"I'm just glad your flute has such a nice scent," said Helaine, smiling once again at Nadja. "I mean, if you had been, say, a trombone player, I would have requested a roommate change."

"Why? What do trombones smell like?"

Helaine's nose wrinkled. "You don't want to know."

"Wait a minute," said Nadja, snapping her fingers. "How do you get through the day? I mean, sound is everywhere. Even when you're alone, there is still the sound of the breeze, or your heartbeat, or even the sound of your clothes rubbing together as you move."

"That's not too much of a problem. Let me think of how to explain this," Helaine rubbed an index finger back and forth in the space between her lower lip and chin. "Have you ever noticed how some places have particular smells? Like, the copper mine smelled different than our home or even the conservatory."

Nadja nodded in understanding.

"But you stop noticing the smell once you have been there for a while," continued Helaine. "It's kind of like that. The smells I get from all the background noise is faint already. And even when they blend into something unpleasant, unless something dramatically changes, I stop noticing it after a while."

"That has to be a relief."

"It is. And Grandmaster Westbrook has found some resources in the archives which he thinks may help me better manage my condition. We'll be meeting once a week for what he's calling 'personal development.'"

At that moment, a low rumbling interrupted their conversation.

Nadja raised an eyebrow and crooked half of a smile as Helaine giggled and squeezed her pillow tighter against her middle.

"I guess all that talk of cinnamon apples has made my stomach realize how late it's getting," Helaine confessed.

"And all that talk has me wondering what exactly *that* smelled like," teased Nadja.

Helaine gasped and hurled the pillow she had been hugging towards Nadja. It limped through the air before landing, rather anticlimactically, on the floor between the two beds. The two of them burst into laughter.

"Come on," said Nadja, rising from her bed and heading for the door. "Let's go see what they're serving in the dining hall tonight."

Chapter Thirteen

"I overheard one of the expert-level students saying it's the same every year," said Helaine.

Nadja and Helaine made their way down the long hall of doors which marked the living quarters of the conservatory students. On this first day of classes, they, along with every other student, were going back to the Concert Hall for a half-day class conducted by Grandmaster Westbrook. As the dean of the school, most of his duties were outside of teaching. However, his Harmony in Permaculture lecture and workshop was a once-a-year requirement for every student.

"No wonder they all look so sullen this morning," replied Nadja.

"You'd think Grandmaster Westbrook would consider changing things up a bit to keep people interested."

"I guess there are only so many ways to say, 'use your talent wisely.'"

Helaine glanced at Nadja's empty hands. "You don't plan on taking notes?"

"No. Do you think I should? I thought this was mostly group problem solving and thought experiments."

"Oh. Probably not then. I'm always overly prepared for everything, anyway." Helaine's notebook was clutched tightly to her chest.

They paused at the top of the open staircase and gazed at the crowd below. A mass of people funneled into the Concert Hall. One in particular caught Nadja's eye.

Unlike the rest of the students who were heading into the hall, Pax leaned against the wall near the entrance door, surveying the crowd as it passed. He appeared to be looking for something, or someone.

"You know, on second thought," said Nadja, backing away from the stairs, "it's better to be overly prepared than under prepared. I'm going back to the room to get my notebook. I'll catch up with you in a few minutes."

"I'll save you a seat."

Nadja retraced their steps and grabbed her notebook. Avoiding Pax wasn't convenient, but the less contact they had the better. By the time she made it back to the Concert Hall, the entrance was empty, and Pax was nowhere to be found.

She cracked the door and peered into the hall. The faculty were arranged on the stage much as they had been during the Apprentice Assembly. She scanned the room, looking for Helaine, and spotted the pretty blonde on the opposite side. An empty seat was next to her as promised.

Nadja slipped through the door and took a few steps towards Helaine before she recognized the man seated behind that empty seat. Pax. Nadja's hands clenched. That man was relentless.

She knew her shy roommate would miss her bolstering presence during the class. Sending Helaine a mental apology, Nadja sank into a seat near the door just as Grandmaster Westbrook's calming voice silenced the hum of the crowd.

"For over a thousand years, growth, development, and change in Amrantir have all been driven by the way we as a people interact with and utilize music. While our neighbors in Grenyan to the west of us, and our neighbors in Pantomaria to the east of us have developed along a different path, music is the constant around which we define ourselves as a society.

"But, this was not always the case. There was a time, long before even your great-great-great-grandparents took their first breaths, that the music of man resided exclusively in the realm of art. It wasn't until an ancient race known as the Mevocali befriended Man, and taught him how the properties of music and sound can interact with nature to great effect, that the destiny of our people began to change.

"The Mevocali had the ability to alter the world around them through the means of song. Like us, Mevocali could manipulate the natural world. But, their talent reached deeper than that. They could also heal physical wounds as well as mental ones. This vocal talent was passed through bloodlines, and therefore, not something which could be taught. And though every Mevocali carried the seed of that talent within themselves, that seed did not sprout and bloom in each offspring. Those whose gift did not manifest often applied their knowledge of the science of music to playing instruments. Eventually, the Mevocali instrumentalists saw fit to share their skills and knowledge of instrumental music-making with Man.

"There is a stained glass panel which hangs in the ceiling above the atrium. You apprentices may have noticed it upon your arrival, and some of you older students may pass beneath it every day, hardly seeing it at all anymore. The next time any of you chances to enter the atrium, I encourage you to look up. For in that scene you will see depicted the moment the destiny of Amrantir changed. You will see a Mevocali and a Man, palm to palm, a symbol of the sharing of knowledge and skill. The beginning of a mutually beneficial and supportive relationship.

"Master musicians, as the instrumentalists are now called, concentrated their efforts in the stewardship of natural resources. They focused on things like farming, fishing, and mining. They manipulated the weather, diverted insect plagues, and broke ground. At the same time, the Mevocali, whose blood right was made manifest, utilized their skills as healers and counselors. They tended to wounds, counseled the hurt and grieving, and presented a calming influence in times of trial.

"For hundreds of years, Man and Mevocali coexisted peacefully using their combined talents to improve the world around them. But, little more than two hundred years ago, their relationship crumbled.

"The Mevocali's abilities started to grow and change. A new generation emerged who had the talent to do more than influence the mood of those around them. Some were soon able to alter perception and even insert concrete thoughts into the consciousness of individuals.

"As the new Mevocali skills emerged, so too did their new malcontent. No longer happy living in peace with the rest of Amrantir, they sought to dominate it. Since the uniqueness of the Mevocali's talent rested in their ability to heal, dozens of deaths from illness and injury were linked to Mevocali apathy and the desire to subdue Man.

"Man was not without fault, however. Across the land, Mevocali mind control became the most claimed defense in crimes ranging from petty theft to murder. It was impossible for Man to know whom amongst themselves to trust. Everyone was at equal risk of falling under Mevocali influence.

"The people viewed this mind manipulation as an act of war. Under the leadership of the Venerable Siris Cullen, Man carried out a preemptive strike against the Mevocali. Complete and utter annihilation of all Mevocali was deemed the only definitive solution. All other options led only to the eventual subjugation, enslavement, and the possible end of Man.

"The initial strike was well coordinated and perfectly timed. The Mevocali were neither great in number, nor skilled in fighting. Most died during the first strike. However, a small group managed to escape and fled for the eastern border of Amrantir.

"Siris Cullen and his army caught up with them in the Gardens of Annuay. It was on that spot where a great battle ensued. Cullen commanded his master musicians to attack the Mevocali with full force, without regard for the land around them. Through the din of battle, plants and animals alike fell victim to the conflict. The natural passage of seasons increased at an alarming rate, causing full cycles to repeat in a matter of moments. Some master musicians attacked with floodwaters pulled from the earth and sky, while others upturned the ground in an attempt to bury their foe.

"In the end, the Mevocali were defeated—their existence extinguished forever. Man had won the day and our continued survival but at great price to the land. The once lush and thriving Gardens of Annuay lay in chaos and ruin. The delicate balance which was once the foundation of a thriving ecosystem was destroyed along with the enemy, never to be restored.

"Today the land upon which the Gardens of Annuay once flourished is known as Cullen's Waste. Let it stand as the prime example of what can happen when our skills are used in a free and reckless manner. Regardless of the grim state of our circumstances, we must maintain a balance between what needs to be done to solve our problems, and the effect those changes will have on the natural world.

"Perhaps Siris Cullen could have accomplished his goal with a more tactical solution. Perhaps not. But never let it be said that you do not understand how your future actions may impact our world. The stronger you grow in your abilities, the more responsibility you have as a steward of them.

"Are there questions?" he asked, his eyes sweeping over the crowd.

"Some say the Mevocali weren't totally defeated. That some survived," a man called out from the middle of the room.

Grandmaster Westbrook chuckled. "There are also some who say Siris Cullen rode into battle on the back of a great winged beast with three heads and eyes blazing with fire. I am afraid neither is true." His eyes softened. "Whether for good or ill, the last of the Mevocali were destroyed that day."

When no further questions were offered, Grandmaster Westbrook began rearranging the papers on his podium, and the crowd resumed its low murmur.

The story told by the dean was as familiar to Nadja as her own reflection, but it wasn't the whole story. A niggling worm of irritation began in her belly and wriggled upward. The consequences of that battle stretched beyond the land of Cullen's Waste, consequences which were of a personal nature to Nadja, yet Grandmaster Westbrook had neglected to mention them. The annoyed little worm worked its way into her throat, and before Nadja could swallow it down, she opened her mouth and released it.

"What of the other people?" she called out.

The crowd hushed, and a hundred heads turned to face her. Nadja's own face grew hot as she immediately regretted calling attention to herself.

Grandmaster Westbrook's eyes searched the crowd for the source of the question. "To which people are you referring?"

Nadja chose her words carefully. "If the Gardens of Annuay were once as fertile as you say, there must have been people living there. What happened to them?"

The dean's eyes found hers at that moment, and his understanding nod was accompanied by a sad smile. "Ahh. An excellent question. Your assumption that the region was once populated is correct."

He turned his attention back to the crowd. "In the months following the Battle at Annuay, as the once green and abundant gardens gave way to the barren and desolate Waste, most of the inhabitants moved west and settled in other regions of Amrantir. All except for one group.

"The small border village of Dunnan was the site of the Battle at Annuay. The few hundred villagers who lived there bore witness to the battle itself and saw firsthand the effects of music used as warfare. Escaping to a place of safety before the battle ensued, they watched their homes and lands destroyed in a matter of minutes. In the end, the

Dunnans abandoned all music-making and fled Cullen's Waste in search of a new home.

"But, choosing to turn their backs on the foundation of the Amrantirian way of life made them outliers. Unable to reintegrate comfortably into a society with whom they held fundamentally opposing core beliefs, the Dunnans adopted a nomadic lifestyle, always moving from place to place, and never staying long in any one location. And now, over two hundred years later, they are still moving, though they have long since lost the Dunnan moniker. Today, they are known as the Wanderers.

"So you see, the price of the abuse of the master musicians' talents has a long-lasting effect on not only the land, but the people as well."

The grandmaster looked back at Nadja with kindness in his eyes. "I hope that answers your question."

Nadja nodded dumbly, and the dean resumed shuffling his papers.

The crowd's attention having mercifully turned away from her, Nadja sunk into her seat. She lowered her head and pretended to write in her notebook. Only when Grandmaster Westbrook began the next part of his lecture did she lift her eyes. A tingling on the right side of her face and neck pulled her chin in the same direction. She turned her head and her muscles stiffened.

On the opposite side of the room, a pair of narrowed, stormy-blue eyes gazed back at her, probing, studying. Pax's brow was furrowed as if working through a puzzle. Then, in an instant, his face relaxed and his tight lips melted into a crooked smile. Nadja sucked in her breath when he winked at her before turning his face and attention back to the lecture.

After watching him for a moment to ensure he wasn't going to resume his unwanted study of her, Nadja let out the breath she'd been holding. If she wasn't more careful, Pax would be an even bigger problem than she'd anticipated.

Chapter Fourteen

The ethereal tone floated over the class, leaving a hint of melancholy in its wake. Nadja shifted in the uncomfortable wooden chair, craning her neck to get a better view of the glass. The movement caused her face to prickle with warmth. The crisp autumn air had led her to choose a seat on the left side of the building near the forge's hearth, which glowed red with coals ready to spring to life with a touch of the bellows. But, that position made it difficult to see her instructor.

Grandmaster Rafe Gilmoren, the conservatory's metal craftsman in residence, was, by all accounts, a short man. His ebony skin, already smudged with soot in some places, only seemed to camouflage him more in the early-morning shadows. His stocky frame, made thick and hard by decades of metalwork, hunched over a dainty stemmed glass. He extended one beefy finger. His hands looked like they could snap a man's neck in a matter of seconds. But instead, that one finger drew a delicate circle around the rim of the glass producing the sad sound.

"Resonant frequency." Grandmaster Gilmoren's deep and sandpapery voice interrupted the movement of his finger. His long braided beard, which matched the color of his skin, bobbed up and down as he spoke. "Everything has one. Resonant frequency is an object's natural frequency, or vibration. It's based on the object's physical attributes. And what is sound?" He looked out over the forge floor, surveying the apprentices who were seated in pairs at tables arranged in a sort of ordered chaos.

As his gaze passed over the table claimed by Nadja and Helaine, Nadja was startled to see a pair of emerald-green eyes shining out from under his heavy, dark brows. They were identical to her own. Until that moment, she had never seen anyone with eyes like hers. Of course, she'd spent most of her life in the relative exclusivity of the Wanderers, so there were probably others. But something about this shared trait piqued her curiosity.

"Come on. Anyone?" bellowed the grandmaster, jerking Nadja from her thoughts and back to the task at hand.

A voice piped up from somewhere to her right. "Sound is . . . one or many tones which we sense with our ears."

"No."

Nadja glanced over her shoulder in time to see the young man slink down into his chair and try to look busy. She remembered seeing his face on the day of the auditions, Petrin something-or-other. In fact, all the students in this class now looked familiar to her, since Beginner Sound Theory was a requirement for all apprentices.

As Nadja turned to once again face her instructor, she spotted Pax seated in front of Petrin. He was flanked on either side by Selina, who was constantly sneaking glances at him through lowered lashes, and Vatara, who sat at the table beside him, wearing a sulky expression. Nadja assumed it was because she hadn't been able to claim the seat now occupied by Selina.

Pax was an island surrounded by a sea of women. In the few days the apprentices had been in residence at the conservatory, this had become a common sight. At mealtimes and in classes, there was a small group of them who seemed to have united in the cause of all things Pax. Nadja would almost feel sorry for him, if he didn't seem to be enjoying the attention. His warm personality and flirtatious smiles only encouraged their adoration. Though he hadn't singled out a particular lady yet, Nadja knew it was only a matter of time.

For her own part, Nadja thought the whole group was rather ridiculous, but she smiled to herself as she focused on Grandmaster Gilmoren. Pax's group was an excellent distraction and only made it easier for her to avoid him.

"Would anyone else like to tell me what sound is?" asked the dark, gruff grandmaster.

When no one else dared to guess, he continued. "Sound is vibration which travels through the air and is perceived by our ears and interpreted by our mind as something we hear."

He dipped his finger in a pitcher of water which rested on the edge of the table and circled the rim of the glass once more. The same otherworldly tone rang out.

"My finger on this glass acts like a bow on a string. As I move around the glass, my finger slips and sticks repeatedly in tiny motions along the glass's edge. The constant slipping and sticking causes the glass to vibrate. When the vibrations reach the glass's resonant frequency, it emits the sound you hear."

Curiosity getting the best of her, Nadja leaned over and whispered to Helaine, "What does that smell like?

Helaine's chest rose. "Hmm. Moss, or wet dirt."

Grandmaster Gilmoren lifted the pitcher, filling the glass almost to the brim. He brought his finger back to the rim, but this time the sound was much lower.

"By adding water to the glass, I have changed its physical attributes. The glass with water has more mass than the glass without water. That is why its resonant frequency is a lower pitch." He continued speaking over the sound. "If you look closely, you can see the water vibrating along the path of my finger."

Nadja leaned forward, squinting her eyes. From her position it was difficult to see, but she could just make out tiny ripples on the water's surface. They appeared to be chasing her instructor's finger around the sides of the glass.

"Now," barked the grandmaster, abruptly dumping the contents of the glass onto the dirt floor and startling the attentive crowd. "I don't have to touch the glass to make it vibrate."

He placed the empty glass on the table. Turning his back to the class, he bent to retrieve a second, identical, glass from the cabinet behind him. As he placed it on the table, he also swiped a tiny metal rod from a box of metalworking materials situated atop the cabinet. He balanced the rod, which was no bigger around than the shaft of a duck feather and no longer than his thumb, across the top of the second glass so each end of the rod just touched the rim.

Wetting his finger, he placed the first glass close to the second and once again began the mournful music. At first, nothing happened. Then, as he gradually increased the volume, the metal rod began to quiver and fell into the glass.

"As you can see, since sound is vibrations which travel through the air, tones produced by one source can affect other objects."

Grandmaster Gilmoren cleared the second glass and rod from the table and pulled a trumpet from beneath it. "The more volume, or energy, behind the tone, the more the object will vibrate."

He positioned himself behind the glass and aimed the bell of the trumpet directly at it. His short but compact frame expanded by at least half as he drew in a deep breath.

The sound blaring from the instrument was an exact pitch match to the resonant frequency of the glass. The class watched intently. Their instructor's chest and abdomen deflated as the volume of the trumpet continued to increase. Some students lifted their hands to shield their ears from the noise.

Just when Nadja thought he couldn't possibly continue to play, a sudden *pop!* interrupted the trumpet's attack, and the glass shattered, sending shards skittering across the tabletop.

The grandmaster lowered the trumpet and inhaled. "If an object vibrates enough, it can rattle itself to pieces." He put away the trumpet, using the brief interlude to regain his breath.

"This idea of resonant frequency and how sound vibrations affect objects is the foundation of the way we approach music at the conservatory. If you don't get it, find someone to help you get it, or you'll have a tough time getting anything else." He scanned the class with a raised eyebrow, making eye contact with each student. When he completed his survey, he nodded his head in satisfaction.

"Now for your project. Each of you will partner with another student in this class to design and build an original instrument. It must produce at least one full octave of pitches, and it needs to be out of your own imagination. You will have until the last class before we break for the Candlefire Celebration to complete and demonstrate your instrument."

Helaine looked at Nadja, her eyebrows raised and her expression hopeful. Nadja smiled and gave an affirmative nod.

"Since this assignment results in a finished, working instrument," the grandmaster continued, "you'll need to partner with someone from the opposite track. So, one musician to one craftsman. You'll need both areas of expertise to create a good finished piece. So hurry up and pick your partners," he finished as Helaine and Nadja shared disappointed looks. "Before you leave, I'll come around to make note of who's partnering with whom."

"I hate group assignments," sighed Helaine, as the room buzzed. "The only thing worse than relying on someone else for your grade is taking that chance with a stranger. I don't even know anyone in the craftsman track yet."

Nadja's eyes panned across the room. Pax's corner was swarming with activity, and she chuckled to herself, imagining the posturing which must be going on as at least half of his admirers nominated themselves to be his partner. "What about Petrin?" she said, her focus shifting to the lanky, fair-skinned man. "I'm pretty sure he's concentrating on String Craft, so you'd be well matched."

"Oh, no, I don't think I could ask him," stuttered Helaine, a rosy glow rising to her cheeks.

"Why not? It looks like he's just standing around waiting for someone to pick him, so I'm sure he'd agree to it. And I was impressed he volunteered an answer to

Grandmaster Gilmoren's question. The grandmaster is pretty intimidating."

"I know," agreed Helaine. "I was hoping the whole time he hadn't learned our names yet. I'd hate to be called on by him for an answer I didn't have."

"So . . . Petrin?" Nadja grinned at Helaine. She could tell by Helaine's initial reaction to the suggestion that her roommate had already noticed him on her own. "Come on. He's beginning to look like a lost puppy. Why don't you go put him out of his misery?"

"Oh, no, I really couldn't! I mean, I haven't even actually met him yet. I'll just wait and see who is left without a partner once everyone else has paired up."

Nadja raised an eyebrow and gave her friend a stern look. "You just said you hate relying on some stranger for your grade, but since classes just started, and neither of us has gotten to know many other students yet, you're going to have to do just that. At least with Petrin, you know he's got a bit of courage, which must be a good thing."

"But what about you?"

"I'll wait for the leftovers." Nadja smiled. "Now, you'd better hurry. It looks like that short, blond man is headed his way."

The threat of a missed opportunity was enough to get Helaine moving, and she weaved through the crowd towards Petrin.

Nadja was so absorbed in finding a partner for Helaine she didn't hear the weighty footsteps approaching. She glimpsed her stout instructor out of the corner of her eye just before he spoke.

"Who will you be partnering with, Mr. Raynor?" he asked.

Mr. Raynor?

A heavy hand landed on Nadja's shoulder.

"I'll be partnering with Miss Machinal."

Nadja spun to face Pax, knocking away his hand. She stared at him in stunned silence for a moment as the amusement in his eyes belied the mask of innocence he wore. She opened her mouth to say something, but closed it again when her mind refused to cooperate with her lips.

Instead, she whipped back around to tell the grandmaster there was a mistake, and she would most certainly *not* be partnering with Pax. However, by this time her instructor was halfway across the room, speaking with Petrin and a beet-red Helaine. Nadja desperately scanned the rest of the class, now only a handful of people since most of the students had already left. Finding everyone else paired off, she faced Pax, her eyes blazing.

"I did *not* agree to be your partner."

Pax feigned surprise. "Oh, I'm so sorry. I thought that was why you were standing over here clearly not looking for a partner. You seemed to be waiting around for someone to come over and claim you."

"You have some nerve," she seethed.

Nadja had struggled to live comfortably within the male-dominated society of the Wanderers her whole life. One of the few benefits of no longer living among them was the equal footing she now held with all of her peers. "I don't know about where you come from, but here in Cantio, women do not wait around for men to claim them."

Pax must have sensed he'd touched a nerve, because he changed tactics.

"Please, you have to help me," he whispered, the teasing tone gone from his voice. "This assignment is a large part of our grade in this class. I need to tackle this project with someone who is smart and resourceful. I don't want to waste my time with someone who is more interested in what I had for breakfast than in getting this project done." He flicked his eyes over towards the remainder of his followers, most of whom were eyeing Nadja suspiciously.

When she did not immediately respond, Pax played his last card. "Besides," he whispered, reaching out and lightly tapping her forearm. "You owe me."

With those three little words, Nadja knew he had her. She swallowed hard as a fresh wave of guilt washed over her. She did owe him. Likely her very life, not to mention a handful of his possessions. All he was asking for in return was help with a class assignment. It was the least she could do.

And, if it would repay the debt she owed, she doubted she would get a better, or simpler, opportunity. She sighed and closed her eyes.

"Fine," she conceded. Then she looked pointedly at him and said, "But once this assignment is complete, we're even."

A slow smile spread across Pax's face. "Deal."

Chapter Fifteen

The crisp autumn breeze battled with Nadja's cloak. Dodging fruit which had long since lost its grip on the trees above, she picked her way through the grove towards Pax. Though a cozy spot by the fire seemed more ideal to her now the summer heat was long gone, Pax suggested they begin work on their project in the apple orchard along the northern wall of the conservatory. Despite her red-tipped nose, she had to give him credit for his location choice. While other teams packed themselves into practice rooms, the dining hall, or one another's private rooms, which was not an option as far as Nadja was concerned, the orchard offered a relatively secluded space which would allow them to work uninterrupted and without the need to keep their voices low.

She spotted Pax on one of the stone benches hidden throughout the orchard. It was situated beneath one of the taller apple trees, whose low-hanging branches offered a modicum of privacy. Pax reclined against the back of the bench with his long legs outstretched and feet crossed at the ankles. He was steadily scribbling away in a sketchbook, and his eyes were narrowed in intense concentration.

Nadja took in his profile appreciatively for just a moment, then chided herself. True, she was grateful for the help and kindness he'd given her. And she would be lying if she said she didn't find him very attractive. But their previous encounter left her current situation open to unwanted questions. And besides, Pax seemed less and less like the one-woman kind of man.

As she neared him, Pax lifted his chin towards her with a welcoming smile. Nadja's cheeks stung as they erupted into twin blooms of pink and red. She clenched her teeth and hoped the effect would pass for a slight windburn. She cast her eyes down at his sketchbook and jumped right to work.

"Are those some of your ideas for our instrument?"

"Well, hello to you too." Pax slid over to make room on the bench, and Nadja seated herself on the empty end, leaving a respectable space between them.

"And yes. These are some rough ideas," he continued, passing the sketchbook to her.

She studied his drawings, happy to discover his artistic skills extended to paper and charcoal.

"Sticking with wood. That's a good idea, considering your skill set."

"And, I thought a wind instrument would be best, considering yours." Pax mimicked her businesslike tone.

Nadja turned the page and paused, pondering a strange configuration. "What's this one? It looks a little like an oddly shaped bass recorder, but how do the strings fit into it?"

Pax grinned, dropping the serious tone, and scooted closer to her, his body breaking the onslaught of the breeze. "It was something Grandmaster Gilmoren said about making objects vibrate without touching them." He reached across her body and pointed to the different parts of the sketch. "I was thinking we could install a set of strings here and here which could be tuned to vibrate sympathetically with the notes produced by the wind part of the instrument."

"Like melding a wind instrument with a stringed instrument."

"More like a wind instrument with strings attached." Pax chuckled.

Nadja smiled, looking up from the book to find her face only a few inches from his. The corners of her mouth wavered slightly, but she straightened her back and took a deep breath. "It's brilliant, actually."

Pax's taut form relaxed back against the bench. "I was hoping you'd like that one."

"I do. Very much, in fact." Nadja passed the sketchbook back to him. "I thought the plan was for us to come up with ideas together, but you've already done a lot of work. To be honest, I think we could sit here all day and not come up with another idea half as good as that one. I'm wondering what my contribution to the project is."

Pax closed the book and set it beside him on the bench. "Since we have some extra time," he said, giving her a pointed look, "why don't we get to know each other a little better?"

"You don't know when to give up, do you?" Nadja jumped up from her seat and stalked back towards the conservatory. Couldn't this man take no for an answer? She hadn't made it a half a dozen steps before she felt Pax's strong hand wrap around her upper arm, stopping her in her tracks.

"Come on, Nadja." Pax's words hissed through his clenched teeth as he leaned towards her ear. "I find you half-dead in the middle of the forest, alone, with barely enough supplies for an overnight trip, let alone a week's worth. I patch you up as best as I can, offer to get you better care, and in the morning wake up to find you've disappeared along with some of my supplies. What am I supposed to make of that?"

Nadja whirled to face him, raising her fist between their bodies. "Make whatever you'd like. We had a deal. I agreed to be your partner on this assignment, and you agreed that made us even. I'm sorry about taking your things, but I hope the payment I left behind was enough to cover it. Let me know if the cost is greater, and I will settle up. But other than that, I owe you nothing."

Their silent standoff seemed to go on for ages. Eventually, the determination on Pax's face gave way to resignation.

"You're right. We have a deal." He released his grip on her arm. "But it's not about the supplies, or you owing me something. How do you think I felt when I woke up that morning to find you gone?" His eyes softened. "This strange little phantom who had appeared as if by magic then disappeared just a quickly. For all I knew, you were wandering the woods, bleeding out or dying of infection. Or someone had come and stolen you away during the night."

Nadja swallowed hard at his last comment. How close that could have been to the truth. She knew he'd been worried about her. His care and attention to her and even his ill thought-out plan to take her to his mother for further aid was evidence of that. Guilt churned her insides.

His eyes held a mixture of hurt and concern, and she knew he was right. Like it or not, they would be spending a lot of time together over the next few months. And he'd already proven himself more determined than a dog with a bone. This dance of attack and dodge wasn't one they could keep up forever. She didn't have to tell him *everything*, but if she wanted to keep him from poking into her business, she needed to tell him something.

"Fine," she sighed, and walked back to sit on the bench.

Pax did his best to hide his emotions, but Nadja spied his smug grin threatening to break forth as he hurried back to join her.

That manipulative little —

Nadja closed her eyes and took a calming breath. Whatever his tactics, she still needed to offer something to placate him. "What do you want to know?"

"To begin with, what were you doing in the woods when I found you?"

"I already told you I was headed west. I had just stopped to refill my canteen at the spring when that ghost cat came out of nowhere."

"Where were you coming from?"

"A small village in the Seven Steppes."

"If you were planning to travel all the way from the steppes to Cantio, why did you pack so little?"

Nadja clamped her mouth shut, and her lips flattened into a thin line. Then, the memory of the other letter her mother had penned flashed in her mind, and she let it guide her reply. Pax had already shown himself to have a soft spot for a lady in distress. Perhaps she could use that to her advantage.

She arranged her features in what she hoped was a sincere look of helplessness and fear and leaned into him. "Please, if I tell you, you must swear not to tell anyone else."

Pax blinked, surprise at her sudden change in demeanor written plainly across his face. "I give you my word."

"The village I come from isn't a village as much as it is a people. I was born into the Wanderer tribe." She paused for dramatic effect.

When Pax said nothing, she continued. "As you know, my people don't believe music should be used as it is in the rest of Amrantir. In fact, within the tribe it's a crime. As a woman, my life was laid out for me. Marry, have children, and follow the role of my husband. But, I couldn't do that. I wanted to experience life outside of the confines of the tribe and the rigid expectations for my life. So, I ran."

"That must have been a difficult decision."

"You have no idea." Nadja looked out across the orchard, her gaze passing beyond the north wall and landing on the Delegates Hall. All the warmth left her body as the memory of the real reason she fled froze the blood in her veins. Baulo's face, contorted and bleeding as he crumpled to his knees, floated in front of her eyes. She shivered as the cold and the memories fused together in an attack against both her body and mind.

"Hey." Pax's soothing voice broke through her trance, and he placed a sturdy hand on her knee. "You're all right."

The warmth of his touch drew her attention back to the present, and she breathed deeply, dispelling the muscle spasms. She gave Pax a reassuring smile.

"People just don't leave the tribe. It happens rarely, if ever, and it's an option only afforded to men. Women don't have that choice. So, for me, leaving meant breaking tribal law. I knew they would be looking for me as soon as they realized I was missing. That's why I had to keep moving."

"That explains a lot." Pax nodded, but his look remained puzzled. "Why didn't you pack more supplies if you knew you were leaving? And how did you end up at the conservatory?"

"My leaving was a last minute decision. The night of my . . . of this big celebration, everything kind of came to a head. I saw every day for the rest of my life laid out in perfect order before me, and I knew I couldn't do it. So, I slipped away when no one was looking, tossed a few things in a bag, and left."

Why did she hesitate to tell Pax she had been betrothed?

"And the conservatory? How did that fit into your plans?"

"Oh . . . well . . ." Nadja licked her lips.

She didn't want to say it was a convenient hiding place. His presence here proved he valued the use of music differently than she did. He would likely find it offensive she was using her coveted position within the conservatory just to keep out of sight.

"Like I said, the Wanderers don't believe music should be used to manipulate the natural world . . . but I do," she lied. "I want to use my talents to be a help to my friends and family and society." There, the answer of a good little apprentice.

"Wow." Pax puffed out a deep breath. "I can't imagine what that must have been like for you—leaving the only life you knew and cutting all ties." His hand slipped off her knee as he leaned back and considered all she'd said.

Nadja played her final move. "Please," she reached out and took his hand. "You won't tell anyone, will you? You don't know what they would do if they ever found me."

Pax's eyes reminded Nadja of the cobalt eddies where the Nostirivin River empties into the Shadow Sea. She saw the moment he made up his mind.

Tugging her towards him, Pax wrapped his arms around her in a protective embrace. "I gave you my word."

Nadja's body relaxed against his firm chest. A small sigh escaped her lips as the fear of Pax uncovering the truth disappeared. She felt the muscles beneath his shirt flex and harden as he tightened his embrace. Her eyelids fell closed. She breathed in his now familiar scent of earth and pine and allowed herself a single moment to imagine the what-ifs.

Her scalp tingled as Pax's hand began stroking her hair. How protected she felt in that moment. How nice it must be to have someone else share your burdens. Someone to lean on. Someone to protect you.

Someone to speak for you.

No!

Nadja sat up and pushed away from Pax. The last thing she needed was to wind up under the control of another man. To have no say in how to live her own life. To always ask permission as if she was still a child.

How could she have even entertained that idea?

"I'm sorry," she stammered, "I shouldn't have . . ."

"Shouldn't have what?" Pax eyed her curiously.

"Shouldn't have burdened you with my troubles."

Pax smiled. "I didn't leave you with much choice in the matter."

Exactly. "No, you didn't."

Nadja scooted over, desperate to put more space between them. She pulled her cloak tightly around her middle, anxious to close the conversation. "Your turn."

"For what?"

Nadja lifted her chin and shot him an accusatory look. "The last time I saw you, the only thing on your mind was finding the Auldwood Oak and bringing honor and riches to your family, or something like that. It seems to me that would have been more than a couple-weeks' job. What happened?"

That crooked grin once more appeared on Pax's face. He stretched his legs out into a reclining position and laced his fingers together over his stomach. "You."

"Me?"

Pax sighed and looked up into the branches above them. "You know how I told you I come from a long line of woodsmen? That's true. That's what my family does and has always done. When I was too small to be much help with the felling and splitting, I would gather up leftover scraps of wood and carve things with them. Toys, mostly. Little ships or whistles, that sort of thing." He smiled at the memory.

"As I got older, I became more interested in carving instruments. Simple ones at first, and then more complex. And I was good at it. I decided I wanted to be a craftsman."

Pax looked at Nadja and chuckled. "But, you know how this part goes. It wasn't what was done. The Raynor family have been woodsmen for as long as anyone can remember. My father discouraged any ideas I had about becoming a craftsman. He said my work was good, but not good enough to be accepted into the conservatory. I don't blame him. He has always wanted to see his two sons take over the family business like he and his brother did from his father. And, I think maybe he didn't want me to deal with the disappointment of not getting accepted if I did apply.

"And then, one day I was in the woods minding my own business when I heard this woman locked in combat with a ghost cat. Not exactly how I was expecting to spend my afternoon." He flashed Nadja a grin. "And you called me a craftsman. You were a stranger judging my work for what it was.

"So, I found the tree and mapped its location before heading straight home. I knew it was probably too late in the year to apply for admission, but I crossed my fingers and submitted some of my pieces anyway. Two weeks before classes started, I got my acceptance letter in the mail."

"And what about your father? Your family?"

Pax's face contorted as if being squished on one side, and his voice rose in pitch. "Well, let's just say they weren't all that excited for me to leave. But, they are happy I found the tree. And my mother and sister, at least, wished me well."

"That must have been hard."

"I'd be lying if I said it was easy. But, my brother will get over it soon enough. And my mother has always known I'm a craftsman at heart. My father," Pax looked down at his hands, "well, time will tell."

The breeze picked up speed and whirled Nadja's hair into an obsidian tornado. Pax reached out and tucked the errant strands behind her ear, wearing an almost sorrowful expression. "At least I can go home."

His touch was soft and gentle, yet her skin burned in the trail left by his fingers. Guilt and something else, something not unpleasant which stirred low in her belly, collided in a sickening combination which sent a wave of anxiety through her body. Nadja inhaled a sharp, icy breath and replied curtly, "And for that, I am glad."

With quick movements she smoothed her hair back and twisted it into a knot, pulling up her hood to hold it in place. "Please don't pity my circumstances. I shared my story with you because you demanded an explanation, not because I need your help or sympathy. The only thing I ask for is your silence."

"You have it," Pax reassured her once more.

"Thank you."

Nadja rose from the bench. Swaths of pink and orange which now colored the sky caught her eye. "It's getting late. And I believe we've done all the work we can today. Your idea is brilliant, and I look forward to its completion. Good night."

With those words, Nadja spun on her heel and hurried towards the conservatory, leaving Pax staring at her back. She meant what she had said. This project couldn't be over soon enough. Why had she agreed to be Pax's partner? She'd sentenced herself to countless hours alone with him. It was one thing to indulge in the memories of their kiss when he was just someone from her past, but quite another to deal with his very real existence in her present. She didn't like the storm of emotions he could conjure within her with a simple touch of his hand.

He could be too easy to care for and rely on. Too tempting to trust.

Just when she had gained her independence, Pax had appeared, offering a return to the life she left behind.

No thank you.

Nadja pushed back her hood and unfastened her cloak, allowing the chilling twilight winds the victory they had fought for all afternoon. She invited the brisk current to dance across her face and neck, and twist up her skirt and around her legs, chasing away all warmth and frustration and leaving only cold resolve in its wake.

Chapter Sixteen

The notes emanating from Nadja's flute were anything but pleasant. She struggled through the Pantomarian folk song for the hundredth time since sitting down for her lesson in Grandmaster Kero's office.

" . . . five, six, seven, one, two, three . . ." Meliina Kero counted the beats of the random organization of notes and rhythms which had been giving Nadja a headache from the moment she began learning it. The morning sunlight streamed through the windows and flashed a steady beat across Meliina's mop of white curls as she bobbed her head in time. Her short, unruly mane stood out as the single untidy feature within her office, which was arranged in a comfortable, though minimal, presentation. Bookshelves and cabinets covered the walls, filled to the brim with books, music, and instruments. But, though the paraphernalia was numerous, every book, baton, reed, or paper was neatly ordered in precisely the space it ought to occupy.

Nadja stopped playing and fidgeted in her straight-backed chair, glaring at the music before her. The lack of ink on the page had duped her into believing the Pantomarian piece would be easy to learn. However, its atonal nature and irregular rhythms soon taught her that music is rarely what it seems at first glance.

"It shouldn't be this difficult," she snapped.

The feelings of self-doubt which had troubled her the day of auditions returned full force. She remembered hearing the other hopefuls playing their pieces with such perfection and grace. Songs much more difficult than this simple Pantomarian tune soared through the air as a testament to the skills and proficiencies of their performers. Yet, somehow *she* had managed to get in. And now, that mistake was revealed. Now, they would finally discover she had fooled them. They would know she was a fraud.

"I can't," she whispered, defeated.

Meliina regarded her with thoughtful scrutiny, then nodded her head. "Why do you think you were accepted into the conservatory?"

"I was wondering that myself." Nadja shook her head. "I heard some of the other auditions. I know how good most of them were—much better than I am. My audition wasn't perfect, and my song choice was probably less difficult than two thirds of the others. Honestly," she said, deciding to come clean, "I think maybe you made a mistake."

"Are you questioning our judgement?" Meliina challenged.

Nadja thought she couldn't feel any smaller than she already did, but Meliina proved that false. Her face heated, and she looked down at her flute as she stumbled over her words. "Of course not. It's just that, well, I know I'm not as good as most of the other students here. Maybe I had a lucky audition. I don't know."

A dainty hand closed over the top of her own, and she looked up to see a smile softening the pair of eyes ringed by thick-rimmed glasses. "You think you were given a lucky break?" asked Meliina.

"Yes."

As quick as a whip, the tiny hand smacked the back of her own. "Nonsense."

Nadja looked at Meliina's suddenly stern face in surprise, unsure of how to respond to the abrupt, though innocuous, blow.

"It's true your audition wasn't *technically* one of the best we heard. But you play with heart and feeling, something most of other auditions lacked. Heart is just as important as technique, especially in the way we use music, but much more difficult to teach. You already have that natural tendency within you. As for the technique, we have four years to improve on that point. And I have no doubt you will." Meliina's harsh expression softened once more, and she relaxed back in her chair. "Now, enough foolishness." She smiled. "Why do you think I assigned you this piece in particular?"

"I have no idea. It's not melodic. It's not easy on the ear. I can't find any pattern or reason within the song. It has no steady rhythm, so it's difficult to feel."

"Ahh, and there you have it." Meliina wagged her finger at Nadja. "All of the things you said are true. This is an older Pantomarian tune, and they had disparate ideas about musical structure and composition. The musical fundamentals upon which this song is built are foreign to the ears of most Amrantirians, which is why we fail to find its 'feel.' But, the same could be said of much of the music created and played by master musicians all over our land.

"Not every piece of music used in our work has a nicely packaged melodic line. The musicians in the northern Viridian Mountains near the Gelid Highlands utilize the wind flowing down through the maze of gorges there to produce tones through enormous pipes. The tones produced are low, droning sounds, which would hardly be called inspirational. But, by opening and closing valves at specific intervals, the musicians can play the exact tones needed to move the cool, moist Highland air down to the southern mountains, so they get the rain they need to keep green all year long. It's not a song you're likely to catch yourself humming the next day, but it gets the job done.

"Even if the notes on the page don't immediately inspire your heart, learn them. Spend time studying them and playing them. It will come."

Meliina rose and paced the floor. "One thing which might be helpful is learning to sing the piece before

177

playing it. Are you familiar with 'The Green, Green Grass in Spring'?"

"The children's tune?"

"Yes."

"Very."

"Good. Then, if I played it for you now, on any instrument, you could tell me if I was playing it right or wrong based on your familiarity with the tune, not because you had the music in front of you. Set aside your flute for a moment and let's try to sing your piece instead."

Meliina padded over to the small studio piano which occupied one corner of her office and plinked out the first line of the melody. "Sing that to me."

Nadja took a deep breath and began, "La, laa, di, daa, laa, da—"

"No, that 'daa' needs to be higher." Melina played the line once more. "Try again."

"La, laa, di, daa, laa—"

"No, still higher on the 'daa.' Again."

A burning irritation ignited in Nadja's belly as her frustration returned. She gritted her teeth against it and tried again.

"La, Laa, Di, Daa, Laa, Da—"

"Higher."

"La Laa, Di, DAA, Laa, Da—"

"Yes, but your pitch fell on the 'di' this time. Again."

Nadja closed her eyes and tried to focus on the notes even as the frustration flamed within her, warring for her attention. "LA, LAA, *DI*, DAA, LAA, DA, LA, DA, DA," she spat.

She braced herself for another correction, but Meliina was silent.

Nadja cracked her eyes and peered at Meliina through blurry slits. Startled, she opened her eyes wide.

Scarlet tinted Meliina's fair features, and the muscles in her jaw pulsated as she clenched and unclenched her teeth. A grimace twisted her lips, and the overall effect caused Nadja concern. She knew she didn't have the melody right yet, but she didn't think she had done *that* badly.

As Meliina continued to stare wordlessly at her, Nadja's back weakened and shoulders slumped. Meliina knew. For all her encouraging words, she knew Nadja was a fake. She couldn't even get the first line of a simple folk song correct. Of course she didn't belong at the conservatory.

Meliina blinked a few times as if emerging from a haze. "That will be all for today." She turned her back to Nadja and moved to one of her bookshelves, running her fingers along rows of spines.

Stung and ashamed by the abrupt dismissal, Nadja gathered her belongings and hurried from the room.

"Oh my."

The unfinished wood passed like silk beneath Nadja's fingertips as she ran her hand down the length of the barrel. There was no denying Pax's craftsmanship. He had the makings of a master.

Their new instrument prototype looked every bit like his finished sketches, save the detailed decoration and ornamentation. In the few weeks which had passed since their first meeting, they'd tweaked and refined his initial design, taking into account not only Pax's eye for aesthetics and construction, but also Nadja's perspective on playability and tone quality. Now, it was her turn to test its functionality and suggest any final changes which might need to be made.

"It will probably still need some adjustments, but it *is* pretty good," agreed Pax.

Nadja glanced up at him, raising an eyebrow. It was one thing to be an unwitting fool to hubris, but quite another to be confident in one's obvious strengths and talents. Nadja still wasn't sure on which side of that coin Pax resided. She was leaning towards the latter, but she didn't need to tell him that.

"Yes, 'pretty good' about sums it up." She smiled as his smug grin faltered. "I'll get to work on the testing and let you know how it goes."

She was bending down to wrap the instrument in its protective woolen cloth when Pax's hand shot out to stop her. She turned to find his nose inches away from her own.

"Allow me," he said, his eyes twinkling with mirth.

His woodsy scent overwhelmed the crisp autumn breeze whipping through the orchard and ignited her senses. She pulled up straight and watched him rewrap his work. He took great care to weave tiny strips of wool between each string before swaddling the entire piece in a neat package. Then, tucking the bundle under his arm, he asked, "Where are you headed?"

"Back to my room."

"Great. I'll walk you there."

Nadja sputtered, "There's no need." She'd maintained a comfortable distance from Pax these past few weeks, and she wanted to keep it that way. It felt too personal to let him accompany her to her room.

"It's no problem. I'm headed that way, too."

Before she voiced another objection, Pax's long stride had taken him halfway down the orchard path, leaving her no choice but to follow.

"You know," he began, once she came alongside him, "we've put in a lot of work on this project over the past few weeks. I think we need a break."

Pax's suggestion hung before her like the possibility of a refreshing rain shower after months of dry heat. Of course! Why hadn't she thought of that? Now the design phase of their project was complete, and the prototype was crafted, the bulk of the work remained with her testing. They wouldn't need to meet as often. In fact, they would only need to exchange the instrument once she had completed testing so he could put the finishing touches on it. She doubted she'd find anything in the design which needed to be changed.

Nadja smiled up at him, nodding her head in agreement even as she tried to push aside a niggling sense of disappointment riding the coattails of her new hope. "That's probably a good idea."

Pax grinned. "There's a Harvest Bazaar happening in the middle ring tomorrow. They're inviting farmers and merchants from all over Amrantir to come and set up stalls for the next two days. There'll be food and performers and artists. What do you say?"

"It sounds like fun."

"Great! Why don't we head that way after lunch tomorrow? Or, even better, we could get there early and see what food we can find in the stalls."

Wait, what?

Nadja's toe caught a rogue tree root, but she righted herself well enough. Her uneasiness returned as she realized her mistake. Pax didn't want to take a break from her. He wanted to take a break *with* her.

"Oh, I thought . . ." She trailed off, searching her brain for an excuse.

Pax reached out and pulled open one of the back doors, ushering Nadja through the opening with a light hand on the small of her back. Even through her cloak, she felt a pulse of energy spark at that point and shoot tingling trails across her skin.

"You thought what?" Pax prompted.

"I thought when you said we need a break you meant we didn't need to be meeting as often."

"You're probably right about that," agreed Pax. "Now you have the prototype, we'll be doing most of the work that's left on our own. All the more reason for you to join me tomorrow. I'm going to have to work harder to come up with excuses to spend time with you."

Nadja's heart did a flip-flop in her chest, for which she cursed it. Yes, he was handsome and kind and generous and talented. He was also a flirt and a ladies' man and not at all what she needed.

Just before rounding the corner, she caught a flash of red hair disappearing into one of the practice rooms. And, like a small present which had fallen out of the sky and into her lap, she had her excuse.

"That's sweet of you," she demurred, "but don't you think that would be unfair to Laurel?"

It had taken only a few days for the beautiful one-woman welcoming committee to attach herself to Pax, much to his followers' chagrins. She had become a regular fixture at his table in the dining hall and on his arm. This hadn't deterred the rest of his fans—yet—but it was assumed the two of them were a couple. And who could blame him?

Pax's steps slowed, and Nadja detected a change of color in his cheeks. "What does she have to do with anything?"

"I assumed the two of you were together."

Pax sighed. "We're just friends."

"Really? Well, that's a surprise to me, and likely anyone else who has seen the two of you together. Are you sure it wouldn't be a surprise to her, too?"

"Look," said Pax, stopping and coming around to face Nadja. "I'm friends with lots of women, and Laurel is one of those friends. But that's all she is."

"If I were 'just friends' with a man as friendly with me as you are with Laurel, I would think his intentions reached beyond friendship," she snipped.

Why was she getting so irritated at this line of discussion? Pax with Laurel was a good thing.

Nadja smoothed her features into a mask of placidity before continuing. "You and Laurel make a lot of sense together, and I wish you all the best. You and I, on the other hand, we don't make sense."

Pax's free hand reached up and grasped her chin, squaring her eyes with his own. He took a step closer to her and lowered his voice. "I don't want Laurel. I want—"

"I thought that was you!" The sweet and musical voice floated down the hall towards them, heralding Laurel's approach.

Pax looked over Nadja's shoulder and dropped his hand. Nadja thought she heard a small groan before he pasted on his now familiar smile.

"What are you two doing, lurking in the halls?" asked Laurel through yet another tight-lipped smile as she ducked under his free arm and draped it across her shoulders.

Before Pax could respond, Nadja jumped in. "Pax was just passing along the instrument we're working on for our Sound Theory class."

"Oh yes." Laurel's smile relaxed. "That project has been keeping him completely tied up lately. It's like he hardly has time for anything else." She reached up and patted him on the chest.

"Well, he's passing the work along to me now, so it shouldn't be a problem anymore. In fact," she continued, as an idea struck her, "he was just saying something about going to the Harvest Bazaar tomorrow. Since he's not so busy with our project anymore."

Over Laurel's head, Pax shot her a warning look.

Nadja plowed ahead, ignoring him. "I'm sure he would love some company. I hear it's supposed to be pretty lively."

Pax opened his mouth to interject, but was cut short by Laurel. "What a great idea! They always have the best food, and musicians and entertainers from all over Amrantir. And there are contests, and, oh, they clear out a section near the counting houses each night for dancing." She turned her radiant smile upon Pax. "It looks like you can finally show me those two left feet."

Satisfied with herself, Nadja reached out and took the package still tucked under Pax's other arm, all the while avoiding his withering glare. "It appears you two have some things to discuss, so I'll just be on my way."

With a curt nod, she stepped around the couple and made her escape.

Once back in the safety and solitude of her room, Nadja felt a tiny pang of guilt for throwing Pax into Laurel's path the way she had. Probably because she got the sense Laurel's determination and ambition was bound by nothing, not even friendship.

But, it was for Pax's good as well as her own. Laurel wasn't Nadja's favorite person, but Pax would enjoy himself. Of that she had no doubt.

She seated herself on the bed and unwrapped the woolen bundle, eager to begin work on their creation. Bringing the instrument to her lips, she blew a few notes. The sound was high but mellow, and the strings hummed along behind the wind notes like the faint echo of some enchanted and elusive woodland creature. It was a pleasant effect and caused the hair on the back of her neck to stand at attention.

After she played a series of notes, it became clear at least one of the strings was out of tune. She laid the instrument across her lap and inspected the metal cords.

"Why, you arrogant . . . ugh," she muttered to herself.

The strings were fixed. She and Pax butted heads over this particular feature repeatedly throughout the design process. He thought fixed strings would eliminate the need for tuning or human error, while she believed the effects of weather, temperature, and temperament would require tunable strings.

The final design showed tunable strings.

Evidently, thought Nadja, *Pax thought he could prove his point in practice.*

Clearly, this was not going to work.

Frustrated she wouldn't be able to continue testing until the issue was resolved, she examined the two end caps. The strings were connected to screws, so surely they could be adjusted at least a little.

Spying Helaine's violin case lying at the foot of her bed, Nadja crossed over and opened it. She hoped Helaine wouldn't mind her borrowing a tool or two. Lifting the lid of one of the small compartments lining the inside of the case, she found a small screw driver.

She moved to the table in front of the fireplace and laid the instrument on its back. Inserting the screwdriver into one of the screws for the top string, she gave it a gentle twist. She played a few more notes and smiled. That did the trick.

The fourth string was the only other rebel, so she tightened one of its screws as well. Another play-through revealed the string was still just shy of tuned. She placed the instrument back down on the table and once again inserted the screwdriver.

This time, however, as she tightened the screw she heard a loud *crack*! Bits of wood splintered as one end of the string went flying, whipping her across the back of her arm.

"Oh no!" she gasped.

The once pristine creation now looked as though someone had slashed it across one side of its face with a jagged knife, leaving behind a sort of maniacal half smile. Tiny wooden shards pointed in all directions around the wound, and the initial damage affected the surrounding area, leaving the three bottom strings dangling lifelessly.

"No, no, no, no, no."

Nadja grasped at limp strings, vainly attempting to put them back in their proper places.

Pax was going to kill her.

No, think. There had to be a solution.

Nadja began pacing. This was the conservatory after all. Plenty of other students and teachers had the skills to repair the instrument.

Of course, getting help from someone at the conservatory almost guaranteed Pax would find out about the damage. And the last thing she wanted was for Pax to learn it had taken her a matter of minutes to destroy what it had taken him weeks of hard work to create, especially after she had just fed him to the wolves. Or, to one wolf in particular.

Just then, Nadja heard the familiar cadence of Helaine's footsteps approaching in the hall. With no time to hide the instrument, she snatched it off the table and tucked it behind her back just as the doorknob turned.

Chapter Seventeen

The tinkling brass bell announced Nadja's entrance as she pushed against the weathered door. The scents of wood and oils tinged with a metallic note and something else she couldn't identify filled the air of The Broken Chord instrument repair shop.

It had taken no time for Helaine to discover the cause of Nadja's distress and, after being sworn to secrecy, just as long to offer a solution.

Nadja had avoided leaving the conservatory grounds since the day she moved in. But, the repair shop was located in the middle ring, and it was the best bet for getting the instrument fixed without Pax knowing.

She had enjoyed picking her way through the Harvest Bazaar. She kept an eye out for Pax and Laurel, but it was easy for her to blend into the crowd. Being cooped up in the conservatory for weeks had started to get to her. But, having seen no hint of the Wanderers since her arrival in Cantio, moving freely through the bustling marketplace had given her a sense of joy and liberation she had not felt since fleeing her home.

Once inside the door, Nadja paused, wide-eyed. From the outside, no one would guess how many things were packed inside the small building. Piles of sheet music and books were mounded here and there, interspersed with stacks of crafting materials. They reached so high they seemed to support the ceiling, which dripped with instruments of all shapes and sizes, each in varying stages of repair.

Two narrow paths presented themselves, one to the left and one to the right, both leading into different parts of the jungle. A rustling sounded ahead of her. Unable to see past the mess, Nadja tottered down the left path, trying not to bump into any of the precariously assembled stacks.

"Hello?" she called into the disarray.

The rustling stopped. Then, after a beat, it started again. Perhaps an animal? She could easily imagine a family of small rodents making a home under one of the piles for some time before anyone noticed. With nothing else to go on, she continued along her path, choosing the forks and turns which led her closer to the noise.

"Hello?" she called again.

"There you are!" exclaimed a disembodied voice.

Nadja jumped, then turned towards the sound.

A shock of wiry gray hair bobbed above one of the shorter piles, and a little man stepped into view. He hurried away from the pile, smiling down at something in his hand and murmuring to himself. Intrigued, Nadja followed.

"Excuse me," she began.

"Now if I can only find your sister, we'd be on to something," he muttered. Then, a little louder, "I'll be right with you."

Nadja followed the path around a corner and into a clearing. A large worktable sat at its center surrounded by more mountains of objects, though these looked better organized. The wee man stood behind it, bent over a jumble of metal tubes. He moved his hands deftly over the tangle, all the while muttering and clucking like a mother hen.

". . . has to be more comfortable for you . . . cooperation would be helpful . . . brass might be more to your liking . . . what can I help you with?"

Unsure if this last comment was directed at her or the mass on the table, Nadja looked on in silence.

"Ah," said the man, clapping his hands together and sliding the tubes to the side. He looked up at Nadja.

She swallowed a giggle as she met his gaze. He wore a magnifying glass on a band over his left eye like a myopic pirate. The giant grapefruit-sized eye reminded her of some of the larger fish she'd encountered in the Shadow Sea.

The man remembered his now superfluous accessory almost at once and replaced it with a pair of thick, black-rimmed eyeglasses.

"That's better," he chuckled. "Now, what can I help you with, my dear?"

"Are you Morris?" she asked.

"Morris Alrhen, at your service. So sorry for your wait. I was in the middle of a side project. Nothing of great import."

The lines on his face and lack of hair on top suggested to Nadja he was around the age of her grandfather. And the way his blue eyes twinkled as he spoke gave her the same sense of warmth Goran had always given her.

She placed her bundle on the table and unwrapped it.

"Ahh!" began Morris, as he examined the instrument. "What have we here? Mmm . . . maple body, very nicely crafted, but unfinished . . . joins are smooth and snug . . . these strings, what a mess . . . screw placement not reinforced, well that's your problem . . . never seen one like this before. Where did you get it?"

"It's an original creation, for a class assignment."

"So you are a student at the conservatory!" Morris beamed at her. "Rafe Gilmoren's class, no doubt. What is your name?"

"Nadja Machinal."

Morris nodded, knowingly. "I see." He removed his glasses and cleaned the lenses with hem of his shirt before replacing them. "Yes, I see. Nadja Machinal, lately of Grenyan, I believe. Niece of Tau Machinal. And how are you faring at the conservatory, my dear?"

Taken aback by his intimate knowledge of her, Nadja stuttered. "Uh, well, sir. I'm sorry, how do you know I'm from Grenyan?"

"Oh, like many others, I make it my business to keep abreast of the goings-on at the conservatory. Makes sense, considering my line of work, wouldn't you agree? And, as an alumnus myself, I do have more personal reasons."

"You were a student at the conservatory?"

"Many, many years ago."

"What did you study?"

"Oh, this and that . . . nickel!"

In a flash, Morris disappeared once more into the looming stacks. A moment later, he reappeared holding a small valve.

Nadja watched curiously as he bent once again over the tangle of metal tubes. He removed two screws and inserted the valve, replacing the screws when he was finished. "Much better," he declared.

Before he could run away again, Nadja brought his attention back to her problem.

"Sir. My instrument, can you repair it?"

Morris gripped the barrel and brought the string section up to eye level for a closer inspection.

"Of course I can."

"Thank you, but . . ." Nadja flushed, unsure how to phrase her next request.

"What is it, my dear?"

She took a deep breath and rushed on, "You see, I didn't actually craft this instrument. My partner did. It is my fault it's broken, but he doesn't know."

"And you don't want him to know, is that it?"

Nadja cringed. "Yes. Is there any way . . ."

Morris chuckled once more. "Have no fear. When I'm finished with the repairs, it will look like nothing ever happened." He gave her a wink.

Nadja's shoulders relaxed. "Thank you so much."

"You may pick it up tomorrow."

"You can have it done so quickly?"

Morris's eyes twinkled. "Of course, my dear."

"Oh, thank you, sir."

"And no more of this 'sir' business," he chided, waving her away. "Call me Morris like everyone else. And give your uncle my best the next time you see him."

And just like that he disappeared again into the jungle, instrument in hand.

Nadja retraced her steps until she found the door.

The brisk autumn breeze whipped around her as she stepped onto the porch. It carried with it smells of roasted corn and spiced fruit, making her mouth water. As she crept down the porch steps, she decided to indulge herself by taking a stroll through the bazaar on her way back to the conservatory. It wouldn't be hard to blend in with the crowd. She should be fine as long as she didn't draw any extra attention to herself. She grinned as she pulled up the hood of her cloak and practically skipped down the road.

Miles of colorful bunting draped back and forth across the road, its little flags waving a cheery welcome. Stalls lined either side of the street, dotted with every type of produce imaginable. Baskets of apples, gourds, figs, and dates, and even an occasional gemfruit, all the way from the Gelid Highlands, dotted the walkways. The harvest had been good in Amrantir this year.

Giant slabs of preserved meats and wheels of cheeses were sold by weight, while the street performances were free. To her left, a musician whipped up a small whirlwind, spinning crisp red and orange leaves around in a miniature tornado, much to the delight of a crowd of children. As she meandered down the road, the music around her morphed from relaxed folk melodies to rollicking jigs and back again.

A stall selling little balls of fried apple dough topped with cinnamon and sugar drew Nadja in with its delicious scent. She bought a small sack and munched happily on them, savoring the warm sweetness and cozy feeling accompanying every bite.

A group of acrobats caught her attention, and she moved along to join the small crowd which had gathered to watch their performance. She oohed and aahed along with the crowd while the performers flipped and stacked themselves into human pyramids and towers. Nadja watched in amazement as the smallest acrobat, a boy who looked no more than nine or ten years old, climbed to the top of one tower and produced a baton from thin air, which he set aflame and twirled above his head.

The crowd erupted in applause. Nadja did to, almost knocking the rest of her fried dough from her hand. As she fumbled with the sack, trying desperately not to lose one precious bite of the sugary deliciousness, a musical laugh floated above the cheers and grabbed her attention.

Nadja snapped her head towards the sound. Only a few steps away stood the ever-lovely Laurel Willowcroft, her arm linked with Pax's. Nadja shifted back behind a large gentleman, hoping they had not seen her. She peered around the man and saw that both Laurel's and Pax's attentions were directed at the diminutive fire twirler, not at her.

Just then, Laurel's chin dropped. Her eyes followed and landed on Nadja.

Panicked, Nadja jerked around and worked her way to the edge of the crowd. That was too close. She was almost certain Laurel had recognized her. Would she say something to Pax? Nadja couldn't take that chance. Stuffing the remaining fried dough into her mouth, she disposed of the paper sack and took the fastest route out of the bazaar.

Leaving the festivities behind, Nadja wound through narrow paths between businesses and government buildings. With most of the city gathered for the bazaar, the side streets and alleyways were empty and quiet. The afternoon sun did little to warm the air. Instead, it made the taller buildings cast long shadows which enveloped the world around her, bringing with them colder air and making it more difficult to see. Eager to curl up next to a fire in the comfort of her own room, she pulled her cloak tighter around her shoulders and turned her steps towards the conservatory.

With the sounds of the bazaar now a faint hum in the distance, Nadja wondered about Laurel and Pax. They looked the part of the cozy couple, standing arm in arm, sharing warmth. Pax may have said he wasn't interest in Laurel as more than a friend, but their body language and the delighted expression he wore told another story.

But, that was good, right? As long as Pax was focused on Laurel, he wouldn't have time to focus on her.

So why did she have a knot growing in the pit of her stomach?

Just then, Nadja heard scuffing behind her. Freezing, she turned and glanced over her shoulder. She narrowed her eyes, searching the dim alleyway.

Nothing.

It was probably a stray animal searching for something to eat or for shelter from the cold. Smart animal. If you weren't soaking up the warmth and activity of the bazaar, the best place to be was somewhere out of the wind and cold. Nadja picked up her pace. Up ahead, there was a break in the buildings, and she could see little beams of sunlight streaming diagonals across the otherwise darkened alley.

The moment she turned the corner, a gust of crosswind hit her with full force, lifting the hem of her cloak and flapping it like a wild bird. She stumbled back. The gust dissipated as quickly as it had appeared, and she paused to adjust her cloak. Just then, she felt a sharp pain on her left side.

Nadja grunted and sucked in a breath through clenched teeth.

She looked down. The world stopped.

A dart, about the length of her palm, protruded from her side just above her hip. The eerie familiarity of the little stinger made her blood run cold.

Without another thought, she pulled out the dart, tossed it on the ground, and broke into a sprint. A cold, dead feeling surrounded the wound spreading outwards in every direction with each step she took. Her head swam and her vision began to blur around the edges. Her gait became irregular, and by the time she had gone no more than thirty paces, she stumbled to the ground, having lost the use of her left leg.

Nadja clawed at the hard-packed dirt, trying desperately to pull herself forward, but it was no use. Her vision was darkening. Her left arm was gone, and she was rapidly losing the use of her right.

Diamphoria.

It was the Wanderer's poison of choice for taking down large game. Luca had taught her about its use during their time together. It paralyzes the muscles of the prey, eventually killing it. But the disorientation it caused was unexpected.

Her cheek hit the dirt as she struggled for breath, no longer able to raise her head. Through the syrupy thickness of her hearing, she could make out the drumming thud of approaching footsteps.

She pried open her eyelids. If she was about to die, she wanted to see the face of her killer.

A pair of dark leather boots came into view, and someone knelt beside her.

Her surprise and disbelief forced a rueful chuckle from her lips as the last thing she saw before fading into oblivion was Luca's cold stare.

A bone-rattling bump jarred Nadja into consciousness. Through the mist which clouded her mind, she could discern the lazy rhythm of horse's hooves, though she couldn't open her eyes. She was on her back, lying on a hard surface, and her body felt . . . well, it didn't. The effects of the diamphoria were in full swing. But, the irregular rocking and sporadic bumps reminded her of riding in a boat.

The rocking slowed, then stopped.

A low, muffled rumble met her thick ears. Maybe distant thunder?

As she slipped away again, her mind drifted into a dream. *My sister . . . sick . . . taking her home.*

Brisk wind ruffled her hair, and the hard surface vibrated beneath her. They were moving faster now. Still unable to open her eyes, the darkness beyond her eyelids told her the sun had set.

Did you pay him?

How long ago that had happened, she had no idea. Was it still the same day? The same week?

Of course.

The sensation of having no body was disturbing, but perhaps it was a blessing, if it really was as cold as she imagined.

Probably more than his servant salary for an entire year.

At least she wasn't dead yet though she was beginning to wish she was. Being trapped in her body, winking in and out of consciousness, was maddening.

Should be enough to buy his silence, too.

As her window of awareness closed once again, she hoped the diamphoria wouldn't take much longer to finish its job.

Nadja awoke to a thousand tiny pinpricks dancing across her face. Surprised by feeling anything at all, she tried to lift her hand to touch it.

No, she still couldn't move.

Was it possible the diamphoria was wearing off? She had never heard of that happening before, but there was no denying the tingling sensitivity beginning to spread throughout her whole body.

She pried her eyelids open. Another good sign.

A host of twinkling stars filled the cloudless sky. They were a beautiful assurance that yes, she was alive. A lump formed in her throat, and she tried to swallow it, but her throat was raw from breathing the cold night air.

Still unable to move her head, she tried to figure out where she was. The short, wooden rails on either side of her, along with the jostling and the sound of horses' hooves, confirmed she was lying in the back of an open cart. She lifted her eyes and saw the dark heads of two men bobbing above the driver's seat. Luca's long ponytail gave him away at once, but the short-haired man offered no distinguishable features from the back.

"What do you think he'll do with her?" asked Luca.

"He's not a man to stray from tradition." Nadja didn't recognize the other voice. "He'll push for full and exact punishment. After what she did, I can't say I blame him."

Who were they talking about? Nadja would have thought, of all people, Luca would have been the man most injured by her disappearance. Of course, her decision to leave the Wanderers was not only injurious to Luca, but a slap in the face to everyone in the tribe. By abandoning them, she had essentially offended all of their beliefs, traditions, and their whole way of life.

Surely they weren't talking about her grandfather, Goran. As the Speaker for her family, he would have been the most dishonored by her decision to flee. But, he had always championed his daughters' and granddaughters' independence. Perhaps her choice to leave was one step too far.

At that moment, the man with the short hair glanced back over his shoulder. Nadja snapped her eyelids shut and clenched her jaw to stop the chattering. Her best course of action would be to appear unconscious and unmoving. Hopefully she could glean some more information from her captors. And, if escape was at all a possibility, it was in her favor to hide the fact that feeling was returning to her body.

"This looks like a good spot."

The horses slowed to a standstill.

She listened as the two men began unloading the cart and making camp for the night. Within minutes, the sound of a crackling fire reached her ears. They seemed to pay her no attention, which was a good thing at the rate she was regaining sensation and mobility. She could wiggle her fingers now and was surprised to discover, though her face was frozen, her body had been wrapped in a warm, heavy blanket. Not as nice to discover were her bound hands, stiff joints, and aching muscles which were the result of being knocked around flat on her back in a hard wagon bed.

Just then, a pair of large hands wrapped around each of her ankles and yanked her towards the back of the cart.

"Take it easy," came Luca's level voice, mercifully covering her muffled groan.

Her legs dangled off the back at an uncomfortable angle, pinching her spine, and she fought the urge to pull up her knees.

"Huh. I would have thought you, of all people, wouldn't care what happens to her," said the other man.

"I don't," replied Luca. "I just want to make sure we deliver her to the Elders as ordered. We don't want it to look like we passed judgment and sentencing on our own."

Nadja's backbone relaxed as Luca slipped one arm under her knees and the other under her shoulders, lifting her out of the wagon. A few months ago, the thought of being held so intimately in his arms might have made her heart flutter. But now, she was terrified. For all of his gentleness, she'd heard what he'd said. He didn't care what happened to her. He was looking forward to her judgment.

The crackling and popping of the fire grew louder as they drew near. Nadja hoped Luca would at least be kind enough to put her close to it.

As his steps slowed, he unexpectedly lurched forward. Nadja's eyes flew open with a gasp as she felt her body being lifted, then dropped, then cradled once more in a pair of sturdy arms.

"Fonso! Get this bag out of the way and over there with the others," barked Luca. "I almost broke my neck."

Biting the inside of her cheeks, she closed her eyes and smoothed her features once more, hoping Luca had been too distracted to notice her slip.

The warmth of the fire washed over her as he knelt and laid her on her side, facing it. He tucked the blanket around her, blocking out the cold. Just when it seemed he was finished with her, his body stilled.

Nadja held her breath.

The leather of his boots creaked as he shifted next to her, and the heat from the fire disappeared, blocked by something solid.

She felt his breath on her cheek.

"Don't move," he whispered.

Chapter Eighteen

Obeying Luca's command proved to be more difficult than she expected. The effects of the diamphoria had long since worn off, and her shoulder and hipbone throbbed from bearing her weight against the ground. She longed to roll, stretch, anything, but Luca's warning held her firmly in place.

Robbed of her vision, her ears allowed the rest of the evening's activities to play out in her mind. Her captors settled in, one near her foot and the other near her head. They said little to one another. She held her breath as they filled their bellies, defying her stomach to growl and give her away. After the meal, a quietness descended upon the camp as her captors tucked into their bedrolls. Within a few minutes, the only sounds of their presence in the forest were the snapping and hissing of the fire and the echoing boom of Fonso's discordant snores.

No longer able to bear the darkness, Nadja cracked her eyelids. The camp was much as she had expected. Fonso's lumpy silhouette rested on his back at her feet, mouth agape as he projected his nocturnal symphony to the stars. She knew of him, but that was as far as their acquaintance went. He was many years older than her, unmarried, and, being a scout, spent much of his time away from the Wanderer camp.

She slid her eyes upwards. The bedroll at her head was empty.

Strange.

She remembered hearing Luca lie down. Then nothing.

Without warning, a hand clamped over her mouth and nose, muffling her involuntary rasp. Luca flipped her onto her back, straddling her body and pinning her arms to her chest. Nadja struggled against his weight, but couldn't free herself. She tried to draw breath for another scream, but his hand pressed against her face harder as he bent over her.

"I said, 'Don't move,' woman," he hissed. "This won't end well if Fonso wakes up."

Right on cue, Fonso snorted as if in agreement and rolled onto his side.

Nadja froze. Memories of Baulo and Kizzy flashed in her mind's eye. Except, in her imagination, their faces were replaced with hers and Luca's.

"I'm not going to hurt you." Luca whispered low and deliberately. "Now, I'm going to move my hand, but don't make a sound."

Wide-eyed, Nadja wiggled her head in agreement. Luca released his grip, and she sucked in a deep breath.

Right away her teeth began to chatter. Whether from fear or the cold, she didn't know.

Placing a finger to his lips, he climbed off of her, eyeing her warily. She thought for a moment she might be able to land a solid kick to his groin, but, though her legs were free, her hands were still bound. And the possibility of waking Fonso and having two men to contend with was more than she could handle.

Luca gripped her elbows and pulled her to her feet. Taking hold of the rope tied around her wrists, he jerked his head towards the woods. He led her away from the campfire and into the darkness, stepping lightly and motioning for her to stay quiet.

As the shadows swallowed them, Nadja's mind raced with scenarios of how the night might play out. She was no match for Luca's strength. Running was an option, but again, she knew she wouldn't get far. And she knew he wouldn't kill her. He had said as much to Fonso.

No, the night would unfold as she had feared.

Tears streamed down her face, and she bit her bottom lip. The idea of the two of them coming together had once filled her with a sense of curiosity and intrigue. Now it filled her throat with bile as her stomach revolted against the possibility.

She looked back. The glow of the campfire had completely disappeared. Only the moon and stars lit their way.

"That's far enough," said Luca, stopping under a break in the forest canopy. He turned around to face her, and closed the distance between them, his eyes narrow. "Are you all right?"

Caught off guard by his supposed concern for her welfare, Nadja only stared back in response. She had expected his approach to be more forceful.

"Please speak," he said. "We're far enough away from camp. Fonso won't be disturbed." He released her wrists. Reaching up and cupping her face with his hands, he traced his thumbs under her eyes, wiping away her tears.

Nadja stiffened at the unexpected gesture, her heartbeat racing. She opened her mouth to speak, but nothing came out. She licked her chapped lips and swallowed. If she had eaten a handful of glass shards, it would have been less painful. She winced, then repeated the motion a few more times until her throat was lubricated enough to produce sound.

"I'm fine," she croaked.

"Are you sure?" he asked. "The diamphoria seems to have run its course, but I'm less familiar with the symptoms and duration of the nightshade."

"Nightshade?"

"Yes. The healer gave mother a nightshade tincture to help her sleep. It works fast, and she sleeps like the dead. But sometimes it has strange side effects if not taken properly. Visions, hallucinations."

"That explains a lot." Nadja wearily closed her eyes.

Luca must have tipped his dart with the nightshade as well as the diamphoria. She vaguely recalled the dreams she had in the back of the cart. Something about—

"I only hope I slipped Fonso enough to keep him down for as long as we need."

Nadja's eyes snapped back to Luca, once again aware of their nearness. She was suddenly angry with him. Angry he had shot her. Angry he had pretended concern and sympathy to make her lower her guard. Angry he had transformed from the kind, safe man she had grown to care for into a reflection of the cold, heartless man she had killed. She clenched her jaw and rose up on her toes, coming a hair's breadth from his face.

"Then get it over with," she spat.

Confusion and annoyance washed over Luca's face. He dropped his hands and took a step back from her. Then, grabbing her wrists once again, he led her over to a fallen tree.

"Sit," he commanded.

Nadja obeyed, keeping her chin high and her eyes locked on him. Even if she couldn't defend herself against him physically, she would protect her heart and mind. He may hurt her body, but he would not touch her spirit.

Luca walked a few paces away from her, then spun on his heel.

"What in the world happened?"

That was unexpected.

Nadja blinked. "Excuse me?"

Luca began pacing. His voice pinched as he struggled to keep his tone even. "One moment we're celebrating our future together, and the next moment, you're gone. Just like that. No warning. Not even a hint of discontent. Leaving your mother holding some letter about how you needed to see more of the world and other nonsense."

"Oh," Nadja exhaled, her mind spinning. "I thought—"

"Did you?" demanded Luca. "Did you really think? Was this something you planned over days? Weeks? Or was it a last-minute decision?" His pacing slowed as he considered her. "Maybe motivated by something that happened that night?"

"Did you really drag me away from camp just to question me?" she asked.

"I need to know what happened. The truth, without the chance of Fonso overhearing. Why else would we be out here?"

"I mean . . ." Nadja stuttered, looking down at the forest floor. "I just thought . . ."

"You thought what?" asked Luca, coming to a halt. His voice was suddenly quiet.

An uncomfortable silence stretched between them.

Finally, Nadja looked up. The anguish written across his face ripped her heart in two, and her terror-induced nausea was washed away by a wave of guilt.

"Do you know me so little?" he wondered. He turned away from her and peered up at the stars through the canopy opening.

She had known Luca since childhood. They'd grown up together. He had never shown her anything other than gentleness and patience, kindness and dependability. How could she suppose anything different from him?

And yet, though she didn't know Baulo as well, she'd have never suspected him capable of the things she had witnessed that night. How easily he hid his depraved nature behind a mask of tradition, lawfulness, and false morality.

Nadja didn't know how to answer Luca's question, so she avoided it. "So, you came to bring back the runaway?" she asked, glad her mother's letter had done its job.

Luca sighed. "No. I came to bring back the woman wanted for attempted murder."

If it was possible for Nadja's blood to run any colder, it did just that. Attempted murder? Surely he wasn't talking about Baulo. Baulo was dead. She had killed him and seen his corpse with her own eyes.

But, who else could he be talking about?

Her breathing came harder, and her teeth resumed their involuntary nervous chatter. If Baulo was still alive, then she hadn't killed him. She wouldn't be charged with murder. Attempted murder. Yes, that's what Luca said.

She may yet live.

Then, she recalled the last time she saw Baulo. His bulging eyes, the blood pouring from his face. She squeezed her eyes shut in a failed attempt to block the vision. If he managed to survive, it would be worse for her. As the victim, he would hold great influence with the Elders in her sentencing. She couldn't imagine that a man capable of the acts she had stopped would want anything less than for her to endure the same torture. Nadja pulled her hands to her chest and rocked back and forth on the fallen log.

Kizzy! What about her cousin? And her mother? Perhaps the runaway note had saved Jamila from any implication, but perhaps not. What had they suffered since she fled? A sob escaped her lips as she imagined the worst.

A pair of strong arms came from behind her, wrapping around her chest and arms and applying gentle pressure. Luca's chin rested at her shoulder as he shushed her, slowly rocking and calming her breathing.

"I know *you*," he whispered. "And you're not a murderer." Her breaths became more even, and he released his hold, coming around to take a seat next to her. "If there is any way for me to help you, you need to tell me what happened that night. Why did you run?"

Was he truly offering to help? She no longer had any claim on him. Her decision to leave the tribe had severed any promise bond they once shared. He couldn't still want her after this, not a woman accused of attempted murder.

But, he'd always had a deep sense of duty.

And he was offering to help.

Nadja looked at him. His dark eyes were filled with nothing but concern and kindness.

"Please, how is my mother?" She had to know the fate of her family before they talked of anything else.

"Your mother is well. She brought your letter before the Elders the morning after you left. It wasn't until other events came to light that her possible involvement was suspected. But, no evidence has been found to support that, so she has not been charged with anything."

The relief which flooded Nadja's body was fleeting as she formed her next question.

"And what of Kizzy?"

Luca face grew puzzled. "Kizzy . . ."

"Yes, my little cousin," she prompted. "Harman and Pili's daughter."

"Oh, yes. She is well as far as I know." He was thoughtful for a moment, then added, "As I remember, she took to her bed ill for the first few days after you left. But she is better now."

Nadja's shoulders collapsed as she released the breath she'd been holding.

"Thank you," she said. Her mother and cousin were alive and well. That knowledge alone gave her strength and something akin to hope.

"You said I am charged with attempted murder?"

"Yes."

"By whom?"

"Baulo Oramen."

If Nadja had held on to any sliver of hope Baulo was still as dead as when she left him, Luca's words smashed it to pieces.

She steadied her voice. It was in her best interest to find out as much as she could before deciding whether to tell Luca anything. "And what exactly does he accuse me of?"

"Baulo says he saw you leaving his tent as he returned early from our betrothal celebration. Knowing you had no business being there, he searched his tent but found nothing missing. So, he assumed you had lost your way in the dark and walked into his tent by mistake. Then, he says, he drank a glass of wine and went to bed.

"That's where one of the Elders found him the next day. He was barely conscious and had been bleeding from his nose and ears. The healer said it appeared to be caused by some sort of poison.

"A week later, when he finally came out of his tent, he formally accused you of attempted murder, saying you poisoned his wine. His accusations were supported by your disappearance the same night he was poisoned."

Nadja began shaking her head halfway through Luca's tale, and by the time he finished, it looked like a flag flapping in the breeze.

"No. No. No. No!" she exclaimed, jumping up from the log. "None of that is true!"

"Then tell me what is true," said Luca, coming to stand in front of her.

Bitterness tinged her voice. "It doesn't matter."

"Yes, it does. The truth always matters."

"Oh really? He's an Elder and the tribe's delegate to the capital. Who am I? Nadja Filamen, the only daughter of a single woman with no standing. It's my word against his." Nadja threw up her hands. "You're telling me any contradicting account I offer will be taken seriously? Maybe elsewhere in Amrantir, but we both know I don't stand a chance in a hearing before the Elders."

Luca looked on in silence as Nadja ranted, bouncing back and forth between her feet. Her initial shock had given way to frustration and rage. Yes, she was glad to know she hadn't killed a man. But, now that man was determined to punish her. For what? For preventing him from committing horrible acts against an innocent child.

"It doesn't even make sense," she continued. "Did he say why I supposedly poisoned him? Hmm? Did anyone ask him that? And if he saw me leave his tent, why didn't he try to question me? I clearly remember there was no moon that night. That can be verified. He would've had to be really close to someone to identify them."

"Yes, his story has holes," said Luca. "Fill them in for me."

"You are not bound to me." Nadja voiced her thoughts aloud without realizing it. "I disappeared and left you alone on the day of our betrothal celebration. You are well within your rights to bring me back to camp and demand reparation for the shame I brought to you. Why do you even care?"

"Because I love you!" Luca cried, gripping her by the shoulders and giving her a light shake.

Nadja snapped to attention, looking up into his face. His angular jaw clenched, and his eyes flamed with intensity and determination.

He had said those words to her once, the day before she ran away. At the time, she'd taken him at his word because he was an honest man, not because of any grand display of affection on his part. This time was different. She felt the heat of his emotion radiating off of his skin, warming the air between their bodies. His grasp on her shoulders was firm but gentle, and she became suddenly aware of how close they stood. What she had once believed to be true in her head, she now believed with her heart.

The why of the matter would have to wait. If he loved her as he said, he may be her only hope of coming through this mess alive. And she needed to act fast.

Going with her instinct, she told Luca everything that happened the night she ran away. She watched the muscles in his jaw flicker when she described how she found Kizzy and Baulo in the smokehouse, but otherwise his face was a mask of stone. When she got to the part about her scream and its effects on Baulo, Luca's eyes narrowed. He dropped his arms and slowly backed away from her.

"I don't know how or why it happened. I was so afraid. The only thing I could think about was stopping him from hurting Kizzy and me. I didn't mean to hurt him, and I certainly didn't intend to kill him. I mean, I didn't lay a finger on him, but I know I was the one who did that to him." She stopped her tale right before the moment her mother found them, feeling it best Jamila remained above suspicion.

For what seemed like an eternity, Luca's silent scrutiny held her captive. After a while, his gaze weighed so heavily on her she almost fled into the darkness. But, just as she was about to run, he spoke.

"I believe you. Your story is incredible at best, but I know you, and I know you are neither a thief nor a murderer." Luca sighed and set his sights on something beyond her right shoulder.

"There have been stories," he murmured, "rumors really, about Baulo's proclivities for years now. But rumors are all they have been. No one has ever accused him, and no evidence has ever been brought forward."

Nadja straightened her spine. "Until now."

"Yes," he agreed.

"So now what?"

Luca crossed to the fallen log and slumped onto it. "We must tread carefully. Baulo is a powerful Elder. You cannot simply march into camp and accuse him of what you described, even with my support. As you said, it would still be your word against his.

"If we could convince your cousin to come forward, we may have grounds enough to be taken seriously by the Elders. Accusations from both the victim and a witness must carry enough weight to prompt an investigation, regardless of Baulo's standing."

Nadja groaned inwardly. She knew the false sense of security which came with living in the shadows, hiding from the thing that would seek to destroy her. If Kizzy had hidden Baulo's attack behind a feigned illness, she had likely done her best to put the whole incident behind her.

"Isn't there any way we can leave her out of this? She's just a child. Do we have to put her through remembering and retelling her attack in front of the whole tribe? If no one else knows about it, I'm sure she'd like to keep it that way."

"Without a word from Kizzy, we have no hope for her. Or you. Or any other girl Baulo may set his sights on. I understand your concern for your cousin, but if she will not stand and accuse her attacker, fear and regret will follow her the rest of her days."

He was right.

Nadja knew deep within her bones. Hadn't she dealt with the same thing ever since she'd run away? And if being kidnapped by Luca and Fonso had taught her anything, it was that living in fear and hiding was not something you could maintain long-term. No matter the precautions she had taken, her past had caught up with her.

And it would catch up with Kizzy.

"She will not be alone." Luca's voice broke through her contemplation. "I will speak with Harman, and share with him what you told me. And I will stand with her as well. She will have our protection and support if she can find the courage within herself to face Baulo."

Nadja nodded in agreement.

"But as for you," Luca began, rising from his seat. He slid his right hand up the side of his leg and gracefully unsheathed the hunting dagger he wore at his belt. Standing in front of her once more, he let his eyes roam the curves and angles of her face as if committing it to memory. He raised the blade between their bodies.

Nadja gasped as the knife sliced the bonds holding her wrists.

"You need to go. Now is not the time for you to return—not bound and drugged and accused of attempted murder." He replaced his dagger and paced the surrounding area, head down, as if searching for something. "You need to wait until charges are brought against Baulo, and you are named as a witness."

"But what about you?" Nadja protested. "Won't you be in danger for letting me go?"

"This should do it." Luca bent over and retrieved something from the ground. Then, turning back to Nadja, he said, "But I didn't let you go. You escaped."

She looked at the limb he was offering her, puzzled. The smooth shaft was an arm's length and as big around as one of Jamila's walnut cookies. It tapered on one bushy end while the opposite end was splintered and jagged where it had separated from the tree.

"Unfortunately, I misjudged the diamphoria and nightshade dosages. You awoke in the middle of the night.

I heard you trying to escape and chased you into the woods." Luca chuckled. "Too bad for me, you were armed." He reached out and took Nadja's hand, wrapping her fingers around the broken end of the limb. "I never even saw it coming."

She gasped. "You're crazy," she sputtered, dropping the limb and stepping back. "I'm not hitting you with that."

Luca's eyes steeled, and he picked up the discarded weapon. "Yes you are. Then, you will take one of the horses and ride north, away from here and away from Cantio. Whenever an opportunity presents itself, you can double back, but your trail must continue north, away from the capital. This is imperative. Fonso isn't as good a tracker as I am, but he's no fool. He should be out until morning, so you have a small head start. Don't waste it."

"That all sounds wonderful. But I still don't see where me batting you over the head with a tree branch is part of the plan."

"No offense, but no one would believe you outran me. And you besting me in combat is even less believable. It has to look like a surprise attack. For your sake as well as mine." He held out the limb to her once more, his eyes imploring her to comply.

Reluctantly, she gripped the crude cudgel.

In Luca's face, she saw the same strong, quiet boy she had known her whole life, but now with fresh eyes. In the light of the cold, late autumn moon, the boy who had once seemed so stoic and aloof was transformed into a man who loved her more than the rules and traditions he held in such high esteem. He was a man willing to put himself in harm's way, even sacrifice his own body, to protect her.

Suddenly overcome with emotion, Nadja rushed forward, wrapping her arms around his waist and burying her head in his chest.

"Thank you," she sighed into his shirt as a tear slipped down her cheek.

Luca held her tight for but a moment, then stepped back. "There's no time to waste," he said, huskily.

Nodding, Nadja raised the branch over her shoulder.

"And, Nadja," said Luca, with a weary half smile, "I'd rather do this just once. So make it count."

He braced himself.

Nadja took a deep breath and swung. "I'm sorry," she whispered right before the branch connected with the side of his head.

Chapter Nineteen

The pounding of the horse's hooves marked the time and distance Nadja put between herself and her captors. Finding the river had been easy enough since they had been heading south towards the coastal city of Chansey where the tribe favored the more temperate winter climate.

Nadja stuck to the main road, following the river north and leaving a clear trail. Between her cloak, the heat from the horse, and the adrenaline pumping through her body, she kept the feeling in her fingers and toes. When she caught sight of the moonlight bouncing off the curves and angles of the capital city, a renewed hope swept through her, and she urged the horse onward.

An hour north of Cantio, she stopped to water her horse. She slipped off of the beast's back, and her muscles turned to jelly when she hit the ground. Her roles within the tribe never required a horse, and until Luca began training her as a hunter, she had never ridden one. He taught her the basics, but building up the strength and endurance to make the ride she had just finished took more than a few lessons.

On wobbly knees, she led the horse to the river's edge. She dropped down beside it and took a few sips of the icy water herself before stretching out on the soft bank. Strips of violet and pink announced the breaking dawn, and small boats began to appear on the river.

Nadja mulled over getting back to Cantio. Putting as much distance between herself and her captors was her singular focus as she rode, but now the new day was beginning, she wondered about Luca and Fonso.

Thankfully, Luca was conscious when she left him. But the branch had done its job well, leaving a large lump on his head and gashes along his face and neck where the dry brush trailed the initial blow. She winced at the memory.

But what of Fonso? How long would the nightshade last? How long would it take them to pack up camp and follow her trail? A niggling sense of urgency once again took root in her belly as she puzzled through her next steps.

As she thought, she allowed her gaze to wander across the water's surface. A wide, flat-bottomed boat drifted past her, having joined the skiffs which had appeared at sunup. Nadja's eyes narrowed as she considered it. She reached into one of the invisible pockets of her skirt. Relief washed over her when her fingertips found the smooth spheres. Whether Luca and Fonso had searched her was a mystery, considering the amount of time she spent unconscious in their company. Thankfully, the pearls she'd pocketed before heading to the Harvest Bazaar had escaped their notice.

Nadja forced herself to stand and lead the horse back to the road. All the while her joints and muscles protested the movement. She gritted her teeth and hoisted herself onto the back of the horse, turning the animal north once again.

A quarter of an hour into her ride, she passed a small ferry port comprising one dock, two boats, and a little stone cottage, presumably belonging to the ferry operator. The road forked in two directions. One route headed east through the forest. The other followed the river's path towards the Gelid Highlands. Nadja stayed left, continuing towards the Highlands, but kept a watchful eye on the riverbank.

After another quarter hour's ride, she reined her horse to a slow walk and angled towards the water. The forest was still dense and shaded, but the further north she rode, the smaller the trees became. The chill of the season transformed much of the vegetation from emerald into shades of amber and garnet while stripping other trees entirely of their foliage. She stopped her horse at the edge of the river beneath an overhang of naked and spindly branches.

As the horse lowered his head to drink, Nadja flexed and stretched her stiff muscles. Once the animal had quenched his thirst, she turned him to face the road but held him in position.

"Thank you, boy," she said, giving him a hearty pat on the neck. "Now hold still for me for just a minute, and you can be on your way."

She braced her hands on the front of the saddle and leaned forward, swinging her feet up to kneel on the horse's back. The beast huffed at his rider's peculiar movements, but stayed in place. With a grunt of her own, Nadja pulled one leg forward and, fighting against her weakened muscles and spent energy, the second one soon followed.

Centering her weight between her two feet, she stood tall, keeping her knees soft in case the horse shifted beneath her.

She flicked her eyes upwards. The lowest limb was within reach.

Her knees trembled with the effort of keeping her balance. She reached up and laced her fingers around the lowest branch. Her muscles defied her as she pulled the rest of her body up and over the limb.

The hardest part was over. Nadja closed her eyes and rested her cheek against the limb's cool bark. Years spent swimming and diving had made her strong and agile, but a day of riding used muscles in a way she was unaccustomed to. And, if experience had taught her anything, it was that she could expect to feel even worse tomorrow.

She opened her eyes and sat up, balancing on the limb. This wasn't the time for self-pity. She needed to lose her abductors, who were probably following her trail by now, and make it back to the conservatory before she ran into any more trouble.

She slid forward along the limb towards the water and snapped off a long, spiky branch.

"Thanks again, boy," she called down to the horse before swatting it on the hindquarters. "Now go home."

Surprised by the unexpected sting, the horse bolted towards the road and galloped north. Nadja was only a little worried about him. Wanderer horses were used to their nomadic lifestyle and were experts at finding their way along their yearly route. But, as far as she knew, that horse had never been this far north. She hoped Fonso and Luca would be able to track him. In fact, she was counting on it.

She scooted forward along the limb until she hung a few paces out over the water.

Here goes nothing.

Grasping the limb with cold fingers, she swung down and splashed into the frigid river. The water rushed around her, coming up to meet her knees. The sensation of everything below that reminded her of the time she accidentally stepped into a nest of stinging war ants as a child. Those evil little insects had put her to bed for a week.

She pushed the memory aside and focused on making her way back to the ferry port, moving as quickly as she could to get her blood pumping. Since she walked with the current keeping a fast pace wasn't a problem, however keeping her balance was not so easy. She stumbled more than a few times, each time soaking more of the icy river water into her clothes. After a while, her legs lost all feeling, and she had to keep an eye on them to be sure they were still moving.

After an hour of alternately trotting with the current and stumbling down into it, she spotted the port. The morning sun was high and bright as she dragged her numb body out of the water. She kept to the river bank instead of walking along the road. Backtracking towards her kidnappers was a tricky proposition, and she hoped they had not been searching for her long enough to have made it this far.

When Nadja arrived at the port, a motley band of people and animals were boarding the second boat. The ferryman took in her appearance with a curled lip when she attempted to book passage to Cantio. Not that she blamed him. Her skirts and cloak dripped like rain on the dirt beneath her. Her teeth chattered, and she knew that between the events of the previous night and a morning spent in the river, she must look near death. However, the ferryman's skepticism disappeared with a shrug when he spotted the two pearls in her open palm. She knew it was enough to buy passage for an entire family, let alone one woman. She hoped it was enough to keep him from asking questions.

The float down the river was mercifully uneventful. Nadja kept a close watch on the shoreline for a particular pair of men, but they never showed themselves. The river breeze did a fair job drying out her clothes and hair. By the time the ferry anchored along the outer shores of the Cantio docks, she looked much less like a drowned rat, though still not much a member of the living.

With most of the feeling returned to her feet and legs, she plodded through the city rings towards the conservatory. As she was skirting the edges of the Harvest Bazaar, she suddenly remembered her and Pax's instrument. It seemed like an age ago she'd brought it to the repair shop, but Morris had said it would be done by today. No matter. It would have to wait until later to be picked up.

When the gate marking the border between the middle ring and the conservatory grounds clicked shut behind her, Nadja's shoulders relaxed for the first time that day. For now, she was safe.

She circled around the main building towards the back, hoping to make it to her rooms unnoticed. She made her way through the orchard and towards the small wooden door which led inside to the practice rooms.

The door creaked open as she approached, and out stepped Timothy. The young servant had a basket draped over one arm and a long hooked pole in the other. When he spotted her, his face blanched, and the pole he carried clattered to the ground.

"Miss Machinal!" he gasped.

"Hello, Timothy," Nadja said, mustering a weary smile for the lad. She knew her looks must be a fright, and she was sorry she had startled him.

"I . . . I didn't think . . ." he stammered. "I mean, are you all right?"

"Yes, I'm fine," she replied, reassuringly. "Rough night."

He scrambled to pick up his pole and stepped back, pulling the door open for her. "Is there anything I can do for you this morning?" he asked, avoiding her eyes.

It was all she could do to keep her own head up this morning, too. She watched the floor to be sure her feet made it over the threshold. "No, thank you. I'm just going up to my room to rest for a while." She patted Timothy on the shoulder as she passed, then paused in the doorway.

"Are those new boots?" she asked.

"Yes, ma'am," he replied, his face going from white to red in an instant.

Nadja smiled at him, sorry she had now both frightened and embarrassed him in the same conversation. "They look very nice."

Timothy nodded stiffly before closing the door behind her.

The halls were quiet as she made her way up the stairs to her room. She hoped to get out of her dank clothes and into her warm bed without drawing attention, but the faint titter of giggles that greeted her approach told her that wish would not be granted. She sighed and pushed open the door.

Helaine and Petrin were seated at the table, heads together over what looked like a square-shaped viola with twice as many string, and keys adorning the head and neck.

In the time it took Nadja to close the door behind her, Helaine flew across the room and wrapped her in a hug. Nadja winced as Helaine's surprising grip pulled and mashed her sore muscles.

"Where have you been?" her roommate squeaked. Then, pulling away from Nadja, she grimaced and continued, "And why do you smell like low tide?"

"I . . ." Nadja searched her brain for a good excuse. Now that she was out of the open air, the piscine aroma floating up from her clothes and hair strengthened by the minute. Her face reddened as she looked back and forth between Helaine and Petrin, who had by this time risen to his feet.

"Oh, so sorry!" Helaine turned towards Petrin. "I believe we'll need to postpone our meeting until tomorrow."

"That is not a problem," replied the lanky craftsman, crossing to Helaine and taking her hand. "Tomorrow then?"

"Yes," she smiled. A faint tinge of pink colored her cheeks. "Let's get together after lunch, and I'll put that violoma through its paces."

"Tomorrow it is," he said, returning her smile before releasing her hand. Then, turning to Nadja he added, "I hope you're not unwell."

"No, quiet well," Nadja replied, hurriedly. "Just tired."

"I am glad to hear that," he said before wishing them a good day and leaving them to their own company.

As soon as the door closed, Helaine blurted out, "What in the world happened to you? I haven't seen you since yesterday morning. I've been worried sick!"

Nadja decided sticking as close to the truth as possible was her best bet.

"I went to the Harvest Bazaar yesterday afternoon," began Nadja, flopping onto her bed and tugging off her boots. "I ran into some old friends who were in town just for the day, and I guess I let the time get away from me."

"I'll say," said Helaine. "By the looks and smell of you, I'd wager you've had quite a night."

Oh, right, the smell.

"Well, as it turns out, they happened to be staying with my uncle." She unbuttoned her cloak and tossed it on the floor beside her bed.

"The one who runs the shipping company?"

"Yes, that one." The fishy smell only multiplied as she peeled off her socks. "He invited us all to have supper with him. By the time the evening wound down, it was late. So, I stayed there for the night."

Helaine sighed and sank onto her own bed. "I'm glad you're all right. And I know I'm silly to worry. You're a grown woman, and I'm sure you can take care of yourself. It's just that you rarely leave the conservatory." She knit her eyebrows together. "In fact, I can't think of any time you've left the conservatory since we began classes. Even on our free days you're always here."

"I guess the bazaar was enough to entice me out and about." Nadja stood and unfastened her skirt, hoping her sleepy grin was enough to mollify her roommate. She added the offending article to the heap of clothing on the floor.

Helaine thought for a moment. Then, she said brightly, "I'm glad you enjoyed yourself, and you're safe. But, I was wondering one thing."

"Huuuuh?" yawned Nadja.

"Well, unless you have a tiny person hidden in one of your pockets playing a reed pipe at low volume, I'm still wondering about that smell."

Nadja blurted out the first thing which came to mind. "I fell into the river."

"You what?" Helaine bolted up and hurried over to Nadja, whose head was already on her pillow.

"It's fine," she mumbled, shooing away Helaine's hands. Her roommate was poking and squeezing her as if searching for broken bones. "We were walking along the docks, and I got too close to the edge." She managed to get her blankets up to her chin and finally surrendered to her heavy eyelids. "Not to worry. Excellent swimmer."

And with that, Nadja was asleep.

No sooner had she drifted off into blissful oblivion than a series of sharp raps at the door startled her awake. She gazed, bleary-eyed, around the room, but Helaine was nowhere to be seen. The rosy telltale glow of dusk floating in through the windows told her she must have actually been asleep for most of the day.

The rapping came again, and each blow felt as though it landed against her skull instead of the door. Noting that her fishy clothes pile had disappeared, she swung her legs over the edge of the bed and hobbled over to her wardrobe. Her motionless sleep, though much needed, had allowed her muscles to stiffen. She pulled on her robe and limped over to the door, but not before another set of raps boomed through her head.

"Yes!" she bellowed, then winced at the effect and lowered her voice. "I'm coming."

She opened the door and instantly grabbed her robe and pulled it tight around her middle. Standing opposite of her with a plate of food and a lazy grin was Pax.

"What are you doing here?" she asked, unconsciously running a hand through her matted and unruly hair.

"I heard you had a bit of an adventure, so I came to check on you. And since you missed supper, I thought you might be hungry." He brandished the plate of food, and Nadja's stomach rumbled without hesitation. It had been a full day since she had eaten, and the fried dough she'd picked up at the Harvest Bazaar was a distant memory.

Pax leaned back. His smile wavered, and a thin wrinkle appeared across the bridge of his nose.

That smell.

In her exhaustion, she hadn't even bothered to bathe. Even though most of her tainted clothing had disappeared, her long, hard nap had allowed her skin and hair time to marinate. She smelled like the fish market on a warm day.

"I'm sorry, I'm going to need a bath before anything else."

"No problem," he replied, brushing past her and into the room. "I'm not in a rush." He set the food on the table and made himself comfortable in one of the chairs.

"It may take a while," said Nadja, hoping he would take the hint.

"That's all right. I'll wait."

Pax, ignoring the hard line of her mouth, propped his feet up and made himself comfortable.

Nadja walked as gracefully as possible to her wardrobe and gathered a clean set of clothes. She would take care of Pax after her bath.

As the warm waters of the baths soothed and comforted her aching muscles, she considered extending her wash time until the water went cold. Perhaps if she stayed in the baths long enough, Pax would get tired of waiting and leave. Of course, he could also be taking advantage of her absence by poking around all of her things.

In less than a quarter hour, she was back in her room, clean and refreshed.

Pax was exactly where she left him though she doubted he had been sitting there the whole time.

Nadja stood by the open door. "Thank you for bringing me a plate," she began. "That was kind of you."

"It was no trouble."

Nadja shifted her weight back and forth on her feet for a moment, then tried again. "There's no need for you to wait. I'm sure you have other things you'd rather do this evening than watch me eat."

"Nope," said Pax, stretching his arms up and lacing his fingers together behind his head. "Not a thing. Now come sit and eat before your food gets cold."

Reluctantly, Nadja closed the door and settled herself at the table. There was no use in prolonging the inevitable. She would have to face Pax and his inquiries sooner or later. Might as well get it over with.

They sat in awkward silence. Nadja dug in to the beef and potatoes in front of her, all the while doing her best to avoid Pax's probing stare.

Finally he spoke.

"So, how did you like the Harvest Bazaar?"

Caught.

Nadja took a long drink of cider.

"Very much," she said, stabbing another piece of meat. "I particularly liked the street performers."

"Mmm." Pax reached over and plucked an apple slice from her plate. The crunch sparked the air as he bit into it. "I heard you ran into some old friends while you were there."

"And where do you get your information?" snapped Nadja, fed up with his scrutiny. Why did she feel the need to explain herself to him? And how was it any of his business, anyway? "Have you been pestering Helaine?"

"No," he said, looking genuinely appalled at the suggestion. "Our roommates spend a lot of time together. It's only natural you occasionally come up in conversation, much like you did tonight over supper."

Petrin. How could she have forgotten?

Pax's and Petrin's living arrangements had only recently come to light during a late-night study session between her and Helaine.

"See, I thought it was interesting you happened to run into some old friends, considering your past. I mean, I'm pretty sure the Wanderers are usually halfway to Chansey by this time of year, so the odds of you bumping into someone you know are, what?" He polished off the apple slice. "One in a million?"

"Yeah, it's pretty incredible," replied Nadja, staring at her plate while shoving another potato into her mouth.

"Oh, come on, Nadja." Pax leaned across the table and stopped the fork on its way to her mouth. "You purposefully cut ties with your past, yet you happen to meet and spend time with 'old friends'? You show up back here looking like you've been through more than just a dip in the river, and then you sleep half of the day away. And don't think I didn't notice the trouble you're having just making it from one side of the room to the other. Cut the garbage and tell me what really happened."

Nadja clenched her jaw and glared at his fingers wrapped around her wrist.

"Sorry," he muttered, releasing his grip and rubbing his face.

When she didn't say anything, he continued, "Nadja, you are my friend. I care about you. I want to help you, but you have to let me in. I know you've had a difficult past, and you're looking to make a new start. I'm not trying to stand in your way, but I don't want to see you get hurt either. You trusted me with your past. Trust me with this."

Friendship? Was that really all he was offering?

Nadja thought back to all the time they'd spent together. He'd saved her in the forest and cared for her injuries asking nothing in return. Yes, he kissed her once. But, that was a thoughtless moment of celebration, nothing more. He sought her out as a partner because he wanted someone to work with, not someone to fawn over him. And in all the time they spent together, not once had he behaved as more than a good friend.

Did he care for her? Obviously.

Were his feelings more than platonic? Nadja was beginning to doubt that.

Perhaps it was never Pax's intentions she was avoiding. Perhaps she had been running away from her own feelings this whole time.

If growing up as a Wanderer had taught her anything, it was that no one could do it all alone. Within the tribe, each person has a specific task. When the burden of survival is shared among everyone, the tribe thrives.

If Pax felt for her truly as a friend, then she could keep her own emotions in check. He was offering to share her burden. It was time to stop carrying it all on her own.

"All right," she sighed, setting down her fork. "I'll tell you."

Chapter Twenty

Nadja's boots thumped a steady march along the cobbled street which painted a straight line from Cantio's southeastern city gate to the docks, neatly bisecting the wharf. The main thoroughfare was as crowded and bustling as it had been the first day she arrived. This time, however, she knew exactly where to go and moved with purpose towards the Naval Headquarters.

It had been two days since her escape from her would-be abductors. Two days since she confided in Pax the details of her disappearance, omitting the wanted-for-attempted-murder part. As far as he knew, the Wanderer scouts were tasked with retrieving a runaway, nothing more.

His reaction was as she suspected, surprise and anger at her ordeal, but not at her. He appointed himself her on-call bodyguard at once, insisting on coming along any time she left the conservatory grounds. Pax's friendship and loyalty comforted her, and she was happy to have someone to confide in. But sharing one's burden meant just that—sharing. Not dumping it all on someone else's shoulders. So, she kept today's outing to herself.

When she approached the imposing facade of the Naval Headquarters, she turned off of the main road and followed a small footpath around the left side of the building. Behind the headquarters stood a large rectangular patch of land surrounded by a stone wall. She strode up to the set of heavy wooden double doors marking the wall's only entry. The doors were reinforced with iron and were big enough for a drove of horses to pass through, six abreast. The outline of a smaller door was visible within the door on the right with a little hooked handle just below the melon-sized one. She tugged at it, and the small door swung open with ease.

She crossed the threshold and found herself alone in the Naval Headquarters's training ground. A great, open dirt floor took up most of the space. She wandered into the middle and took in her surroundings. Leather and straw archery targets and thick wooden training dummies stood at attention along the far wall. Benches lined the perimeter, and a small shaded area in one corner offered spectators a place to view the training yard shielded from the elements.

Something shiny caught Nadja's eye, and she strolled over towards the wall opposite the archery targets to inspect the source. Three weapons racks, laden with every imaginable armament, stood gleaming in the early afternoon sunlight. Bows and arrows, axes, swords, and knives stood pristine and resolute, waiting for an experienced hand to bring out their full potential.

Nadja's eyes moved across the array and settled on an axe. Its curved head was different from any she'd seen and the decorative detail on its handle demanded closer inspection. She lifted the axe from its resting place, feeling both a sense of awe at the beauty of the craftsmanship and dread at the kind of damage it could do to a man.

All at once, a beefy hand clamped over her mouth as another arm snaked around her waist, knocking the axe to the ground and pinning her back against a wall of muscle.

"Lesson one," chuckled a mirthful baritone. "Always be aware of your surroundings."

Angrily, Nadja wriggled free and spun to face her attacker.

"Was that really necessary?" she growled.

Wheedler's solid body blocked out the sunlight and cast her in shadow. The jerky rise and fall of his shoulders belied the look of mock innocence he wore.

"I told him you wouldn't appreciate that. No one likes to be taken by surprise." A voice Nadja didn't recognize came from behind Wheedler.

Wheedler stepped aside and looked over his shoulder, revealing a slim but muscular form topped with cropped, dark auburn hair. "Maybe not, but I'll bet that's one lesson she won't forget."

"That remains to be seen," the person replied with a distinctly feminine tone.

Wheedler grinned and turned back to Nadja. "Nadja, this is my partner, Brooks. She's the best guard at Montgomery & Co." He paused and wiggled his eyebrows at her. "Except for me, of course."

Brooks snorted and rolled her eyes as Wheedler picked up the fallen axe and replaced it on the weapons rack.

"Speaking of Montgomery & Co.," said Nadja. "I mentioned in my letter I'd like to keep our sessions private. That means from everyone, including my uncle. Is that going to be a problem?"

Wheedler scratched his chin. "Well, that depends. You planning on practicing your new skills on him?"

"No."

"Then I don't see any reason to bring it up. Your uncle's a fine captain. One of the best, I'd say. When I'm doing a job for him, he likes to know everything that's going on, and that's fine by me. But what we do on our own time is our business. Besides, he's captaining one of his runs to Chansey right now, so he's not in town."

Nadja glanced over his shoulder at Brooks.

"Look," snapped the bored-looking woman. "We know how to keep our mouths shut. Now, are we going to stand here chatting all afternoon, or are we going to get to work?"

Nadja nodded. "Let's get to work."

Wheedler led the trio away from the weapons rack and towards the practice yard. "All right, sugar, show me the goods. I need to see what we have to work with."

Nadja unhooked her cloak and draped it over a bench, revealing three straight wooden rods tucked into her belt. She slipped them out and fastened them end to end. When she'd received Wheedler's reply letter agreeing to train her, he asked that she bring along any weapons she was comfortable using. Her blowpipe was the only thing she could think of. It was more of a hunting weapon than a defensive one, but it was the only real weapon she'd ever used.

Once the blowpipe had been assembled, she removed one of the cone-topped darts from its small leather pouch and made her way across the yard towards the archery targets. She planted her feet and inserted the dart into the mouthpiece. Sliding her left hand down the length of the shaft, she lifted the pipe, stabilizing it with her right hand and bringing it to her mouth. She closed her left eye and lined up the sight, aiming for the target's red center. After a few breaths to steady her nerves, she filled her lungs.

A tiny *thhhhpt* was all that could be heard as the air exploded from her lungs and through the blowpipe. The dart shot through the air and embedded three quarters of its length into the target. It missed the bullseye by a hand's width, but being a few months out of practice, Nadja was pleased with her attempt.

She walked over to the target and removed her dart, then returned to Wheedler and Brooks. The former wore a contemplative, if puzzled look, and the latter regarded her with one raised eyebrow and a bemused expression.

"Well, that's a first," said Wheedler, stroking his chin. "May I?"

Nadja handed him the blowpipe. He paced away from the two women, tossing it up and down.

"For a ranged weapon, it's not ideal, but you could make it work." Brooks nodded towards the pipe. "What's the maximum distance on it?"

"About twenty paces."

Brooks snorted again. "That's it? That won't get you far in a fight." She flipped open the leather pouch and held up one of the darts. "These look like they'd be more of a nuisance to an enemy than do any real damage."

A banging sound caught their attention, and they both turned to see Wheedler beating the blowpipe against one of the practice dummies. Nadja cringed hoping she'd get her weapon back in one piece.

"It's used for hunting," she said, turning back to Brooks. "The darts alone are not terribly lethal, unless they hit just the right spot. Most of the damage is caused by whatever poison you dip them in."

Brooks nodded, then stepped back and sized up Nadja. "Better that you try to avoid close combat, anyway. You won't best anyone when it comes to size or strength."

She circled Nadja. "But being small isn't always a bad thing. It's easier to play hide-and-sneak. And if you're quick enough, you can outmaneuver a larger opponent."

Brooks completed her circle. "Just don't let anyone get close enough to surprise you."

As soon as the words left her mouth, Brooks's right hand arced towards Nadja's face, palm open.

Nadja saw the movement just in time, stepping back and crouching to avoid the blow. She felt Brook's hand ruffle the hair on top of her head as it passed.

"Not bad," said Brooks, eyes narrowing.

"This is an interesting little stick you've got here," said Wheedler, walking back towards the women and spinning the blowpipe like a whirling clock face.

"I'm thinking short staff," he said to Brooks.

"My thoughts exactly," she replied.

Wheedler looked at Nadja. "This blowpipe will work well for stealth attacks," he said, walking over to the weapons rack. "But it'll need to do double duty if you want to defend yourself."

He reached into the rack and removed a pair of wooden poles. They resembled the blowpipe in size and shape though the poles were a little longer. He tossed one to Nadja.

She caught the staff, surprised by its weight. It was heavier than her blowpipe, but not by much. The wood was sanded smooth, and the weight was evenly balanced.

"Your best chance is to avoid being attacked all together. But if you can't, using your blowpipe like a short staff will give you a better chance of coming out on the good side of a fight. Now, hold the staff above your head with one hand at either end. Spread your feet apart, one in front of the other, and bend your knees slightly."

Nadja did as instructed. Her muscles were already warm from her brisk walk from the conservatory, and the aches and soreness from her overnight horseback ride a few days earlier were all but gone.

"Lesson two," said Wheedler, with a grin. "Don't get hit."

As soon as she was in position, Wheedler swung his staff above his head and came down hard, connecting with hers. She felt the vibrations from the blow tremor through her hands and arms, but she kept her staff in position.

"Good," he said. "Again."

Wheedler ran her through a half dozen blocks over the next hour, drilling each move over and over before proceeding to the next. Muscles which had only just recovered were once again strained and sore. Her head pounded with each block, and her failed attempts could be numbered by the purple patches now mottling her skin.

"I think that's enough for your first session," said Wheedler, swiping a hand across his forehead. Nadja, for her own part, was drenched in sweat.

"Just a minute," piped up Brooks. For most of the training session, she had remained a silent, sour-faced observer, watching their progress from one of the benches. Now, she rose and took the staff from Wheedler, claiming his position in front of Nadja.

"Ready?" she asked.

It was more of a warning than a question. Before Nadja could reply, Brooks began a series of slow attacks. The difference this time was that, with each attack, she took a step towards Nadja, forcing her to retreat. The speed of her attacks increased with each blow, and Nadja stumbled on the hem of her skirt as Brooks continued to press forward. Nadja tried to regain her footing, but only managed to get even more tangled in her skirt. In less than a minute, she was disarmed and on her rear, squinting up at Brooks.

"Lesson three," said the leather-clad woman. "Lose the skirt."

Without another word, Brooks retrieved Nadja's staff and headed to the weapons rack. Nadja glared at her back.

"She's right, you know," Wheedler said lightly, offering Nadja a hand.

Nadja accepted his help up, brushing the dirt from her backside and straightening her skirt. "She didn't have to be such a boor about it."

"Don't take it personally. She may not be skilled in social graces, but she knows what she's talking about. And there's no one else I'd rather have watching my back." Wheedler looked approvingly at his partner, who was busy cleaning and replacing the staffs. "But, yes, it would be a good idea to rethink your clothing. Long skirts will just get in your way."

As they headed towards the practice dummies, Nadja fished a pearl from her pocket. "Thank you for your help," she said, offering the payment to Wheedler.

He pushed her hand away. "No way."

"I'm not looking for any handouts," said Nadja, extending her arm once more. "I appreciate you agreeing to train me. The least I can do is pay you for your time."

"Look, in your letter you didn't say why you wanted to learn to fight, and I didn't ask. But, the fact you want to learn makes me think maybe you need to. Now, what kind of gentleman would I be to take advantage of a lady in her time of need?" He offered her a charming grin. "Besides," he continued, "your uncle has always been good to me. The least *I* can do is help out his niece."

Nadja considered him for a moment, then nodded and put the pearl back in her pocket. "Thank you."

"Uh, don't thank me yet," he muttered, running a hand through his sandy hair as they approached the blowpipe. Now that Nadja was close enough to really see her weapon, she could tell something was wrong.

"Your blowpipe will make a good staff substitute if you're caught in a bad situation. But, it's a blowpipe not a staff. The hollow core makes it weaker than a solid staff, and I may have been a little too rough on it." Embarrassment colored his face as he handed her the blowpipe.

The pipe looked to be in decent condition, but there was a long crack running from the sight straight up the bottom third of the weapon. It was now useless as anything more than a glorified walking stick.

"Look, I'm really sorry about that. But take it up to Sil, the armorer who works in the market district. He can patch it up good as new. Tell him to put it on my tab."

"You have a running tab with the armorer?" Nadja asked, quirking an eyebrow.

"What can I say, I've always played rough with my toys." Wheedler walked Nadja to the doors. "Once you get your blowpipe fixed, you can use it for solo practice. But for sparring and training here, we'll stick with the real things. No need to damage your weapon if you don't have to."

Nadja thanked him again and raised a hand to Brooks in a half-hearted farewell gesture before exiting the training yard. With a trip to the armorer added to her to-do list, she now had two stops to make before returning to the conservatory.

A few minutes later she found herself once more winding through the disordered stacks of The Broken Chord. She didn't bother to call out to the owner, instead choosing to follow the same route as before, presuming he'd be near his worktable.

Morris's mutterings met her ears before the table came into view. "You are about as uncooperative as a hornet in a vinegar bath . . . going to lose your position if you don't change your ways . . ."

When Nadja rounded the last curve, she spotted the little man hard at work on a modified cornet. This time, however, he was seated on a tall stool, wearing some sort of multitooled glove on his left hand. A set of tubes ran out of the glove and into a box on the table next to him. Another larger tube connected the back of the box to a turnip-sized leather bulb. Each finger of the glove was topped with a different tool which appeared to work in a mechanized fashion. Each stopped and started as needed with a flip of one of the five switches on the box. The glove made a puffing sound each time Morris flipped a switch, and he paused in his work every so often to squeeze the bulb.

Nadja studied him, not wanting to disturb his concentration and assuming he'd acknowledge her when he was able. But, after a few more minutes of muttering and tinkering, it became clear the repairman had not the slightest awareness of her presence. She cleared her throat.

Morris looked up in surprise, then smiled his cheery smile. "Miss Machinal," he beamed, his blue eyes sparkling. "I had wondered if I'd ever see you again. Wondered if perhaps you meant your instrument as a gift for me."

"I'm sorry," said Nadja, returning his smile. "I had a change in schedule which prevented me from getting here sooner."

"I see," said Morris, giving her a knowing wink. "Be right back."

He removed the glove and disappeared into the chaos. He reappeared a moment later, instrument in one hand, small jar in the other.

"Here you are, my dear," he said, passing the instrument over the worktable to Nadja.

Nadja held it up and examined the repair. It was as if Morris had wound time backwards to a point before she had nearly destroyed Pax's work. The wood was hard and strong where there had once been a mishmash of splinters and debris. There were no lines of demarcation to suggest the wood was ever in any state other than solid. The once lifeless strings were now strung taut and secure around matching screws at both the top and bottom.

Nadja stared in disbelief. "It's amazing!" she exclaimed. "How did you get it to look so perfect?"

Morris nodded appreciatively. "Practice makes perfect. Or so they say. Of course, practice does make better, but only perfect practice makes perfect. I've been perfecting my practice for many, many years."

"It is perfect," she replied, resting the instrument on the table and reaching into her pocket to retrieve his payment.

"And what else have you brought me today?" he asked.

"Excuse me?"

"That's not something you see every day. In fact, I haven't seen a blowpipe in years. You know, this *is* more of an instrument repair shop, but I don't mind taking a job that's out of the ordinary now and then. Keeps things interesting." He held out an expectant hand.

"Well," began Nadja, passing him the weapon, "I was going to the see the armorer once I leave here."

"Psh," said Morris dismissively, studying the crack. "Sil will keep you waiting for at least a week before getting anything finished and charge you double what he ought. This crack is straightforward. Right along the seam. Give me just a few minutes, and you can be on your way."

Before she could protest, Morris once again disappeared. Over the next few minutes she busied herself with a browse around the shop. While her first impression had suggested Morris had just piled up his hoard of odds and ends to clear enough floor to walk on, closer inspection made her think there was indeed some organizational system in place. A quick study of the instruments hanging from the ceiling, and she could see they were grouped according to type and size.

Her survey was interrupted now and then by a blend of bangs, bumps, and murmurs coming from elsewhere in the building, and in less time than she thought possible, Morris reappeared at his worktable.

"And there you go," he said, setting the blowpipe before her.

Just like with the instrument, the blowpipe's repair was solid and seamless.

"You are a master," Nadja gushed. "How much do I owe you for this repair?"

"Oh, nothing," said Morris with a wave of his hand. "Consider it covered in the cost of your instrument repair. It was a pleasure to get to work on something different for a change. Just be sure to come back and see me again sometime, would you?"

His genuine smile again reminded Nadja of her grandfather, and she returned it with an affirmative nod.

She paid Morris, gathered the instrument and blowpipe together in her arms, and turned to leave the shop.

"Aren't you forgetting something?" Morris called after her.

"I don't think so," she said, turning back to the worktable.

Morris reached over to where he had placed the small jar and slid it across the table towards her.

Nadja picked it up and eyed it curiously. "What's this for?"

"Your muscles," he said, wandering back into the stacks. "Twice a day should do the trick." His voice floated back to her as he disappeared. "You'll feel right as rain in no time."

Nadja studied the jar for a moment longer before slipping it into her pocket and heading for the door. Something told her it was better not to ask.

Chapter Twenty-One

Nadja wound through the maze of hallways towards Grandmaster Kero's office. Their weekly lessons had become a familiar part of her routine at the conservatory, but after her embarrassing performance last week, she was hesitant to face her teacher again. Fortunately, despite her abduction and subsequent addition of thrice-weekly training sessions to her schedule, she still found time to work on that blasted Pantomarian folk tune. She hoped it would be enough to regain some respect in the eyes of her teacher, especially since this was their last lesson before the winter break.

She approached Meliina's office door with her hand poised to knock when she heard voices coming from inside. She was early, so the previous lesson was probably still in session. Deciding it best not to disturb them, she leaned against the cool stone wall opposite the doorway, waiting for her turn.

Moments later the door opened, and Nadja was astonished to see the swarthy figure which emerged.

"Uncle Tau!" she exclaimed.

One of his heavy eyebrows lifted in surprise while the other remained stubbornly nonchalant. "Good afternoon, Niece."

"What are you doing here?" she blurted out.

He gave her a short nod. "It is a pleasure to see you."

"Oh, I'm sorry," she stammered, "I am glad to see you too. I just wasn't expecting to. I thought you were in Chansey."

She realized her slip too late and tried to cover it. "Or Wailing Gap or somewhere else, just not here. That is, I tried to pay you a visit this week and discovered you had not been home for a few days. Naturally, I assumed you were captaining a barge somewhere or other."

His eyes narrowed, and she bit the inside of her cheek. How could she have known he was gone for days? She would have had to get that information from Branson. Uncle Tau would ask Branson if she'd been there, and he would say no. Oh well, the damage was done. She crossed her fingers, hoping her uncle wouldn't check her story.

Tau blinked a few times, then gave Nadja one of his rare smiles. "A visit from you would be lovely. The Candlefire Celebration is almost upon us. While I know your accommodations here are much more comfortable than anything I could offer you, please join me for a meal or two during your time off. If you would be kind enough to send me a letter specifying the dates, I promise I will have my pantry stocked with more than its usual fare."

"Thank you. Yes, that would be nice."

"Good. Then if you'll excuse me, I have a matter which requires my immediate attention. Good day."

Before Nadja could say another word, Tau turned and marched away. She watched him disappear around a corner, then collected her thoughts and knocked on Meliina's door.

"Come in," called the grandmaster.

Nadja pushed against the door and entered the tidy office.

"So good to see you, Nadja," said Meliina, settling into her chair and motioning for Nadja to take the one beside her.

Nadja relaxed at Meliina's warm greeting, and she took her chair, setting up her music on the stand before her and unpacking her flute.

"And how are you?" asked Meliina. Her face wore a look of genuine interest, not polite indifference.

"Well, thank you," replied Nadja. Then, before they could get into the flow of the lesson, she added, "I ran into my uncle on my way in."

"Oh yes," said Meliina. "We've been friends for some years. He stops by to visit from time to time." Then, turning towards the music stand she asked, "And how is the Pantomarian folk tune coming?"

Realizing Meliina would give up no further details about Tau's visit, Nadja focused on the lesson.

"Better, I think. I've been able to internalize the melody, and I believe I have a better grasp on it than I did last week."

"Very good," said Meliina, warmly.

Nadja raised her flute, then paused. "Would you like me to sing through the melody first?"

"No," Meliina snapped. Then, in a gentler tone, "I don't think asking you to sing the melody was the wisest course of action. It's a useful tool for some students, but not always. At this point, I believe it may be more of a hindrance than a help."

Nadja nodded and raised the flute once more.

Unlike her performance the week prior, the notes rang from the flute with much more ease. The tune itself was still awkward and foreign sounding to her ears, but she played it with precision. When she finished the piece, she lowered her instrument and waited for the verdict.

Meliina sighed, and Nadja's shoulders slumped.

"Wonderful," her teacher said.

Nadja looked up to see Meliina nodding in approval. "I can tell you've worked hard on this piece over the past week. True, the feeling isn't there, yet. But you have mastered the technical aspect. Now, it's time to *season* the piece, as it were."

Meliina rose and crossed to her desk, producing a piece of paper and a pen. She scratched down a few lines.

"I am assigning you some light reading over the break. This is a list of books which can give you more insight on the history of Pantomaria, as well as some more history on our own music." She handed Nadja the paper. "You can find everything you need in the Archives."

Nadja took the paper and skimmed the list of titles: *Pantomaria: Our Neighbor to the East, Folk Tunes of the Northern Realms, Musica Antiqua and Other Lost Arts.* This looked like more than light reading. But, it wasn't as if she had any other plans to occupy her time over the break, save a few meals with Uncle Tau.

"Thank you," she said, and tucked the list into her pocket.

The scent of metal and smoke hung heavy in the air as the students took their seats for the last Sound Theory class before break. Grandmaster Gilmoren had stoked the forge's firepot into a blaze which kept the early-winter freeze at bay and warmed the whole smithy to a comfortable temperature.

Pax and Nadja sat shoulder to shoulder watching the other partners demonstrate their original instruments. Some were better than others. The giant sand drum, whose pitch could be changed on demand by filling or emptying sand from its kettle, was impressive and prompted a lot of questions from the rest of the class. On the other hand, the nasophonium, a wind instrument played almost exclusively by the nose, drew little more than confused looks and a snicker or two from the crowd.

Nadja held their finished project in her hands. It was stained to a luscious deep walnut color, which emphasized the intricate detail work Pax had carved into the wood. She had convinced Pax to convert the fixed strings to tunable ones, reinforcing each end with metal backing plates and replacing one set of screws with pegs which were easier to manipulate.

"Are you nervous?" whispered Pax, leaning closer to Nadja.

"A little," she replied. "You?"

"Nah," he said with a reassuring smile. "We've got something good here. And you play it beautifully."

"Miss Machinal and Mr. Raynor," boomed Grandmaster Gilmoren's deep voice.

Nadja jumped, and the two of them looked back over their shoulders at their formidable instructor.

"You're up," he barked.

Nadja and Pax took their position at the front of the room. As Nadja passed in front of the forge, the heat from its flame amplified her already elevated temperature, nearly taking her breath away. As if sensing her anxiety, Pax placed his hand lightly on the small of her back in a calming gesture.

"What's the name of your instrument?" asked Grandmaster Gilmoren.

"We call it a gale harp," replied Pax.

"Begin your demonstration whenever you're ready," said the grandmaster.

Nadja inhaled a shaky breath, steadying herself as she raised the instrument. They had chosen an easy lullaby tune as their demonstration piece. The minor key and slow tempo lent itself well to the haunting sound of the strings as they vibrated sympathetically with the wind notes. The simplicity of the melody also made it easy for Nadja to master in what little time she had to learn how to play it.

The evocative blending of mellow wind tones and humming strings cast a net of peacefulness and contemplation over the class. In the moment following her last note, no one stirred. Then, Grandmaster Gilmoren's voice once more shattered the silence.

"Very nice," he said. "Now, please explain your design."

With her part of the presentation now complete, Nadja's muscles relaxed as Pax took over explaining the technical aspects from concept to finished product. Garnering a "very nice" from the grandmaster was high praise, so she had little doubt their project would score well.

Once their presentation was over, Nadja and Pax resumed their seats, their relief tangible in their slackened posture and loose muscles. They observed the remaining presentations, silently cheering as Helaine and Petrin demonstrated their violoma, which also seemed to go over well.

Once all the presentations were complete, Grandmaster Gilmoren marched to the front of the room and addressed the class.

"Thank you for your hard work. Your finished products are as varied and original as I expected. Some, more so than others," he cast a sidelong glance at the team responsible for the nasophonium. "Remember, change and innovation are important parts of our roles as musicians and craftsmen. We must always strive to improve what we do and how we do it. With that said, when we return from the break, you will begin researching ways your new instruments might be used in the field. Keep that in mind as you're enjoying your time off."

With those parting words, he dismissed the class.

Helaine stood and rushed over to Nadja and Pax.

"I absolutely adored your gale harp!" exclaimed Helaine. "It made me feel happy and sad all at the same time." She sighed.

"Impressive design," said Petrin, joining them. He shook Pax's hand and nodded to Nadja. "And well played, too."

"I could say the same to you both," said Pax, clapping his roommate on the back.

"Yes," agreed Nadja. "I have a feeling more than a few string players will want to have a go at your violoma. You two form a great partnership." She shot Helaine a sneaky grin while Petrin was distracted. Her roommate's face bloomed into a brilliant shade of crimson.

"Are you all right, Helaine?" asked Petrin, placing a hand on her arm.

"Oh, yes," she stammered. "I think the heat from the forge has proved to be more than I can handle at the moment."

"Let's walk, then," suggested Petrin, gathering up both his and Helaine's books as well as the violoma.

The four of them left the warmth and shelter of the smithy and stepped out into the chilly air. The frozen ground was hard beneath their feet as they circled back through the orchard.

"What a relief," said Petrin. "Now that our instruments have been completed and demonstrated, I'm looking forward to a nice long break."

"Do you have any special plans for the Candlefire Celebration?" asked Helaine.

"No," he replied. "Just heading home to spend it with my family. A few days spent in front of the fire with a good book or two and a belly full of my mother's cranberry cake. That's my idea of a nice vacation. What will you all do?"

"My father has sent an escort to bring me home," said Helaine. "I love living along the Highland border, except for this time of year. I mean, the summers are nice, but the winters are just bitter. The winds coming down from The Veil will freeze your nose off in a second."

"That sounds terrible," said Nadja.

"You do have to dress for the weather," said Helaine with a sniff. "But it makes the Candlefire Celebration even more inviting. They keep a bonfire blazing in the center of town for the whole week. And there's nothing like coming in from a snowstorm to a warm house filled with those you love."

"We don't get much snow at our home," said Pax. "But, we'll keep the fires going just the same." He paused before muttering, "It'll be cold enough."

Nadja wondered if his comment held a double meaning. She knew he, like most of the other students, had not been home since classes began. But she also knew he was returning to face some strained relationships.

"What about you, Nadja?" asked Petrin.

"I'll be staying here over break," she said. Then, she hurried to add, "But I have plans to see my uncle during the holiday."

"Of course," said Petrin, apologetically. "Grenyan is too far away to make the trip for so few days. Well, I'm glad you do have some family nearby."

They approached the back entrance and Pax held open the door, ushering his companions into the conservatory and out of the cold.

"May I help you carry your bags, or has your escort already taken care of that?" Petrin asked Helaine as they filed in.

"Oh, no. Nadja and I still have Music History to attend before we're finished with classes," said Helaine.

"That's right . . ." replied Petrin.

"But I need to drop off the violoma in my room before heading that way." Helaine gestured to the instrument tucked under Petrin's arm.

"No problem. I can carry it up for you." Petrin smiled, obviously glad to have an excuse to spend a few more minutes in Helaine's company. He said a brief farewell to Nadja and Pax and followed Helaine.

"And you need to take this," said Nadja, handing Pax the gale harp.

Pax opened his mouth to protest, but Nadja cut him off. "I know you are on your way to Wood Craft, and I think Grandmaster Drake would like to see what you've been working on." Pax's skill was inarguable. She wanted someone else to affirm that before he left to spend two weeks with a father and brother who discouraged his passion.

Pax took the gale harp without further protest.

"I don't like you being here alone for the holiday," he said, dropping the corners of his mouth into a frown.

"I'll be fine," replied Nadja. "Other than visiting my uncle, I have no reason to leave the grounds." *Except for when I go down to the wharf for training.* "Grandmaster Kero has assigned me extra reading over the break, so I'll probably spend most of my time in the Archives. There's not much trouble I can get into down there."

"But you'll be traveling to and from your uncle's home. There won't be anyone around to accompany you." Then, as if struck with an idea, he said, "I'll stick around here. I promise not to be in your way, but if you need to go anywhere, I can make sure you get there safely."

"Oh, no you don't," snapped Nadja. "You're going home to spend time with your family. Don't try to use me as an excuse to get out of it."

Pax's eyes grew stormy, so she softened her tone before continuing. "You need to see them. Whatever disagreement you may have with your father and brother, this may be the perfect time to work through it." She placed a hand lightly on his chest. "Go home, Pax. I'll be fine. I promise."

He reached up and placed his hand on top of hers, giving her fingers a squeeze. Nadja felt his heartbeat under her palm, and for a moment they stood in silence, locked in one another's gaze.

When Nadja realized her own heartbeat was vying for her attention, she shook her head, breaking the trance, and slipped her hand away from his.

"All right," Pax sighed, defeated. He turned and strode down the hallway towards the wood shop.

Nadja watched his back. As he turned and disappeared from sight, she felt a tight, tugging sensation in her chest. She was surprised to realize how much she was going to miss him.

Chapter Twenty-Two

The conservatory was eerily quiet as Nadja wound her way up and down the infinite stacks of books, scores, and sheet music which stretched from floor to ceiling in the underground labyrinth that was the Archives. The vast information repository, though much warmer than the weather outside, retained a slight chill, even in the summer months. She'd been told the constant temperature aided in the preservation of the texts and was one of the main reasons the Archives had been constructed underneath the conservatory.

About a week had passed since classes had ended, and the Candlefire Celebration was in full swing. Even the Archives, though tucked out of sight from most of the population, did its part to embrace the festivities. Though food and drink were strictly forbidden among the shelves, a small table of treats was set up in the entryway. Nadja could still taste the deliciously sweet walnut tart she'd gobbled up on her way in.

The fireplaces dotting the perimeter of the room blazed brightly, inviting visitors to enjoy the reading nooks which were arranged in front of them. These fireplaces were only in the sections which housed the newer books and music. Some of the older materials were too fragile to handle the warmer temperatures. In the older sections, hundreds of tiny candles arrayed the tables, creating an inviting feeling without the heat. Each candle wore a small glass shade, should some engrossed researcher get his ancient manuscript too close to the flames.

In the days following the break in classes, Nadja read her way through *Pantomaria: Our Neighbor to the East*. It wasn't the most interesting read, but it gave her insight into the culture and musical foundations of the country lying just beyond the Waste. She hoped the other two books would be more interesting.

Nadja slowed her pace and faced one of the shelves, running her finger along the book spines.

Fe . . . Fi . . . Fl . . . Fo. Folk. There it was, *Folk Tunes of the Northern Realms*. She lifted the heavy tome from the shelf. It contained not only histories and descriptions of folk tunes from Pantomaria, Grenyan, and Amrantir, but the latter half held a collection of every song mentioned in the first half.

She lugged it over to a long wooden table and set it down. Having just plodded her way through one boring book, she debated starting another one so soon. After eyeballing the volume before her, she decided to seek out *Musica Antiqua and Other Lost Arts* and compare the two.

She left the book on the table and followed the signs towards the *M*'s.

The smell of paper permeated the air, and Nadja sniffed the pleasant aroma. Cheery lanterns placed at regular intervals made up for the lack of windows. And, though the Archives was spotless, each beam of light revealed a ballet of fiber and dust motes leaping and twirling through the air.

Before long, she found herself strolling along shelf after shelf of *M* books. This section was much bigger than the *F*'s, but it wasn't difficult to locate the specific book she was after. She slipped *Musica Antiqua* from its place on the shelf and returned to the table to compare it with her other option.

A quick skim of each book easily determined her choice. While *Folk Tunes* was formatted as a reference book, *Musica Antiqua* was more of a narrative. *Musica Antiqua* it was. She hefted the weighty *Folk Tunes* and replaced it in the *F* section, then made her way to one of the reading nooks.

At once she was swept away into a tale of the ancient civilizations of the northern realms. She read about how the music of Grenyan and Pantomaria developed independently of each other, from unsophisticated, yet intentional tribal tunes into more structured systems, with rules and constants. She was surprised to learn the ancient peoples of Amrantir were Grenyan immigrants who crossed the Viridian Mountains thousands of years ago before the mountain range became impassable. But it was the stories of the Mevocali which truly captured her attention.

"The Mevocali, Amrantir's original inhabitants, were well settled when the first Grenyans arrived. They lived in the northern part of the Seven Steppes, and went undiscovered by Amrantir's newest inhabitants for hundreds of years until population growth and expansion forced the two societies into acquaintance. After a brief period of unrest and distrust between the two groups, an era of peace blossomed.

"Naturally, intermarriage between the two people groups began to occur. However, if a Mevocali and a Grenyan native joined, their union came at a cost. Any offspring produced from such a match had as much potential of manifesting the vocal abilities inherent to the Mevocali people as any pure-blooded child. Thus, the Grenyan parent and all children which followed were bound to the Mevocali for the rest of their lives, living as they did and adopting their culture and tradition.

"Since their vocal abilities could emerge at any age, it was important for Mevocali children to be surrounded by other members of their race. Children and young adults in whom the vocal gift manifested trained to control and properly use their gifts. Failure to gain control had the potential to carry with it devastating results. Infant and very early developers were sequestered from the rest of the population and handled by specially trained Singers until such a time as they were deemed mature enough to begin training."

Nadja continued reading about how the Grenyan and Mevocali approaches to music gradually melded to form the music of modern-day Amrantir. She read in detail about the early master musicians, and how the skill passed from the Mevocali instrumentalists to the men and women of the new Amrantir. Her mood darkened as she read about the emergence of new Mevocali skills and the uprising of Man against them. She could hear Grandmaster Westbrook's low tenor reading the words aloud in her head. It was just as he described.

"And so the Mevocali disappeared from existence. But, can it really be so? Can a civilization once as mighty and flourishing as theirs truly be gone? As with all ancient stories, rumors and fantastical tales have been woven among and around the truth, picking and choosing what to remember and what to discard. Herein I have presented the facts as I know them. Any further suppositions are of your own doing."

Nadja rubbed her eyes. Looking back down at the pages before her, she was surprised to see she had already read through half of the book. She stood up from the deep and cushiony chair and stretched. She needed a break, and if her stomach was any indication, a meal as well. She tucked the book under her arm and left the Archives, pausing just long enough to grab another walnut tart on her way out.

She stopped by the dining hall and picked up a plate of food to carry back to her room. Boiled chicken and potatoes, a roll, and a chunk of cheese. With most of the students away, and the conservatory minimally staffed during the holiday, the food and service reflected the temporary downgrade in circumstances.

Nadja munched on her roll and cheese as she made her way back upstairs. She had taken a few steps into her room when her boot crunched over something. She looked down and found a letter under foot. It must have been slipped under her door while she was in the Archives. She set her plate and book on the small table and then bent to retrieve the paper.

"Miss Machinal,

Many happy wishes of the season to you. I have it on good authority you are in town for this year's Candlefire Celebration, and I have something of importance to discuss with you. Please stop by and see me at your earliest convenience.

Warmth and light,
Morris Alrhen"

It was disarming how that funny little man always seemed to know her business. Still, he had been nothing but kind to her, and the letter piqued her curiosity. She glanced at the table. She would pay him a visit that very afternoon. The rest of her reading could wait until later. Her food, however, could not.

The streets of Cantio were decorated with the warmth and welcome inherent in the Candlefire Celebration. Smoke billowed from every chimney top. Flickering candle flames in every single window of buildings both public and private watched passersby like friendly sprites. Swaths of evergreen bundles draped over doorways and rails, along rooftops and footpath borders, accented with ribbons of purple and gold.

Those decorations which were exposed would soon be covered in more than a dusting of white, if Nadja was reading the sky correctly. The clouds hung dark and low with the promise, or threat, depending on who you were asking, of Cantio's first snow of the season. She hoped she would make it to The Broken Chord and back before it started.

For all of her layers, she still felt naked as she walked through the market district. She was thankful her uncle had insisted on including several pairs of pants in her wardrobe. Circumstances now necessitated their use, at least outside the safety of the conservatory. And she knew she wasn't *actually* naked. A quick peek down confirmed that. The tightly woven wool pants did well keeping her warm, tucked into the tops of her boots. But there was something about them which made her feel both liberated and vulnerable at the same time.

She made her way along the busy market streets, leaning against her blowpipe. At her most recent training session, Wheedler noted the blowpipe, much like a staff, could easily be hidden in plain sight if used as a walking stick. Unlike the staff, her blowpipe could be broken down and stored in a small pack. But, since it had only been a few weeks since her escape from the Wanderer scouts, she felt it best to keep her weapon at the ready.

She reached Morris's shop without incident and let herself in. The now familiar and quirky interior was a welcoming sight. The tinkle of the little brass bell did its best to proclaim her entrance, but it was lost to the conversation Nadja heard coming from the general direction of the workbench. With no desire to interrupt the other customers, Nadja chose the left path this time, leisurely investigating a section of the shop which, until now, had remained unexplored.

As she wound her way along the path, a man's voice morphed from a muddled murmur into something intelligible.

"There have always been stories of them popping up from time to time further south, you know. But now people are saying they may already be all over Cantio, and we just haven't realized it."

"Stories, stories. People do love a good story. Keeps things interesting." Nadja recognized Morris's voice.

"But what if they ain't just stories?" asked a woman, lowering her voice excitedly. "What if it's all true?"

Nadja stilled behind a giant pile of reeds and strained to listen as the woman continued.

"Just last week Finley Doveshill was arrested for stealing five hundred gold pieces from Shep's Pawn. Claims he didn't do it, but they have witnesses who say they saw him creeping out of the shop in the wee hours of the morning. And no one has seen bit nor bauble of that gold."

"He's probably hidden it away somewhere," said the man.

"Naw," said the woman. "He's as law-abiding as they come. Stealing's not in his nature."

"Perhaps not. Gambling is, if other stories are true," said Morris.

"I say gambling and stealing are two different things," proclaimed the woman. "As sure as I'm alive and standing here, ol' Finny wouldn't steal unless he was *under the influence* of some evil persons."

"Even if he was 'under the influence,' there's nothing we can do about it," said the man.

"And why not?" asked the woman, her voice rising in pitch and volume. "I say we root them out. All of them. Have every person in Amrantir pass a test or something. Any true citizen would be proud to prove they are a real Amrantirian."

"What kind of test would you propose?" asked Morris.

"Oh, I don't know," said the woman. "Some say they all carry a special mark on their bodies. If we could learn what that mark is, finding them would be easy."

"Still just more stories and hearsay," said Morris.

"What if we could identify them," said the man. "Then what? What would we do?"

"I say we lay them to rest with their ancestors!" exclaimed the woman. "There's no telling what damage they've already done with their mind manipulation."

"You would have them all killed?" asked the man. "Not exiled, or something less brutal?"

The woman's voice lowered once more. "There were good reasons they were eliminated in the first place, and Amrantir has been better for it these past few hundred years. What would you do, Master Alrhen, if one of them came into your shop?"

"Considering I'm just an old man who specializes in repairing instruments, I don't see my services being sought out to fix a broken voice box." Morris chuckled. "And speaking of repairing instruments, here is your dulcimer, pegs intact and freshly strung."

"Beautiful," gushed the woman.

"A job well done, as always," said the man. "There's no one else who does as high quality work as you."

Nadja heard the chink of coins being placed on the counter.

"My pleasure," replied Morris. "Just be sure to use a proper mount if you insist on hanging it from a wall."

Nadja noted the familiar shuffle of Morris's feet fading away towards the back of the shop.

"Yes, yes, lesson learned," said the woman.

"And give my best to your family," Morris called out as the couple departed down Nadja's usual route of choice.

No sooner had the bell signaled their exit than Nadja heard Morris's footsteps returning followed by a clunk of something hard striking the worktable.

"So glad you got my letter," he called out.

Nadja bit her lip and emerged from her hiding place, a sheepish look on her face. "I didn't mean to eavesdrop," she said.

"Of course you didn't."

"I mean, I didn't want to interrupt your conversation." She hesitantly approached the worktable.

Morris's eyes twinkled at her. "Observation and discretion are rare but precious gifts." He gave her a nod and a wink. "Gifts! Yes, and so I have one for you."

He reached down and grabbed a cloth lying across the worktable, yanking it away with a flourish.

Underneath the cloth lay a shiny silver rod. Nadja recognized it at once as a blowpipe, but one unlike any she had ever seen. Decorative details were etched into the metal on either end of the pipe while the middle remained smooth and glinted with an almost mirror finish. Padded leather grips, about two hands in width, wrapped around the barrel on opposite ends between the etchings and the middle.

Without thinking, Nadja reached out to pick up the blowpipe, then stopped, her hand hovering over the barrel.

"May I?" she asked, wide eyed.

Morris smiled. "Of course."

Nadja grasped one of the leather grips and hefted the blowpipe, surprised at its weight.

"It's so light," she said incredulously.

"It's a new metal I've been playing with. Recently discovered in Grenyan. Lev—Levi-something-or-other. Managed to get a sample brought up from a friend. Helps to know people, you know. It's lightweight and alloys beautifully with steel. I believe you'll find this one to be much stronger than your wooden one, but just as light."

Nadja spun the pipe in her hands. The metal flashed in the firelight. She brought the mouthpiece up to her lips, but something gave her pause.

"Oh yes," said Morris. "I almost forgot. Both ends are protected with stoppers which you can remove when you're ready to fire. They will help keep the inside of the barrel clean until you're ready to use it."

"Brilliant," said Nadja, as she removed and then replaced the mouthpiece stopper. It was cork wrapped in leather, both larger and more decorative than the stopper in the opposite end. It lent the feeling of a richly appointed cane to the blowpipe's appearance.

"I hope it serves you well," said Morris.

As if suddenly waking from a fantastical dream, Nadja's eyes snapped to Morris and her mouth fell open.

"It's beyond imagining," she said, "but I couldn't possibly accept this with nothing to give you in return. The time you must have spent on it, and the cost of the materials alone . . . I wouldn't even know how to repay you."

"Psh," harrumphed the old man. "That's why it's a gift. Besides, it was a joy to create. Every day it's 'repair this string,' 'remove this dent,' 'fix that valve.' The brain gets very mushy with nothing new to entertain it, you know. The challenge of something new and different. That's living. That's keeping sharp . . . sharp . . . hmm . . . aha!"

The wiry white head dropped beneath the edge of the worktable, only to reappear a second later, this time wearing another grin.

"Wouldn't be of any use without these," he said, plopping an embossed leather pouch on the table. He unhooked the pouch flap and tossed it back to reveal a dozen shiny metal darts in two neat rows, securely flanked by two empty glass vials. "The pouch has an adjustable strap, so it can be worn however and wherever you like."

"I don't know what to say," said Nadja, running her fingers along the rows of darts.

"'Thank you' is the most commonly used expression, I think," said Morris.

"More than thank you," said Nadja. Touched by the old repairman's thoughtfulness and kindness, her eyes were filled with gratitude when they met his.

Morris nodded in understanding then shuffled over to a nearby shelf and removed a small bottle. "Just remember to oil it after each use. Keeps it in top shape." He handed the bottle to Nadja, who was slipping the pouch strap over her head and across her shoulder. Then, giving her an appraising look he added, "You look ready to take on the world."

Nadja smiled at the compliment, though his words sounded more like an omen.

"Warmth and light, Miss Machinal."

"Warmth and light, Morris."

Chapter Twenty-Three

Thwak! Thwak! Thwak!

Nadja's metal blowpipe slammed a series of blows against the practice dummy. Her strength and skill with the makeshift short staff had improved greatly over the past couple of months. Her movements were becoming more instinctual and had developed a comfortable feeling of fluidity.

Great clouds of steam puffed from her mouth with each strike, and a thin layer of snow blanketed almost every surface of the city. Though the weather was frigid, the walls of the training ground did a fair job protecting her from the occasional burst of wind.

Nadja stepped to an adjacent dummy and removed her cloak, wrapping it around the dummy's shoulders. Cold or not, her muscles were warming up, and the cloak was more of a hindrance than a help when it came to fighting. Her layered top and woolen pants kept her warm enough as long as she kept moving.

Once everyone had returned from the winter break, she gave in to wearing pants almost exclusively. Partly because her original decision to wear them only a few hours a week for private "study sessions" was likely to raise as many questions as eyebrows, and partly because the more she wore them the more comfortable she felt in them. She could move with ease, and against the cold weather, the pants won out over the skirts with little competition.

Helaine had noted Nadja's change of fashion upon her return, to which Nadja commented on the standard garb of Grenyan women, and the practicality of pants in the winter. That was the last she heard on the topic.

She returned to the first dummy and drilled against it once more.

Pax's return was more unsettling than she had anticipated. The feelings which flooded her senses when she saw him again were unnerving. Relief, happiness, and anticipation, tinged with regret. The emotional concoction was different from the general pleasure she felt at seeing Helaine again. He had greeted her with a warm smile and friendly handshake, but something about his demeanor had changed. She couldn't pinpoint what exactly was different, but whatever it was tugged at her heart. And she didn't like that.

Tingling vibrations thrummed up the metal and through her gloved hands and arms with each strike as she channeled her confusion and frustration towards the dummy. Coming to her training session early had been a good idea. She cleared her mind and focused on her breathing and technique, her breaths coming faster and creating a great cloud in front of her chest.

Out of the corner of her eye, she saw a thin wisp of steam float over her right shoulder. She spun around to her left and swept her blowpipe upwards, blocking the wooden staff heading straight towards her.

"Nice," said Brooks, bearing down on Nadja's staff for a moment before releasing her.

"Lesson number one," said Nadja.

"Someone's an early bird today."

"I wanted to get in some extra practice."

"Anyone I know?" asked Brooks, inclining her head towards the dummy.

"No. Like I said, I just wanted to get some extra practice."

"Mmm hmm." Brooks strode over to the benches and removed her cloak, stretching her neck and arms. "Glad you're already warmed up. We can get right to work."

"Aren't we going to wait for Wheedler?" asked Nadja, glancing towards the large double doors.

"No. He's helping your uncle with one of his runs to Chansey. It's just you and me today."

Nadja didn't like the sound of that.

She got along well with Wheedler. Though demanding, he was a good and patient teacher. He fit Nadja's imaginings of what it might be like to have an older brother.

Brooks was another thing altogether. Though she had never been openly hostile towards Nadja, there was something about her which made Nadja uncomfortable. She was blunt and sarcastic and tough. Quick to judge and slow to compliment. She reminded Nadja a little of Grandmaster Gilmoren, but less likable.

It was obvious Brooks didn't like her, and she wondered why Brooks agreed to help with her training. She had always given Nadja good instruction, but never bothered to temper it with kindness or caring. Nadja could tolerate her presence when Wheedler was there, but she cringed at the thought of an entire training session alone with Brooks.

"Why aren't you with them, too?" Nadja asked. "I thought you and Wheedler were a team."

"Usually," said Brooks. "But Tau only required one man this time."

"And you got the short straw?"

Brooks eyes narrowed, and Nadja could have sworn she saw a smile threaten the corners of her mouth. "You could say that."

Brooks took an offensive position in front of Nadja. "Ready."

At Brooks's nonquestion, Nadja spread her feet apart and prepared for the blow.

Brooks gripped her staff like a bat and swung down hard towards Nadja's head. Nadja instinctively spread her arms wide and lifted her staff above her head, blocking the hit. Brooks moved thorough a few more attack combinations, and Nadja effectively blocked each one. Brooks's attacks carried more weight behind them than Wheedler's usually did, and Nadja suspected the jovial giant had been taking it easy on her.

Brooks increased the speed of her attacks and began varying the combinations. Nadja zeroed her focus in on Brooks's chest and shoulders as Wheedler taught her, trying to anticipate each blow before it landed. Her confidence grew as she skillfully blocked blow after blow.

Without warning, Brooks took a quick step backwards, swung her staff over her head with one hand, and slammed it down in a diagonal at Nadja's foot.

Nadja's knees went weak as the end of the staff connected with the side of her boot. She dropped her arms and grunted in pain, sinking to the ground. "That was a cheap shot," she spat.

"Your opponent won't fight by the rules," said Brooks, lowering her staff. "He won't attack you with strikes he knows you can block. Just the opposite. Technique is good. Drills are good. Adaptability is essential." She offered Nadja a hand.

Nadja ignored Brooks's outstretched palm. Instead, she planted the end of her blowpipe in the ground and pulled herself up.

Brooks shrugged. "Nothing's broken."

Nadja clenched her teeth against the pain. "How do you know?" she hissed, shifting her weight off of her throbbing foot.

"Because I didn't hit you hard enough. And you're standing. It'll hurt like anything for a few minutes, but it won't last long. Shake it off."

Brooks walked over to the bench and took a drink from her canteen. Nadja rolled her injured foot a few times and gingerly tested her weight on it. Brooks was right. Much like a stubbed toe, the initial pain was ebbing.

Brooks returned empty handed. "Put away your blowpipe," she ordered.

"Why?" asked Nadja. She warily propped her blowpipe against the dummy still wearing her cloak and returned to face Brooks.

"Adaptability is essential," Brooks repeated. "There is no guarantee you'll have your blowpipe assembled and ready when an attack happens. What would you do if someone came at you while you were unarmed?"

Brooks lunged at Nadja, who threw up her arms in front of her face and jumped back.

Brooks grunted. "Let's try this another way. Attack me."

Nadja lowered her arms and set her legs into a fighting stance.

"What are you waiting for?" taunted Brooks. "Attack me."

Nadja pulled back her right arm and swung it towards Brook's face.

Brooks reached across her body and caught Nadja's wrist, glaring at the open palm. "What is this?"

"This is me attacking you," challenged Nadja.

"With a slap?" Brooks eyed her incredulously. "I intend to end you, and the best you can do is a slap? This should be a fist at the very least."

"It was the first thing I could think of."

"Why?"

"I don't know."

"Yes, you do. Think. Why is this," Brooks jerked her head towards Nadja's open hand still in her grasp, "the first thing you thought of?"

Nadja dropped her gaze to the snow-covered ground beyond Brooks's body and searched her mind. She was given a free pass to attack, and she had gone with a slap to the face. Thinking about it now, that didn't make much sense. She considered other times in her life when she'd injured someone, whether accidentally or on purpose. The answer came to her in a flash.

"I didn't want to hurt you."

"Exactly." Brooks released her wrist and took a step back. "If someone attacks you, hurting you is not something he's trying to avoid. No man is going to go easy on you just because you're a woman. Take advantage of every opening. You may not get many, and if you squander them, you'll get yourself killed. Now try again."

They got back into position. Once again, Nadja swung her right arm. Once again, Brooks caught her wrist.

"It's a fist at least," said Brooks, "but choose another place to land it. You're much more likely to be fighting a man than a woman. And while I know punching the side of my face might be something you really want to do, you're likely to break the little bones in your fingers against a big man's jaw. Aim for a softer spot, like the nose, or stomach."

Nadja tried again, this time, leading with her left arm and landing a decent blow to Brooks's midsection.

A sharp exhale of steam puffed from the guard's mouth on contact. "Exactly," she grunted.

Brooks showed Nadja the proper way to form a fist, a few ways to strike an opponent with her hands and feet, and how to take a hit.

As the end of their training session drew near, Nadja and Brooks once again took up their staffs and faced off in a sparring match. At first, Nadja attacked and defended herself well against her trainer, but after a dozen moves, she found herself disarmed and lying on her back on the frozen ground.

"What will you do?" Brooks looked down at her, staff in hand.

Nadja hesitated.

Brooks landed a blow against Nadja's knee. Nadja cried out as pain radiated up her thigh to her hip.

"What will you do?" demanded Brooks.

Nadja scrambled backwards. On the ground with no weapon, she was at a severe disadvantage. She rolled over and got up on her hands and knees just as Brooks's staff connected with her ribs, knocking the air out of her lungs.

"Adapt!" yelled Brooks.

The frozen snow tingled beneath her hands. Without thinking, she crushed a handful of it into a tight ball. She rolled over onto her back and aimed it at Brooks's face.

The frozen projectile found its target and splattered frosty bits across Brooks's eye and nose. It didn't do any damage, but the surprise attack bought Nadja enough time to put a little more distance between the two of them. She rolled back onto her hands and knees and reached up to feel her ribs. When she did, her hand brushed over the leather dart pouch she wore around her waist.

Brooks's bitter laugh echoed off the stone walls of the training ground. "Nice try, but you'll have to do better than that."

With her back to Brooks, Nadja jumped to her feet and deftly released the small clip which fastened the pouch's strap. Gripping the end of the strap, she spun around, swinging the pouch like a whip towards Brooks's head.

The guard didn't see the improvised weapon until it was too late. The pouch landed a solid blow against her cheek. She staggered backwards, stunned.

Nadja raised her fists, readying herself.

A small stream of blood trickled from the corner of Brooks's mouth, likely from a cut left by the pouch's buckle. She reached up and wiped it off.

She looked at the blood on her fingers.

Then, she grinned and looked up at Nadja.

"Well done."

Chapter Twenty-Four

"Ooo, this looks like a good one!" exclaimed Helaine, pulling Nadja into yet another dress shop. It was the fourth one they had been into that day, and while Nadja enjoyed beautiful dresses as much as the next woman, she didn't think anyone enjoyed them as much as Helaine.

"What do you think, too much?" the cheerful blonde asked, running her hand down a fluffy confection of pink organdy and white satin ribbons.

"For a spring wedding, no. For an informal lunch date, yes," replied Nadja.

Helaine sighed and strolled along the row of dresses, letting each one slip through her fingers as she passed.

"Do you know where he's taking you?" asked Nadja.

"No," replied Helaine, creasing her brow. "That's what's making this difficult. If we're going to The Hen and Harp, then anything would do, really. But if he's taking me somewhere like Trio's, that's a whole different matter."

The two restaurants Helaine mentioned represented opposite ends in the range of culinary choices available in Cantio's middle ring. Of course, the wharf offered its own particular style of food and atmosphere, but the idea Petrin would consider one of those eating establishments for their first official date was absurd.

It had taken the lanky craftsman a few weeks to work up the confidence to ask Helaine out on a proper date once everyone had returned from winter break, and Nadja had watched the whole awkward dance with amusement. Without their project creating the perfect excuse to spend time together, Petrin began popping up regularly in Helaine's day-to-day routine: between classes, at mealtimes in the dining hall. Helaine interpreted his continued presence as a gesture of friendship, while Nadja knew better.

But getting two shy people to admit they have feelings for one another is like trying to push together two identically charged magnets. One has to go against its true nature before they can snap together. Here, it was Petrin whose courage finally won out over his nerves, and their date on the following day was the result.

"Ooo!" Helaine squealed.

She was standing in front of a mirror holding up a long-sleeved cotton dress in ice blue. The bodice had just enough detail embroidered along the neckline to add a pretty bit of interest without overdoing it, and the color complimented Helaine's skin and hair perfectly.

"That's lovely," said Nadja.

"It's perfect," said Helaine, grinning at herself in the mirror.

Helaine paid the shopgirl, arranged to have the dress delivered to the conservatory, and breathed a sigh of relief as she and Nadja exited the store.

The market district was more crowded than usual. The quarterly delegates meeting was in progress, and between the delegates and their entourages, the middle ring was a hub of activity.

Right now, sitting in an assembly in the Delegates Hall, was Baulo. Nadja shuttered at the thought.

"All that shopping has made me hungry," said Helaine. Then, she halted and grabbed Nadja by the arm. "Oh! I overheard Selina and Vatara talking the other day about a stall selling a new frozen sweet cream. It sounded delicious. Let me treat you. As a thank-you for coming along with me today."

"Frozen sweet cream? In the middle of winter?" Nadja smiled. "That sounds wrong and right all at the same time. Where's the stall?"

"Somewhere in the western fifth." Helaine's face lit up. "It shouldn't be too hard to find."

Nadja felt a twinge in the pit of her stomach. That would put them near the government district and the Delegates Hall. But, seeing the excited look on Helaine's face, she brushed the feeling aside. The bustling streets should make it easy enough for them to go unnoticed, and as it was not yet supper time, the delegates would still be in session.

She smiled at Helaine. "Lead the way."

The temporary population increase, which always accompanied a delegates meeting, meant most of the roads and pathways were compacted by a steady stream of foot traffic. Though the roads were cleared by conscientious shopkeepers, there were invisible ice slicks every so often set like inadvertent booby traps, so Nadja and Helaine stepped carefully. The occasional burst of winter wind blew puffs of white powder down from rooftops onto unsuspecting pedestrians below, giving Nadja the perfect excuse to keep the hood of her cloak snug around her face.

"So, what about you and Pax?" Helaine asked, casually.

Nadja almost stumbled. "Um, what about us? Not that there's an 'us.' I mean, there's a him and there's a me."

"Really? Because I would have bet my best bow there was something going on between the two of you before we broke for the Candlefire Celebration."

The sudden pain in Nadja's chest took her by surprise, much like it had done when she said goodbye to Pax before the break. And she had no wish to follow this line of conversation down whatever path it might lead.

She leaned in and gave her friend a conspiratorial wink. "There was something going on."

Helaine's eyes widened. Nadja glanced around to make sure no one else was listening, then whispered, "We were working on a class project together."

Helaine straightened and rolled her eyes. "I know that. But, what else?"

"I don't know what you want me to say. Pax and I are friends, but that's as far as it goes."

"Petrin says he speaks very highly of you."

Nadja's first instinct was to ask for more details, but she quickly realized that didn't matter. Friends should speak highly of one another.

Helaine pressed on. "Do you mean to tell me that, in all that time the two of you spent together, not once were you the teensiest bit tempted to run your fingers through that gorgeous head of hair?"

"Helaine!"

Nadja's face warmed at the memory of sitting in the orchard with Pax, his arms around her and his fingers running through *her* hair. Even though it was only in a comforting, friendly kind of way.

"What? I'm not blind, Nadja. Anyone with eyes can see Pax is a very attractive man."

"Yes, I'm not denying that. But, in case you haven't noticed, I don't go around throwing myself at every attractive man who crosses my path." Nadja attempted to shift the conversation once more. "Lucky for you, or else you'd have competition on your hands."

"Now, really!" Helaine looked appalled for the briefest moment before dissolving into giggles. "Petrin is handsome, isn't he?"

"Absolutely. And it's a good thing too, because I'm afraid once he sees you in that dress, he won't be much for conversation."

"Oh, stop!" Helaine swatted Nadja's arm.

"Speaking of your dress, how do you plan on wearing your hair?"

Helaine cut her eyes at Nadja, but allowed the change in subject. She began listing various hairstyle options and the pros and cons of each. Nadja relaxed. Since Helaine required little contribution from her on the matter, she mulled over her friend's original question.

What about her and Pax?

They were exactly as she wished. Good friends.

But something had changed. Pax was as kind and friendly as ever, but something had been missing since his return from the winter break. There was a sort of emptiness in their encounters which caused her heart to ache. The level of intimacy they had shared before she had sent him home had evaporated, replaced by a cordiality she secretly loathed. Even more, she hated herself for loathing it.

After a quarter hour of weaving their way through shoppers and businessmen and sidestepping black ice and miniature avalanches, they stopped in front of a colorful stall. A jolly man bundled in leather and fur stood behind the counter taking orders while two smaller versions of himself ran around filling them. The line was long, but if the steady flow of customers towards the stall was any indication, the frozen sweet cream was sure to be a treat.

Nadja and Helaine queued up. The stall owner and his sons scurried around like crabs running with the tide, keeping the flow of customers moving. After a few minutes waiting in line, the crowd around the stall and in the streets grew exponentially.

The buzz of activity and conversation hummed all around them. Nadja caught bits of phrases which escaped above the din.

"The new old threat . . ."

". . . uncontrollable . . ."

". . . still people, just like us . . ."

Puzzled, she leaned in to Helaine. "Is it just me, or is there more tension in the air than usual today?"

"Yes," said Helaine, eyeballing the menu board and waving her hand dismissively. "It's the great Mevocali debate." She rolled her eyes. "My father said it pops up about once every generation. Old rumors resurface. People get anxious. Then nothing comes of it. It's silly, really. I mean, the Mevocali have been gone for hundreds of years. I guess some people just aren't happy unless they have something to worry about."

Nadja nodded, remembering the couple she'd overheard talking with Morris at The Broken Chord. She was glad it was nothing but rumors. After growing up with an aversion for how music was used throughout the rest of Amrantir, she was finally becoming comfortable with her new life as a musician. Like any gift, it had to be wielded with wisdom.

Thankfully, it had its limitations. Instrumental music could manipulate the natural world, but that was the extent of its use. It couldn't heal people, and it certainly couldn't affect people's thoughts and minds. And, it was a skill available to anyone who wanted to learn, not something reserved for a select few.

"In fact," continued Helaine, half of her attention still fixed on the frozen cream flavor options, "I'm pretty sure that's the main topic of discussion at the delegates assembly."

A crisp gust of wind blasted down the road, sending a chill through to Nadja's bones. She shivered, tucking her chin.

Finally, the two women reached the counter. With plenty of time in line to study the menu, they didn't waste a moment placing their orders. Helaine requested the caramel and walnut flavor while Nadja went with cinnamon sugar. Almost as soon as Helaine placed the coppers into the stall owner's hand, two frosty cups appeared on the counter before them. Molded snow and ice formed the cups which were filled with mounds of a stiff and slick concoction of cream, sugar, and spices. A thick, flat ice shard stuck out of the top of each cream, and a cursory glance at previous customers told them it served as a kind of spoon.

They thanked the stall owner and stepped aside. As soon as they were on the edge of the crowd, Helaine raised her icy cup and took a bite right off the top of the creamy mountain. Nadja watched in amusement as her roommate's eyes rolled back into her head before fluttering closed.

"Ohhh myyy woord," Helaine sighed, elongating the words as if savoring the taste of each.

"That good?" Nadja laughed as she spooned a bite into her own mouth.

The frozen creation was silky and sweet, and Nadja thought she had never tasted anything like it in her life. She appreciated Helaine's reaction as her own eyelids fell closed. The cinnamony cream numbed her already cold face and lips as it slowly melted in her mouth.

"Thith hath got to be one of the motht delithith thingth I have ever tathted," said Helaine. Her hand flew to her mouth, and she dissolved into a fit of giggles.

Nadja joined in her roommate's laughter, noting Helaine had already eaten half of her cream.

"Agreed," she smiled, taking her time to savor the next bite.

They strolled around the edge of the crowd back towards the main road, taking their time and enjoying their treats. The kitchen staff at the conservatory would serve dinner soon, but Nadja doubted anything would ever taste as good as what she held in her hands.

They emerged from the stall crowd. As soon as Nadja's feet landed on the main road, another surprise burst of wind swept down the street and blew back the hood of her cloak. She felt the hairs on the back of her neck stand at attention. As she reached up to replace her hood, she turned her face into the oncoming wind.

In the space of a second, the frosty air penetrated to her core and sucked the breath from her lungs. She froze in midmovement, the fingertips of one hand lightly touching the edge of her hood, while the grip of her other tightened around her cup.

No more than twenty paces away stood a figure at once familiar and foreign to her. An old man with dark eyes and a white beard was engaged in a lively group discussion along a pathway between the frozen sweet cream stall and the border of the government district.

Nadja squeezed her eyes shut against the wind, unsure if what she was seeing was real or a creation of her own paranoid imagination. Opening them again, the reality of the situation pressed in on her.

Baulo.

Not the strong, fearsome monster who attacked Kizzy and whom Nadja had almost killed, but an older, rougher, more worn version of the man. It had been just two seasons since their encounter, not long enough for his dramatic change to be merely due to the passage of time. His salt-and-pepper beard and mustache now mirrored the color of the snow. The lines on his face had deepened, and deep purple shadows colored half-moons beneath his eyes.

As if sensing her presence, Baulo's eyes drifted casually over the crowd until they locked with her own.

Unable to look away, Nadja stared at him, frozen in place. Her pulse quickened and her vision darkened around the edges. What now? Would he order her arrest? Could he even do that within the borders of Cantio? Would he come at her himself? Her disassembled blowpipe was tucked into her pack. Would she even have time to put it together if he did come?

Then, he did the last thing she expected.

He smiled.

If she had any lingering doubt the old man was indeed Baulo, the familiar rows of crooked teeth put that doubt to rest.

Her eyes widened. His smile broadened as he bobbed his head in acknowledgement before turning his attention back to the discussion.

A light popping sound, followed by sharp pain in her wrist broke Nadja's trance.

"Oh dear!" exclaimed Helaine through a mouthful of sweet cream.

Nadja looked down at the hand holding her frozen cup, now clutching a few broken pieces of ice and a sticky mess. A thin line of red blossomed across her wrist just above the cuff of her glove where a jagged piece of ice sliced the skin.

"I guess that cup wasn't as sturdy as it looked," Nadja sputtered with an embarrassed laugh.

"And you've cut yourself," said Helaine, grabbing Nadja's hand for a closer look.

"It's nothing," said Nadja. She pulled away from her friend's grasp and examined her injury. The blood welled slowly, and her eyes followed its path over the edge of her wrist.

Two red drops stared up at her from the white snow below. Baulo's face flashed in her mind. Not the old man who stood paces away from her, but the monster, blood pouring from his eyes as he advanced on her and she . . .

What had she done?

Screamed, yes. But no scream could have done that to a man. There had to have been something else.

"But you're bleeding," she heard Helaine protest. "Oh, that looks like more than nothing to me. Should I fetch a doctor? Mind your clothes!"

Nadja squeezed her eyes shut at the gruesome memory and shook her head. This was not the time to get lost in thought. Lesson one: Always be aware of your surroundings.

She jerked her chin up and cast a sidelong glance towards the chatty delegates.

"No, no, I'll be fine," she muttered absently.

The group was still deep in conversation, but with one small difference. Baulo was no longer among them.

Nadja's senses went on high alert. Her eyes scanned the crowd, but found no sign of him.

"You don't look fine," said Helaine. "You've gone as white as a sheet." She took her friend's arm. "Let's go back to the conservatory and get you cleaned up properly."

"All right." Nadja offered her roommate a weak smile and pressed her uninjured hand over the cut to halt the bleeding. They hastened their steps towards the center of the city.

The conservatory was the safest place, and the crowded streets would provide a relative amount of protection as they traveled back. This was neither the time nor place for a confrontation. Baulo was too calculating to attempt anything less than honorable in so public an arena.

Still, the hair on the back of Nadja's neck stood tall as her eyes darted over the street, failing to find their mark.

No doubt he would soon learn of her attendance at the conservatory—if he didn't know already. And then what? His reaction to seeing her both puzzled and terrified her. There was no way to predict his next move.

One thing was certain, however. He would make a move. Never a man inclined towards mercy and forgiveness, Baulo had always favored swift justice. But what he might consider justice with regards to Nadja left her with an inescapable sense of doom.

Chapter Twenty-Five

The geese drifted through the azure sky in a wide, lazy arc headed for one of the ponds which dotted the farmlands outside the walls of the capital city. Like the other flocks which had begun to appear in the past few weeks, their return from the warmer climates of Grenyan confirmed spring had finally come to Amrantir.

Nadja watched their aerial display through the conservatory's window with divided attention. The birds' yearly cycle of travels from north to south and back again, ever chasing warmer climates, reminded her of her old life—of the Wanderers. They couldn't be farther away from her than they were now, preparing to leave the coast soon and turn northward into the steppes.

Her mother would be making her last dives of the season, collecting fat oysters from the deeper waters of the Shadow Sea. Some would be eaten right away, while the rest would be set out to dry in the sun, then added to the food stores. They would be enjoyed later in the year when the briny sea air and sandy coast became a distant memory.

Goran, her grandfather, would be working alongside Jamila. At his age, his activities were confined to the shallows, trapping crabs in inlet waters and casting nets for schools of blue arrowfins which favored the surf at tide's change.

Nadja's mind drifted to Kizzy. As a gatherer, the winter and early spring months were largely uneventful for her, which was a good thing. She would have been able to take as much time as she needed to recover privately.

But Nadja sensed things were not going as planned.

When she'd parted with Luca, he'd promised to tell Kizzy's father, Harman, the truth of what had happened. Luca promised to stand with them and protect Kizzy if she would come forward. However, seeing Baulo in his capacity as Wanderer delegate at the midwinter meeting led her to believe Kizzy wasn't convinced. Or worse, she'd made her accusations, but the support of Harman and Luca wasn't enough to convince the Elders to charge Baulo.

Though her heart ached at the thought of her family so far away, Nadja's consolation was that Baulo should also be among the tribe. The next quarterly Delegation wouldn't take place until midseason, so unless Baulo contrived another reason to be in Cantio, she was safe for the time being.

But Baulo was not to be underestimated. It was because of this she had left the conservatory grounds only twice since seeing him. She suspended her training sessions with Wheedler and Brooks and spent her days off within the walls of the conservatory.

Nadja continued to practice her combat skills in the early-morning hours in a secluded area of the back orchard. She knew she could not best Baulo, despite her moderate level of training and his altered physical state. But, she didn't want to lose the strength and skills she had already acquired.

She was a small child playing with a jack-in-the-box, completely at the mercy of that smug-faced harlequin, waiting for it to jump out at her when she least expected it. The best she could do was stay hidden and wait to hear from Luca.

"Do you not agree, Miss Machinal?"

Grandmaster Xavier Pennequois's annoyed tenor penetrated her distraction, and she snapped her eyes to the front of the classroom. A single raised eyebrow accompanied his look of disdain.

Heat crept into her cheeks as she stared back at him. She had no idea how long she had been gazing out the window, and no clue what he was talking about.

"Oh, I am sorry," he said, feigning remorse. "Did I interrupt your daydreams? Or perhaps you find no value in singing?"

Ah, singing.

"No, singing is very valuable," she mumbled, lamely.

"Quite so."

He gave an exasperated sigh ensuring everyone in the class was well aware of his disappointment. Nadja slunk lower in her chair. From the seat next to her, Helaine shot her a pitying look. Xavier Pennequois was the kind of teacher who expected much from his students, yet always assumed they'd fall short of those expectations.

He turned his attention back to the rest of the class. "If any of you bothered to read the syllabus distributed at the beginning of the year, you already know you'll be giving a performance in one week's time during the Heartstide Festival. This class is called Music for Enjoyment for a reason. Please choose a piece you believe will connect with the audience. It doesn't have to be a happy song, per se. Melancholy songs can be enjoyable in their own right. You may perform solo, or in a small ensemble."

A low murmur came over the class as students began grouping together and discussing song choices.

Grandmaster Pennequois raised his hand and spoke over the noise. "Just be sure each person has an opportunity to sing solo."

The talking ceased at once, and everyone regarded the grandmaster with collective surprise.

Nadja's stomached clenched.

A hint of a smile crept over his lips, highlighting his already conceited expression. "Oh, didn't you know? These will be vocal performances."

He waited for the news to settle over the stunned class before continuing.

"It is true we focus on instrumental music here. However, since vocal music is not utilitarian in nature like instrumental music is, it's the perfect medium for exploring music purely for the sake of enjoyment."

The class once again began to murmur, and the grandmaster once again raised his hand.

"And I want to hear no complaints of, 'But I can't sing!' Any idiot with working vocal cords can sing. Singing is just speaking with greater range."

Without warning, he launched into an aria from "The Night of a Thousand Moons." His voice was strong and sure, and he performed with gusto, emoting with a flourish like a professional upon the stage. Nadja hated to admit it, but he was good.

When the song was over, he paused for dramatic effect. A smattering of applause, led enthusiastically by Laurel, stroked his vanity.

"Of course, not everyone who sings can do so with great skill." He bestowed a gracious smile upon the class, aiming particularly at the ladies. "Skill will factor little into your final grade. The point of this exercise is for you and the audience to relish in the music for its own sake."

He dismissed the class with a wave of his hand, giving no chance for questions or argument.

"Singing. Well, I didn't see that coming." Helaine said.

"Me either," Nadja mumbled, her stomach now at a full roll. Memories of her last vocal performance came to mind.

"What's the matter?"

"It's easy for him to say anyone can sing when he does it so well. Let's just say there's a reason I play an instrument."

"Oh dear, don't worry! You heard what he said. Skill won't matter much to your grade. You must sing a duet with me. I love to sing." Before Nadja could agree, Helaine began planning the whole thing. "We can take turns, and I can take on any difficult parts. In fact, you choose the song. Pick whatever you like. Something you're comfortable with."

Nadja was glad for her friend's offer to help, but didn't want to mess up other plans which might already be in motion. "Thank you for the offer, but wouldn't Petrin be disappointed? I'm sure he's already making plans to sing with you." She scanned the classroom for Helaine's spindly beau.

"Oh, he's a bit under the weather, poor thing. Hopefully he'll be well in time for the Heartside Festival, but he may have to make up the assignment." Helaine sighed. "I'll take him some food after Music Theory. I hope it's nothing too bad . . ." Then, she shook herself, flashing a smile at Nadja. "But I want *you* to sing a duet with me."

Nadja couldn't help but smile back. "Of course."

Helaine snapped her fingers. "You know, Grandmaster Pennequois said solo or small ensemble. We could do a trio or quartet if you like. That way we could spread the solo parts around even more."

Nadja's eyes flitted over the class. Most of the students were already grouped together or had left the room. Her gaze paused on a couple towards the back corner of the classroom.

Pax's angular profile captured her attention as he leaned across one of the long tables, resting on his forearms. The months spent away from the physical demands of the forest had done little to diminish his impressive form or the sun-baked hue of his skin. She watched the strong line of his jaw bob up and down as he spoke. He grinned, and tiny crinkles accented the corner of his eye.

A high musical laugh broke through the buzz of conversation. Laurel sat across the table from him, wearing a smile which enhanced her already impossibly perfect features. She reached out and traced her slender fingers down the length of his arm, bring it to rest in his open palm.

Nadja flinched.

She dropped her eyes to the floor and blinked a few times, then looked up and gave Helaine what she hoped was a reassuring smile.

"No, I think a duet is just the thing."

"No!" exclaimed Nadja.

She looked at Helaine's face, cheeks flushed and eyes brimming with unshed tears.

"I'm so sorry," croaked Helaine. "Here I am, letting you down in your time of need. What a wonderful friend I turned out to be." She buried her face in her hands.

Nadja's shoulders slumped. Her best friend was sitting in bed propped against the headboard, fevered and in pain, and Nadja's first reaction had been self-pity at the loss of that evening's duet partner. A wave of shame washed over her, and she softened her voice.

"No," she said. "I shouldn't have shouted. I was just surprised that's all. How are you feeling?"

"Like someone set fire to my throat," Helaine whispered.

Nadja sat on the edge of the bed and placed her hand across Helaine's forehead.

"No," said Helaine, pushing her hand away. "I don't want you to catch it."

"You are burning up." Nadja stood and crossed the room to the water basin, returning with a cup of fresh water. "Drink this. I know it hurts, but you need it. I'll go down to the dining hall and bring you back some soup. Would you like me to send for Nurse Silvers?"

"There's no need," said Helaine, taking a small sip of water. "I know what it is." She raised her eyes to meet Nadja's, and she bolted up in bed. The tears which had been threatening to escape finally broke free.

"Oh Nadja, it's all my fault," she cried, her voice sounding like sandpaper. "I knew better, but I just couldn't help myself. And now I'm not the only one who will pay for my foolish actions. I hardly ever get sick. I guess that's why I was so arrogant. Stupid. Completely preventable."

"Woah," Nadja crooned. She grasped Helaine gently by the shoulders. "Slow down. What are you talking about?"

Helaine took a deep breath which trembled as she released it. "It was Petrin. He was just so pitiful. Like a helpless little boy lying there. The worst of it was over, and I thought it wouldn't be catching by then. I just couldn't seem to help myself. So I . . ."

Nadja nodded slowly. "Ah." She released Helaine's shoulders. Then, stifling a grin she asked, "Couldn't keep your lips off him, could you?"

Helaine shook her head and sniffed. "See what I mean? Stupid. And now I'm sending you out on that stage all alone when I should be there right beside you."

Nadja chuckled, and Helaine glanced up at her with a puzzled look.

"It's fine, Helaine, really." She reached out and patted her friend's hand. "I could sing this song in my sleep, duet or solo. Don't worry about me. Just promise you'll get some rest this evening." She paused and looked pointedly at her roommate. "And don't even think about sneaking out to Petrin's room, no matter how irresistible his kisses are."

Helaine let out a giggle which sounded more like a hiccup, and Nadja saw her shoulders relax.

"Are you sure?" asked Helaine.

"Yes," said Nadja, placing her hands on Helaine's shoulders once again and leaning her friend back against her pillows. "Now, you relax, and I'll get you that soup."

She stood and headed for the door.

"Besides," she called back, "it'll do me good. I need to stop hiding behind my own insecurities and just lay it all out there. What's the worst that could happen?"

Chapter Twenty-Six

Nadja rolled her flute back and forth between her palms. The coral instrument, cool when she removed it from her pack, had warmed to match her own temperature due to copious amounts of fidgeting.

She sat with the rest of her classmates at one of the small wooden tables positioned in front of the modest stage at The Hen and Harp. The rest of the room was filled to overflowing with celebrants, most at tables or at the bar, with a few choosing to prop against walls or support beams when seats were not to be found. Couples made up the majority of the crowd, heads leaned together, seeing little more than each other. One large table was filled entirely with women, imbibing pints of the pub's special festival brew and conversing boisterously with one another.

The pub itself was decorated from top to bottom in honor of the Heartstide Festival. Basketfuls of spring blooms adorned almost every nonfunctional surface in the building. Chains of heavenly scented lilac and snowdrops spiraled their way up beams and railings. Festoons of pink crocuses and cheery daffodils dipped and swayed back and forth across the ceiling. The flowers, symbolic of the spring's new life and the bloom of love, adorned the hair of many women.

Nadja was not one of those women. While that night's patrons gathered to indulge in the more tender feelings of the heart, all Nadja wanted to do was get her performance over with. Unfortunately, she would have to wait.

Grandmaster Pennequois had ordered them all to meet in the Music for Enjoyment classroom an hour before they were due at The Hen and Harp. He noted each song to be performed, then ordered them as he saw fit.

If Nadja hadn't been so caught up reworking her duet into a solo, she would have made it on time. As it was, she'd slipped into the classroom a few minutes late. The grandmaster had been annoyed by her tardiness, and even more annoyed he would need to rework the set list. In the interest of time, however, he had begrudgingly tacked on Nadja's song at the end.

The dread of having to sit through everyone else's performances first, stomach rolling and palms sweating, had been mitigated slightly by the fact she hadn't had to travel to the pub alone. She'd navigated the dusk-shadowed streets of the market district safely ensconced in a pod of her peers.

And now, one hour and a dozen or so songs later, her turn had come. She sat, head down, mentally going over each transition in the music as Vatara's sweet soprano offered a touching rendition of "The Lady with the Long Dark Hair" in the background. Nadja had chosen to lend her flute playing to her own piece in the absence of a duet partner. She told herself it would add interest and perhaps help camouflage her less-than-expert vocal skills. In reality, it was a crutch she used to prop up her courage.

The clapping and cheers shook Nadja's concentration, and she looked up, wiping her clammy hands on her pants. Vatara bowed with a smile and returned to her seat. The host took her place center stage.

"Next up is Miss Nadja Machinal. She will perform 'The Tide of Love.'" The host led the room in applause and gestured for Nadja to take the stage.

Nadja rose from her seat and gathered her flute and the small stack of music which sat on the table before her. She walked to the side of the room and took the small staircase which led onto the stage one step at a time. She distributed her music to the house band, hoping they didn't notice the way the papers shook as she handed them out.

"The Tide of Love" was a familiar song, and Nadja had chosen to sing it because it reminded her of home. Her mother taught it to her as a child and sang it often. Jamila said it reminded her of Nadja's father, and Nadja, having never known her father, clung to it as if it were a piece of him. She loved the sweet story. But, mostly, she loved the way her mother's face looked when she sang it, wistful yet content. She was one who had known great love, and though she had lost it too soon, she was better for it.

She turned to face the crowd.

The band struck up at once, surprising Nadja. The shock sent a jolt of adrenaline through her body and she breathed deeply, trying to calm her raw nerves. Instinctively, she raised her flute to her lips. Almost as soon as the instrument was in place, she realized the flute part didn't come until after the first verse. By then it was too late. The moment had passed.

Nadja looked over her shoulder at the band leader and grimaced. "I'm sorry," she whispered. "Can we try again?"

He nodded and cued the band who stopped in perfect unison before picking up at the beginning once more.

Nadja turned back towards the crowd, offering them a tight-lipped smile. The whole situation felt eerily familiar. She remembered the last time she sang in front of an audience. She had missed her entrance then, too. Only that time, she didn't have her flute with her. No. She had sent Kizzy to fetch it. But Kizzy had never come back with it. While Nadja had been performing for her party guests, Kizzy had been enduring unspeakable acts at the hand of Baulo.

Baulo.

Nadja's eyes widened as they darted back and forth across the crowd. The table of women smiled and whispered amongst themselves. A few of the couples diverted their attention in her direction, but most were still engrossed in their partners.

Of course, Baulo had no business being in Cantio. It wasn't midseason yet, at least not for a few more days. But, as the Wanderer delegate, he could create an excuse to come into the city any time he saw fit.

As this thought crossed her mind Nadja spotted a lone figure seated at the end of the bar. The figure was dressed simply enough, but wore a long, hooded cloak, which was odd for the season. The man's body, for that size and build could only belong to a man, was turned towards the bar, but his head faced the stage.

Though Nadja couldn't see his face, she could feel his eyes on her. Studying. Scrutinizing. She studied him in return, unable to look away. His form and bearing was all too familiar. Panic rose in her throat as she realized her ability to stay hidden from Baulo had come to an end.

The music coming from behind her faded away as a great rushing sound filled her ears. She tore her gaze from the man and found every eye in the room trained on her.

Why were they all staring?

Did they know?

Had he told them?

Were they *helping* him?

Nadja felt like she was standing at a mark, waiting for him to give the order to fire.

Without warning, a strong arm snaked around her waist, and a hand wrapped firmly around her side. Nadja gasped, nearly dropping her flute.

"May I join you?" Pax whispered low, his breath tickling her ear, his caramel-coated voice soothing her

316

nerves. She turned and looked up at him in surprise, her head clearing as she inhaled the scent of freshly hewn wood and rain.

She heard the band clearly now, vamping the same bar, waiting for her entrance.

Nadja felt a rush of embarrassment. No wonder everyone was staring.

Pax turned his winning smile on the crowd and launched into the first verse, still holding her to his side, as if sensing she needed the support.

"My love came to me like the rising tide
Gracefully she approached, bearing treasures so sweet
With a love as deep as the sea is wide
That summer's day two hearts did meet."

Pax's voice swept over Nadja like the spring breeze. He was surprisingly good, his smooth baritone coating the room in a wash of warmth and tranquility. She smiled inwardly at the way he deftly changed "he" to "she" in the verse as if this had been the plan all along. As he sang, the tension melted from her body, and she leaned into him ever so slightly.

She thought of their first meeting, how he appeared out of nowhere and saved her, much like he was doing now. That time had been a matter of life or death. And this time may well be, too. She chanced a quick peek at the bar. The cloaked man still sat much as he had before, but perhaps a little more intent.

As Pax neared the end of the verse, he glanced down at her and winked. The worry-induced tightness in her gut transformed into something fluttery and moved lower in her belly. She turned to the audience before her feelings showed on her face and joined him on the refrain.

"The waves may crash and roll and roar
But I am my love's forevermore."

Pax's hand gave her a gentle squeeze.

"Your turn," he whispered, before dropping his arm to his side and slipping the flute from her grasp. A tingling sensation bolted up her arm as their hands connected. He set the flute on a nearby music stand. Then, he pulled her to face him and took both of her hands in his. She looked up into the endless blue of his eyes.

"Don't worry about them," he breathed. "Just sing to me."

He was coaching her through it.

Right before her eyes that perfectly polite yet aloof Pax of the past few months dissolved into the Pax she had come to know and care for. His face was open and supportive, and his grip on her hands was firm, yet gentle as he rubbed his thumbs back and forth across her knuckles.

She inhaled and closed her eyes.

"Face to face, and hand to hand
Lips to lips, in joy and love
There we played upon the sand
Heart to heart, 'neath blue skies above."

Opening her eyes, her gaze came to rest on his mouth. She thought of their kiss. Hasty, but full of joy. Though it had been many months, she still replayed that moment often in her mind. Her cheeks prickled as she thought of his hands on her face. She unconsciously licked her lips. Pax leaned towards her and parted his.

His voice carried the refrain solo this time. Nadja startled, embarrassed to have been caught staring at his mouth. Pax's eyes met hers, his encouraging expression replaced by a questioning look which carried with it an undercurrent of heated intensity.

She knew that look. She had seen similar ones color his features before, and she had always run from them.

But this time was different. This time, she didn't want to run.

From the time she had left the tribe, Pax had been the one constant in her life. He treated her with nothing but kindness and caring. He was like the Auldwood Oak—strong, protective, persistent, and rare.

Why had she run?

She didn't want a man to speak for her, to play proxy for her to the rest of the world.

But, Pax never offered that. Yes, he wanted to protect her, but he never discounted her.

How she longed to feel the security of his arms around her again, to lean into his powerful body and share her worries like she had done that day in the orchard.

She looked at his mouth again, his full lips unmoving.

She wondered where they were in the song when Pax's eyebrows drew together and the corners of his mouth pulled down. He released her hands and stepped back, turning away from her to face the audience. A chill swooped in to replace the warmth of his nearness causing Nadja's heart to ache. His voice, low and melancholy, brought her back to the present.

"Then ever like the fickle moon
Which pulls the tide back out to sea
My love was gone, but over-soon
And brokenhearted there left me."

She didn't want him to pull away. Her heart pulsed in time to the music as it swelled and permeated the air with longing. She reached out for Pax and drew him back to her, threading her fingers through his and singing the final verse.

"But come again, my love, my heart . . ."

She dropped her mask of indifference. Her feelings shone on her face as clearly as the sunrise.

"My arms will enfold you once more . . ."

Nadja's fingers outlined the solid muscles in his arms as they traveled upwards to rest on his shoulders. Pax brought his hands to her waist, pulling her against him, his jaw clenched, his eyes flashing with a desire matching her own.

"And kiss your lips and never part . . ."

He reached up and cupped the back of her head, weaving his fingers through her hair. They leaned in, their foreheads coming to rest against one another.

"Like the tide along the ocean shore."

Nadja's eyelids fell shut once more as his breath washed over her. The room spun, threatening her ability to remain standing. She slid one hand down across the hard plane of his chest. She could feel his heart racing and knew hers beat just as quickly. Their chests rose and fell together as Pax's voice joined hers in the final refrain.

"The waves may crash and roll and roar
But I am my love's forevermore."

With their faces inches apart, Nadja held her breath as the band played the outro.

The moment of silence following the final note was broken by a smattering of enthusiastic applause. Reluctantly, Nadja stepped away from Pax, and they both turned to bow to the crowd. When she stood up again, she noticed many things at once.

A flash of movement at the bar caught her eye. The cloaked man hurried across the room towards the door. As he neared the exit, a beam of lantern light pierced the darkness beneath his hood and, for a second, illuminated the face hidden there. It wasn't Baulo's. Nadja puffed out a quick sigh of relief before something else caught her attention.

The entire demeanor of the room had changed. The crowd itself, including the conservatory students, had diminished in size. Half of the women at the large table were gone as were some of the other patrons. The remaining singles fidgeted uncomfortably in their seats.

The couples, on the other hand, were more intimately engaged. Nadja was shocked to find most of them locked in ardent embraces, faces pressed together, lips and hands roving. True, she had never been in the capital city during a Heartstide Festival, but she was surprised at the blatant public displays of affection.

Was she really that bad?

Nadja knew her vocal skills left something to be desired, but most people had the common courtesy to at least feign attention. And, no one had ever thought her singing terrible enough to leave in the middle of a song.

Or maybe they had, but were just kind enough to keep that opinion to themselves.

Nadja's heart sank.

All the insecurities Pax had helped her defeat only moments ago came rushing back. She turned to him, seeking reassurance. The scene before her stole the breath from her lungs.

Pax, his broad back facing her, was bent low, and a pair of slender arms wrapped around his neck. Nadja stood rooted in place, staring as the seconds ticked by. Finally, he straightened and shifted his weight, giving her a clear view of the person to whom the arms belonged.

Laurel stood in front of him, eyes glistening, with a beautiful smile shining up at him. Nadja thought she heard Laurel praising Pax's performance, but she couldn't be sure. Her mind was fighting a war between what her eyes and ears were telling her and what her heart refused to believe.

Laurel looked past Pax's shoulder. She met Nadja's eyes and giggled before turning back to Pax.

The air, sweetly scented with new spring blooms, became sickening. Nadja swallowed, forcing down the supper threatening to escape her belly. She couldn't face him. Not now.

Before he had a chance to turn around, Nadja leapt from the stage and hurried out the door.

Chapter Twenty-Seven

Nadja lay beneath the warm water moving her arms back and forth and letting the temporary current rock and soothe her exhausted body. Her head pounded and her muscles were tighter than a drum head.

She'd spent most of the day fighting invisible enemies in her little corner of the orchard. Her hurt and frustration found release, and her mind escape, as she jumped, rolled, struck, and dodged. One tree in particular had taken a bashing, and Nadja hoped she had done no irreparable damage.

Bubbles broke the surface of the water as she sat up and smoothed back her wet hair. After a quick survey of the bath, she was glad to find herself still alone. Thankfully last night's performance had preceded their day off. By keeping to the untrodden areas of the grounds and away from the dining hall, she'd avoided seeing anyone. And by anyone, she meant Pax.

Her mind flashed to the night before. The heat in his eyes. His body pressed against hers.

Nadja groaned and slipped below the water's surface once more, reaching out to turn on the cold tap as she did so.

It hadn't been real.

How could she have been so stupid?

She recalled Laurel congratulating Pax on his performance. And that's all it had been. A performance. One he had played convincingly enough to fool her. And if Laurel's praise hadn't been enough to prove Nadja's foolishness, the memory of seeing the two of them kiss, on stage for the world to see, was.

Nadja released a few air bubbles, and the tightening in her chest subsided. She wondered if she could stay on the bottom of the tub for the rest of her life. She could definitely make it for a few minutes more.

When the cold water had done its job, Nadja reluctantly emerged from the bath, shivering as she toweled off and got dressed. She made her way back to her room, avoiding the glances of people she passed in the hallway.

"There you are," said Helaine as Nadja entered the room. She was propped against the pillows in her bed, and the hoarseness in her voice was little improved. "I've been wanting to talk to you all day."

Nadja gave her roommate an exhausted half smile.

Helaine had not been in their room when Nadja had returned the night before, for which she had been glad. And Nadja had slipped out early that morning before Helaine had woken up. She hadn't been ready to talk yet.

But after putting a day's time between herself and last night's performance, she was ready to handle whatever questions Helaine might pose.

"My, you look positively brown!" her roommate continued.

Nadja walked over to her nightstand and picked up the silver mirror, a warm reminder of her mother. How she wished she could talk to her.

Instead, she peered into the mirror and inspected her face. The fallow coloring she had developed from weeks spent mostly indoors was transformed into a deep tan. The effect gave her skin a radiant glow which stood in stark contrast to the gloom she felt on the inside.

"It was such a lovely day. I spent most of it enjoying the outdoors."

"It must have been nice to keep you out until sundown. Not that I blame you. If I could have gone out today, I would have. I think the fresh air would do me good, but Petrin thought otherwise." Helaine smiled shyly at the mention of her beau.

"I'm sure he prescribed a more enjoyable remedy," said Nadja, arching an eyebrow at her roommate. Helaine would balk at the insinuation, but she was just so easy to tease, Nadja couldn't help herself.

True to form, Helaine's blush stretched up from her neck all the way to the tips of her hair. "Certainly not!" she croaked, then giggled. "But he did bring me supper." She gestured to the table where a bowl of stew, a roll, and a glass of water sat untouched.

Nadja's empty stomach rumbled at the sight of the meal.

"You can have it if you like," said Helaine. "I just can't right now." She reached up and patted her throat.

Helaine didn't need to offer twice. Nadja sat down at the table and scooped up a large spoonful of the stew. The lamb and potatoes were seasoned to perfection, and she ate greedily, just now realizing how hungry she had been.

Helaine didn't waste another minute. "Tell me about last night," she chirped.

Nadja's chewing slowed as she studied her stew, trying to find the right words. She decided on a banal reply. "There was a nice turnout."

"I'm sure. But how did *you* do?" Helaine's eyes sparkled with mischief.

"Oh, well . . . I—"

"Because I heard you had quite the effect." Helaine sat up straight and grinned at Nadja.

Nadja was puzzled and more than a little hurt her friend would take pleasure in her public humiliation. She had been the only performer who actually drove away paying patrons with her singing. "Quite the effect" was putting it mildly.

Nadja swallowed her mouthful. "Things didn't go exactly as I had hoped."

"I should think not," said Helaine, bouncing on the bed. "I mean, it sounds to me like you gave Music for

Enjoyment a whole new meaning. 'Steamy,' is how Vatara put it."

"Vatara?"

"Yes, she stopped by to check in on me this morning. She said you and Pax practically set the stage on fire." Helaine giggled. "I didn't know you got him to fill in for me. Of course, I doubt our version of the song would have carried the same *feeling* as the one you two sang last night."

"It was a last-minute decision," Nadja mumbled, then shook her head. "Wait, I don't understand. Pax is a great singer, yes, but me, hardly. And, steamy? Half of the crowd walked out in the middle of the song."

Helaine giggled again. "So I heard. Well, I don't know about *all* the people who left, but Vatara said Selina and Quinton snuck out to find a more private location."

"Huh? Quinton, the percussionist Quinton? I didn't even know they were friends."

"No! Selina would barely give him the time of day, what with him being from the edge of the Waste and her fancying herself above all that. Evidently, they've both been secretly admiring each other for a while, but never did anything about it. I guess you and Pax *inspired* them." Helaine's giggles grew irksome.

Nadja furrowed her brow and rubbed her hand across the ridges there, remembering the scene in The Hen and Harp right after her performance. The missing people, the kissing couples. Was it possible her performance hadn't been as awful as she'd imagined? Maybe it had even been good?

"Oh, he stopped by here around lunchtime looking for you."

"Quinton?"

Helaine sighed. "No, silly. Pax." She gave Nadja a knowing look.

Nadja's stomach dropped. She was glad she'd been out all day. She wasn't ready to face him. Not yet.

Nadja looked back down at her bowl. "I wonder what he wanted," she said noncommittally, before shoving the roll into her mouth.

"Hmm," said Helaine, tapping a finger on her chin. "Yes I wonder what he wanted. Maybe he wanted to study, or return your music, or discuss the weather. Or *maybe* he wanted to see you. Since, you know, you two are obviously more than just friends. At least, based on what Vatara saw."

"Vatara doesn't know what she's talking about," snapped Nadja. "The next time you see her, please correct her before she goes around gossiping about things which aren't true."

"I'm sorry," said Helaine. Her scratchy voice, barely above a whisper, carried with it none of the cheerful exuberance it had a moment before.

"No, I'm sorry," said Nadja, rubbing her forehead again. "I didn't mean to snap at you. I'm just exhausted, that's all." She stood up from the table and trudged over to sit on the edge of Helaine's bed. "We did give a convincing performance, so it's no wonder Vatara is confused."

"It must have been a good one because she's sure you two are a couple."

"If you have any trouble persuading her otherwise, tell her to talk to Laurel."

"Why Laurel?"

"Because as soon as we finished singing, Laurel and Pax celebrated with some kissing of their own." The words tasted sour in Nadja's mouth.

"Oh." Helaine's shoulders drooped. "I'm sorry."

Nadja forced a laugh. "Why? We're just good friends, after all." She patted her roommate's leg before rising and moving to her own bed. "But enough talk about that. You need to get some rest."

Helaine fell back against her pillows and groaned. "I can't. I've only managed a few minutes here and there all day. I can't seem to get comfortable. Every time I close my eyes all I can think of is how much my throat hurts and how much I'm missing because I'm stuck in bed." She stuck out her lower lip.

"Anything I can do for you?" asked Nadja.

"No," Helaine pouted. She punched her pillows a few times before snuggling down into her blankets.

Nadja made a round about the room, blowing out the lanterns. She returned to her bed and nearly fell into it. Her joints and muscles were paying for that day's workout. She'd pushed herself too hard. She would have to skip training tomorrow to give her body time to recover.

Nadja yawned and stretched out before curling up on her side. She pulled the soft blankets over her head in a feeble attempt to smother all the thoughts swirling around inside her mind. The memory of being wrapped in Pax's arms juxtaposed a vision of Laurel in his embrace. She squeezed her eyes shut and rolled over to her other side.

"Nadja?" Helaine's crackled whisper hung in the darkness.

"Yes?"

"Will you sing me a lullaby?"

Nadja laughed at the ridiculousness of the request. Not a bitter laugh, but a true belly laugh which eased the tension in her shoulders and neck. "Are you sure you know what you're asking?"

"Of course," said Helaine. "I have heard you sing before, you know. We did rehearse together for the festival." She paused as Nadja's chuckles died down. "My mother used to sing to me when I was little, and it helped me fall asleep. And you do have a nice voice whether or not you believe it." Helaine yawned. "And it has such a lovely smell. Like honeysuckle." She sighed.

Nadja rolled onto her back and put one arm behind her head. She stared up into the darkness, contemplating Helaine's request, her eyelids heavy with fatigue. "What did your mother's singing smell like?"

"Nothing. Never smelled anyone's singing before. Yours is the first."

Strange. But then again, Helaine's condition—talent?—was also something of a mystery. Perhaps it was evolving, responding to a new set of sounds. Nadja hoped not, for Helaine's sake.

"All right," Nadja yawned. "How can I refuse a sick friend?"

Nadja's eyes drifted closed. She sang her lullaby, sweet and low, all the while fighting the gentle grasp of sleep which threatened to pull her into its blissful oblivion. Her head swam and the darkness was palpable. Errant yawns punctuated phrases here and there, but she managed to stay awake long enough to carry the tune through to its completion.

When she finished singing, the room was hushed and still.

"Helaine?" she murmured.

A light snore came from Helaine's bed.

Nadja smiled and rolled over. Sleep overtook her in seconds.

Nadja slept fitfully all through the night. A menacing thunderstorm sprang up sometime after midnight, buffeting the shutters with rain and powerful gusts of wind. Bizarre visions of Baulo and Pax swam through her dreams, twisting and overlapping until she didn't know whom she was running to and whom she was running away from. The storm raged on until the wee hours of the morning as she slipped in and out of her restless slumber. As soon as a hint of indigo lightened the dreary sky, she gave up on sleep.

She climbed out of bed and crept to the wardrobe. At this early hour she didn't light any lanterns, making it difficult to see. But Helaine was still sound asleep, and Nadja hoped she would stay that way for at least a few more hours. The storm was moving on, and with Helaine's recovery still in the early stages, she could use as much sleep as she could get.

Nadja pulled on a pair of dark-gray pants and a burgundy tunic. At least, she hoped that's what they were. In the predawn darkness, everything was varying shades of the same color. She soaked a cloth in the cold water from her basin and tried to scrub the sleepiness from her face. The shock of the chilly water against her warm skin helped to rouse her and chase away a bit of the fog in her head. She hoped the cup of strong coffee awaiting her in the dining hall would take care of the rest of it.

Nadja hung the cloth over the side of the basin and turned back towards her bed. She had taken no more than two steps when her toes caught some invisible obstacle and sent her flying into the table and chairs. Her cup and bowl, right where she had left them the night before, leapt over the edge of the table and scattered across the floor. She managed to catch herself from following suit, but not before her chin slammed into the back of one of the chairs, sending it toppling over with a crash.

So much for making a stealthy escape.

A metallic tang swept across her tastebuds as blood leaked from where she had bit her tongue in the fall.

"Sorry," she ground out, righting herself and shuffling over to her bed. "I'll just be a minute." She hoped Helaine would be able to go back to sleep.

Nadja picked up the lantern from her bedside table and lit it. Her boots, the cause of all the commotion, were right where she had dropped them last night instead of under the edge of her bed where she normally kept them. Grumbling under her breath, she picked them up and put them on.

After putting the table in order, she went back to the basin to rinse out her mouth. Nadja frowned. The bleeding had already begun to subside, but the cup of coffee she was looking forward to would have to be postponed.

"Can I get anything for you before I go?" she called out.

Helaine gave no reply.

That was odd. The ruckus caused by Nadja's early-morning acrobatics had been loud enough to wake the dead, yet Helaine hadn't moved.

"Helaine?"

The silence which met her ears caused the skin along the back of her neck and shoulders to tingle in apprehension. No one could have slept through that.

An unexpected gust of wind slammed into the shutters, propelling her towards Helaine's bed. The sound of her boots on the stone floor magnified in the utter stillness of the room.

"Helaine," she said, this time louder.

Still, nothing.

The pretty white coverlet, one of Helaine's many personal touches, was a mound of ghostly gray in the middle of the bed. Nadja reached out and pulled it back.

Her friend lay there, unmoving. The lantern in Nadja's hands cast a trembling glow over Helaine's soft features. Nadja reached out, gripped Helaine's shoulder and shook it. Softly at first, then forcefully.

Nothing.

Nadja slammed the lantern down on the bedside table and patted Helaine's face.

"Helaine!" she shouted.

Still nothing.

Her stomach clenched.

Nadja shoved her hand under her friend's nose and froze.

Time stopped. Nadja held her breath. Even the lantern light, which bends to the will of every wayward breeze, stood unnaturally motionless.

Then, she felt it. The soft puffs of breath tickled her fingertips.

Nadja exhaled and placed her hand on Helaine's cheek.

"Helaine, wake up."

Chapter Twenty-Eight

Doctor Corinson stepped out of the infirmary's office. He gave Nadja a tight nod, then strode from the room.

Nadja rubbed her eyes with the pads of her hands, trying to blot out the weariness threatening to pull them closed. She leaned against the stiff, wooden chair back and stretched out her legs. A cramp seized her right calf, and she yanked her knee to her chest, grabbing her toes and flexing her foot. The hard seat had caused her rear end to go numb, and the sudden movement made her fleshy rump feel like the world's largest pincushion. She groaned.

"If you keep that up, I'll order you into one of the empty beds. We have a few to spare." Nurse Silvers surprised her. His guttural voice sounded more threatening than it was. "Besides, you look like you could use some rest yourself."

The infirmary was well equipped to handle several patients. With the foundation of Amrantir's society and culture resting firmly on the Music Conservatory's graduates, the current delegate prime felt it prudent to provide the best medical care possible to the students. Nurse Silvers was in full-time residence to handle most complaints, and the doctors living within the city were available at a moment's notice should an emergency arise requiring skills exceeding Nurse Silvers's. Doctor Corinson was one of those doctors. He and Nurse Silvers had just finished conferring about Helaine's condition.

Nadja looked up at the brawny man standing next to her, checking Helaine's temperature. His fingers, bearing a striking resemblance to a plate of giant sausages, tenderly grasped Helaine's wrist, checking her pulse before tucking her arm back under her blanket.

"What did you find?" asked Nadja.

The candlelight bounced off of his shiny head as he shook it. Nadja wondered if the impressive, if not slightly foreboding, red beard he wore on his chin had ever extended all the way to the top of his head. Hardly the image of "nurse" Nadja had in mind when she had first met him, his gruff appearance belied a tender heart. Nurse Silvers's knowledge and bedside manner were impeccable, and Nadja knew Helaine couldn't be in more capable hands.

"Isn't there anything else we can do?" she asked.

"Right now, there's nothing *to* do other than keep her comfortable," he replied. "It doesn't appear to be a complication caused by the throat infection. Her symptoms are subsiding and her temperature has returned to normal. Her heartbeat and breathing are strong and regular. Her pupils are responsive, and her movement isn't impaired. If she was comatose, we would expect to see the opposite."

He reached up and ran a hand down the length of his bushy beard. A deep *V* formed between his eyebrows. "If I didn't know better, I'd say she was asleep."

"Then why can't we wake her?" Nadja demanded.

"That's an excellent question. And one we are working on." Nurse Silvers patted her shoulder. "Doctor Corinson has gone to consult some of the other physicians. I expect they'll all be paying us a visit soon."

Nadja stood up, her spine popping and creaking as it realigned, and paced to the end of the bed, rubbing the back of her neck.

"And that was an honest offer," said Nurse Silvers, gesturing to an empty bed in the corner of the room. "You need sleep. Better yet, why don't you go back to your room? I'm sure you'll sleep better there, and I will send for you if there's any change. I'll have Timothy bring up some supper."

The young servant had been checking in on them from time to time, carrying messages and fetching things as needed.

Was it already supper time?

"There is nothing you can do here."

"Mmm mmm." Nadja shook her head. Helaine was more than her roommate. She was her best friend. Nadja wasn't about to run off and leave her alone. Not now.

What would she be like when she woke up? If she woke up? Nadja needed to be there to reassure her.

"Suit yourself," said Nurse Silvers. "But the offer doesn't expire. That bed is yours if you want it."

Nadja nodded. "Thank you."

A sound at the door drew their attention.

Petrin rushed into the infirmary and straight to Helaine's bedside. Worry etched lines across his thin face, and his eyes searched her body, looking for an explanation.

"What happened?" he asked.

"She won't wake up," sighed Nadja.

"Why not?"

Nadja shrugged. "She seemed all right when we went to bed last night, but this morning . . . " She held her palms up, empty of any answers.

Petrin turned to Nurse Silvers and began peppering him with questions. As his body shifted, Nadja spotted someone over his shoulder. Pax stood in the doorway.

Nadja's feet moved towards him of their own accord.

In three strides, he closed the distance between them and wrapped his arms around her, crushing her against him. Nadja leaned into him, burying her face in his chest and allowing him to support her weight. Her shoulders relaxed as he hugged her.

Neither of them spoke.

For a few beautiful moments Nadja savored the solace of his embrace. In the security of Pax's strong arms, there was nothing too terrible which couldn't be overcome.

But Pax's comfort was just for the moment. His heart belonged to Laurel.

Nadja stiffened and pulled away from him. She refused to torment herself any longer with thoughts of things which would never be. With a quick nod she turned away, but not before catching the troubled expression in his eyes.

She returned to Helaine's bedside where Petrin was finishing his interrogation of Nurse Silvers.

"Thank you for staying with her," said Petrin as Nurse Silvers returned to his office. "I would have come sooner if I had known she was here." He shot Nadja an accusatory glance.

"How did you find out?" she asked.

"Grandmaster Gilmoren. He asked if I'd deliver his best wishes to her when she wakes up. You can imagine my confusion."

Nadja felt a twinge of guilt. She had been so worried about Helaine, she hadn't even thought about letting anyone else know. She told Petrin as much.

"I know," he sighed. "It's all right." He reached out and took Helaine's hand. His eyes were forlorn as he studied her face.

Nadja squeezed his other hand. Then, she moved away from the bed to give him time alone with Helaine.

For all of its stark and sterile appearance, the bed in the corner was looking more and more appealing to

Nadja. She shuffled over to it and flopped down on the edge. The mattress was much kinder to her rear end than the chair had been. She was about to lie back when Pax joined her.

The mattress sank under his weight, shifting her balance and causing her to lean inadvertently against his shoulder. The unexpected contact sent goosebumps racing down her arm, and she clumsily shifted away from his touch.

"How are you?" he asked.

"I'm fine," she replied. "It's Helaine you should be worried about."

"I am. We all are. But Nurse Silvers is doing his job taking care of her." His eyes searched her face. "When was the last time you slept?"

"Last night," she said defensively, " . . . some."

"Listen, Petrin wants to stay here with her tonight. Why don't you go back to your room and sleep in your own bed?" He bounced up and down on the mattress, grinning. "Though, I know this one is very tempting."

Nadja rolled her eyes and returned his grin with a weary look. "I don't want to leave her. She'll need a familiar face when she wakes up."

"And Petrin can be that, if she wakes up tonight."

He was right. Helaine would be just as happy to see Petrin as she would be to see Nadja. Maybe even a little more.

Nadja conceded. "All right." As she rose from the bed, Pax jumped up beside her.

"I'll walk you to your room," he said, taking hold of her hand.

"No," she snapped. Nadja jerked back as if she had been stung. Her hand tingled from his touch.

Pax frowned.

"What I meant was," she said, steadying her voice, "I can make it there myself, thank you." She turned and marched out of the infirmary. She needed to put as much distance between herself and Pax as she could. And fast. Why did his touch do such things to her? She knew he didn't have feelings for her. But her body wouldn't accept the truth.

"Nadja, wait," Pax called after her.

She felt his hand on her elbow and gritted her teeth. He came around in front of her, and she ordered her features in as placid an arrangement as possible.

"Look," he began, "about the Heartstide Festival—"

"Yes," Nadja interrupted. "I appreciate you coming to my aid. I hate to admit I have a bit of stage fright when it comes to singing." She clenched and unclenched her hands. Under no circumstances did she want to discuss their performance.

"I was glad to help. Listen—"

"That's why Helaine and I were planning a duet," she hurried on. "Of course, our delivery would have been different. But your performance was convincing." *Why did she say that?* She hurried on. "At—at least if the gossip is to be believed." *That wasn't any better.*

Nadja bit the inside of her cheek. This is exactly where she did not want the conversation to go. She mustered up a smile and said brightly, "So, anyway. Thank you again."

She moved to step around him, but he countered her. "Nadja," he said, forcing her to meet his gaze. "We need to talk."

Her shoulders slumped, and she closed her eyes. "Please," she whispered. "Not now."

"Why not?"

"I just . . . I can't."

Because she couldn't handle his gentle letdown. Because hearing him talk about his feelings for Laurel while her best friend lay unconscious in a bed in the next room was too much heartache for one day.

A sudden, panicked yell from inside the infirmary rang through the hall. Nadja's heart stopped. She spun around and ran back into the room with Pax on her heels.

Nurse Silvers rushed from his office while Petrin frantically gestured towards Helaine. When Nadja approached her bed, she saw the cause of the commotion. Helaine's previously tranquil face was contorted and distressed. Her breathing was punctuated and irregular, and her eyelids bumped and rolled as her eyes darted back and forth behind them. No wonder Petrin was in a panic.

Nadja breathed a sigh of relief and reached out to Petrin, giving his arm a gentle squeeze.

"She's just dreaming," said Nurse Silvers, placing his palm against Helaine's forehead and cheek before checking her pulse once more.

"Dreaming?" Petrin's voice was strained. "That must be a terrible dream."

"She's been doing this every few hours," Nadja reassured him. "It's nothing to worry about."

"Is everything all right?"

All four heads turned towards the door as Grandmaster Kero entered the infirmary.

Nadja winced. In her concern for Helaine, she had forgotten about her lesson. It was one thing to skip out on her regular classes. They would go on with or without her body at a table. But, it was another matter to miss a private lesson.

Meliina noted their concerned expressions. "Evidently not," she said, her small strides hurrying her over to join them.

Nadja took a step towards her and said in a low voice, "I am so sorry I missed our lesson."

Meliina shushed her with a wave of her hand. "Nonsense. With Helaine in such a state as she is, it's no wonder you took the day off." Then, with a gleam in her eye she added, "Just be sure you don't make a habit of it."

Nadja nodded. "How did you know about Helaine?"

Meliina's eyes grew wide. "Silly girl. The entire faculty is informed whenever any student visits the infirmary, even if for something as benign as a bee sting.

Next to the instruction you receive here, keeping you well is one of our highest priorities. We all knew about Helaine's condition within an hour of her arriving here this morning."

"That explains how Grandmaster Gilmoren knew," said Petrin. "I had wondered."

"Has there been any progress?" Meliina asked Nurse Silvers.

"No, ma'am. Doctor Corinson has gone to research and confer with some of the other physicians. I hope to see him again by morning."

"Mmm." Meliina nodded. "When was she last awake?"

"Last night," Nadja answered.

"You were with her when she fell asleep?"

"Yes."

Meliina's eyes narrowed. "Can you tell me what happened before she went to sleep?"

"I was away most of the day. She was in bed when I returned, still not feeling well. She said she had not been able to sleep much all day. She probably fell asleep around—"

"No, no, more details please," said Meliina. "What exactly happened when you returned?"

"Oh. Well, as I said, Helaine still wasn't feeling well when I returned. Petrin had brought her a plate of food, but she couldn't eat it, so I did."

The corners of Petrin's mouth drooped. Nadja just shrugged.

"We talked for a while about," she cast a sideways glance at Pax, "some things. She mentioned Vatara had also been to visit her earlier that day.

"Once we finished talking, I put out the lights and got into bed. That's when Helaine said she was having trouble sleeping." Nadja snickered. "She asked me to sing her a lullaby."

"A lullaby?" asked Petrin, with a wistful glance at Helaine.

"Yes, I know. Funny, huh?"

"And did you?" asked Meliina.

"Yes. By the time I finished, she had fallen asleep. It wasn't until the next morning when I tried to wake her that I discovered there was something wrong."

Meliina's lips pulled into a thin line.

"So it wasn't her food," offered Pax. "What about her medicine?"

"That was one of the first things I checked," said Nurse Silvers. "Nothing amiss there. It's quite the mystery."

"Yes," said Meliina thoughtfully. She studied Helaine for another moment, tapping one of her small fingers against her chin. Then, she straightened. "Well, it looks like you have everything in hand, Nurse Silvers, as always. Please, let me know when she wakes."

"Yes, ma'am."

"And the rest of you, get some sleep." She looked pointedly at Nadja. "Especially you."

Meliina reached up and patted Nadja on the cheek, a troubled look flitting across her eyes. Then, she turned and left the room.

"I will stay with her tonight," said Petrin. "Grandmaster Kero is right, you need a break."

Seizing the chance to make a clean escape, Nadja nodded. "You're right. I could use time to myself." There, now Pax couldn't follow her without seeming ungallant. "Please come get me if there is the slightest change in her."

Petrin nodded. "You can depend on it."

Chapter Twenty-Nine

The next day passed much like the first. Helaine slept on while Nadja and Petrin took shifts at her bedside. Doctor Corinson paraded in half a dozen other physicians to examine Helaine, but none of them found anything medically wrong with her.

On the morning of the third day, while Petrin and Pax were attending their String Tech class, Nadja sprawled out on the bed next to Helaine's and plodded her way through *Folk Tunes of the Northern Realms*. It was the final, and by far most substantial, book Grandmaster Kero had assigned her to read before the winter break. She had put it off because it was as dry as toast. But, since she suddenly had an abundance of time on her hands, she thought she ought to put it to good use.

She'd rather be playing music instead of reading about it. Nurse Silvers said it would be a welcome change to the usual quiet ambience of the infirmary, and they didn't have to worry about disturbing Helaine. But, Nadja had misplaced her flute, and she had searched her room thoroughly with no luck. The last time she remembered seeing it was during the Heartstide Festival. She'd asked Pax about it yesterday, but he didn't know where it was. A trip back to The Hen and Harp was in order as soon as Helaine recovered.

Nadja rubbed her eyes and tried to focus on the words in front of her.

"The Grenyan Cogs Reels, a colloquial derivation from the rightly named Cruxnik Reels, is a subset of dance songs originating from the late Tynan Era known as Pastoral Industry Songs, or Industry Songs. This type of song seeks to impress upon the listener a sense of the rural worker at his everyday task, while emphasizing the delight which comes from reaping the fruits of his labor.

Cogs Reels can be best identified by the incessant quarter note rhythm, commonly carried along the bass line, which attempts to mimic the steady tick-tick-tick-tick of gear teeth set in perpetual motion above a millstone by the miller himself.

Not to be confused with Kogs Reels, Cogs Reels lack a substantial . . ."

"Ugh," Nadja groaned, letting her head fall onto the book with a thud. She took a deep breath. The scent of paper and leather filled her nostrils. If she wasn't careful, she'd fall asleep right there and wake up in a puddle of drool.

"Nadja?"

Her head snapped up. Helaine's dark eyes stared back at her through heavy lids.

"Oh my—" said Nadja, scrambling off her bed and over to Helaine's. "Helaine!" She reached out and smoothed Helaine's hair back from her face. Her forehead was cool and dry, not a trace of fever.

Helaine smiled up at her. "What are you doing?" Then she blinked, taking in her surroundings. Confusion overtook her relaxed features, and she tried to sit up. "Where are we?"

"You're fine," said Nadja, placing her hands on Helaine's shoulders and helping her to lie back. "We're in the infirmary."

"Why?" Helaine's voice rose in pitch, her confusion transforming into panic. "Is something wrong with me?"

Hearing the sound of voices, Nurse Silvers rushed from his office.

Nadja sidestepped the question. "You were sleeping. How do you feel?"

Helaine swallowed hard, then thought for a moment. "Heavy. Like I weigh a ton. But my throat feels so much better now." She turned her head. "Nurse Silvers," she said, offering him a weak smile. "It's so nice to see you, though I would have rather not seen you under these circumstances. Of course, I'm not sure what these circumstances are."

Nurse Silvers completed his cursory examination. He smiled down at Helaine. "We are glad to have you back from your little vacation to dreamland, my dear. You've been asleep for some time, so it's natural you should feel foggy and a little out of sorts."

"How long have I been asleep?"

"Three days."

Helaine bolted upright in the bed. "Three days?! I don't understand. How does that happen? Is something wrong with me? I mean, I know something *was* wrong with me, but I thought it was just a sore throat. It doesn't hurt anymore. Petrin had the same thing. Oh no, Petrin! Is he all right? Did the same thing happen to him?" Her hands gripped and released the sheets over and over as she searched the remaining beds for any sign of him.

"No, no, no," Nadja cooed, reaching over to still Helaine's frenetic hands. "Petrin is fine. In fact, we've been taking turns staying with you while you've been here."

Nurse Silvers chuckled. "That's a lot more spunk than I would have expected so soon after waking. It's a good sign. From what I can tell, you appear in good health. But, you need to try to relax. We all have a lot of questions, and I know Doctor Corinson will want to examine you as soon as possible."

The infirmary became a hive of activity. Nadja sent Timothy to notify Petrin that Helaine was awake, and he returned with both Petrin and Pax. Doctor Corinson was not long behind them, poking and prodding Helaine, and asking her the same questions she had already answered over and over again. The grandmasters stopped by as their schedules permitted, so Nadja wasn't surprised when Grandmaster Kero scuttled in the door.

"How are you, Helaine?" Meliina asked, patting Helaine's hand in her calming manner.

"All of this fuss is making me nervous, but I really do feel fine."

Meliina smiled and nodded. "Good."

Doctor Corinson swooped in to do yet another test, and Meliina stepped away from the bed, pulling Nadja along with her. "Would you join me in my office, Nadja?" she asked. "I haven't seen you in a few days, and we have some catching up to do."

"Of course," said Nadja, collecting her book from where it lay open on the bed. She had already missed two lessons, so there was certainly work which needed to be made up. She followed Meliina down the slate-tiled hallway, trying to come up with the best way to tell her she'd misplaced her instrument.

Meliina ushered Nadja into the tidy office and closed the door behind her.

"Would you like some tea?" Meliina asked.

Nadja was surprised. Meliina had never offered her refreshment. "That would be nice," she said, hesitantly.

"Please, have a seat," said Meliina, pointing at one of the two soft chairs near her desk instead of the hard-back chairs they usually assumed for lessons.

Surprised again, Nadja sat and rested the book across her lap.

"You can put that on my desk. I know how heavy it is," said Meliina with a twinkle in her eye.

Nadja obeyed, hoisting the book onto the desk and resuming her seat. She should be pleased at the seating arrangement. It meant there would be no playing today.

Maybe that would buy her enough time to find her flute before Grandmaster Kero was any wiser. Still, something about Meliina's demeanor gave Nadja a sinking feeling.

"How have you been?" asked Meliina, handing Nadja a sturdy mug filled with a sweet smelling herbal brew.

"Well," replied Nadja before taking a sip. Peach and ginger. Delicious. "Tired, but fine."

Meliina sank into the seat opposite Nadja and sipped her tea, studying Nadja with interest. "And Helaine? Tell me about what happened when she awoke."

Nadja recounted the events of the morning while Meliina listened intently, at intervals offering small nods of encouragement.

At last, Nadja finished her narrative.

"And she remembers nothing?" asked Meliina.

"Nothing after I finished singing to her. Actually, she was already tired. I'm pretty sure she was asleep before I finished."

"More's the better," Meliina muttered.

Nadja flushed. She knew how the grandmaster regarded her singing. And, in her own opinion, rightly so. Still, the comment stung.

"What about you?" asked Meliina.

Nadja cast Meliina a questioning glance above the rim of her mug before taking another sip. "What about me?"

"How were you feeling that night?"

Nadja thought back to her day spent fighting herself in the orchard. It seemed like ages ago, but her muscles had only just recovered from the abuse.

"Exhausted," she said finally. "Like I could sleep for days. We turned in at the same time, and I hardly remember finishing the song before I fell asleep, too."

"Ahh," said Meliina, giving Nadja a knowing nod as if that explained everything. Her eyes turned thoughtful and Nadja looked down into her mug, avoiding her gaze. The air between them was suddenly heavy with something unspoken, and Nadja didn't want to be the one to break the silence. Whatever it was, she feared it was something best left unsaid.

Meliina reached towards the book atop her desk and ran her fingers along its cover. "How is your reading coming along?"

Relieved by the change of subject, Nadja's tension eased. "I'm almost done. But I have to admit, *that*," she said, pointing to the book, "is not what I would consider light reading."

Meliina smiled. "No, I suppose not. But, it is worth your time to study. Tell me," she paused, taking another sip of tea, her forceful gulp audible. "What did you think of *Musica Antiqua and Other Lost Arts*?"

"Much better," said Nadja, brightening. "It was enlightening, and much easier to read. I didn't realize Amrantir was originally settled by immigrants from Grenyan."

"Yes, the land of your forefathers," said Meliina, arching an eyebrow.

"Mmm hmm." Nadja's affirmation echoed in her mug as she downed the rest of her tea.

"But, they weren't the first ones here."

"The Mevocali."

"Yes. A fascinating people, don't you think? The Battle at Annuay was a tragedy."

"Maybe," said Nadja, tilting her head. "It would be sad for that to happen to any people. But then, what would Amrantir be like if they had survived? I think most people assume we'd all be under some kind of Mevocali mind control by now. The Mevocali would still be alive, but would our lives even be worth living?"

"One wonders. But nothing in their history suggests any tendency towards violence. The Mevocali were, from what we can tell, a peaceful people. They used their gifts mainly to heal the body and mind, something we master musicians have never managed. Until their powers evolved, the only thing about them which could be troublesome were the untrained young ones."

"Yes," agreed Nadja. "But, according to *Musica Antiqua*, they had rules in place to prevent that from being a problem."

"True," said Meliina. "But, what if someone broke those rules?"

Nadja chuckled. "Then I suppose they'd be in for trouble on all fronts."

She smiled at Meliina, but the grandmaster's face was full of something Nadja couldn't comprehend. Worry? Reluctance? Definitely not mirth.

That heavy air settled between them once again, and Nadja swallowed hard. She rubbed her damp palms along the top of her thighs as a sinking sensation pulled at her stomach. For what reason, she did not know.

At last, Meliina spoke. "It was the Pantomarian folk tune which first caught my attention."

Again with the abrupt change of subject. Nadja wondered where this new line of conversation was going.

"Usually, when my students have trouble internalizing a piece, I have them learn to sing it first. The mind can more clearly focus on the essence of the song when it's not also burdened with the technicality of manipulating the instrument. So naturally, I asked you to do just that."

Nadja cringed. "But that didn't work for me. I know it frustrated you."

Meliina set her unfinished tea on a round, flat piece of cork situated equidistant between the class notebook and wooden metronome neatly arranged on her desktop.

"No, *I* wasn't frustrated. You were."

"Well, disappointed. Or angry. I could see it on your face as clearly as a full moon at midnight."

"No," Meliina repeated. "That was you."

"What are you talking about?" asked Nadja, a hint of annoyance lacing her words. How could Grandmaster

Kero sit across from her and deny her reaction when it had been so obvious at the time?

Meliina leaned forward, resting her hands on her knees. "How did *you* feel about it?"

"Frustrated. I wasn't getting it, and you kept pushing. Like trying to milk a bull," Nadja smiled wryly, "you weren't going to get what you hoped for. But you had me sing it over and over again."

"And every time I corrected you," Meliina interrupted, "you became more agitated. I didn't notice it at first. The oppressive weight bearing down on my shoulders. The way the air in the room warmed until I began to sweat. My feelings were suddenly not my own. I grew more angry and frustrated and defeated every time you tried to sing a phrase. I fought this overwhelming urge to grab you by the shoulders and shake you, all the while knowing it was not *me* entertaining such thoughts. They were coming from you."

Nadja stared at Meliina incredulously. Was her teacher having a mental break? It was one thing to feel empathy for someone. But that burden lay with the empath, not the person projecting their feelings. It was impossible to force your emotions on another individual.

"Then this happened with Helaine. Simply a lullaby." Meliina spoke the words with a dismissive wave of her hand. "But how were you feeling when you sang for her?"

Nadja didn't reply. She held her breath, trying to slow her increasing heartbeat.

"Like you could sleep for days," Meliina said softly, repeating Nadja's own words back to her. "The doctors can examine Helaine all they want, but they will not find the cause of her long sleep. Not unless they look to you."

The mug in Nadja's hand trembled, and she banged it down on Meliina's desk, heedless of the precision with which the grandmaster's notebooks and music paraphernalia were arranged. She shot up from her seat and paced over to a bookcase.

"You're blaming Helaine's illness on me?" she practically shouted. "That's a stretch. How could I have caused her condition?"

"Nadja," said Meliina, rising smoothly from her chair and folding her hands in front of her. "Why do you think I asked you to read *Musica Antiqua*?"

"To further my education, obviously," said Nadja sarcastically.

"There's a reason Mevocali stayed amongst their own people. If the ability manifested itself and the wielder was not properly trained, it could have damaging effects. The power behind the gift depends as much on the emotion of the singer as on the song itself."

Nadja whirled on Meliina. "What are you saying?"

Meliina smiled sadly at her. "Come now. You're a bright young woman. Haven't you pieced it together?"

No.

"That's impossible," Nadja spat. "The ability is passed through bloodlines. I couldn't be what you think I am."

"That's why I sought out your uncle. I hoped he might illuminate the situation," said Meliina.

Nadja froze, remembering the day she ran into him coming out of Meliina's office. Her pulse slammed against the sides of her head like two drum mallets beating a quick tempo. She took a ragged breath.

"And what did he say?" she asked, meeting Meliina's eyes.

Meliina pursed her lips. "I think it's best you speak to him about the particulars."

No!

Nadja didn't need to speak to him. Whatever he'd said had done nothing to dissuade Grandmaster Kero's suspicions. Could it be true? Was she really what Grandmaster Kero suspected?

Mevocali.

As soon as the word entered her brain, the room started to spin. She reached out and steadied herself against the bookcase. Her mind flashed through all the times she sang in recent memory. One by one, events locked into place.

The Heartstide performance with Pax. Her feelings for him ran deep and strong, and she had allowed that to come through in the song. Could it have been more than just the song choice which led the audience in an amorous direction?

Then there was the night after she had fled the Wanderer camp. She'd been alone and afraid. She had known she was saying goodbye to the only life she had ever known, and she'd poured out her grief in song. The next morning, every living thing around her was dead.

Dead. Could she have killed Helaine? The thought struck her like a knife to the gut, making her suck in her breath. She had almost killed Baulo.

Baulo!

Suddenly it made sense. She hadn't sung to Baulo. But Grandmaster Kero said it was as much the emotion behind the song as the song itself which held the power. And behind her strange vocalizations—her scream—she had only one thought. And she had felt it with an intensity she had never felt before.

Stop.

Stop what you are doing.

And he did.

Stop being . . .

And he almost had.

Nadja pinched the bridge of her nose. She had been wrong. She did need to speak with her uncle. Her entire world just turned on its head, leaving her with countless questions. And he was one person who might have answers.

She stumbled to the door, still dizzy from the revelation.

"Where are you going?" asked Meliina, reaching out a steadying hand.

"To see my uncle."

"You won't find him today, I'm afraid. The Delegation has convened, so he's in Chansey."

Nadja's eyes narrowed. Clearly, her uncle's relationship with Meliina was closer than she thought.

She jerked away from Meliina's hand and gritted her teeth. "Then I'll pack for warm weather."

Chapter Thirty

As Nadja passed out of the city gates onto the wharf, she was struck with the same tingling sense of anticipation she'd felt the first time she'd crossed that threshold. Just like before, her whole life was a jumbled mess, and her uncle held the key to setting it right.

The wharf was as lively and noisy as ever. The hot midday sun glinted off of her blowpipe as she walked. With the Delegation in session she must remain vigilant. Baulo was in Cantio, and until she got out of the city, she would have to watch her back. It would be easy enough to go unnoticed in the horde, which could be a good or bad thing, depending on whom she ran into.

Everyone was too focused on their own business to take notice of her. She made her way easily to the Montgomery & Co. office. Instead of going inside, however, she circled around the building to the back door. She leaned her blowpipe against the side of the building and pulled her pack around in front.

She had gone straight to her room when she'd left Meliina's office earlier that morning. After she had dug her pack out of the back of her wardrobe, she packed lightly, just enough for a couple days. As she had tossed in the small tub of Pax's healing ointment and pocketed some of the pearls her mother had given her, she'd formulated a plan to get to her uncle.

Getting to Chansey as fast as possible was the goal. Boats filled the Cantio harbor, moving things in and out of Amrantir every hour. But those carrying passengers only departed twice a week, and Nadja didn't have time to wait two days for the next departure. Fortunately, she knew someone who had plenty of boats. Unfortunately, he never allowed passengers.

Nadja reached into her pack and removed the small key her uncle had given her when she had lived with him. Then, it had been mostly so she could keep herself locked in. Now, it would help her leave.

She tossed a quick glance over her shoulder to make sure no one was paying attention before she slipped the key into the lock. A slight turn, a smooth *click*, and she was in. She slipped through the door as silently as possible, pulling her blowpipe in behind her. Once she was in the little stairwell, she settled her blowpipe and pack against the back door and eased the boots off her feet.

Since he kept the back door locked, and Branson manned the front desk like a grumpy, immovable boulder, Uncle Tau never bothered to lock his office door. Nadja stepped softly as she entered the office, thankful for both her light frame and the rug covering most of the floor. Her boots probably wouldn't have made noise, but she didn't want to risk tracking in any evidence of her clandestine visit.

As she moved towards the imposing mahogany desk, she felt guilty to be sneaking through her uncle's private business. But, Branson would never give her the information she sought, even if she was Tau's niece.

Nadja sifted through the papers and notebooks on top of the desk with no luck. She carefully opened and closed the desk's drawers, picking through each one, being careful not to rearrange anything.

She found what she was looking for in the bottom drawer. The leather-bound notebook was soft, and she laid it on top of the desk, flipping through the pages until she found one marked with the current date. The page was divided into two columns, one titled Arrivals and the other, Departures. Nadja ran her finger down the Departures column looking for a barge headed to Chansey. There. Nereid's Wake. Departing in a few hours.

Nadja closed the notebook and placed it back in the drawer. She arranged the papers and books the way she had found them and crept back to the stairwell. Slipping her feet back into her boots, she shouldered her pack and picked up her blowpipe before easing her way back outside and locking the door behind her. She took a deep, calming breath and surveyed the area. Then, she headed towards the docks.

Until she began searching for the barge which would take her to Chansey, she hadn't realized how considerable her uncle's shipping company was. Nearly a third of the berths in the dock held barges baring the Montgomery & Co. flag. After a half hour of walking along the dock, she spotted Nereid's Wake.

The ship was abuzz with activity as four dockmen loaded crates into the bottom hold of the barge. The barges which ran the deeper waters of the Nostirivin were modified with the addition of large holds which sat below the water level. These holds allowed the boats to carry more cargo than the other flat-bottomed barges which traveled along the Kalmari. Nadja noticed one man standing guard near the gangplank, arms folded across his chest, keeping a watchful eye on the workers. The wooden boxes rocked back and forth, their contents jingling as the men carried them from the freight cart onto the boat with practiced steps. A worn, but sturdy-looking mule was hitched to the cart, staring at the wooden planks of the dock as if they were the most interesting things in his small world.

Keeping her stride as casual as possible to avoid any unwanted attention, she continued strolling past the boat for a minute or two before turning away from the dock, then doubling back. Now that she had found the boat, the next question was how to get aboard.

The dock swarmed with people and beasts, loading and unloading cargo from freighters and fishing vessels. The air carried an unmistakably fishy aroma. While the Montgomery & Co. barges limited their travels to the Nostirivin and Kalmari Rivers, some of the smaller fishing boats sailed directly into Cantio with holds full of saltwater fish pulled from the Shadow Sea.

Mountains of crates and barrels covered with sheets of canvas and burlap dotted the inland edge of the dock. These shipments were prepared for loading but awaiting the arrival of their respective freighters. Nadja glanced around before darting into one of the piles and pulling the cloth down behind her.

She stood motionless, waiting for someone to reach under the covering and snatch her out. But no one came. Keeping low, she inched her way towards the front of the pile, squeezing between boxes and around barrels. She knelt where two of the larger crates sat crosswise, creating a small, triangular patch of open ground. She brought her blowpipe forward and laid it across the top of a crate, using the far end of the pipe to lift the edge of the tarp just enough to see out.

Her position gave her a good sight line to Nereid's Wake. The berth next to the barge was empty, but there was no way to board from that side without being seen by the guard.

The mule nickered as the weight in the cart shifted, pulling against its harness. Nadja studied the animal; the one unpredictable variable in the well-rehearsed routine.

Sliding her right hand to her waist, she felt the soft leather of her dart pouch. She slipped out a dart and inserted it into the mouthpiece of her blowpipe, aiming the opposite end at the mule. She brought the pipe to her mouth and waited.

Nadja's breathing became shallow as the crowd of people flowed back and forth along the dock. Her clear shot flickered open and closed, open and closed, as bodies passed continuously between her and the mule. She had one shot.

She took a steadying breath and closed her eyes, listening to the sounds of the activity around her. When she opened them again, she took a deep breath and held it. Sighting the mule, she focused on its hindquarters. The next moment her shot cleared. She forced the air from her lungs in one swift blast, sending the dart through the crowd and directly into the mule's rump.

The animal's eyes rolled back in surprise. It let out a terrified bray and bolted down the dock, spilling boxes from the back of the cart. Passersby dove out of the way to avoid being trampled. The stunned dockmen dropped their crates and scrambled to intercept the mule, shaking their fists and shouting obscenities and death threats at the poor animal.

One of the crates laid broken where it fell. Silver serving pieces spilled out, creating a sparkling puddle upon which the splintered bits of wood floated. Nadja smiled. So that explained the jingling.

The guard warily eyed the silver. Nadja figured he could handle two or three would-be thieves, but if the crowd moved en masse, it would be easy pickings. The guard must have thought the same. He moved down the gangplank, snatching up a canvas tarp along the way. Nadja seized her opportunity.

As the guard swept the tarp over the mangled cargo, Nadja slipped from her hiding place and stole down the pier separating Nereid's Wake from the empty berth. The crowd was still in an uproar. Everyone's attention was focused on the mule, making it easy for Nadja to go unnoticed as she hopped over the side of the barge and scrambled down into the hold.

Nadja opened her mouth to breathe as the thick, stale air filled her lungs. It was cooler out of the sun's beaming rays, but the solid walls and lack of windows denied the river breeze entry into the humid room. The ceiling hung low, which wasn't a problem for Nadja, but she imagined most of the dockmen couldn't stand up straight in the room.

The hold was about half-full. Crates were marked with their destinations and arranged accordingly, creating thin walkways between each set. She slipped to the back of the room and hunkered down in a nook which she hoped would remain undisturbed until they reached Chansey.

A few hours later, with the recovered cargo stowed, the hold door closed, plunging Nadja into darkness. Finally, alone and without fear of discovery, she rolled her shoulders, ridding herself of the tension knotting her muscles.

The thoughts she'd kept at bay for most of the afternoon came flooding back with glaring intensity under the cover of darkness.

Mevocali.

The word sounded beautifully insidious as she mulled it over, luring her in with its musicality only to sting when she considered its full ramifications.

But how? And why hadn't her mother ever mentioned it to her? If Jamila knew of Nadja's abilities, she had never breathed a word. Maybe she didn't know. Not all Mevocali manifested their abilities. Perhaps Jamila merely passed it along to her daughter.

Or maybe it came through her father's line. Nadja wished, not for the first time, her father had lived long enough for her to know him. He was an only child, and his parents had died years ago. She was the last of his line. Perhaps she could have found a clue in her memories of him if he had lived.

One thing was certain. If she truly was Mevocali, she had inherited it from an ancestor. A person didn't *become* Mevocali like one might become a baker or a blacksmith. But, the strict rules which guided intermarriage between Man and Mevocali eliminated that possibility. If one of her Dunnan ancestors had married a Mevocali, they would have been required to stay with the Mevocali people. She would have never been born a Wanderer. In fact, the very possibility of her existence would have been eliminated when the Mevocali were destroyed.

Unless . . .

What was it Meliina said?

"What if someone broke those rules?"

Nadja pressed her fingers to her temples and squeezed her eyes shut trying to soothe the pounding which had set in. It was no use trying to figure it out now. All she had were questions. Her uncle was the one with the answers.

Muffled voices and the sound of footsteps overhead told Nadja they were about to cast off. She disassembled her blowpipe and tucked it under her pack, fluffing the bag up like a pillow. She stretched out and leaned her head against it. It would take two and a half days to reach Chansey. She might as well get comfortable.

Chapter Thirty-One

The sound of a latch being lifted startled Nadja awake. The gentle motion of the boat had lulled her to sleep minutes ago? Hours ago? In the windowless room she had no idea of the time.

She heard the door open, but no light entered the hold. Hours it was.

Her sleep-induced fog disappeared in an instant, and her senses went on high alert. She sat up and pulled her knees to her chest, making herself as small as possible.

The door closed, and Nadja breathed a sigh of relief. She began to relax against her pack once more when a warm glow lit up the far side of the hold. Snapping back to attention, her ears strained to pick up anything.

Faintly, she heard footsteps. Slow. Deliberate. The light grew brighter, pausing every few steps as if the intruder was making a methodical sweep of the room. His footsteps were nearly silent, and Nadja wondered if he was trying to keep his presence in the hold a secret. With nowhere else to go, she ducked her head between her knees and willed herself to become invisible.

A board creaked, and she flinched. Whoever he was, he was almost on top of her. Would he turn her in? Would they bring charges against her for stowing away? Would they drop her at the next port?

Nadja lifted her head and peered over her knees just as the lantern appeared around the corner, blinding her. She winced and threw up her hand to block the light. A large shadowy figure loomed behind the lantern, but Nadja couldn't make out his features.

"Look," she stammered. "I—"

"Shhh!" The figure swooped towards her, pressing his fingers to her mouth.

Nadja recoiled as the lantern lowered and the intruder's face came within inches of her own.

Her eyes widened.

Pax smirked at her. "Surprise," he whispered.

A mixture of relief and displeasure washed over Nadja, fighting for dominance against the apprehensive desire which always appeared when he did.

"What are you doing here?" she hissed, brushing away his fingers.

"I could ask you the same thing."

"I'm on my way to Chansey. Obviously."

"Why?"

"Business."

"And what was so important you needed to stow away instead of waiting a few days for one of the passenger boats?"

"*Personal* business." She glared at him. Why wouldn't he leave her alone? "Your turn. Why are you here?"

Pax gave her an exasperated look. "I should think the answer to that was also obvious."

Nadja regarded him flatly.

His eyes turned tender as he gathered his thoughts. "When Grandmaster Kero returned to the infirmary without you, I got concerned. She said you needed to speak with your uncle." Pax tilted his head and studied her. "You spent every waking moment with Helaine while she was unconscious. But, the minute she wakes up you disappear?" He shook his head.

"How did you find me?"

"I went to the shipping office. Saw you leaving out the back door and followed you to the docks." He flashed her one of his winning smiles. "That's quite a number you did on that mule."

Nadja was glad he couldn't see her face redden in the dim lantern light. He'd been watching her the whole time? Annoyance flashed in her eyes.

"Look," she said. "I don't know what you think you're doing here, but one stowaway is hard enough to hide. Two is just begging to be caught."

Pax leaned back and raised his eyebrows. "Then it's a good thing there is only one."

Nadja's eyes narrowed.

Pax spread his arms wide. "You are the only stowaway aboard this fine vessel," he continued, placing a hand over his heart. "I am just an honest sailor taking advantage of an opportunity."

"What are you talking about?"

"I'm talking about that stunt you pulled with the mule. One of the crew was injured trying to calm down the stubborn beast. The captain was in a bind to find someone to fill the spot so close to castoff time. So I volunteered."

Nadja bit her lip as her stomach clenched. Her actions had hurt someone. Guilt threatened to well up in her throat, but she swallowed it down. Pax had said "injured," not killed, and there was nothing she could do about it now. She pushed the thought aside and focused on her current problem.

"But you're not a sailor," she said, crossing her arms.

"Sure. I've always wanted to be a sailor. Just looking for an opportunity."

When Nadja didn't respond, Pax shrugged. "Well, that's what I told the captain."

"And he hired you like that?"

"Yep. Who knew the captain had a soft spot for green young men wanting to make a life at sea? You are looking at the newest deckhand of the Nereid's Wake," he said, inclining his head.

Nadja rolled her eyes. Even weathered boatmen weren't immune to Pax's silver tongue.

"Now come on. What's this personal business?"

When Nadja didn't immediately respond, Pax reached out and took her hand. This time she didn't pull away.

"Let me help you. Not that you need it," he added hurriedly when her hand twitched. "I know you're perfectly capable of taking care of yourself. But maybe I need to help you for my own sake." His gaze bounced back and forth between her eyes, probing, searching. His face was open, and his eyes were wide and hopeful. She felt her resolve weakening. "Haven't I proven you can trust me?" he asked.

Nadja sighed and glanced down at their joined hands. "It's not that. It's just . . ."

"Does it have something to do with your past?" He traced his thumb over the back of her hand in a soothing circular motion.

She nodded. "Grandmaster Kero shared some things with me I'm still trying to work through. I'm not ready to discuss them with anyone yet. I don't know if I'll ever be." She looked up at him and smiled weakly. "I don't understand it, and the more I think about it the more questions I have. One thing is certain though. My uncle has some of the answers I'm looking for."

"All right then. We'll get you to your uncle." Pax shifted his weight and stood, pulling Nadja up with him. As he stood, he dipped his chin to avoid hitting his head on the low roof, bringing his face close to hers. Goosebumps prickled the back of her neck.

"I need to get topside before someone wakes up and discovers me missing," he whispered. His breath stirred the hairs framing her face, sending a shiver down her spine. "Do you need anything?"

Nadia swallowed and shook her head, not trusting her voice.

"You should be fine down here. No one has any business in the hold until we dock in Chansey." Pax reached up with his other hand and tucked a stray hair behind her ear. He looked like he wanted to say something else but thought better about it and dropped his hand. "There's rain headed our way, so it'll get bumpy. Just do your best to keep quiet and stay out of sight. I'll check on you again tomorrow night." He lifted her hand to his lips and brushed a soft kiss across the back of her fingers, his eyes never leaving hers. Nadja sucked in a shallow breath as she watched him, too stunned to move. A faint smile tugged at his lips. "Get some rest."

Pax released her hand and bent to retrieve his lantern. As he turned to leave, Nadia watched the yellow glow grow dimmer and dimmer before vanishing. She heard the click of the latch signaling Pax's exit.

With a hard exhale Nadja sank to the floor and shook her head, trying to order her thoughts.

Three days ago Pax was embracing Laurel at the Heartstide Festival, and tonight he was following Nadja to Chansey, handing out ambiguous kisses along the way. Perhaps he was freer with his affections than she had thought.

But that didn't make sense. Pax was flirtatious, yes. Maybe he was just being affectionate, trying to soothe her nerves. He hadn't kissed her on the mouth like he had Laurel.

Not that any of that mattered, anyway. As soon as he found out what she was, he'd put as much distance between the two of them as possible. In fact, he may not even have to worry about doing that much. If her heritage became common knowledge, it was likely she'd be arrested, if not killed.

Nadja curled up on her side, pulling her knees to her chest once more. The ramifications of what she was assaulted her brain. She knew what happened to the Mevocali all those years ago. Why would anything be different now? She remembered the woman she'd overheard in Morris's shop. *"There were good reasons they were eliminated in the first place, and Amrantir has been better for it . . ."*

Nadja thought about Helaine. *She* would have been better if not for Nadja. And Baulo. Well, she had stopped his attack on Kizzy, but she'd almost killed him in the process. And if it wasn't for that, she would have never left the Wanderers in the first place.

Nadja blinked back tears as the rain moved in, peppering the boat with taps and pings. Somewhere in the early hours of the morning she finally succumbed to the soothing sound of the rain and slipped into a deep sleep.

She spent most of the next day alternately sipping from her canteen and lying down to ward off the nausea which had overtaken her when she'd awoken. The gentle pitter-patter she'd fallen asleep to the night before turned into a powerful rainstorm, pelting the barge with an infinite number of tiny, gravel-like droplets. Once or twice she crawled out of her corner and peeked towards the door. The dark skies beyond refused the sun its due and painted a gray outline around the door, never giving a clue as to what time of day it was.

Even though the hold had no windows, Nadja knew the river was swollen. The boat dropped and rolled beneath her, traveling much more swiftly than it had at the beginning of their journey. Occasionally it dipped sharply to one side, causing the contents of the crates to shift and jingle. Nadja's stomach rolled with the boat, and she squeezed her eyes shut in a poor attempt to manage the dizziness which clouded her head. The irony of the situation wasn't lost on her. How was it someone so at home in the water could be almost useless riding on it?

It was during one particularly large dip that Nadja noticed a change in the commotion going on above deck. The voices of the deckhands, though muffled by the rain and walls, were raised and urgent. Footsteps pounded overhead in a mad dash towards the back of the barge.

Suddenly, the boat lurched to the left. Nadja's eyes flew open in time to see a crate slide off the stack near her feet. She rolled to the left just as the crate crashed down, cracking open and sending silver sliding across the floor. The high-pitched noise rang in her ears, briefly masking the sound of the rain overhead. There was no way the crash had gone unnoticed by the men topside.

A few minutes later, Nadja felt the boat slow, then stop. It still bobbed up and down in the river's swift current, but all forward progress ceased. She slunk back into her corner as far as she could as footsteps approached the hold door.

Chapter Thirty-Two

The door to the hold swung open and Nadja listened, heart in her throat, as the footsteps drew closer to her hiding place. She slipped her pack over her shoulder and across her chest in case she needed to make a run for it.

"By the sound of it, I thought it would be a lot worse," said a gruff voice.

A boot scraped across the wooden floor, colliding with silver. Apparently, the crate next to Nadja wasn't the only casualty of the rainstorm.

"Blast that tree," came another voice. "If it hadna been uprooted like that, the captain wouldna had to pull so hard to port, and we'd be docking in Chansey by now."

"There's no use whining about it," replied Gruff-Voice. "You get to work repairing this crate and I'll take a look at the one back there."

Nadja pressed herself into the shadows of the wall as the gruff-voiced man came into view. As he reached down to recover the splintered bits of the crate, he caught her cowering form out of the corner of his eye. Shocked, he jumped back and nearly tripped over the spilled cargo. After regaining his balance, he cocked his head to the side and eyed Nadja. "Well, well. What do we have here?"

Nadja was afraid to answer. The boat continued to dip and sway, though it was going nowhere, and her seasickness was no better. Saliva filled her mouth. She swallowed it tentatively, willing her stomach to keep its contents. Opening her mouth was sure to bring what little was in her stomach back into the light.

"Whadja find?" asked the second man, coming to investigate.

Gruff-Voice lifted an eyebrow. "Looks like we have ourselves a stowaway."

Moments later, Nadja was hauled up on deck by the same guard who had overseen the loading of the vessel. His grasp around her bicep was firm, but he wasn't hostile. After a day and a half cooped up in the hold, the rain splattering against her face and body was refreshing and helped assuage her nausea.

The barge was anchored along the eastern bank of the river. Cliffs rose on the opposite side taller than any building Nadja had ever seen. It was one of the most distinct features of the Nostirivin. The river ran like a great partition separating the sandy shores of the east from the craggy cliffs of the west, which grew taller as they approached the Shadow Sea. Cliffs this tall meant they must be close to Chansey. But with the foggy rainstorm limiting visibility to sixty paces, there was no way to be sure.

"What's this?" barked a commanding voice.

The guard spun Nadja around to face the captain. Water soaked the slick deck, and the abrupt motion made her lose her footing. The guard righted her. She lifted her head, and raindrops slid down her forehead and into her eyes, clouding her vision. The wizened captain stood, hands on hips, glaring at her through the storm. Just over his shoulder she saw Pax. His eyes widened, and he clenched his teeth, unable to do anything but watch the scene unfold.

"We caught this woman down in the hold," yelled Gruff-Voice above the rain. "Looks like she's been hiding there ever since we left Cantio."

The captain strode towards Nadja. "Explain yourself."

The boat dipped again. Nadja, unlike the boatmen who spent the majority of the trip on their feet, pitched forward. If it hadn't been for the guard at her elbow, she would have fallen headfirst onto the soggy deck. Nausea welled up inside her once more. She reached out her free arm and grasped the side of the boat to steady herself, swallowing twice before attempting an answer.

"I . . . I need to . . . need to get to . . . Chansey," she managed between swallows.

"Don't we all?" The captain glared at her. "It appears you mistook my barge for one of the passenger boats." He huffed, then seemed to have another thought. "Well, no harm there. Just show me your ticket and we can get you transferred to the right vessel."

The guard next to her grunted.

"Well?" bellowed the captain.

Nadja squeezed her eyes and tried to keep her head as still as possible. What was this about a ticket? With her head swimming and stomach spasming, she couldn't make sense of what the captain had said.

"Oh, no ticket?" he said in a mocking tone. "Well then, that makes you a stowaway." The captain sneered, drawing snickers from the rest of the crew. All but one. Pax stood motionless, his forehead creased with worry.

"Come here," demanded the captain, pointing to the deck in front of him.

The guard released her arm, and she shuffled towards the captain, focusing her eyes on the wood beneath her feet. She heard the captain yelling about all the ways they handle people who stow away aboard his ship, but Nadja couldn't make out what he was saying. She was so focused on staying upright and not vomiting that the laughter of the crew was almost lost on her as well.

Without warning, the boat dropped sharply to the right. The force of the motion coupled with the slippery deck and her dizzy head sent Nadja careening over the edge of the barge and into the rushing waters below.

The churning, chilly waters enveloped her in a violent bear hug. The suddenness of the plunge shocked her body, dispelling her nausea almost immediately. As she broke the surface of the water, she thought she heard another splash, but wasn't sure. The roaring of the river filled her ears. Instinct kicked in, and she rolled over onto her back, filling her lungs with air and pointing her feet downriver. Her pack, the strap still wrapped across her chest, floated to the surface next to her. She silently thanked Morris for crafting a blowpipe which was so lightweight.

A hand clamped down on her shoulder like a vise. Surprised, she twisted her neck to look behind her and saw Pax's face. His head bobbed up and down along the surface. He gasped and sputtered, spewing mouthfuls of water each time he surfaced. With a gritty look of determination, he got his other arm under her shoulder and tried to stand.

Nadja shook her head furiously. "No!" she cried, water filling her mouth. She spat. "Don't stand up!"

But he couldn't hear her over the thundering river. Clearly he wasn't thinking straight. Even this close to the bank, the river had risen well above his head. The well-meaning oaf would wind up getting pulled to the bottom, and he would take Nadja along with him. No sooner had he dropped his feet than the undercurrent whipped his legs out from under him. His arm wrenched away from Nadja's body and his head disappeared below the surface.

"Pax!" she screamed.

A wave washed over her head. As soon as the water cleared, she filled her lungs with air once more. She could hold her breath for several minutes, but she doubted Pax could hold his for more than one.

The river pulled her towards the middle. Rain and river water splattered her face obscuring her vision.

Blinking the moisture from her eyes, she desperately scanned the rapids for any sign of him. She counted the seconds as they passed.

At twenty seconds, the fear gripping her chest became painful.

Come on Pax, where are you?

At forty seconds, the corners of her eyes pricked with the threat of tears. There were other dangers besides the rushing water which lurked within the depths of the river. Fallen trees and large rocks littered the bottom of the Nostirivin like components in a giant sieve, capturing debris while allowing the water to flow past.

At sixty seconds, a sob escaped Nadja's throat as her last shred of hope dissolved. The threatening tears sprang forth, mingling with the raindrops on her damp cheeks.

No . . . no, nooo!

Another wave washed over her face, bringing her back to attention. She had to get ahold of her emotions, or she would end up just like Pax. Taking another huge gulp of air, she squeezed her eyes shut. Her throat burned against grief withheld.

Nadja opened her eyes and focused on her current situation. The middle of the river appeared to be the least treacherous place to ride out the rapids. She peered through the wet, gray fog which hung like a thick curtain among the driving rain. A shadow emerged to her left. She could make out a silhouette of buildings looming ahead. Chansey. She needed to get to shore before the Nostirivin swept her out to sea.

She started to position her body towards the eastern shore when an arm shot up from the water to her right. A soggy mop of brown hair followed the arm before once more ducking beneath the surface.

It was Pax!

Nadja's heart leapt at the sight of him, and the pain she'd been holding back forced its way out of her mouth in a cry of relief. She angled towards him.

A short distance ahead, he surfaced again, flailing his arms as if searching for something to hold on to. He was much too close to the western bank. The waters which ran parallel to the cliffs were overflowing with jagged rocks. They stuck up out of the river like the teeth of a great sea monster hungering to crush the bones of men.

As if the thought was made manifest, Nadja watched in horror as Pax's body dashed against the side of one of those rocks. He bounced off like a child's dolly flung at a tree before he slipped under the water once more.

Nadja's muscles burned as she fought the rapids in a desperate attempt to reach him. She made progress, but not nearly fast enough.

Pax resurfaced one more, still ahead of her. Another rock lay directly in his path. Nadja winced as he slammed into the second one. But this time, his hands found purchase, and he clung to it with unbelievable determination.

Nadja struggled to get close enough to him without getting sucked into the rocks herself. She was almost there when the current shifted and sent her barreling into his back. His hands slipped with the unexpected impact, and she latched onto his shoulders. Pax scrambled to regain his grip, then turned his head to look behind him. The hard lines of his features softened slightly, and the corners of his mouth lifted.

"Fancy meeting you here," he yelled above the din, his chest heaving from the exertion.

Nadja wanted to kiss him and punch him at the same time. How could he joke at a time like this?

"Are you insane?" she yelled back, bringing her mouth close to his ear. "Why did you jump in the river?"

"To rescue you," he shouted.

"And how is that working out?"

"I've been in better situations."

Nadja tightened her back muscles, pushing against the current and dropping her feet straight down. Keeping a firm grip on his shoulders, she maneuvered directly behind him. The force of the river pressed her body into Pax's back.

"This is hardly the time for a piggyback ride," he shouted.

"Very funny," replied Nadja. "We need to get away from these rocks or we're going to get crushed." She scanned the surface of the river. "There," she said, pointing over Pax's shoulder to a twisting pattern of water not far from them. "If we can make it to that little run, it should carry us back towards the middle."

"Sounds easy enough," said Pax. Nadja caught a glimpse of his profile when he turned to look at the current. The muscles in his face were taught, belying his carefree tone.

"When I count to three, we need to push off of this rock towards that current. Together." she shouted.

Pax's eye twitched. Then, he tossed her a grin over his shoulder. "Aye aye, Captain."

Nadja turned her hips to the side and pulled up her knees, planting her feet on the giant stone. Pax shifted in front of her, getting into position.

"Ready?" she called.

Pax nodded.

On three, they kicked off from the rock. Pax let out a rough growl as the rock fell away from them and they headed towards the little current. They became separated for a moment, but Nadja managed to grasp a handful of Pax's shirt. Within moments they were pulled back to the center of the river.

Pax slapped at the water, struggling to keep his head above the surface. Nadja pulled herself towards him, getting into position behind his head. In one swift movement, she released her hold on his shirt and linked her forearms under his armpits, keeping him from going under. "Stop fighting!" she yelled.

Pax flailed, sending them both under the water, but Nadja maintained her hold on him. When they surfaced again, she brought her mouth to his ear. "Relax," she said in a soothing tone. "I've got you."

Pax stopped thrashing, but his muscles were strung tighter than a bow.

Nadja filled her lungs and slid her body underneath Pax, easing him onto his back. He acquiesced, alternately holding his breath and panting as they bobbed along.

At that moment, Nadja felt the water shift. She was so focused on keeping them afloat she didn't notice the city pass them by. The cliffs fell away, and the Nostirivin emptied into the Shadow Sea.

Their chance to make it to the eastern bank was gone, and fatigue was setting in. As they were pushed further out to sea, Nadja felt for the first time she wouldn't make it back to shore. If she only had herself to worry about, getting back to land wouldn't be a problem. But getting herself and Pax both out was looking like less of a possibility.

Nadja tilted her head back and closed her eyes, sensing the water around her. The tide was coming in. That was a good thing. If they could get away from the mouth of the river, at least they wouldn't be fighting against the tide.

Abruptly, the water shifted again. This time it pulled them in the opposite direction. Nadja looked over her shoulder. They were headed right for the cliffs. As they got closer, a large black hole appeared in its face. It emerged through the rainstorm like the mouth of a giant whale, swallowing everything in its path.

Nadja's heart raced. Her lungs and muscles burned as she vainly tried to kick out of the current. She cursed herself for not paying attention as she tried to free them from the water's pull. But the current was too strong. With Pax weighing her down, there was no way to break its hold.

The water picked up speed as they approached the mouth of the cave. Nadja was glad Pax hadn't looked back. The last thing she needed was him pulling her under again.

The sun chose that exact moment to break through the clouds. Nadja lifted her chin towards it, relishing the warmth shining down on them. She took a deep breath and looked back over her shoulder again.

With the cliffs at their back, Nadja relaxed her legs and tucked her chin, resting her cheek against Pax's hair.

"Hold on," she said, as darkness engulfed them.

Chapter Thirty-Three

Nadja rolled onto her side, panting. The small cobblestones, made smooth by centuries of changing tides, were hard beneath her. Water lapped around her thighs. The sea deposited her and Pax within the cave, still pushing her forward with the incoming tide.

"Pax!" she called, pushing herself up and squinting into the darkness.

"That's what they call me," came a throaty reply.

Nadja blinked, waiting for her eyes to adjust. The thin beam of light which squeezed into the space between the water and the top of the cave's mouth lit the surrounding area. She spotted Pax lying on his back just out of reach. His chest heaved up and down as he struggled to catch his breath.

"Are you all right?" he asked between breaths.

Nadja ran her hands down her body. There was a scrape along her forearm where she had hit the railing when she fell overboard. Her muscles were aching and her strength was spent, but she found no other injury.

"Yes," she replied. She climbed to her feet, wobbling on her weakened knees, and walked over to Pax.

By this time, he was sitting up.

"How are you?" she asked.

"Alive, thank you," he replied rubbing his face with his hands. "What was that?"

Nadja glanced towards the entrance. "Some kind of rogue current." She shook her head. "I should've seen it coming."

"It's not like you had anything else to worry about," said Pax.

Nadja turned back to him. He was standing now, leaning heavily on his right leg.

"You're hurt," she said, taking a step back and looking down at his left leg.

"It's just my ankle."

Nadja reached down and felt the area around his foot. The skin around his ankle, already puffed with swelling, strained against his boot. Pax hissed when her fingers met a sensitive spot.

"That boot needs to come off. I can't get a good look," she said. "Can you walk on it?"

Pax shifted his weight onto his left leg then grunted and clenched his jaw, abandoning the idea. Nadja reached out to steady him, wrapping her arm around his waist. Pax turned his head and looked down at her with a cheeky grin.

"Looks like you'll have to play doctor."

As Nadja ducked her chin, thankful the low light hid her features, Pax peered over her shoulder. The smile fell from his face, and his eyebrows lifted. "That must be some rogue current," he murmured.

Nadja followed his gaze and her jaw dropped. "Oh my."

The narrow cave entrance led up a steady incline into a larger, open area. Stone walls on either side of them bore matching horizontal stripes. The wall below the stripes was moist and dark, marking the crest of high tide within the cave. The light faded as it followed the watermarks further into the darkness, but not before highlighting the cave's most intriguing feature.

Boxes, sacks, baskets, crates, and piles of driftwood littered the cavernous room. Some rested along the water line, but most had been pushed up onto the dry floor by those closer to the water. Nadja followed the cobbles further into the cave.

The containers were in varying states of decomposition. Some appeared to be almost new, while others were dark and decaying, covered in mildew and long since having lost their original shape. The ones further in the cave were in better condition than their soggier brethren closer to the water.

Nadja approached one of the newer-looking crates and ran her hand along the wood. It was damp and broken along the outer edge. She peeled back the cover and looked inside. A cache of metal gears, now red and brown with a thick layer of rust, made up the contents of the crate.

She angled the lid towards the cave entrance, barely able to make out the markings on top.

"Grenyan Trading Company," she read aloud.

She inspected more similar-looking crates, all bearing the same insignia. Then she approached one of the older-looking containers. The markings were almost unintelligible, but she was just able to make them out. "Ferris Bros. Trading," she said.

Then, realization dawned.

"Shipwrecks," she said matter-of-factly, looking up at Pax.

"That would explain all the broken wood," he agreed.

"The cargo must have been caught in the same current we were." She surveyed the room. "Some of these must be decades old."

"That's much longer than we'll last," said Pax, in a rare moment of earnestness.

The light coming into the tunnel faded as the tide continued to rise. If the waterline on the walls was any indication, the cave entrance would be completely under water in a few minutes.

"We need to get higher," said Nadja, making her way back down the incline to Pax. "Lean on me," she said, slipping one arm around his waist and bracing her other hand against his abdomen. Pax grunted at her touch but allowed her to support some of his weight.

They picked their way up the incline. As they approached the large room, the cobblestones gave way to the smooth, solid stone floor. Once they put a comfortable distance between themselves and the water, Nadja helped Pax lower himself into a seated position propped against the wall. When she withdrew her hand from his abdomen, her palm was sticky.

"You're bleeding!" she exclaimed. She dropped down beside him and squinted in the fading light.

"I did have a personal encounter with a few river rocks," Pax joked.

Nadja shuddered at the memory of his body being slammed against the boulders. He hissed as she lifted the edge of his shirt, revealing a gash across his belly stretching from his navel to his ribs. It was wide and ugly, and blood flowed freely from the wound.

"We need to stop the bleeding," she said. She pulled her pack over her head and set it on the floor beside her. It was drenched but still intact. Pax shifted, and she looked up just in time to see him remove his shirt.

Nadja's mouth went dry as she stared at his shirtless form. Even in the disappearing light, she could make out the hard lines of the muscles defining his torso. The fluttering in her stomach began to stir, and her face and neck flamed with heat.

Pax wrung the water out of his shirt and balled it up. He cringed as he pressed it against the wound.

Yes, his wound!

Nadja chided herself. She should be focused on his well-being, not his well-defined physique.

She glanced away and pushed herself up. "I need to get a fire going before we lose the rest of our light." She busied herself gathering the drier bits of driftwood and broken boxes, grateful for a distraction from the half-naked man just a few steps away.

The cavernous room reminded Nadja of the atrium at the conservatory, mimicking its high, vaulted ceiling and making her feel very small. An incessant breeze blew in from the sea, ever pushing them towards the darkness beyond, and indicating the cave had another opening. Though the likelihood of that other entrance being near, let alone reachable, was slim, Nadja took comfort in the fact that they at least had a steady stream of fresh air.

Once she had amassed a sizable pile of wood, she removed the box of pearls and rough stone from her pack. A wistful smile traced her lips as she remembered stealing that stone, among other things, from Pax the first time they had met. Then, he had saved her life. Now, she hoped to return the favor.

Aiming for the smaller bits of wood, she struck the stone against the side of the metal box. Sparks flared in the darkness, and soon she had a respectable fire blazing. It sizzled as the heat evaporated latent pockets of moisture before the flames rose in intensity.

Out of the corner of her eye, she could see Pax illuminated by the firelight. He silently watched her move about the cave, wearing a look which she could only describe as contemplative. She felt as if she was being observed underneath a magnifying glass, and her palms began to sweat.

Pretending to ignore his study, she attended to his ankle. He grunted against the pain as she maneuvered the boot off of his foot. A mottled purple stain covered the skin around his ankle as if someone had spilled a glass of wine into his boot. She needed to elevate his foot to help with the swelling.

Nadja retrieved her pack and emptied its contents, arranging them around the fire to help them dry. Her extra clothes were soaked, but made for a decent pillow on which to rest his ankle. The dried meat was wet, but still edible. The berries had turned to jam while the bread had completely disintegrated. She gathered some meat, her canteen, and the tin of healing ointment Pax's mother had made—another pilfered item—and returned to check on him.

"How is it?" she asked, kneeling beside him and avoiding his gaze.

Pax peeled the shirt away from his wound, never taking his eyes off of her. The cloth shone bright red in the firelight, but a close inspection of the gash revealed the bleeding had all but stopped. She opened the canteen and poured a small stream of fresh water along the edge of the gash, rinsing away bits of sand and salt.

The temperature in the cave dropped as the water flowed in, completely covering the entrance and eclipsing the last rays of light. It was somewhere just past midday now, but in their little cliffside alcove, the fire would be their sun until the next low tide.

A chill ran up Nadja's spine. She capped the canteen and reached for the ointment. The little tin glinted in firelight.

Pax finally spoke. "That looks familiar."

She raised her eyes to his, having the tact to appear somewhat chagrined. "It comes in handy," was the only reply she offered. She dipped her fingers into the creamy salve and began to dab it gently along the length of his wound.

She was suddenly struck by how good this felt, taking care of him for a change. Until now, their roles had been reversed. He'd saved her from the ghost cat attack. He'd appointed himself her bodyguard after she'd been kidnapped. And again, he came to her rescue during the Heartstide Festival.

But now it was her turn. He wouldn't have made it out of the river alive on his own. In the midst of the rapids and the storm, he had listened to her and deferred to her, with no objection. She couldn't imagine any of her tribesmen yielding to her commands, no matter how dire the situation. Pax trusted her. And now, it was her turn to watch over him. And he was allowing her to do it without complaint. It felt balanced. It felt right.

Absorbed in her own thoughts, Nadja's hand slowed in its treatment. She didn't notice Pax's movement until his fingers grazed the back of her hand. Surprised, she looked up.

Her heart stopped when she met his eyes, dark and stormy in the shadows of the cave. Her hand flattened against his abdomen as his hand closed over hers. She felt an overwhelming desire to lean into him and press her lips to his once more. To see if the reality of his kiss matched the memory she carried in her heart.

Then, in a rush, she recalled his last kiss. It wasn't with her. It was with Laurel.

Nadja leaned back, pulling her hand from his grasp. She leapt to her feet and paced across the room to a pile of mangled boxes.

"I need to find something to bind your wound," she stammered. "Our clothes are too wet. Maybe there's something we can use in one of these crates." She began picking and sifting her way through the clutter.

"Why do you always do that?" Pax's voice was low and controlled. His usual mirthful undertone had completely disappeared.

"Do what?" she asked, uncovering another crate of metal gears.

"Run."

She moved to another mound of boxes. The Grenyan Trading Company shipped a lot of metal. Not helpful for binding wounds. "I don't know what you mean," she replied.

"I think you do," he said. "You've been running ever since the first day I met you."

"Yes," said Nadja, unearthing a shipment of linens. Ah ha! The fabric was mildewy near the walls of the box, but the cloth in the center was clean and dry. There wasn't a lot of it, but it would have to do. "I told you." What exactly had she told him? "I was trying to get away from the Wanderers without being caught."

"But you never stopped. Every time you're frightened, you run."

Nadja ripped the linen into manageable strips and crossed back over to Pax. "Don't be ridiculous."

"Tell me you don't. Tell me every time you get in a situation you're uncomfortable with, you don't bolt just like that mule. If you have the chance."

She steeled her resolve and knelt beside him once more, focusing on her task. She wrapped her arms around his waist and passed the linen between her hands. Her face came to within a breath of his chest. The light coating of hair which dusted his sun-kissed skin tickled her cheek, causing her to catch her breath. She pulled back, settling the fabric tightly against his wound. One down.

"And what am I supposedly running from right now?" she asked, reaching around his waist once more. Her heart hummed within her chest. His familiar woodsy scent mingled with salt and sweat, leaving her lightheaded.

Stop it, now. He has feelings for Laurel, not you.

She swallowed hard and wrapped the second layer. Two down.

"I can think of a couple things," he rumbled. This close to him, Nadja felt the low vibrations of his voice. "Something sent you running to Chansey."

"I already told you," she breathed. "I need to see my uncle. Chansey is where he happens to be." She wrapped her arms around him for a third time. The firelight danced across his body, outlining the hard edges of the muscles right in front of her eyes. She fought the urge to rest her head against them. Wrapping the third layer, she let out a shaky breath. "And what else?" she asked, securing the ends of the fabric.

Again, his hand found hers, stilling its ministration. "Me," he said. "Why are you running from me?"

Reflexively, Nadja pulled her hand back, but Pax reached out and grasped her wrist.

Nadja's fingers clenched into a fist, and her breathing increased. "Why are you doing this?" she whispered.

Pax turned her hand palm up. He reached out and peeled back her fingers one at a time. "Do you truly not know?" He brought her palm to his lips and placed a gentle kiss in its center.

Her hand burned. How was it such a simple gesture could ignite such fire within her? "Pax," she murmured, "I . . ."

Then the memory of Laurel's arms around his neck and his head bent low over hers flickered in Nadja's mind. She shook her head and twisted her wrist from his grasp. "You must have swallowed too much salt water. I think you mistake me for someone else."

Pax drew his eyebrows together, frowning. "Not a chance."

"Laurel?" Nadja lifted her chin and looked pointedly at him.

Surprise and then understanding showed in his eyes. "Laurel is a friend of mine, nothing more."

She smiled ruefully. "Please. You must give me more credit than that."

He nodded and rested back against the wall. "Nadja, I have tried my best to be your friend," he said, slowly. "Before I went home for the Candlefire Celebration, you made it clear friendship with you was all I could hope for. I've spent these last few months trying to put you out of my mind. Laurel is a friend of mine, and, yes, she may harbor some fondness for me. But I have never felt anything beyond friendship for her."

"How can you say that when you kissed her at the Heartstide Festival for the whole world to see?"

"Look, I don't know what you think you saw, but I did not kiss Laurel at the Heartstide Festival or any other time. She came to congratulate me after our performance. I don't know, she may have hugged me."

Nadja searched her memory. True, she had only seen the back of him that night. And Laurel's smug face. Was it possible she'd drawn the wrong conclusion?

Pax pushed away from the wall and slowly reached for her as if he was afraid he'd frighten her away. His hand cupped her face, and he ran his rough thumb along her cheek. Nadja didn't pull away.

"I have never kissed Laurel." His eyes held her captive. "I've never wanted to kiss her." She trembled as his thumb traveled down her cheek and across her bottom lip. "Not like I want to kiss you," he whispered.

Nadja's head swam. Could it be true? He had been so distant since his return to the conservatory she'd believed he had given up on her. Was it possible after all the time she had spent keeping him at arm's length, he still wanted her?

"I know exactly who you are, Nadja Machinal. Wanderer refugee. Fighter and survivor. Dreamer. Musician . . . keeper of my heart." He slipped his other hand behind her neck, tangling his fingers through the sensitive hairs at her nape. Nadja's breath caught in her throat as he tugged her towards him. Her shivering had nothing to do with the cold air.

Pax brought his face to hers, his eyes dark and flashing in the firelight. "Say you've changed your mind, Pretty Lady." His husky voice echoed in the cavernous room. "Say it." He brushed his nose lightly against hers. "Tell me I have even the smallest hope."

Nadja finally found her voice. She managed a faint whisper.

"Yes."

Chapter Thirty-Four

Pax's mouth hovered over hers for a moment. Long enough for Nadja to think perhaps he hadn't heard her. Then, with excruciating slowness, he lowered his lips to hers. They were just as she remembered, warm and soft. Her eyelids fell closed.

He was gentle. Testing. He approached her with a tenderness which shattered into a million pieces what remained of the wall around her heart.

When his tongue traced a lazy line along her bottom lip, Nadja gasped. A shock bolted through her body on contact, sending sparks to the tips of her fingers and toes, and a swirl of simmering charges deep into her belly. Her mouth opened instinctively, but Pax continued his slow, deliberate assault on her lips.

Her breathing came quicker, and she brought her hands up to rest against his chest. The pounding heartbeat beneath her palms betrayed his relaxed overtures. She ran her hands up and over the hard planes of his chest. A tight ache was building within her. She needed . . . something more. Her fingers began kneading the muscles of his shoulders, trying to pull him closer.

Much to her distress, Pax stopped his languid seduction and raised his head. As Nadja lifted her heavy lids, he pinned her with his gaze. His eyes were fierce, and the muscles in his neck were taught as if struggling against an unknown restraint. He stared into her eyes, searching for something. Time stopped as the world itself took a breath. Under the weight of his stare, Nadja's heart clenched and a soft whimper escaped her lips. In response, a rakish grin flashed across his face.

Then his mouth was on hers once more. This time with an urgency matching her own. Pax's hands fell from her face, running down her sides and gripping her waist. His lips traced a trail down the side of her neck leaving fire in its wake before returning once more to her mouth. A low growl met her ears, sending her pulse racing. His kisses were hungry and demanding, and she rose to meet him at every turn. With her mind reeling, her body acted of its own accord. She wrapped her arms around his neck and pressed against his torso.

Pax sucked in a sharp breath and pulled back. Dazed, it took Nadja a moment to realize what had happened.

"Oh no! I—"

"Shh," said Pax, placing a finger against her lips. He leaned his forehead against hers and closed his eyes. They rested together like that for a time, his hands encircling her waist and her fingers laced behind his neck. Their chests rose and fell in tandem as their breathing returned to normal.

When they regained control of their emotions, Pax released his hold on her. He ran his hand along his makeshift bandage.

"No harm done," he said, giving Nadja a reassuring smile. He reached out and pulled her to him, tucking her under his arm and nestling her against his good side. The stone wall was cold against her back, but between the heat radiating from Pax's body and the warmth coursing through her own, she barely noticed.

He took her hand, threading her fingers between his own.

"You have no idea how long I've wanted to do that," he murmured against her hair.

"Probably about as long as I have," Nadja admitted, sheepishly.

Pax leaned back, surprised. "If that's true, which I doubt, you did a great job hiding it."

"Are you calling me a liar?" she teased.

"I would never presume." His arm tightened around her, and she snuggled back against him. "Although a statement like that deserves some explanation. Don't you think?"

They sat in comfortable silence as Pax waited for her response. When it came, Nadja was surprised to discover how easily she was able to open herself to him.

"You know about my past. I mean, where I come from." She looked up at Pax for some kind of acknowledgement. He nodded and waited for her to proceed.

"A life with the Wanderers . . . women are always less than. Girls are raised to be obedient and helpful, always deferring to the men around them. A woman may offer her opinion to the man who speaks for her family, but never has an official voice. Once a woman is married, her future is determined by her husband. Her past life no longer matters. She learns his trade and becomes secondary in his household. What he says is law."

"Is this how it was with your parents?" Pax asked.

Nadja shook her head. "That's how it is with everyone's parents. Except mine."

Pax raised his eyebrows, so she continued. "I never knew my father. He died when I was a few months old. My mother never remarried, so the role of Speaker for my family reverted to her father. For some reason, my grandfather was happy to let my mother lead our little family, which is unheard of.

"She's so strong and capable, my mother. And wise. I can't imagine her being secondary to any man. She shouldn't have to be. I shouldn't have to be."

Nadja let her words hang in the air between them.

Pax placed his fingers under her chin and tilted her face towards him. "I would never ask you to be."

"I know," she said, meeting his gaze with confidence and affection. "I haven't always, but I do now." His lips brushed against hers again, instantly transforming her insides into quicksilver.

When they separated, contentment filled Nadja's heart, and she leaned her head against him. It fit neatly in the groove between his shoulder and chest, and she marveled at the rightness of it all.

"It only took looking death in the face to get you to come around," chuckled Pax.

"Not quite," Nadja replied, absently gliding her fingers over the hard bumps defining his abdomen.

"Well, whenever it happened, I'm glad it did. I fought so hard against my feelings for you. I even began to believe I had put you out of my head for good. Then you stood up at the Heartstide Festival. In that moment, I knew I was lying to myself. When you sang, it was like you were singing only for me. Like you were pouring a part of yourself into my soul. You sparked this small flicker of hope within me that I'd been wrong. That there was a chance for us to be together."

Nadja's hand stilled, and her heart clenched. Pax's words hit her like a kick to the gut. In the halo of their passion, she'd forgotten anything existed in the world but the two of them. Now, reality came rushing back in a black tidal wave of anxiety and despair.

Of course his feelings returned when she sang. She was Mevocali.

"And now, to have you in my arms," said Pax, breaking her introspection. He leaned down to kiss her once more.

Her brain was spinning. It wasn't real. His feelings for her had faded before that dreaded performance. She remembered the effect her song had on the audience. Of course it would have the same effect on him.

Nadja savored the taste of his lips on hers, knowing it would be the last time. She couldn't take advantage of him. She would not. Wasn't this the most hideous thing about what she was? This ability to bend others to her will. To infiltrate and influence their minds.

Tears stung the backs of her eyes, and a lump rose in her throat. She sobbed against his mouth, breaking their connection.

"I can't," she cried, scrambling to her feet.

Surprise and confusion washed over Pax's face. "What can't you?"

"This. You and me. I can't take advantage of you like this." She moved away from him and began pacing the floor.

"Take advantage of me? What are you talking about?"

Nadja's head pounded in time with her footfalls. "This isn't real. Your feelings for me aren't real."

"I'll be the judge of that," he said, sounding annoyed. Then, changing his tactics, he shot her a cocky grin. "Why don't you come back over here and I'll show you how real they are."

"No, they're not," Nadja protested. "I did this to you, and I'm sorry. I didn't mean to. It just happened, and I don't know how to take it back. I would if I could."

"You'll do no such thing." Pax struggled to his feet, teetering on his right leg. "Nadja, you're not making any sense. Come back over here and sit down. You can tell me what's bothering you and we can work it out together." He reached a hand towards her.

"No!" she shouted, jumping back and circling around to the opposite side of the fire. She couldn't bear to be close to him now. It hurt too much.

Pax looked as if she'd slapped him, and her tears finally broke free.

"You don't understand," she sobbed. "It's why I'm on my way to Chansey. Why I need to find my uncle. It's why Helaine was in the hospital and why you think you have these feelings for me." Her voice shook as she spoke in hushed tones. "I am Mevocali."

Pax looked as if she'd sprouted an extra head. "That's not possible."

"Apparently it is," she choked. "It was Grandmaster Kero who figured it out, and she made it clear my uncle knows something about it. Things happen when I sing. I don't mean for them to, but they do. Just like at the Heartstide Festival." Nadja took a shuddering breath and closed her eyes as the confession left her lips. "Yes, you felt like I was singing only for you because I was. But everyone else in that room felt the same way. Those were my emotions you were feeling, not yours."

"The devil they were!" Pax boomed. "I know what I feel for you, Nadja. And regardless of who you are—what you *may* be—that has never changed."

"You said yourself you'd put me behind you until that night."

410

"A fool's fantasy," he sputtered. "If I had been honest with myself, I would have admitted the truth. But I wanted to believe the lie because it was easier."

She cast him a mournful look. "I'm so sorry." She was thankful his ankle prevented him from closing the distance between them. It took every ounce of her resolve to turn him away.

"I don't want your apologies," said Pax. "I want you to give up this idiotic notion that what we have between us isn't real."

There was no convincing him otherwise. Nadja realized she had to make him see her for the aberration she really was. Then an idea sprang to mind.

"I almost killed a man," she blurted out. Her words rang through the air, silencing Pax's protestations.

His lips parted as his thick eyebrows knit together. The crackling of the fire which separated them was suddenly overpowering as he considered her words.

Finally, he sniffed. "Tell me."

"I haven't been completely honest with you." Nadja recounted to him the night she had fled the Wanderer camp, going into detail when she described Baulo's physical response to her. She watched his face metamorphose through looks of shock, anger, and sorrow as she told her tale. When she finished, she waited for his reaction.

"That must have been horrible," he said. "I'm so sorry."

No. Not pity. She could bear anything but that. Where was his disgust? His loathing?

"Were you listening to me? I just told you I almost killed someone."

"It sounds like he had it coming," snorted Pax. "He attacked your cousin and was about to do the same thing to you. Seems to me you reacted in self-defense. Besides," he said, limping his way around the fire towards her, "I know you, remember? You're not a murderer."

Nadja sighed and dropped her head. "But I am Mevocali. Maybe that's just as bad."

"That may be what you are, but that's not who you are." Pax stood beside her now, close enough to touch her. She felt his nearness like a thousand tiny pinpricks against her skin. He raised a hand towards her face, but she shied away from his touch.

He dropped his hand. "You believe my feelings for you are something of your own creation. I disagree. We are at an impasse." He studied her guarded expression for a moment, then leaned back. "And I am making you uncomfortable."

She made no move to deny his words.

"Consider the matter tabled."

"Good."

He turned and hobbled his way back towards the wall.

Nadja watched his back, and a twinge of guilt squeezed her chest. She walked over to him and helped him back to his spot, propping his leg on her pile of wet clothes.

"Just remember," he said. "I said tabled. Not settled. Now, I'm hungry. Where's that beef you had?"

Nadja doled out the rations and sat apart from him. They settled into companionable silence as they filled their bellies.

After a while, Pax spoke. "Whatever happened to the man you almost killed?"

The dried meat turned to wood chips in her mouth, and Nadja reached for her canteen, taking a sip before passing it back to Pax. There were so many things she had been keeping from him. But, now that he knew the worst, there was no reason to lie to him anymore.

"It's a long story," she said.

Pax gestured to his ankle and smiled. "I'm not going anywhere."

Nadja told him everything from the time she left his camp in the woods. His face grew stormy when she mentioned her covert training sessions with Wheedler and Brooks. No doubt he was upset about her sneaking into town unguarded. When she told him about seeing Baulo face-to-face in the market district, she gave an involuntary shudder.

"And you're sure it was him? You said the man looked different."

"There was no mistaking him."

"And he did nothing?"

"No."

"And you haven't seen or heard from him since?"

"Not so much as a whisper."

Pax looked thoughtful. "Perhaps he has forgiven you."

Oh, how Nadja wished that was true. But, she knew better. She shook her head. "More like biding his time. I've stayed close to the conservatory since that day. I haven't been alone outside the grounds. Even canceled my training sessions to avoid traveling through the city alone."

Pax opened his mouth to protest, but Nadja held up her hand. "I know, you said you wanted to accompany me whenever I left the conservatory. But, you were so different when you returned from the winter break. I wasn't sure if you regretted making that offer. And besides that, with Baulo back in play, I didn't want to burden you any more than I already had."

Pax's face fell. "I'm sorry you felt like you couldn't come to me. In my heart, I have always been there for you. After the Candlefire Celebration, I just felt like—" He stopped and offered her a half smile. "Well, we've tabled that discussion for now, haven't we?"

Nadja returned his smile with a tentative one of her own.

"But as for this Baulo," said Pax, his eyes narrowing, "there has to be something we can do. You can't keep living in fear of him for the rest of your life. Maybe we can appeal to the Delegation on your behalf. After all, it was an accident. And you didn't actually kill him."

"And tell them what? That I am a Mevocali who used my voice to nearly kill one of their members? The city is already on edge over the possibility they—*we*—still exist. I can't imagine they would be quick to come to my aid. Besides, the Wanderers may be citizens of Amrantir, but they have always maintained legal autonomy within the tribe. And my crime falls under their authority."

"I'm not giving up," he said, rubbing a hand across his face. "Maybe your uncle will have some ideas. We can ask him if we ever make it out of this blasted cave."

"About that," said Nadja. "I think I can get us out of here."

Pax watched her in stony silence as she explained her plan.

"I don't like it," he said. "Didn't you just tell me you've been avoiding being out in the open alone?"

"You're not going anywhere with your injuries," she retorted. "And, it's too risky for me to try to carry you. Besides, the Delegation is in session now, so Baulo is in Cantio. And, he's the person I'm avoiding."

Reluctantly, Pax agreed, and they made plans for Nadja to get help. The tide was just beginning to ebb, but it would be dark before it reached its lowest point. They would stay in the relative safety of the cave for the night, and Nadja would set out at the next low tide.

They passed the rest of the evening discussing everything from music to metaphysics, and by the end of the night, they had regained some of their comfortable congeniality.

Though it was tempting to bed down for the night alongside Pax, given the cool underground air, Nadja kept to her side of the fire. She didn't want to give him any false hope, and it pained her to be so close to him and know the relationship she'd longed for was just an illusion.

The next morning, with the sun and the water low in their courses, Nadja said farewell to Pax and stepped out of the cave and into the Shadow Sea.

Chapter Thirty-Five

The coastal city of Chansey lifted Nadja's spirits with its familiar patchwork. Chansey was a hodgepodge of architecture and people, reflecting both its Amrantirian roots and the influence of the myriad ethnicities and nationalities which visited its harbor on a daily basis. While the law required all imports and exports to pass through Cantio, Chansey is where the people came and went.

Her clothes were almost dry by the time she reached the harbor. The water outside the cave had been only a few feet deep when she'd left, and she'd made it to the east bank of the river without incident. Her blowpipe thumped against the stone walkway, dutifully disguised as a walking stick. Even with Baulo much further north, Nadja took no chances.

It didn't take long for her to reach her destination. The path to the Chansey Custom House was well marked, and she weaved her way through the crowd with relative ease. Once inside, however, her progress stopped.

People, mostly men, packed the floor of the custom house, jockeying for positions in line before one of the six customs agents. The air was hot and stale and smelled of sweat and ink. Nadja paused in the doorway enjoying one last breath of fresh air, when something solid collided with the back of her shoulder, pushing her aside. She stumbled into the room as the man elbowed his way to a position in one of the lines. Undaunted, she plunged into the throng. Since the entrance doors acted as a funnel, drawing newcomers into the center of the room, Nadja shuffled to one of the outside lines.

With each departure, the lines shifted and pressed forward like giant tentacles pulling the waiting crowd towards their collective goal. Nadja stood firm against the bumps and shoves, refusing to give ground lest she lose her place in line. By the time she reached the agent, she was exhausted.

"Papers," droned the agent, not bothering to look at her.

Nadja disregarded his outstretched hand and leaned forward to be heard above the noisy crowd. "I need information."

The agent raised his heavy eyelids and graced her with a blank stare.

Realizing she could expect no response from him, Nadja continued. "I'm looking for Tau Machinal. He captained a vessel from Cantio to Chansey some days ago."

The agent rotated on his stool as if by some form of mechanization and retrieved a book from the shelves behind him. Returning to face her, he placed the book on the counter between them and opened it. After a moment of research, his finger paused on a line of script.

"Tau Machinal. Captain of Mia Fair. Arrived five days ago. No departure claims submitted." Snapping the book closed, he spun on his stool, replacing the book on the shelf and turning back to face her in one fluid movement.

"Next," he said, inclining his head to the person behind her.

The line surged forward, squeezing Nadja aside. Annoyed, she turned and elbowed her way towards the door. She'd have to come up with another plan. Short of canvasing the entire port, she wasn't sure how to find her uncle.

She was almost to the door when a large hand wrapped around her bicep, bringing her to a halt.

"Well, well, what have we here?" crooned a familiar voice.

Startled, Nadja looked up. "Wheedler!" she exclaimed. "What are you doing here?"

"I believe that's my line," the gentle giant smiled at her, releasing his grip on her arm. After the excitement of the past few days, it was a relief to see his familiar face.

"I'm trying to find my uncle."

Wheedler laughed. "Aren't you always?"

Nadja gave him a sheepish grin.

"Right this way," he said, gesturing to the door.

"On, no," said Nadja, fielding another shove. "I don't want you to give up your place in line." She looked over her shoulder and glared at the pushy culprit. "I know how hard they are to come by."

"What's a few more minutes in line when there's a lady in distress?" Wheedler's eyes twinkled as he slipped an arm around her shoulders and led her through the crowd. Nadja was once again surprised by how, even in the press of the custom house, people moved aside, creating an easy path for him.

She gulped a mouthful of fresh air as soon as they stepped through the doors.

"We're set to sail in one hour. Your uncle sent me to clear up business here while he's busy enjoying a nice hot meal." The tone of Wheedler's voice carried none of the envy suggested by his words. "Your best bet is to look in at The Whale's Tale. That's his favorite tavern here in Chansey, and I doubt he'll be able to resist going home without stuffing in one more of Charity's prawn pies first."

Nadja thanked him, and he pointed towards the city, giving her directions to the tavern. Before she left, he stepped around in front of her and held up a hand.

"Look, I know you like to keep your secrets," he began, his usually humorous tone replaced with a quiet seriousness, "and I respect that. I can't imagine what brought you all the way to Chansey by yourself, and I'm not going to ask. But, if there is ever anything you need, I hope you know you shouldn't hesitate to ask."

Wheedler's offer touched her. She reached out and clasped his large, rough hand between her own. "Thank you," she said. "You are a true friend."

She left Wheedler to his business and set out for The Whale's Tale. It wasn't long before its sun-bleached blue-and-gray siding and slate shingles came into view. Quaint little sea-shell wind chimes spiraled downwards from the overhang above the entrance, and the aroma of seafood wafted through the air. The crowded tables and bar proved Uncle Tau wasn't the only person who enjoyed their fare.

Nadja scanned the room and spotted her uncle at a small table in the back corner. And he wasn't alone. Another figure sat opposite Tau, facing the corner. A tingle of familiarity crawled up Nadja's spine as she stared at his back. While a light sheen of sweat from the bright day and balmy sea air covered the rest of the patrons, the stranger wore a cloak with the hood pulled up.

As Nadja approached the table, Tau looked up. His eyebrows shot up, and his mouth dropped open. Then, just as quickly, his features smoothed. He rose from his seat and came around the table to meet her.

"Niece," he said. Concern laced his words, betraying his calm exterior. "What are you doing in Chansey? It is my understanding the conservatory has not yet dismissed for the summer months."

At her uncle's words, Nadja saw the stranger stiffen beneath his cloak. Something tickled at the back of her mind, but it was fleeting and uncatchable.

"I must speak with you privately, Uncle. It's a matter of some urgency."

Tau gave her a crisp nod and bent to speak to the stranger. His voice was low, and Nadja couldn't make out what he was saying. When he rose to face her again, the stranger stood and left the table, keeping his head down. But Nadja's height put her at a rare advantage. As the stranger passed, she saw a hauntingly familiar face and a pair of green eyes flash from underneath the hood.

Recognition hit, jarring her senses. The stranger and the man she had seen at the Heartstide Festival. Could they be one and the same?

"Who was that man?" she asked her uncle as her eyes followed the stranger out of the tavern.

"A business associate," said Tau, waving his hand. Then, he gestured for her to take the now empty seat. "Now, Niece. What is so urgent you left the safety of the conservatory and traveled all the way to Chansey alone."

Nadja saw worry hiding behind his impassive exterior.

"I didn't come alone," she began. "My friend and I fell overboard on our way here. He's injured."

Tau listened intently as Nadja related the pertinent details of the events which led her to find him. She glossed over the fact she had stowed away aboard one of his own ships, leaving him to fill in the details of her transport on his own.

"But why did you come?" he asked again. "What was so important it could not wait until I returned home?"

Nadja glanced around to be sure her next words would not be overheard. "What do you know about the Mevocali?"

Tau gave no sign he knew what she was referring to. "What do *you* know about the Mevocali?" he countered.

Nadja laid everything before her uncle. Against the protesting hammering of her heart, she told him everything she knew. About Baulo. About Helaine. About the Heartstide Festival and even about that night in the woods when she had destroyed every living plant around her. All the while, her uncle's face remained a stony mask of imperturbability.

When she had finished, she sat back, anxiously awaiting his response.

Tau sat in thought for what seemed like an eternity. When he spoke, he chose his words carefully.

"Meliina was right to come to you when she did," he said.

Nadja caught his familiar reference to Grandmaster Kero, bolstering her suspicions they were more than acquaintances.

"Did she speak the truth?" whispered Nadja. "Am I really Mevocali?"

Tau leaned back in his chair and ran two fingers across his mustache, considering his reply. "The answer to that is more than a simple yes or no."

"What do you mean?" asked Nadja. Her blood simmered. After all she had endured to get to this moment, his vague response was more than frustrating. "Either I am, or I'm not. Which is it?"

Tau locked eyes with her. His gaze was heavy with unspoken truths, but Nadja did not waver under it. When he answered, his voice was thick. "You are."

A thousand questions sprang to her lips, but Tau raised his hand. "I know you have more questions, but what we have to discuss will take time. And right now, I believe you have a friend in need."

He was right, of course.

"We will see to his rescue first, and then I will answer all of your questions to the best of my ability."

With that, Tau rose from his chair. Nadja had no choice but to follow. As much as she longed for answers, Pax's rescue was their top priority.

Once outside, Tau glanced up at the sun. "We should be able to reach him on the next low tide. I will collect Wheedler and some supplies, and we will go see to your friend. I need you to go to the Mia Fair and let Brooks know we will delay our departure."

Nadja nodded her agreement, wishing she could be there to help Pax herself, but grateful to know he was in capable hands.

Before he left, Tau reached out and placed a gentle hand on her cheek. Shocked by the intimate gesture, so uncharacteristic of her uncle, Nadja raised questioning eyes to his. His face was awash with unspoken sentiments. He opened his mouth as if to speak, but changed his mind and patted her cheek instead. "Take care," he said gruffly, then turned and marched down the lane.

Nadja stood there for a moment. As she watched her uncle's retreating form, her eyes burned as unbidden tears threatened to surface. She blinked them back in surprise. Confused by her reaction, she shook herself and straightened her spine. She had a job to do, and she needed to get to it.

The Chansey harbor surpassed the one in Cantio in both size and industry. As a child Nadja had enjoyed what little time the tribe spent near the port city. The excitement, which was a natural side effect of the bustling harbor, thrilled her young sensibilities and brought to mind fantastical daydreams of adventures awaiting those who set sail from the banks of her homeland. But today, the heat and smell of the crush, even this late in the day, were oppressive as she pressed her way towards the docks.

She hoped Uncle Tau and Wheedler made good time to the cave. Considering Pax's injuries, she'd left her pack of supplies with him and made it to Chansey with only her blowpipe. The little food and water which had not been ruined by the river or used to clean his wound would last him a day if he rationed. For herself, she looked forward to delivering her message to Brooks and imposing upon her hospitality for some food and drink. Hopefully the barge was well stocked for the trip back to Cantio.

The crowd leaned into her from all sides. Eye level with shoulders and chests, Nadja could barely see the tops of sails belonging to the larger ships. She was trying to decide the best direction in which to begin her search when an idea struck. A nearby cargo stack provided the required asset, and she scrambled up onto one of the crates. The added height afforded her a clear view of the docks, and she scanned the area for a clue as to the whereabouts of the Mia Fair.

Shielding her eyes from the midday sun, she searched up and down the docks for a few minutes. Then, not too far from where she perched, she spotted Brooks emerging from the hold of a barge. Brooks lifted her head towards the port, pausing for a moment as her gaze passed Nadja, then continued her survey.

With her destination fixed, Nadja hopped down from the crate. As soon as she stood, she felt a sharp pain in her right side.

"One word and I'll gut you where you stand."

All color drained from Nadja's face as an arm snaked around her waist. There was no mistaking that voice. She'd heard it enough in her nightmares.

Baulo yanked her against his side. Her hip dug into his thigh and her shoulder crushed underneath his arm.

"Walk," he commanded. His breath was moist in her ear, smelling tangy and stale.

Somehow her leaden feet obeyed his command, and they wove through the crowd and away from the docks. Passersby might have mistaken them for a father and daughter trying their best to not get separated in the crowd. But the blade threatening to pierce her tunic, and subsequently her flesh, proved nothing could be further from the truth.

She pressed her blowpipe against her side. The surrounding mob made it impossible to use. But, the feel of it in her palm gave her a small, if false, sense of security.

A hundred questions flew through her mind. What was Baulo doing in Chansey when the Delegation was in session? How had he found her? Was he alone? What was he planning to do with her?

They headed east, and within a quarter hour approached the gates of the port. Once through their relative safety, it would be much more difficult to signal for help. As they passed through the iron gate, Nadja looked at one of the guards. Her eyebrows knit together above her intense gaze. She mentally projected her plea for help as if he might hear her if she tried hard enough. The guard glanced at the pair before turning his attention to the cart full of Pantomarian textiles coming up behind them. Baulo and Nadja passed under the arched gateway and out of the city.

Baulo remained silent as they walked the well-traveled road, turning away from the coast and into the forest. As twilight descended, he turned off the main road and tugged her down a less traveled path. The trees parted, revealing what amounted to a sorry excuse for an inn. The thatched roof, worn almost bare in places, was patched together haphazardly, much like the brightly painted woman who manned the front door, leering at the two of them. Baulo ignored the woman and drew Nadja around behind the building to the dilapidated lean-to which served as the inn's stables.

The lean-to was empty, save for three horses huddled in the small patch of shade provided by the roof. Away from the suggestive gaze of the inn's hostess, and with the road out of view, the sinking feeling which had been Nadja's constant companion since Baulo had grabbed her wormed its way up her throat. With no witnesses, she was at his mercy. They approached one of the horses.

"You will ride in front where I can see you." After a half hour of silence, his grating voice startled her, sending her rapid pulse into a gallop. A vision of being seated atop the horse with her back pressed against Baulo, his breath on her neck and his intentions muddy at best, lethal at worst, made her shudder.

Before she could consider the consequences, she clasped her blowpipe with both hands and swung it like the pendulum of a clock. The bottom of the pipe connected with Baulo's shin just before her heel slammed down on his instep. He let out a grunt as his hold loosened just enough for her to wrench free.

Nadja ran. She made it two steps before a sharp pain sliced across her lower back, bringing her to her knees. A cloud of dust puffed into the air when she hit the ground. Scrambling to her feet, she spun to face him, sliding both of her hands down the pipe and swinging it like a bat towards his head. Baulo threw up a hand to block the blow and growled, spiraling his arm around the shaft of the pipe and yanking it towards him.

Her grip held fast. Baulo's motion propelled her face-first into his chest. He hugged her tightly against him. Her nose pressed into his shirt for only a moment, but it was long enough to get a lungful of his musty scent. She choked against the fabric. With another twisted jerk, the blowpipe slipped from her grasp.

Nadja shoved against his chest in a fruitless attempt to break his hold. Warmth trickled down her backside where his knife had left its mark.

Her hands vibrated against him as a low rumble burbled up from his chest and erupted into laughter.

"Stupid girl," he hissed.

The side of her head exploded in a blinding white fire which pierced her brain and robbed her of her sight.

Chapter Thirty-Six

Bits of fiber scratched the back of Nadja's throat, choking her as she came crashing back into consciousness. Lanolin coated the roof of her mouth, and neither her tongue nor her gag reflex could expel the woolen mass. Her hands were roped together above her head and tied to the tree behind her. Her boots were gone, and her feet were bound at the ankles.

Baulo shifted somewhere to her right, and Nadja cracked her eyes to find him with his back to her. She squinted in the darkness, her head still pounding from his beating. As if sensing her gaze, or perhaps in response to the muffled retching, Baulo turned from his work and faced her.

The flickering firelight cast ominous shadows across his sunken face, highlighting his sharp angles and deepening the hollows of his eyes and cheeks. Even though she had seen him in the market, the shock of his transformation hit her full force. Gone was the powerful orator who spent his youth as one of the tribe's best warriors. The withered old man before her was a shadow of his former self.

Withered, maybe, but not decrepit.

If she had any fantasies of being able to match Baulo physically, those vanished the moment he had disarmed her and used her own weapon against her.

"Good. You're awake," Baulo said, crossing to where she lay on the ground. "We can begin."

He knelt beside her, bringing his face close to hers and studying her with a critical eye. Dirt ground into the gash on her back as she squirmed under his scrutiny. She winced and grunted against the gag.

A ragged smile curled the edges of his thin lips. "*Tsk-tsk,*" he said. "Don't start without me."

Nadja heard the blade ring as he unsheathed his knife. Her breath caught in her throat. The wad of wool absorbed her protests, and the rope bit into her wrists and ankles as she fought against her restraints.

"I'm sorry, was there something you wanted to say?" Baulo sneered. Nadja raised her chin and cast her eyes towards her mouth.

"Idiot," he spat. "Do you really think I'd let you speak when your cursed mouth is the whole reason we're here?"

Nadja's eyes grew wide.

"Yes. Take a good look at your work." Swinging a leg across her body he sat astride her supine form. Her stomach strained against his weight, and she struggled to breathe. The twisted smile which haunted her dreams

431

reappeared on his face. Her body trembled as Baulo leaned down and brought his lips to her cheek. Nadja bit back a sob.

"I don't know what you are, but whatever it is, you're an abomination," he whispered. "How dare you attack me?"

"Me!" he shouted.

Her eardrum rattled and rang.

Baulo sat back against her hips and snickered. "Worthless. Just like the rest." He rested the blade of his knife against the hollow of her throat. The steel was startlingly cold in the balmy evening. Nadja's breathing grew ragged. Then, slowly, he pressed the blade against the tip of her collarbone. Every muscle in her body contracted, squeezing salty tears from the corners of her eyes and clamping her teeth down on the gag.

Baulo released his pressure and traced the knife up her neck. She froze, fearing the slightest movement would assist the blade in its murderous intent.

"And what a position you left me in," he sighed. "The idea you could have such an effect on me is preposterous. But even if it weren't, how could I continue to command the respect I deserve if everyone knew you— you, a fatherless nobody with an undeserving mother— somehow did this," he held his free hand palm up, "to me?"

With a flick of his wrist, the knife sliced the skin beneath her earlobe. Nadja's body jerked as she screamed. The stifled sound lodged in the back of her throat.

"You know the punishment for attempted murder."

Yes, she knew all too well. And if Baulo continued his torture much longer, she would wish for it.

"Whether it's carried out here or amongst the tribe makes no difference. You must pay for what you've done."

Baulo lowered his knife to her shoulder and split the fabric with ease. He yanked her sleeve up, baring her arm. Nadja thrashed beneath him, trying to roll away from his grip. A wash of shadow danced across the trees.

Baulo hooked his feet back over her legs and leaned down to press his forearm across her shoulders, pinning her to the ground. "Be still, girl," he hissed through his teeth. "Just like your mother. Neither of you know your place." He flipped the knife, pointing the blade towards her upper arm.

Nadja's back arched as the blade sliced a thin, shallow line from her armpit to her elbow. The muscles in her neck tightened, and she fought back another cry.

Though painful, none of her injuries were yet enough to do any lasting harm. Baulo's end goal may be to kill her, but one thing was clear. He would take his time doing it. And she would suffer all the while.

A blur of darkness passed in front of her eyes. With a surprised gasp, Baulo tumbled to the ground. Nadja sucked in salt-laced air, finally able to fill her lungs. She craned her neck to see two forms locked in combat. The darkened sky made it impossible to both discern whom Baulo's opponent was and distinguish between the two. A sound like a mallet pounding meat turned her stomach as they traded blows.

Then, as quickly as the fight began, it ended. Silence shrouded the camp interrupted only by the distant sound of crashing waves. The bodies of the combatants lay between Nadja and campfire, dark, appearing as a single amorphous mound of nothingness. Then, a form rose from the darkness, separating himself from the mound and finding his feet.

"He's out. For the moment," said a familiar voice.

Nadja sputtered as Luca removed the gag.

"How?" she rasped before running her tongue around the inside of her mouth, willing the moisture to return.

"Easily," he replied, kneeling and slicing the rope fastening her to the tree. With two more deft movements of his knife, her wrists and ankles were free.

Nadja threw her arms around his neck, ignoring the searing pain where the open flesh of her upper arm pressed against his leather tunic. Her pulse pounded in each laceration as her panicked heartbeat gave way to relief. Luca's arms came around her waist, and his head dropped to her shoulder. Nadja imagined she felt his lips brush against her neck, but knowing Luca's respect for tradition, that couldn't be true.

"I don't understand," she said, pulling back. "I've heard nothing from you since we parted last autumn. How are you here now?"

Luca dropped his chin, gazing at his chest, but he did not answer or release her right away.

"I saw Baulo at the winter Delegation," she prompted.

"I suspected," he said, raising his eyes to meet hers. "When he returned home, he was much changed. I had not seen him in such good spirits since before you left." His gaze flickered over her shoulder, and his eyes widened. Releasing his hold on her, he gripped her chin and tilted her head back and forth. His face hardened as he surveyed the damage. "We must tend to your injuries."

Nadja shook her head and pulled his hand away from her face. "Later. Please, what about Kizzy? When I didn't hear from you, I feared the worst. Were you able to bring charges against Baulo?"

Luca sighed. "No."

Nadja's shoulders slumped, and she nodded. "She couldn't be persuaded."

Luca shot to his feet. The anger flashing in his eyes caught her by surprise as she mirrored his movements.

"Kizzy is braver than half the men in the tribe," he snapped. "She confirmed your account, and she was more than willing to come forward to stand against her attacker. But, your Uncle Harman . . ." Luca's lip curled, and he kicked a log which had fallen to the edge of the fire. Sparks shot like burning dust into the night air. "Fool," he spat, slamming a fist into his open palm, giving Nadja a rare glimpse of unrestrained emotion. "He would not stand with her."

"He didn't believe her?"

"I don't know. It does not matter. He said the risk to his family was too great. If the charges could not be proved, he feared reprisal from Baulo. And, to have Kizzy's shame made public would cast them all in an unfavorable light."

Nadja gaped. "*Her* shame?"

"His words."

Nadja nodded at Luca's knife, holding out her palm. Once in her possession, she set to work cutting a strip of fabric from the bottom of her tunic. Luca remained quiet as she bound her upper arm, taking advantage of the distraction to process his news. Once more, the faint sound of crashing waves punctuated the silence.

"So, nothing has changed?" she asked.

Luca shook his head.

"And I still can't return home." It was more of a statement than a question. Strangely, though, the words didn't bring as much sadness as she had thought they might.

She took in Luca's form, smeared with dirt from his brawl with Baulo, but none the worse for wear, and allowed her mind to wander. Where would they be now if Baulo had never attacked Kizzy? Happily married? Spending their days stalking prey together in the steppes and their nights in comfortable companionship at home? Would they be expecting their first child by now?

When they had last met, he'd said he still loved her. Would she go back if she could?

No.

She had changed. Everything had changed. Her home was no longer with the Wanderers. It hadn't been for a while now.

She twisted the ends of the cloth together, holding one end between her teeth. "You still haven't told me how you wound up here," she gritted out, jerking a knot in the makeshift bandage.

"As I said, Baulo's mood had greatly improved since his return from Cantio in the winter. When it came time for his journey back for the spring Delegation, he appeared much more eager. Too eager. I felt certain he had discovered your whereabouts. So, I followed him."

"If he knew I was in Cantio, then what was he doing in Chansey?"

"Following you, in all likelihood."

"But how is that? I only told one person where I was going, and she wouldn't have told him. How did he know where to find me?" Pax had figured it out as well, but the idea he would betray her to Baulo was absurd. Besides, he wouldn't have had time to alert Baulo and catch up with her at the harbor. No, neither Grandmaster Kero nor Pax was to blame.

Luca's face twisted. "Probably the same way Fonso and I did."

Nadja arched an eyebrow, waiting for him to continue.

"It doesn't take much coin to persuade a servant to keep watch on you. Especially one who is young and ambitious."

Nadja shook her head. That still didn't make sense. She'd spent her last days at the conservatory cooped up in the infirmary, taking shifts with Petrin and Pax. She hadn't even ventured into the dining hall for meals. They were all brought in by—

"Timothy," she gasped.

"I believe that was his name."

Nadja squeezed her eyes shut and pinched the bridge of her nose.

"If it's any consolation, I don't believe he thought you were in any danger," said Luca, taking a step towards her.

Nadja threw her hands in the air. "Thank you. That makes me feel a thousand times better. Knowing the whole time I thought I was safe within the conservatory walls, my movements were being reported first to you, and then to him." Nadja pointed past Luca to where Baulo lay. She froze midsentence, her finger hanging in the air.

Baulo was gone.

"Luca," she hissed in warning.

Luca's head turned to follow her arm. At the same moment, a sickening thud punctuated the air. Luca's body stiffened and his mouth dropped open, gaping at Nadja in surprise.

"No!" she shouted, rushing forward to catch him as he crumpled to the ground. She wrapped an arm around his waist. He grunted as her hand brushed against the smooth knife handle protruding from his back. Nadja's eyes snapped up in time to see Baulo emerging from the trees.

Luca gripped her shoulders roughly and pushed her away. *"Run!"*

Chapter Thirty-Seven

Nadja leapt to her feet and ran towards Baulo, putting herself between the two men to draw his attention away from Luca. She needn't have bothered. Baulo clearly had only one target in mind. He lunged at her with surprising speed. When she was a mere two paces from him, she veered to the right, slipping through his outstretched fingers. Her sudden change in direction took him by surprise, giving her a lead of a few seconds as he stumbled to adjust his trajectory. The trees enveloped her like a favored ally. Away from the campfire, her eyes struggled to adjust to the early-morning haze. She stumbled over roots and around saplings as the sound of her pursuer drew closer.

The sea called to her. The sound of the crashing waves beckoned her to the shore with a familiarity and certainty which fortified her courage. She could retreat into its waters. Or if not, she could at least meet Baulo on familiar ground.

The new sun peeked over the horizon when Nadja broke free from the forest. Her pace slowed as her feet met with shifting sands. She adjusted her gait to compensate, hoping Baulo would not adapt so easily. A few more steps and her bare feet connected with the wet, hard-packed sand left by the retreating tide. Dark footprints trailed behind her as her feet, now bleeding and bruised from her bootless dash through the woods, pounded towards the surf. The water swept over her toes, then up her shins, slowing her progress. A growl of frustration rocked her chest. She kicked her legs wide and brought her knees higher, leaping over the rolling waters like an ungainly doe.

Nadja's breath flew from her lungs in one sharp punch as Baulo's body connected with her back. His knobby arms hugged her thighs, sending her headlong into the water. Salt burned her nostrils and stung her open wounds. She planted her palms against the sea floor, digging her fingertips deep in the sand, and pushed up. Her face cleared the surface, and she sucked in a soggy breath. Baulo moved up her body and gripped the back of her skull, shoving her head back in the water and grinding her face into the sand. The minuscule bits of rocks and shells scoured her skin and forced their way up her nose. She writhed against his hold.

The water shifted, destroying Baulo's tenuous balancing act, and he toppled sideways into the water. Nadja kicked free from his grasp. She struggled to stand, blowing the sand from her nostrils. Her mind flashed back to their first confrontation, and once more her instinct took hold. She turned and faced him.

Just as before, the soaring sound emanating from her mouth grew louder as she called on the sea to help her.

Baulo regained his footing.

Come, wave, come!

The words repeated themselves over and over in her mind as her body trembled and her sight dimmed. The sounds of a hundred crashing waves faded away replaced by a single roar which crescendoed at Nadja's back. For an instant, the water surrounding the pair disappeared, and they stood face-to-face on dry land. The next moment, Nadja was off of her feet. Her body was thrust forward, then backward, rolling and tumbling like a seed in a shaker. She lost all sense of direction as the water tossed her to and fro. She had spent most of her breath calling the wave, and now her lungs burned, craving fresh air. As the initial impact subsided, her body began to float. Twisting herself upright, she kicked her legs as fast as she could.

When Nadja broke the surface, her eyes darted around. They were much further out than she had hoped. She cursed herself for not being more specific when she called the wave.

She spotted Baulo treading water not far from her position, blocking her path to the shore. He saw her at the same time, and that haunting, sinister smile again twisted across his lips. He dove forward and began a series of long, determined strokes in her direction.

Nadja had wondered if the inner workings of Baulo's body were as much changed as the outside. He wasn't as robust as he had once been. Still, he bested her in strength and dexterity at every turn.

But she could stay in the water half the day before growing tired. She doubted he could say the same.

She tore her eyes away from Baulo as he closed the distance between them and once more searched the sea. The early-morning sunlight reflected off of the dark water like a thousand tiny mirrors. There, to her right and not too far away, she saw her escape. She swallowed a gulp of air and ducked her head beneath the water, bolting for salvation.

Nadja's strokes were quick and sure, and she put distance between herself and Baulo. After a few moments, the water shifted and its temperature dropped as the rip current caught her. She slowed her effort and allowed the rip to pull her further away from the shore. Rolling onto her back, she searched for Baulo.

She saw his face change the moment he entered the rip. His grim look of determination faltered, slipping into confusion, then fear. She continued to watch him as the water pulled them both further out into the deep. He glared first at her and then back at the shore. She could almost hear his mind debating between pursuing her, or turning back before he was pulled too far out.

With a raging roar which shook Nadja to her very soul despite the distance between them, he turned his body back towards the sand. His fatal mistake.

The rip ran its course for a moment more before spitting her out into calmer waters. Diving down and keeping the shore to her left, Nadja swam until the water grew warm once more. When she broke the surface, she turned back and watched with grim fascination.

Baulo struggled in vain against the current. The harder he pushed forward, the more he seemed to stay in one place. After a while he began to falter, slipping under the murky water before coming up once again, struggling for air. The cycle repeated itself over and over; each time Baulo remained under longer. Nadja's stomach clenched in sickening trepidation.

Too late, he changed his tactics, following her lead and swimming in her direction. But the rip would not release its hold. Baulo surfaced again, spitting water and flailing without course. His eyes locked onto hers. She saw the moment he recognized his fate.

As if willing his voice to carry the same power as hers, his scream bit through the air, gurgling as he slipped beneath the surface for the last time.

Nadja trudged up the slanted shore and away from the sea. The sky, now a bright and gentle blue, seemed to smile down on her as if the events of the past few hours were only a figment of her imagination. She turned to face the waters one last time and found them in the same state as they ever were. Dark and taciturn, accented with cresting white caps, showing no sign anything was amiss.

Her bandaged arm told her otherwise.

As she approached the edge of the forest, her ears perked at the sound of footsteps.

Tau burst forth from the trees, beating a straight line for her. He swept her up in his arms and pressed her to his chest, heedless of her sodden state.

"I thought I'd lost you," he choked into her hair, pressing kisses to the top of her head. "Not again," he whispered. "Never again."

At his words, Nadja lost her grasp on the thin mantle of control she'd been holding tightly around her. The weight of everything, her freedom, Baulo's death, her uncertain future as a Mevocali, the good and the bad, came crashing down on her, and she crumpled in his arms. Sobs racked her body while her uncle supported her, murmuring soothing nonsense and stroking her salt-matted hair. Her uncle: the stoic, reserved, statue of a man. Yet, here he was, comforting her with a tenderness which reminded her so much of her mother. Nadja's cries began anew.

When her weeping dwindled to scant hiccups and sniffs, Tau released his hold on her and steadied her on her feet.

"He's dead," she sniffed, unable to meet his eyes. She was back where she'd started. Baulo was dead, this time for good. And it was her fault. Yes, he had done terrible things to her and Kizzy. And they likely weren't his first victims. But, even that knowledge was not enough to assuage her guilt.

Tau cradled her face in his hands and tilted it upwards, fixing her with a look which was both compassionate and hard. "Do not blame yourself. And do not lament his passing." He pulled her in for a quick, stiff hug. His eyes searched the Shadow Sea, finding nothing of significance. His voice was distant when he spoke. "There are many who owe you a debt of gratitude, and I am chief among them."

His words made her wonder, but before she could form her question, a more urgent thought came forward.

"Luca!" she cried, shoving her uncle aside and stumbling forward.

"Woah." Tau caught her and stopped her progress. Understanding swept across his face. "Luca Tulmen? Timpor and Naaro's boy?"

"Yes, please, he's hurt," said Nadja, pulling him with her towards the trees.

Tau cursed under his breath. He kept a steadying hand at her elbow and matched her strides back to camp. "Wheedler is seeing to him. He is conscious, but his injury is grave. We must get him back to the Mia Fair as quickly as possible."

Nadja's heart leapt at the news that Luca was still alive, but she quickened her pace at her uncle's warning.

Tau's stride lengthened as well. "Brooks is there tending to your other friend as we speak."

Nadja stopped short, causing Tau to stumble to avoid colliding with her. "You found Pax!" she squealed, throwing her arms around her uncle in a most ungraceful attempt at a hug. In all the chaos, she had almost forgotten about Pax.

"Yes," huffed Tau, regaining his footing and extracting himself from her grasp. "He is as well as can be expected." Taking hold of her hand, they hastened towards the camp once more.

"Thank you," said Nadja, feeling as if the words were more than inadequate. "But how did you know where to find me?"

They stepped from the trees into the small campground, and Nadja stopped. On the other side of the dying fire, now nothing more than smoking embers, sat Wheedler, his usually jovial face now pale and drawn, cradling a lifeless Luca in his arms. A deep red stained the ground beneath them.

"We have much to discuss," said Tau. "But first, we must tend to the boy."

Chapter Thirty-Eight

"Stowaways in the hold."

Nadja snapped her head towards Monty, nearly spilling the warm concoction she cradled between her fingers. Always with impeccable timing, he side-stepped along his perch in their direction. Being the one ship in the Montgomery & Co. fleet exclusively at her uncle's disposal, the Mia Fair had an extended hold which included sleeping room for up to six crew members and a built-in perch and food and water bowls for Monty.

"You think he knows?" chuckled Pax.

Nadja narrowed her eyes at the bird, who cocked his head to the side, regarding her with one unblinking eye. Of course, he had no way of knowing. Still . . .

"Hmm," she replied, denying and acknowledging the possibility in a single syllable. She made her way around to the little stool next to the cot where Pax reclined and offered him the mug. "Brooks said to be sure you drink it all so she doesn't have to come in here and make you."

Pax grinned. "Is that so?"

"I believe her exact words were, 'He can follow the doctor's orders or find out how hard it is to swim upriver with only one good leg.'"

"Ouch," he said with mock offense, placing a hand over his heart. "Such a taskmaster. I guess I'd better not disappoint." He drained the contents of the mug. Wincing, he handed the empty cup back to Nadja and blew out a low whistle. "Next time I might try the river." He leaned back against the wall and rubbed his hand absently over the fresh bandages.

Nadja's own wounds had also been attended to. Her neck and arm were clean and bandaged, but her earlobe required stitching, and the pain medicine the doctor had given her made her light-headed. All things considered, it could have been much worse.

Her eyes wandered to the opposite side of the hold, where Luca lay as still as the dead. If not for the faint rise and fall of the sheet over his chest, she would have thought he'd already joined their ranks. He still may.

Pax followed her gaze. "So, what's the story there?" he asked.

Nadja turned her attention back to him. His eyes were warm and encouraging, and she let out a sigh. Luca was the one part of her story she'd never told Pax. In the beginning, she didn't know why she withheld that part. But as time passed, she understood. Little by little, since the beginning of their acquaintance, Pax had worked his way deep into her heart. She never wanted her relationship with Luca to be a barrier between them. It was in the past.

But now, with the effect of her volatile serenade clearly still weaving its spell over Pax, a barrier was just what she needed.

"Luca was my Promised One. My betrothed," she said.

Pax dipped his chin in a single, slow nod, waiting for her to continue.

"He was one of the scouts who took me from the Harvest Bazaar that day." When Pax opened his mouth to protest, Nadja hurried on. "He also helped me escape so I could return to Cantio and remain in hiding. He knows about Baulo."

"What happened to him?"

She turned her eyes back to Luca's cot. His face bore an unnatural pallor. His dark hair, now loosed from its binding, spread out across his pillow in an ominous halo. A lump formed in her throat.

She swallowed hard. "He was protecting me."

She bit the inside of her cheek, fighting back the lump which would not go away. Foolish man. Why couldn't he have stayed with the tribe? Why risk himself for her, putting both his position and his life in danger, knowing they had no real future together?

"He must love you very much."

And there it was.

Nadja nodded in reply, not trusting herself to speak.

"And you love him, too."

Pax stated the words as fact, but his tone carried the hint of a question.

Visions of the past swept through her mind. A youth of ten or twelve with serious eyes and impeccable manners helping her mother transport the day's catch. A watchful young man, ever on the fringe of activity, while she and her friends were at play. A kind and patient teacher, encouraging and sympathetic as she endeavored to master his trade. A man of courage, standing between her and disaster on more than one occasion.

The warmth of fraternal affection bloomed in her chest and pressed against the lump, causing a single tear to escape down her cheek.

"How could I not?" she replied.

Nadja knew the love she confessed was not the kind Pax wondered about. But one look at his face proved her words had the desired effect. Dismay marred his features and the corners of his mouth curved downward.

Recalling himself, Pax cleared his throat and shook off his temporary dejection. He fixed a firm smile on his face he said, "Then I am even more glad Brooks was able to send help for you."

"As am I," she replied. The day before, when she'd first spotted the Mia Fair in the Chansey harbor, she had wondered if Brooks had noticed her as she surveyed the docks. Apparently she had, and had also noticed Nadja's departure with Baulo. When Uncle Tau and Wheedler returned with Pax, Brooks related the information. Because of her keen eyes and the willingness of the painted lady from the inn to trade information for coin, her uncle and Wheedler had been able to track them.

Without warning, Pax reached out and plucked the cup from Nadja's hands. He placed it on the floor before grasping her hands in his and wrapping his long fingers around them. An involuntary shudder danced across her shoulders at his touch. His face wore a renewed look of determination.

"Listen to me, Nadja Machinal. I know you say what I feel for you isn't real. That it's something which comes from you, and not me. But if what you say is true, then you carry in your heart a love for me that cannot be denied." She tried to pull away, but he held her hand fast. "I don't care what or who came before. Whatever this is between us, whether it's you or me or both of us, it's not nothing. If your heart still belongs to him, then I will step back and wish you all the happiness in the world. But if I can dare to hope otherwise, please say it and relieve me of this heartache."

Oh, how she longed to do just that. But she couldn't be so cruel to him. Once the effects of her song wore off, he might feel the need to honor his words out of a misplaced sense of obligation. No, she had to take the burden of responsibility upon herself.

"Pax, I—"

Just then, the hold door opened. The sound of boots, heavy on the wooden steps, announced the arrival of Uncle Tau, followed by Wheedler and Brooks. Their conference with the doctor had taken longer than Nadja expected.

Nadja slipped her hands from Pax's grasp.

"Did he follow orders, or does Wheedler need to get his throwing arm ready?" quipped Brooks as they weaved their way past the rather small cargo shipment.

Nadja retrieved the cup and turned it upside down, displaying its empty state.

"As always, your wish is my command, Nurse Brooks," said Pax, flashing Brooks one of his winning smiles.

Brooks huffed, but nodded in approval.

With no preamble, Uncle Tau began, "It is time we discussed your situation. Though, we can take our discussion to a more private location if—" he broke off, inclining his head towards Pax.

"He knows as much as I do at this point," said Nadja. "But—" copying her uncle's action, she inclined her head towards Wheedler and Brooks.

"Ah," said Tau, running two fingers across his beard in an unusual moment of hesitation. "They also know as much as you do, and a great deal more."

Nadja stiffened. How much did they already know? And for how long? A sense of betrayal crept up the back of her neck.

"Is that so?" She punctuated each word, looking at the three of them in turn. Wheedler shrugged sheepishly while Brooks lifted her lips in a half smirk. Tau remained impassive, awaiting her permission to proceed. After a moment of consideration, she threw her hands in the air with an indignant sigh. "Fine."

Tau settled himself onto a nearby crate and motioned for Nadja to resume her stool.

"You are Mevocali," he began, "but you are not alone in this."

"I knew it," said Nadja, clapping her hands together and jumping up from her seat. "You are too. That had to—"

"No," said Tau, cutting her off. "But there are others." He waited for her to resume her seat before continuing.

"History teaches us the last of the Mevocali were killed at the Battle at Annuay. Most of them were. However, a small group escaped and went into hiding. They have lived peaceably, apart from the rest of the world, for over two hundred years. They send a few of their number back to Amrantir every so often, and for a short time, as provisions needs arise. Though they have done their best to remain anonymous, this is no doubt why they are rumored to still exist. Because they do."

"If they've been trying to stay hidden for the past two hundred years, how do you know all this?" asked Nadja.

"The Mevocali who went into hiding at the end of the war did their best to reestablish their people. But the number of survivors was too small, and with each new generation, their population has declined."

"It's kind of hard to make babies when every pretty girl is your cousin," said Wheedler.

"Indeed," said Tau. "The Mevocali came to a crossroads. Rejoin society, or face extinction. The choice was clear, but they could not simply walk through the Cantio gates and announce their return. They would need help. And so, a few years ago, they sent a representative to Amrantir to begin making connections with people they hoped would be sympathetic to their cause."

Nadja nodded in understanding. "And that's where you come in."

"Over the years, our numbers have grown." He raised his hand towards the two guards. "Wheedler and Brooks are a part of our network, as are others you know."

Realization struck Nadja. "Grandmaster Kero," she said.

Tau dipped his chin in acknowledgment. "And others. We have been discreetly adding to our numbers and plotting the logistics of their reentry into society. It is why I captain a boat to Chansey a few times a year."

Nadja's eyebrows rose. "I thought you were trying to avoid the Delegation."

Wheedler chuckled.

"Chansey is the central location for all of our activities," said Tau, with a glint in his eye. "Though, I will admit to some personal indulgence when it comes to the scheduling of our visits.

"The Mevocali call us Defenders because that will be our job when the time comes. History has not been kind to them. It has left a baseless but deeply rooted fear in the heart of Amrantir which has lasted for generations. The Mevocali are a people who only ask for the right to live in peace alongside us as their ancestors did. However, because of their particular skill set, they will surely be met with resistance upon their return."

"How soon will that be?" asked Nadja.

"Time to move! Time to move!" squawked Monty.

Brooks snorted.

Tau rose to his feet and crossed over to Monty, who was deeply involved in his bathing ritual. He stroked the bird under the chin. "The manifestation of your abilities has moved up our timetable. Due to the public nature of some of your . . . displays, we must assume there are others who suspect your lineage."

Nadja squeezed her eyes shut, trying to process all her uncle had said. But there were still questions nagging her. "Yes, about that. You still haven't explained how this is happening to me, or what I'm supposed to do about it."

Tau turned to his guards. "Brooks, ready the barge to cast off. Wheedler, see that our two invalids are secure for the trip to Cantio. Nadja," his tone turned soft as he gestured towards the hold door, "come with me."

A sinking feeling formed in her stomach as she followed her uncle. She looked back at Pax, who had remained wide-eyed and silent during Tau's explanation. He gave her an encouraging wink.

The breeze coming off the ocean was soothing and familiar as Tau and Nadja climbed on deck. Nadja turned her face towards the water and stopped short. A familiar cloaked figure stood aft with his back to them. He turned as they approached.

"Nadja," said Tau. "Allow me to introduce you to Alek."

The man bowed at the waist, then stood, pushing his hood back. A fair face and glittering pair of emerald eyes, exactly matching Nadja's in color and intensity, met hers. He studied her with a mixture of curiosity and hesitation.

"I saw you in Cantio," she blurted out, not sure of what else to say.

Alek glanced at Tau, and it seemed an entire conversation passed between them in that moment. Nadja's frustration mounted as the quiet stretched on.

"Will someone please tell me what's going on," she snapped.

Tau ended the silent conversation and turned to Nadja. "Alek is the Mevocali representative and our main contact with them." Tau cleared his throat. "He can introduce you to your father."

Nadja's brows drew together. "My father is dead."

"Fralo Filamen is dead," replied Tau, keeping his words low and steady. "Your father is very much alive."

The warm sea breeze turned cold as his words bounced around in her mind. They made no sense.

"No." Nadja's voice trembled as she spoke. "My father died when I was barely a year old."

"Nadja," said Tau, taking her hands and turning her to face him. "Fralo married your mother, but he was not your father. Mevocali talents are passed through bloodlines. I know your father. He is one of the last Mevocali."

The urge to bolt made her heart pound and skin itch, but Nadja fought against it. She turned her focus away from the hundred new questions racing through her brain. There would be time for that later. Reigning in her control, she dropped her uncle's hands and took a single step back, planting her feet and angling her body to face both of them.

"All right," she said, projecting a calm she didn't feel. "That answers the question of how. Now, what am I supposed to do about it?"

This time, it was Alek's turn to speak. "I would like to take you back with me to train among the rest of the Mevocali. It is imperative newly manifest powers are treated with great care, or there could be dire consequences. You may have already discovered that." There was no hint of sarcasm in his voice, only a gentle sincerity.

Nadja paced the deck. "I can't just pick up and go with you to who-knows-where. What about Luca? And Pax?"

"I'll look after them," said Tau. "There is nothing you can do for Luca now. His recovery is up to him. But, I can promise you I will do everything in my power to see he does recover. Pax's injuries are not extensive. He should be able to return to the conservatory as soon as we make it back to Cantio."

"And what about the conservatory? Final examinations are in a few weeks. If I don't score well enough, I won't be able to advance in the autumn."

The corners of Alek's mouth twitched. "I can assure you the instruction you will receive among the Mevocali will more than make up for your lack of conservatory training."

"I can take care of your absence from the conservatory," offered Tau.

Nadja stopped pacing and folded her arms across her chest. "How long are we talking about?" she asked.

"Six months," said Alek. "A year, maybe. It depends on the trainee."

"A year?" She gaped at him. "Are you crazy? You don't understand. I've finally started to make a life for myself here. At the conservatory. And you want me to walk away from all of it? My best friend, whom I left with no idea of my whereabouts, is probably beside herself with worry." And what of her mother and Kizzy? The news of Baulo's death would surely bring them some relief. If Luca lived, it could be in his power to reveal the truth about Baulo and have the charges against her dismissed. She might be able to see her mother again without fearing capture.

As reasons and excuses swirled around in her mind, Alek's voice cut through the commotion. It struck her how melodic his tone was. The pitch of his speaking voice was slightly higher than that of the average man, but the effect was most pleasant.

"If you do not receive the proper training, any effort spent building this new life of yours may be all for nothing."

With those words, her choice was made for her. What kind of life would she have knowing she could be a danger to herself, or worse, to the people she loved? It would take only a single, careless moment.

"Fine," Nadja conceded.

Tau nodded in approval.

"So now what?" she asked.

Alek smiled. "I hope you don't mind getting your feet wet."

ACKNOWLEDGMENTS

"Self-publishing" is a misnomer, because no one who does it successfully can truly do it alone.

To Mom and Dad: Thank you for fostering my love of reading from the very beginning.

To Aslinn, Jane, Courtney, Katherine and Adam: Thank you for your willingness to plod through my freshman novel and hold nothing back.

To Susan: Thank you for loving on my babies and giving me distraction-free hours to write - whether you knew it or not.

To Deranged Doctor Design: Thank you for a book cover beyond my imagination.

To Keith Morrill at Little City Editing: Thank you for your notes and guidance.

To Ann M. Martin: Thank you for the BSC, the first series I was ever devoted to, and for setting the bar for number-of-volumes-in-a-series unattainably high.

To my Girls: Thank you for all the times you patiently (or impatiently!) waited when I said, "Gimme just a minute."

To Adam: Thank you for being my support, sounding board, cartographer, tech guru, encourager and critic. You are my heart.

To God: Thank you for the Cross, your Grace, Mercy and Love.

And finally, to you, the Readers: Thank you for taking a chance on me.

ABOUT THE AUTHOR

A.K.R. Scott is a musician, actor, and lover of the written word. This native South Carolinian spent her childhood devouring books, whether tucked away in her bedroom, up a tree, or hidden under the dinner table. Now, she lives in Texas with her husband, two daughters, one rascally dog, and an ever-expanding library.

www.akrscott.com

Made in the USA
Middletown, DE
27 June 2017